SLEEPER PROTOCOL

KEVIN IKENBERRY

Sleeper Protocol

First Print Edition: November 2015

ISBN-13: 978-1-940215-60-0
ISBN-10: 1940215609

Red Adept Publishing, LLC
104 Bugenfield Court
Garner, NC 27529
http://RedAdeptPublishing.com/

Cover and Formatting: Streetlight Graphics

This is a work of fiction. Names, characters, places, and incidents either are the product of the author's imagination or are used fictitiously, and any resemblance to locales, events, business establishments, or actual persons—living or dead—is entirely coincidental.

For my girls.

CHAPTER ONE

LIGHT PENETRATED THE DARKNESS. I felt a sensation on my face and recognized it as warmth. Silence became a soft, steady buzzing, familiar and disconcerting at the same time. My eyes twitched under hooded lids while my fingers flexed and found a smooth, cool surface under my hands. The pinpoint of light expanded into blurry brightness. A million reflections of light rippling on water became clear as they danced and sparkled like diamonds. A horn boomed once, and then again, in the distance. Seagulls chattered all around, adding to the cacophony and confusion. I blinked—a slow movement of my sandpaper lids across my eyeballs—and the camera of my mind snapped into focus.

A wide harbor stretched from horizon to horizon in front of me. Recognition fought confusion and won in slow, lingering moments. The warm sun tingled the right side of my face. I glanced away from it, turned to look at the city behind me, and smiled.

I'd been there, to that exact spot, before. For the life of me, I could not remember when. The rough cut of stone overlooking the harbor had a name. Mrs. Macquarie's Chair resembled a wide sofa tucked into the hillside above Sydney Harbor. It sat off to my right, up a slight incline of sidewalk. A faint breeze off the water rustled the leaves of a tree above and behind me, where the birds chirped. The expanded clamshell of the Sydney Opera House pierced the crystal blue sky a few hundred meters away, on the edge of Circular Quay. *Is the small bar on the harbor patio still there?* I had a memory, bright and vibrant, of going there on a tour of the city with three British girls. Sophie, the cute blonde with the Birmingham accent, liked my smile. We'd traded letters for a few months, and then our brief time together had faded into pleasant memories.

I'd been seventeen years old. Across the Quay, past the Opera House, stood the Harbour Bridge, known as the Coathanger by Australians. The bridge, which dominated the skyline, had a constant stream of traffic crossing it and the space above it. *Above it.* I gaped at the hovering and flying vehicles of differing shapes and sizes as they dove and swooped through the sky like barn swallows at sunset.

A pretty girl in a green one-piece uniform bearing red crosses pinned to her collar points stepped in front of me and knelt. Her eyes were emerald green and her perfume light, like the scent of flowers on a morning breeze. The smell of hazelnut-flavored coffee came with her and made my mouth water. A shower of curly blond hair tumbled over her left shoulder. She leaned in with a concerned look on her pretty face and blocked my view. "Are you quite all right?"

Her Australian accent was warm and familiar. I licked my lips and managed to form the words, "How did I get here? To Sydney?"

A small tablet appeared in her hands, and she tapped on the screen with a stylus. "We'll get to all of that shortly, sir."

Just answer my question. There wasn't time to ask her other questions before she stepped behind me, and we moved down the wide concrete path. *A wheelchair?* Panic shot through me. My blanket-covered legs barely responded when I tried to move them. *Am I injured?* I found that I could move my arms and legs, but they were heavy and unfamiliar even in the light cotton garment that fell around my shoulders. It had to be one of those silly things that tied in the back. That was what sick people wore. *Am I sick?*

A flying car banked above us, and beyond it, the skyline of Sydney appeared and took my breath away. All of it was wrong. The buildings rose like a steel-and-glass wall, reaching hundreds of meters into the azure sky—not angular, but rather, like curved wings and sails. The structures all appeared to have one thing in common: even the smaller ones contained immense rooftop gardens like the Hanging Gardens of Babylon. There was something... different. I couldn't place it and quickly lost the thought as dogs and children noisily filled the park around us, and we proceeded down the path. Kids skated on hoverboards. A young girl led a proud cat on a leash. It was the size of a sheepdog. The blooms of a million flowers contrasted with the green grass of the Royal Botanical Gardens—all of it so similar and yet so very different.

"What happened here?" I croaked and gasped for breath. My chest tight, I glanced wildly around the strange city. A large vehicle painted like a city bus roared overhead. The stimuli overwhelmed me until a cool hand touched the back of my neck.

"Let's get you home."

Home. I wondered what that meant as she pushed me deeper into the city. *This is not my home.* I needed to find answers. That I was in Australia, what should have been a friendly land, gave me a little solace. I might be injured, or I could be a prisoner, but at least there was a chance someone would be able to tell me what was going on or that I'd figure it out myself.

Home appeared to be a hospital, though it seemed more like an almost-vacant office building, especially since I saw no patients or medical equipment. The lack of hospital beds and scurrying staff gave the building an empty feel. There were very few private rooms and many large, open spaces with uncomfortable furniture clustered in front of small windows or dusty paintings. My room was small and private. The young nurse pulled me up from the chair and positioned me against the bed without a word. Moving without the chair was much harder than I'd first thought. The rubbery feeling in my limbs remained, and I felt as if I'd been sleeping for days. The walls of my room were the light blue of a winter sky. Pictures of the shoreline and lighthouses hung in creatively random places. There was no television, printed media, or medical equipment that I could see. I doubted there would even be a Bible in the bedside table. Across from the bed, a large screen hung on the wall and remained grey and empty. A small bathroom door stood ajar to my left, and the facilities appeared exactly as they should. Maybe I'd hallucinated the flying cars and alien skyline.

A nurse, much older and not as pretty as the one I'd woken up to, entered the room and stopped. "Can I get you anything?" Her hands came together in front of her and wrung tightly.

"Something to drink, please."

The nurse stared at me with terrified eyes and hustled out the door. Alone, I sat for as long as I could before nature called. I pushed my way out of bed and stood on quaking legs. Using the wall for balance with my left hand, I managed to plod like a drunkard into the bathroom. A check of my reflection in the mirror gave me no clues. I looked the same as ever—at least, that was what I told myself.

The journey back to bed came easier—more balance and less shuffling—which made me feel a little better about my predicament. Nothing hurt. There were no wounds or healing incisions, at least that I could touch or sense. My mind raced. *Why am I in a hospital? What happened to me?*

The wide wooden door opened, and a man in a long white coat walked in carrying a tray, which he placed on a rolling table. His blond hair had some streaks of grey in it, as did his goatee. The sun-kissed man smiled and maneuvered the table to my bedside. "Good morning. My name is Doctor Garrett—I'm your physician. Why don't we have a look at ya?"

"Can you answer a couple of questions for me?"

The doctor kept his distance. "Sure, mate."

"I've met two nurses, and both of them seemed scared of me. Am I in some type of trouble?"

He laughed and ran a hand across his face. "You've certainly got your wits about ya. No, you're not in any sort of trouble. You've surprised them—that's all. Given your condition, we weren't expecting you to wake up for a bit."

I licked my suddenly dry lips. "My condition?"

Garrett nodded. "Let me give you a quick scan, er, examination, and we'll talk about everything, okay?" His easy Australian manner, as he slowly scanned me from head to toe with a small device, was that of a man watching the surf. *Like a smartphone*, my mind whispered. The hum of his breathing as he scanned my back relaxed me. The procedure lasted a full five minutes, and as he finished, he set the device on the rolling table next to a collection of syringes.

"Well," he said with a grin, "you appear to be fully awake and reasonably healthy. All of your vital signs are normal for a twenty-eight-year-old. Your nervous system is still adjusting, but it's coming along fine. Have you felt a little rubbery in your limbs?"

The breath I'd been holding came out slowly. I was in good health. It wasn't much, but it was a start. I laughed and nodded. "Made it to the bathroom, though."

"That's good to hear." He reached for the small device and tapped a few buttons I could not see. He chewed his lip and made two more entries. He could have been ordering my breakfast for all I knew. After a moment, he said, "Let's talk about your condition. How do you feel?"

"Normal except for the heaviness in my arms and legs. Feel like I've been asleep for days. I'm not sure about a lot of things."

"I can imagine, mate. Had quite a shock, I guess."

"Yeah," I said with a sigh. "Care to tell me about the flying cars?"

"What do you think about them?" Garrett crossed his arms and squinted at me.

Outside, the sky was grey, and rain streaked the window. Thunder rumbled in the distance, and I turned back to the doctor. There was really only one explanation. "What year is this?"

Garrett took a deep breath. "That's what we need to talk about, if you are willing to talk about it calmly."

The cars were only a part of it. Sweat broke out on my forehead, and I licked my lips again. *How long have I been asleep? Didn't he say I was twenty-eight? What the hell is going on?* I pulled in a deep breath, closed my eyes for a moment, and let the breath out. When I opened my eyes, I could tell by the look on Garrett's face it was much worse than I'd thought. "Sure," I managed to croak.

"You've been asleep for quite some time. Right now, finding out what year it is could greatly hurt your chances for a complete recovery. There are quite a few pieces that you're going to have to put together on your own."

"Like what? What aren't you telling me?"

"Do you remember anything before waking up by the harbor?"

Panic rose in my chest. He hadn't told me a damned thing. Two could play that game. "No. That's all I can remember."

"Are ya quite sure? Anna said you smiled. There must have been something."

"Do I have... what's it called?"

"Amnesia?" He shook his head. "Nothing like that at all, technically. You have a blocked memory. That's something we've done on purpose. Everything you remember is there, but you are the only person who can sift through it and put it together. We're just here to help you. Can you remember what you were thinking when you woke up?"

"Who's *we*?"

Garrett frowned. "Your friends. You're among friends here. We just want you healthy."

"I'm not sure I believe you."

He opened his hands. "I understand that, mate. I really do. We're trying to help you remember who you are. That starts with answering my questions."

"How about you answer mine?"

He flinched. It was tiny, but it was there. "In time, I'll answer every question you ask. All I want to know right now is what you were thinking when you woke up."

I told him about Sophie and knowing that I'd been to Sydney before when I was younger.

His eyebrows rose, and he tapped a few notes on his tablet. "That's very promising. If you keep doing that, you'll recover your memory."

"How can I keep doing that—having those memories?"

"Experiences. Everything that you experience from now on is likely to trigger a memory. Could be a familiar smell, a sight, or some other type of stimulus. You'll be doing that all by yourself, and it will take time. Lots of time. You just have to do two things."

"And those would be?" I squinted at him. The whole damned thing made no sense, and I'd have to get the answers on my own. That was fine by me.

"Be a good patient, and ask a lot of questions. That's part of my job with your integration."

"Integration?" That didn't sound medical at all.

"Yeah," Garrett said and leaned an elbow on the bedrail. "This whole process of you putting your memory back together. For the moment, I'm the only person allowed to ask you questions. The nurse who went with you for a walk wasn't supposed to say anything at all to you. A memory block failing at the wrong time would make it difficult for you to integrate. Too much stimuli could basically short-circuit your brain and maybe leave you in a vegetative state."

"All because you've blocked my memory?"

Garrett straightened and turned, rolling the small table closer. "Let me ask you a question. What's your name?"

My mind became a vortex of swirling leaves. Red, brown, and orange scraps of memory blew past my fingers. I grasped at them but came up empty-handed. I didn't feel helpless, nor did I feel lost. I ran a hand through my short, coarse hair and scratched my head. My name was there, on the tip of my tongue, and while it mattered to me, it was not all that important. "I don't know."

His eyes followed my every move, and he relaxed and smiled again. "It's all right, mate. That's part of the process." Garrett took his hand from the edge of the table and its contents, pushing it aside so he could sit in a chair beside my bed.

"I take it some people don't react too well to that question?" I pointed at the tray of syringes.

Garrett laughed. "No, they don't. Precautions are necessary in a case like yours, ya understand?"

"Do you know my name?"

The easy smile on his face faltered slightly. "No, I don't. This is all up to you. Considering that you don't know your name, and that things are very different outside, how are you feeling?"

There should have been some anxiety, but there wasn't. The panic in my chest became muted, and the whole effect of the morning was more numbing than anything—as if none of it mattered despite its importance. There were too many questions. I needed answers, but I hadn't had a single one. My stomach rumbled. "Hungry, I think."

"That's a good thing." Garrett chuckled. "We'll do something about that right now. Take some time, and think through what we've talked about. I'll be back in a couple of hours, and we'll chat some more."

Garrett walked away, carrying his tray of precautions, and left me staring out the window. The low-hanging clouds had become a raging storm. Water ran down the window, cleansing it. The sound of the rain and thunder soothed me, but as the downpour slowly slackened to a drizzle, the unfamiliar skyline caught my eye. Everything was wrong. Changed. Different. *Except for me,* I thought. *But how in the hell do I know that? What in the hell is going on?* I wondered a million things, trying to make sense of it all, but all I knew for sure was that the world was different, and I was alive and alone. The rain strengthened again, smacking the window in thick drops that obscured my view of a world not my own.

The first chance I got, I'd start learning the information they didn't appear to want me knowing. I leaned back against the pillow and closed my eyes.

The vividness of the dream kept my attention though I desperately wanted to wake up. I knew I was dreaming, and as much as I wanted it to stop, I held on for any shred of information I could get.

The heat was unrelenting and everywhere. Grit from the godforsaken desert found my eyes, my mouth, and every nook and cranny of the splotched combat uniform I wore. The relative cool of the headquarters building ran down my sweaty neck, and as I removed my individual ballistic armor—sixty pounds of life-saving ceramic plates—the sweat on my back slicked cold and started to evaporate. I hung my vest and helmet on a series of rigid hooks and negotiated the gathered officers and soldiers toward the front of the building. A plywood bulletin board rested against the front wall with maps and graphics of both current and planned missions. A calendar, days that had passed marked with large black Xs, hung on the wall. One hundred ninety-eight days in Afghanistan—eighty days to go.

The American flag adorned one corner at the front, the Texas flag in another, there as it was supposed to be in our partnering National Guard command's headquarters. I liked the guardsmen. They were solid troops, patrolling with us every day and fighting insurgents and cowards.

I spoke to a few people, some peers, and found my seat on the center aisle. Everyone milled about and waited for the briefing to start. My brigade commander, Colonel Mudge, slapped a hand on my shoulder briefly before striding to the front of the room. The host-brigade commander followed, one of his aides calling the room to attention as the balding colonel clumped to the front of the room like John Wayne.

An officer I did not know introduced Colonel Mudge, who began to brief the mission. Mudge was the kind of guy I'd have followed to hell. He was funny but had a spine of steel. He vigorously protected us from the bullshit requirements of higher headquarters, things like wearing a bright-yellow protective belt for safety reasons—all that did was make you a target. As he introduced the officers, a commotion at the back of the room caught Mudge's attention, and he stopped talking and stared.

A man yelled, "Stay where you are, Lieutenant!"

"No! I need to see Colonel Mudge right now! It's important!"

Urgent and shrill, the voice echoed off the plaster walls, and I was filled with dread. It was one of my platoon leaders, Danny Spencer, just in from patrol. I turned my head and strained to see Lieutenant Spencer pushing through the crowd. Combat uniform dark with sweat and blood, the dark-haired lieutenant limped into the room with his vest undone and his eyes wild. *Class of 2011, Indiana University, degree in history,* my mind whispered. *Engaged, with a child on the way. Not the kind of guy to burst into a high-level meeting looking like he just slaughtered a camel.*

"Colonel Mudge! I need to speak with you."

Mudge glanced at me. I was in for a world-class ass chewing later. "Now is not the time or the place, Lieutenant."

Spencer laughed in a hysterical voice I did not recognize. "You tell us that your first rule is to let you know if someone is in danger, no matter the time or the place."

Mudge squared his shoulders to the lieutenant. "Get to the point, Spencer."

Spencer stopped in the center aisle, a few meters away, and came to the position of attention, but his hands were open and trembling. "Sir, I need to report a terrible crime."

"This isn't the time—"

"The hell it's not!" Spencer yelled. "You want to know when someone is in danger, right? Then you're going to listen to me, goddammit!"

Redness crept into Mudge's face. He stared at me, and I stood.

"Danny, get back to the CQ," I said. "We'll discuss this later. I want you to see the padre before I—"

"Shut up!" Spencer stepped forward, inches from my face. "A woman is dead, and none of you even care!"

"Where, Danny?" I lowered my voice in an effort to calm him down.

The eyes of more than thirty people with higher rank than my captain's bars were focused on me. Anger and embarrassment threatened to take away the last vestiges of my military bearing. That would only make the whole damned situation worse.

"Right here on base. I tried to save her, sir. I really tried. She's in my room. I couldn't save her. He killed her!" Spencer leveled a finger at Mudge. "He killed her! He puts us out there every day and sits back here drinking coffee and all that bullshit! We saw things! They tried to kill us!"

I stepped toward the aisle with the stares of thirty men and women on me. I was never going to live this down. "Danny, knock it off. There's a woman in your quarters?"

"He has to atone for his crimes, sir!"

Spencer stepped around me, and I saw something under his armor, glinting in the fluorescent light. He ran three steps down the aisle toward Mudge. Time slowed down as I went after him.

"He killed her! He killed her!" Spencer screamed, spit flecking my arms as I tackled him from behind and wrestled him to the ground.

I fought to grab his wrists, to keep his hands away from the trigger of whatever weapon he was carrying. Our chests ended up together, and the fetid stench of vomit and blood coated my face. His hand worked between us, trying to get under his vest. This couldn't be happening.

"Bomb!" I yelled, but the crowd didn't move. I yelled louder, and they scattered like rats. "Bomb!"

Spencer's blazing eyes met mine, and there was no recognition, only hatred. There was a flash of light, and then the heat returned, only more ferocious and intense than the desert outside. The light reached up and pulled me into darkness.

As I woke, thrashing, I knocked over a rolling table and crashed to the floor. There was screaming, and I knew it was mine, but I couldn't stop it. Tears stung my face, and I moaned something even I couldn't understand, through spit and snot, as the nurses rushed in. A man in a long white coat followed them with a syringe at the ready.

"Hold him!"

They were going to hurt me.

"We're trying to help you! We're here to help you!" a nurse said in my ear, and as I lashed toward her, a pinch on my neck brought heat and numbness that spread like wildfire through my body.

My limbs didn't respond, and I slumped to the cold tile floor. "What are you doing to me?" I moaned and began to sob. Pins and needles ran over my body as whatever drug they'd given me took full effect. My vision swam, and my mouth dried up. "What am I?" No answers came.

My vision tunneled as I whispered, "Why aren't you helping me?" The blackness returned. *I'm not alive at all. I'm dead.*

CHAPTER TWO

An hour passed before Major General Adam Crawley entered the hospital room. At the door, he paused for a full three minutes to make sure the subject was asleep before walking forward. His dress-uniform shoes squeaked on the polished tile floor. The young man slept peacefully, his mouth slightly open, from the administration of a sleeping agent. Crawley watched him breathe rhythmically. The shock of the nightmare would make it memorable to the subject. As much as Crawley wanted to wake up the young man and tell him the truth, the rules said he could not. If anyone could have overwritten them, it would have been him.

Crawley tilted his chin slightly toward the ceiling and spoke softly. "All sensors disengage. Override Crawley Delta Two."

Outside, in the control areas of the ward, screens would blink into standby mode so that Crawley could have a moment by himself. He trusted his staff, but some things were meant to be his and his alone. Crawley allowed himself a small smile. In his hand was a book familiar to everyone in the Integration Center, though no one knew its importance. The old brown leather was cracked in places and worn smooth in others, and the book stayed closed most of the time, but Crawley carried it like a talisman. "I hope you're worth all the trouble, son."

Crawley believed the young man would be worth it. All of the research, official and not, said he could make the difference. Time was not their only enemy. Then again, without the drastic events of the last conflict, neither of them would have ever been in the same room. If another war was to be won, their interaction was absolutely necessary.

The Styrahi brought the ability to transfer memory from one

generation to the next. In the years before the Great War, the Terran Defense Force imprinted two hundred genetic descendants of twenty-first century soldiers. Not long after, a nefarious alien race known only as the Greys attacked the Outer Rim. The Terran Council believed that the war was a construct intended to make humanity devolve from their mass passivity to something more primitive.

With the war over and the Greys defeated, Earth's leaders had further trimmed their tiny military forces. "Unnecessary expenses in life and money," they said. Earth was trying to withdraw from its role in the galaxy, a move that would have dire consequences if it succeeded. If the Greys returned, there was no question in Crawley's mind that they would not only target Earth but also eliminate it. The Greys were unlike any enemy the sentient races of the galaxy had ever encountered. Their very presence and early offensives sent the collected allies in search of new friends to bring to the fight.

The first alien race to make contact with Earth had been the Vemeh nearly two hundred years earlier. They came in search of the great warriors who'd split the atom, and they found a passive, peaceful planet instead. The Vemeh asked the Styrahi for help in recruiting Earth to help defend the galaxy, counting on the existence of humans who were engaged enough to strongly fight for their beliefs and who would be willing to give their lives to protect Earth. The insectoid Vemeh needed an ally capable of fighting the Greys with powerful weaponry and committed soldiers. They believed that humans were, if anything, able to learn forgotten ways. The Grey assaults on the Outer Rim in the early twenty-third century had been too far away for common earthlings to take seriously. Over the course of human history, when the populace had failed to act, politicians had jumped in full bore. But rather than embrace their new allies and take the race farther into the stars, political leaders had voted unanimously for the opposite approach.

Stupid bastards. "Earth First" had banished all of the Terran Defense Force imprints to points outside the solar system, but that wasn't enough. The hardy souls who'd pushed out and created permanent colonies were also recalled and their ships decommissioned. No one on Earth would study war. The Terran Defense Force accepted the role of training poor imitations of armies called "militias." Critical weapons of war were destroyed by the millions, though none was as conspicuously missed as the ability to lead men into combat. Worse, the very aliens who'd presented the human race with the keys to the galaxy were banned to the outer planets and Luna.

"Sorry to have to do that to you, son." Crawley grimaced and sighed at the same time. "Even dreams can be manipulated. I cannot take the chance you won't remember who you are." He glanced up at the sensor arrays, now quiet by design. That he alone knew the identity of the young man, and what he was capable of, was a fact no one else could know.

Crawley went quietly to the door. Turning his back on the small hospital room, he whispered, "Don't prove me wrong."

My screaming headache told me that the events in my dream had really happened and that my thrashing and fighting were as real as the dream had seemed. A tall glass of juice and a medicine cup rested on the rolling table. I sat up, drank some juice, and stared at the medicine for several minutes before deciding to take it. The staff really had done nothing but attempt to help me. There was no reason to believe that anyone here would hurt me. With more thought, guilt about my reaction to the dream and how the staff had wrestled me to the ground weighed on me, and embarrassment was piled onto that just for fun. I wondered how I could meet any of their faces.

The window was dark, and the lights of downtown Sydney shone through low clouds and fog. The dream felt so vivid that parts of it stuck with me, but others faded with every heartbeat. That I could remember the names of others was strange, considering that I couldn't remember my own. In my dream, I'd been a soldier—that was clear. The young lieutenant, Spencer, had called me "sir."

What does that mean? Was I in a position of authority or something? Nobody in the hospital would answer that question for me. Anything I wanted to find out about myself would have to come from outside. I'd have to ask questions and experience things beyond a boring hospital room. The screen on the wall across from my bed was unfamiliar. I smirked. "How do I turn the television on?"

A weather-radar screen flashed on, and my mouth fell open. "Holy shit." After a minute or so, the radar remained unchanged. "Change channel."

The screen beeped but did nothing. Obviously, that wasn't going to work. I changed tactics. "Find football."

The scene shifted from the clear radar pattern to a soccer match. *Dammit.* At least I was getting somewhere. "I don't want to watch soccer. I want football."

The screen shifted again to something that I recognized, after a few moments of gleeful enjoyment, as being Australian rules football. "What about baseball?"

The screen beeped but did nothing.

"News?"

Nothing.

"Movies?"

Nothing.

"Funny animal videos?"

Sure enough, the scene changed. Apparently, the television, or whatever it was, knew the rules, too. That would make things difficult. "Back to Australian rules football."

At least there was something to watch while I waited for breakfast. I didn't recognize the teams. *The Madrid Matadors and the Toronto Titans?*

"Keyboard?" I asked, but the screen did not change. "Access my medical records."

Text appeared across the game. "Not permitted."

"Show my vital statistics."

"Not permitted."

I scowled and thought about what sequence of words would work until the door swung open.

"Good mornin'." Doctor Garrett entered the room exactly as he'd done the previous morning but without the tray of syringes. "Had a heck of a dream, did ya? Remember anything?"

"How long was I out?" I yawned and tried to sit up straighter on the bed. "All day?"

"About twenty hours now," Garrett answered. "Anything new? You look like something's bothering ya."

I swung my legs over the edge of the bed and told him about my dream, which I recalled with nearly as much clarity as I'd had while I was experiencing it. All of the details were vivid, but nothing resonated. I had to make sense of it. "You're here to help me, right?"

"Yes." Garrett smiled. "That whole response-team reaction is to protect you, mate. It's a standard operating procedure, so to speak. We didn't want you to hurt yourself or anyone else. Dreams are like that. Not surprised you didn't dream about flying or falling, even a car accident or something. First dreams are scary. I mean, you haven't had one you remembered until now, right?"

"No." I paused. "What if it wasn't a dream?"

"Why do you say that?" Garrett asked. "Dreams are very seldom real. You might dream something about people you knew, but the context could be wrong. Or the situation is correct but all the people are complete unknowns. What about it bothers you?"

I told him about the names I remembered. The once-vivid details blurred at the edges. I held tightly to the names and recounted as much of it as I could.

He fell into the chair beside my bed. "Anything from your dream might have been true, like your colonel's name, for example. Given time, you can marry it up with other memories as they return. Some of that dream will fade, but the really important stuff tends to stick."

I wanted to believe him. All of the little thoughts in my head were confusing at best. My trust in Garrett built with every conversation, but I couldn't rely on our conversations alone. I liked the man, but I wanted him to answer my questions instead of asking more of his own. "Can I have a notebook?"

"What?" The curious squint on his face made me laugh.

"A pen and paper? I want to write down what I remember."

Garrett nodded his head. "I can do that for you, mate. You'll have everything you need to help you remember things as they come. Now, I have a bigger question for you." He paused, and the easy smile on his face grew even bigger, if that were possible. "How'd you like to go outside?"

"Now?"

"No, for good." Garrett leaned forward. "Here's the deal, mate. We'd like to send you on a walkabout. Ever hear of that?"

"Dropping me in the outback to survive on my own?" *How did I know that?*

"Indeed." Garrett peered over my shoulder at the window. "Experiences are everything to you. What you see, smell, taste, and feel will do more for this process than anything else. At least, that's what we believe. You have to piece things together yourself in a slow and easy manner. Walkabout is the best way for that. Going outside will be difficult, but you'll always be in contact with us, and I'm reasonably sure it's going to help you put your memory back together."

"Because I've been here, to Sydney, before, and I remember it clearly?"

"Precisely. Everything you see or do outside could affect you. That could be good or bad, I have to say. Maybe we can even get you out of here today."

"Today?" The idea of going outside, on my own, brightened everything. Whatever I was supposed to do, a voice-activated television and a hospital room were not going to help me. The fact that I didn't know my name would not stop me. There should have been fear, but excitement overrode it completely. "I feel like I'm making this up as I go along, but I want to do this. Today."

"We'll get to that," he said, grinning. "How about ya follow me, mate?"

The hallways of the hospital were almost vacant. A few staff members—it was impossible to tell doctors from nurses—hustled from closed door to closed door. The quiet emptiness struck me. "You're not very busy here."

"You're the only patient in this ward right now," Garrett said as we turned a corner into another wide hallway. "Downstairs, there are a few hundred patients receiving other types of treatment. We're treating everything from broken bones to heart transplants."

"What ward am I in?"

"This is the Integration Center. We have a staff of thirty dedicated solely to blokes like you."

"What's that mean? There are more people like me?"

We made our way down a short hallway with windows from floor to ceiling. "Your particular condition is the first of its kind. Those of us who aren't interacting with you during your stay are studying every bit of data we can glean."

At the end of the hallway were an elevator and a bin of umbrellas. "We're going outside?" I asked, smiling.

"Might still be raining. Want an umbrella?"

"I'll take a chance."

We stepped inside the elevator, and the ride was quick and silent. The doors opened to a rainforest. Dank, musty air filled the elevator cabin, and I drank it in. Rain no longer fell, but drops of water tumbled from the large tropical plants and trees. A small path, no wider than a person, led from the elevator in both directions along the rooftop. Palms and other unfamiliar trees stretched into the sky. Everything was deep, bright green and healthy despite the cool temperature. Breathing deeply, I could see a fine mist of my breath in the air.

"Spring or fall?" I asked as we passed into the garden.

Garrett opened his umbrella and fell in behind me on the path. "Spring. A bit cooler than normal today, but summer is coming."

A large palm trunk stretched above us. Something about it seemed out of place. "Palm trees don't like cool temperatures like this."

"They are phytomechanically engineered."

"What?" The palm tree swayed in the light breeze. The rough bark felt no different than any tree I could ever remember touching.

"Phytomechanics," Garrett said. "All of these plants are specifically engineered to remain green and healthy year-round despite extreme temperatures and volatile precipitation shifts."

From the edge of the roof, we looked out over the city. The building was much taller than I'd thought. At least sixty stories in the air, the breeze off the harbor was fresh and cool. Clouds touched the tops of the surrounding buildings, and mist fell in sheets. A garden adorned every rooftop. "Why create something like this?"

"Two reasons. The first should be obvious. What do plants breathe?"

"Carbon dioxide," I replied. "Cleanse the air."

"Precisely," Garrett said. "The other part is the real reason for phytomechanical engineering. This garden supplies more than 80 percent of the fresh water required for this building. The walls store rainwater collected up here, which in turn is an excellent insulator. Twenty percent of the water is used to maintain the garden. We recycle all of the water continuously. That's a standard practice these days."

"Why? You're next to an ocean. Can't you just desalinate?"

"Sure, but that takes a significant amount of energy and effort. Why not just recycle what we use every day? We do desalinate a little, but recycling is better."

That made sense to me. Whatever the year was, I remembered lingering concerns over water rationing and drought conditions. I listened to my mind for a moment more but found no other memories. "The engineering is to help the plants do more with less water—is that right?"

"Partially. This garden also generates 30 percent of the energy we need for daily operations."

"What?" I blinked. "How is that possible?"

"Not a biologist, mate. Something with the way sugars are produced and processed. All living things generate electricity. The garden is built into the roof to access that power and transfer it out to the power grid."

The sheer audacity of the garden overwhelmed me. The thick foliage and vegetation appeared meticulously cared for, and I didn't notice anyone else on the roof but Garrett and myself. The tiny drops of rain collecting on the plants ran down wide, green leaves and disappeared. I couldn't help wondering where it went. I glanced down at other buildings with equally impressive rooftops. "Why show me this?"

"A measure of scope. This is how much the world has changed."

"You're not afraid that all of this would make me want to jump over the edge?"

Garrett laughed. "You can't. Suicidal behaviors or ideations would cause your motor functions to shut down until you could be stabilized. It's happened before."

"You said that I was the first to have this condition. How could suicide have happened before?" I faced him, crossed my arms, and leaned against the roof.

He peered out at the horizon and tilted his head slightly. "You are the first of your condition to wake up, yes, but I'm saying that suicide in this society is no more. We found a way to significantly shut down the ability to take one's life. Millions of people used to die of suicide every year. We've eliminated that on most counts. Look, it's mainly biochemical response control, if I had to name it."

"But you haven't cured it." I wondered for a split second about trying it. Any attempt, and I'd likely not be anywhere close to leaving.

Garrett nodded. "No. If a man is determined to take his own life, nothing can stop him. Like I said, it's happened before, and in similar conditions to yours. There is considerable strength in the human mind. That's something I want you to remember as you go walkabout. Take your time, ask questions, and experience life to the fullest extent possible. You have a very limited time to integrate."

"Why is it limited?"

"Treatment protocols. We try one course of treatment and then reevaluate."

A low rumble of thunder rippled out over the harbor. "How much time do I have to integrate?"

Garrett shrugged. "We've estimated that your memory should return within a year. By the time we're done testing, you'll have a little more than ten months."

"I thought you said I could leave soon." The taste of outside air, neither recycled nor controlled, captivated me. Sitting on my ass for two months would not be easy.

"Yes." Garrett shifted the umbrella between his hands. "Ten months is from when we initiated the process. You're on day forty-two right now."

I recoiled as if slapped. "But I just woke up at Mrs. Macquarie's Chair."

"That's right. You've been in treatment for the last forty-two days. Once we believed you might wake up, the clock started. You're what we call Stage One. Don't worry about what it means just yet. What's important is getting you to full integration."

"What happens if I don't integrate in a year?" Time felt like a noose tightening around my neck. "I come back here?"

"Yes, for reevaluation." Garrett opened his mouth as if he were going to add something but then shut it. The look on his face told me that he'd said more than he wanted to.

"What aren't you telling me?"

Garrett took a deep breath. "It's not going to be easy. But there are some rules that will help you. Most people have a neural implant, like a computer in their head. Most people won't be able to get information about you. You're a null file, and that will scare people."

That sounded fun. "Why?"

"Because they'll know not to touch you, and most people won't even look at you or talk to you just to be safe."

I squinted at him. "Won't touch me?"

"Tactile stimulation, in your condition, could provoke strange responses." Garrett shrugged. "We've used these procedures when dealing with the various sentient races of the galaxy—"

"What?" I shivered. "Did you say aliens?"

"Yes." Garrett tapped his device. "You won't find any on Earth. They were restricted to Luna and the other planets some time ago. Their technology is what helped us wake you up."

Flying cars. Aliens. Try as I might, I couldn't remember either of those existing. The questions in my mind gelled into one. "You said you'd tell me. What year is it?"

He stared at me for a long moment, and I had the strongest feeling he was wishing for his tray of syringes. "The year is 2305, mate. You've been asleep a long time."

The trail of flying cars above the Harbour Bridge paused in midair. Traffic seemed to be as pervasive as cockroaches. "If I go out there, won't I need money?"

A funny look crossed his face as if he were searching for the meaning of the word. "Oh, currency! No, you won't need anything like that." He chuckled and shook his head as if our conversation was fun and not troubling.

"When I leave here, how will I pay for food or lodging?"

"We'll get to the ways of the world soon enough." Garrett stared out over the harbor. "What I can tell you is that you seem to be in perfect health and are about twenty-eight years old. Once we get you cleared for walkabout, I'll make sure you get all of the information you need—either from me or from a protocol—I promise."

I followed his gaze to the dramatic skyline. A driving sheet of precipitation emerged between the buildings and marched down the wide glass and steel corridors. I could smell the wet, clean rain approaching. The insistent drops thumped into the leaves and splattered along the rooftop around me. There were still a million questions in my mind, but none seemed important enough to ask. *Reevaluation* had an ominous sound to it, but I left it alone. The way Garrett had said the word made me think it was equal parts nothing and everything. I felt uneasy about it, but it wasn't going to keep me from leaving the center. Nothing else felt important, and a part of me wondered if that was part of the treatment plan. With no name and barely any sense of awareness beyond my body, I needed to focus on the basics. Three hundred twenty days didn't really matter if I couldn't remember the guy in the mirror.

Rain fell in big, cold drops through the cooling air. The water on my hair and skin sent chills down my spine. *I am alive.* The thought brought a smile to my face. Raising my chin to the sky, I closed my eyes and let the rain wash over me.

"You all right, mate?" Garrett asked. "Sure ya don't want to get back inside?"

I snuck a last long glance at the Sydney skyline. *What will it be like to be out there, surrounded by people I don't know, finding my way without my name?*

Garrett studied me from under his umbrella, his blue eyes watching.

Ask questions, I thought. "Where can I go?"

Garrett pointed toward the ocean. "Anywhere you want, as long as you stay on Earth. The moon is pretty dull anyway, and you're not cleared for interstellar flight yet."

Dull or not, the moon sounded like a perfect place to go. The rules, it seemed, reached far beyond me. "Where else can't I go?"

"There's a list. We'll get the protocol to work that out for you."

"But if I want to go anywhere that's not on the list—and I mean anywhere—I can go?"

"Yeah." Garrett motioned toward the elevator. "Let's get you out of the rain for now."

Walking back to the elevator wasn't so bad. My legs felt better, lighter, than ever. The world was strange enough that I wanted to know more. More awaited me than flying cars, phytomechanical gardens, and the sense that I'd been asleep for a long time. I was alive, and whatever they wanted me to discover, I could find it.

I might not like what I would find out, but I had to know.

CHAPTER THREE

THE EARLY-MORNING FOG AND RAIN gave way to a stunning late-spring day. The afternoon sun streamed through the two windowed walls of General Crawley's office. Five floors below, a young man wearing work coveralls and carrying a khaki backpack strode away from the Integration Center.

Crawley watched until the man disappeared around a corner without looking back. A satisfied grin crept onto his face, and he thrust his hands in his pockets. Here, no one could see him breaking regulation.

A tone from his desk interrupted the quiet moment of accomplishment. Crawley said softly, "General Crawley."

"What did you need, Adam? I'm late for a Council meeting." He could hear the snicker in Penelope Neige's Parisian-accented voice. "Is this official or personal?"

Crawley tried not to smile. He'd known the newly appointed chairman of the Terran Council for more than twenty years, and she rarely made any meeting on time. "Official."

There was a pause, followed by the snick of an electric cigarette lighter. "You've been successful?"

Crawley breathed slowly. "We have a subject awake and preparing for his walkabout. He'll be leaving the center within the hour." Giving him a head start had always been a part of the plan, but his old fair-weather friend did not need to know that. Trust was not something Crawley gave a politician easily.

"Really?" He could hear Neige exhaling a stream of cigarette smoke. "Are you sure this isn't going to be a waste of time and resources, Adam?

This is... what, one hundred years in development, and you're just now giving the Terran Council a possible subject?" She laughed in his ear.

It was melodious and enraging at the same time. Sacrificing the ability to have a family, a loving relationship, and his career in the Terran Defense Force would never be enough in the eyes of some. His team worked with genetic-mapping research that lengthened the human lifespan. They cured cancer and a host of other diseases.

Neige, and those like her, never understood what it was really about. The politicians wrote off the work as research, but Crawley and his precious inner circle knew better. Using a twenty-first-century subject had been the goal all along. The Terran Council wanted soldiers for the defense of humankind, but what they preferred, without saying as much, were docile men and women who would not question or fight without direction. Crawley wanted victory. The Greys wanted to eradicate humanity, and acquiescent soldiers better suited to political machinations would make that possible. Crawley and his team wanted to give Earth a fighting chance. Anything less was unacceptable.

Crawley felt the redness creeping up his neck. "Running off the Greys is hardly a waste of time and resources, Madame Chairman. Without the Terran Defense Forces and our research, the Greys will burn Earth to a cinder when they return."

"If they return." Neige chuckled but said nothing for a moment. Even the Terran Council knew the danger posed by the Greys, no matter how far they shied away from it. "And you're monitoring the subject how?"

"No neural connections. He has a standard guidance protocol instead."

Neige's voice rose above its normal diplomatic tone. "No. He gets a Class Three protocol. We need to be sure he is a valid subject, Adam. I'll have it downloaded immediately."

"I really think—"

"You heard me, Adam!" Neige recovered her composure in an instant. "I'd love to chat about this, but with a coherent subject awake and on walkabout, higher-security protocols are necessary."

Crawley felt anger rising in his chest. "A Class Three protocol is not necessary."

"For the Terran Council, General, I believe it is. Is there anything else?"

Crawley fumed but kept his voice measured. No matter how

much it infuriated him, the woman was predictable to a fault. "No, Madame Chairman."

"I can always tell when you're trying to kiss my ass, Adam. It doesn't suit you." The line clicked off, leaving Crawley resting his chin against his tightly clenched fist.

Damn that woman. A Class Three protocol served no purpose other than to subvert Crawley's own reporting methods. Every move that the subject made would be broadcast directly to Penelope Neige, giving the chairman and the Terran Council the opportunity to interfere at each turn. *Direct reporting,* Crawley thought with a grimace. *Whatever I know, she'll know.* Which was exactly what she wanted. *Unless we can stop it.*

Neige had been an undersecretary of military affairs when they dumped the cloning program in her lap. From the first meeting, Crawley knew she was trouble. The woman would do anything to stay in power, and in this case, she enjoyed the perfect political position. If the experiment failed, she could brush it off as another Terran Defense Force failure. If the experiment succeeded, she had the power to embrace it and leverage it against her political adversaries. The biggest problem was that she didn't believe the Greys intended to attack Earth. The silent aliens had jumped away in 2281 and had not been found since. But failing to prepare for battle with them was a chance that Crawley couldn't take.

He sat at his desk and raised his shiny black shoes to the acrylic surface that doubled as a screen. "Encrypted connection to Livermore. Now."

A synthesized human voice answered sixteen seconds later, the delay necessary to encrypt the transmission and bounce it from Earth to the moon before decoding it. "Livermore, access code, please?"

"Crawley, Four Two November Zero."

"Granted," the voice answered. "Orders, General?"

Crawley stared out the window toward the sun glinting off the skyscrapers of downtown Sydney. One man's journey suddenly felt like the weight of the world on Crawley's shoulders. His long, successful career was in the balance, yet he did not hesitate. There were far greater things to consider. War was coming. The only way to fight it was with men and women who knew what it meant to lay everything on the line, not for king and country, but for the men and women alongside them.

"Get her ready," Crawley said and disconnected the transmission.

Most second-year professors, regardless of institution, made a valiant effort to avoid teaching classes either late in the evening or first thing in the morning. The reasoning was simple: when the students would not get out of bed or put down their beer glasses, they wasted their instructors' time since all second-year professors had to be present and ready to teach whether the room was completely empty or not. But at the age of twenty-six, three years removed from her unprecedented accelerated graduation from Cambridge, Doctor Gwendolyn Bennett welcomed the opportunity to teach at ungodly hours, even a first-period class. Unlike many of her peers, Bennett never worried about whether or not her students would be present for class. Usually, they weren't absent more than once.

The rule was simple: beat Doctor Bennett into the classroom and avoid having to write lengthy reports on highly technical subjects, mainly cybernetic theory and the transmission of varying degrees of information across the blood-brain barrier. The students got the message by the end of the first week or sought a different field of study.

A stainless-steel mug of Earl Grey tea in her hand, Bennett walked with a leisurely but purposeful gait down Hawking Hall toward her first-hour class. She brushed a lock of blond hair away from her face and adjusted the stylish glasses on her nose. They were much more than simple glass lenses. No one wore glasses to see clearly, and likewise, wearable technology had never really hit the mainstream even in the twenty-fourth century. Bennett let her students think her glasses were like the nonfunctional ones the celebrities wore, but they had a purpose other than fashion. She'd made more than a few modifications on them over the years.

Her peers smiled and said hello as they passed, and she smiled brightly. In front of her, a rush of first-year cyberneticists pushed down the hall like a herd of cattle, checking over their shoulders occasionally to gauge their distance. Several gave longing looks at the restrooms but ducked into the lecture hall instead of flirting with the chance Doctor Bennett would not get caught in a hallway conversation.

Such encounters happened fairly often as friendly faces greeted her with handshakes and hugs of congratulations. Three weeks before, she'd received a nomination for the Nobel Prize in Cybernetics. The well-wishers made her feel light and happy, but all of the smiles and encouragement were for naught in her mind. Up against the likes of motor-neural alignment, fourth-generation artificial-intelligence engine design with suppressed emotional control, and complete petabyte transmission of the human brain and genome model, her experiments in laser communications in the .5 nanometer band paled in comparison. Her experiments could not facilitate an instantaneous download in fifty-petabyte range nor stand up to artificial intelligence design, but the interest of the Terran Defense Forces in her communications work allowed her a considerable research budget and private facilities at the university. Not bad, especially for a girl from North America.

Of the considerable faculty, she was the only one from across the pond, and the entire contingent of North Americans numbered fewer than twelve with the exception of the Canadian faculty and students. Many of the other faculty members of Cambridge referred to her as being from the "colonies," which made her laugh on the outside and turned her stomach on the inside. A hundred years after the collapse of the United States of America, the rest of the world pretended it hadn't existed and what had happened there had been a bad dream. Bennett's own family had escaped to the Republic of California when her father was only six, more than forty years after the walls went up. Leaving Canada had been the family's only choice. He'd only told her the story a year ago when she'd asked about it for a millionth—

"Doctor Bennett?" A pudgy man with bright brown eyes stepped in front of her. Professor Higdon Jacks, holder of the Hawking Chair in Theoretical Physics and a fellow Terran Defense Force grantee, caught her arm. "You seemed deep in thought, my dear. Is everything all right?"

Bennett smiled. "Of course, Higdon. What can I do for you?" She blinked twice rapidly. Information began to print on her retina, and she could read it without taking her eyes from his. *Body temperature high, probably from walking fast enough to catch me. Four minutes to class. Higdon needs a checkup on that heart rate. Email his wife and recommend that she make the appointment.* All noted before the professor managed to speak. *Not bad,* she told herself. The experimental neural connection worked almost as well as she wanted it to, but there was much work to do.

"A call came for you. They were unable to connect to your neurals. I told them the campus had a policy..."

Higdon kept talking, but she wasn't listening. With a long blink, she opened her communication feed. A hacking program went through the university's neural protocol block like a hot knife through butter. Almost immediately, a message-waiting icon blinked on her retina.

"I'll call them back after class." Bennett smiled and made for the door of the lecture hall.

Higdon called after her, "You don't suppose it's the big news?"

"Not likely," she called over her shoulder with a wink.

A few more students hustled to the lecture-hall door in front of her. Unlike most days, she did not speed up to watch the first years fall all over themselves. Reaching the door at the same time as a wide-eyed Irish girl with bright-red hair, Bennett smiled and gestured the student inside before she entered. At the ornate lectern, she set down her material and tea before withdrawing twenty strips of paper then went back to the door and handed the strips to crestfallen students as they entered and met their fate. No big weekend plans for any of them.

One student wiped a sweaty brow with a shaking hand and blurted, "I can't prove that!"

Bennett almost laughed. "Why not?"

"Bending space and time is theoretical physics! I'm studying electromagnetic impulse communications, not relativity."

"A good student"—she turned to the seated students, who finished the quote in unison—"has a broad grasp of all possible insights."

With a satisfied smile, she closed the lecture-hall doors and noted that every seat was full for the eighteenth class period in a row.

"Good morning, everyone." She keyed her terminal into the projection system of the lecture hall and the individual desks of her students. They were bright, all of them, and despite what they thought of her methods, she loved them. "This morning, we're going to continue on last period's investigation of the blood-brain barrier and challenges to connectivity. For this period, I'm allowing you to utilize your neurals on local connection only. The first time I catch anyone playing Pac-Man, you'll lose the privilege." They laughed, but nostalgic eight-bit video games were making a comeback. Bennett didn't mind except when the business of learning was at hand.

"Who can tell me the five critical areas of cybernetic connectivity with the human brain?"

Twenty minutes into the period, her students were nodding their heads and taking turns exploring the data pathways of their neurals when the call came and stopped her midsentence. "Just a moment." She paused her lecture, spun away from the class, and activated the connection. She silently replied, "Bennett."

"Doctor Bennett, no-contact order lifted by order of the chancellor," the artificial operator said. "Please remove yourself from the classroom to a private area and turn off audio inputs. Reception of call in two minutes."

Bennett looked up into the amphitheater of students, most of whom sat with their mouths open. They'd be telling their friends that Doctor Bennett figured out a way to get past the university lockout systems. It was better than telling them the truth. "Ladies and gentlemen, it appears that good fortune is smiling upon you. I will post a follow-up to today's lesson in your mails. Class dismissed." She gathered her things and strode out of the room. Butterflies alit in her stomach. Only the Terran Defense Forces—the TDF—called with the expectation that she take the call immediately. A quick search told her the Nobel committee was not meeting for another week, and the odds were still woefully against her. It had to be the TDF.

Her office, across the quadrangle, was out of the question as were the faculty lounges on every floor. She couldn't get outside in less than two minutes, and with the cold autumn rain that was falling, she didn't want that anyway. *Privacy. Absolute privacy.* Her connection and subvocalization would keep the conversation completely secret even if others came and went, but it would be best that no one see her. Nothing circulated a campus faster than a rumor. In the ladies' restroom, she seated herself and her materials in a stall when the call connected.

"Doctor Bennett?" The man's voice was a smooth baritone and spoke in fluent, unaccented English.

"Yes," she subvocalized through her neural translator. "Can I help you?"

"Livermore."

Her hands began to shake. "Can you repeat that, please?"

"Livermore."

Sonofabitch! Three years ago, the Terran Defense Force had come to her, offering money for her research. After all that time and a Nobel nomination, she'd nearly forgotten the arrangement. Shaking her head, she thought, *What arrangement would that be?*

"Affirmative. Subject has departed Integration. Is the package ready?"

"Once I get back to the lab, it'll take five minutes. Standard guidance?"

The voice paused. "No. Series Three guidance protocol initiated."

Damn. That would complicate things. "How much time do we have?"

"Three hundred and twenty days, give or take a few."

They've really done it. The limits on the program, from what she remembered, were finite by order of the Terran Council at the highest levels. There was not much time at all. "How soon will you want a connection?"

The voice paused again. "Immediate background connection to establish telemetry. Be prepared for a physical connection."

Eyes closed, she waved her hands tightly together like an angry child playing in a box. *This can't be happening! Not now!* Measuring her voice silently, she replied, "You are authorizing physical connection? How soon?"

"Better telemetry will flesh that out, but right now, we're tracking our subject in the Sydney area. Can you be ready in a few days?"

Bennett replied. "It may not be easy. Exams are a couple of weeks away. I'll have to ask the university if—"

"We'll handle that. If this is not handled with the utmost care, people will ask questions. We don't want any more than are necessary."

Bennett paused. "I understand. I'll have a background connection in the next thirty minutes. I'll need updated telemetry by then."

"You'll have it. Breaking down this connection." The line went dead, leaving a slight ringing in her ears that cleared within a few heartbeats.

We're going to do it. Forehead in her hands, Bennett took a deep breath. As long as the TDF remained interested in her research, they would fund it, and it would be profitable for her. *Maybe they'll consider increasing my grants.* She pushed the thought aside. Her father would have said something about looking gift horses in the mouth, and he would have been right. This required restraint and attention to detail. The other stuff could wait. She gave the unused toilet a cursory flush—somehow it felt wrong not to—and strode out of the restroom. Out into the cool Cambridge rain, she hardly felt the drops hitting her loose blond hair. With first-hour classes in full swing, and horrible fall weather, the quadrangles and gathering places were devoid of people, which served her mood. The forlorn feeling as she'd left Alexander Hall slowly faded with the rain, and her eyes narrowed in concentration. There was much to do.

Connecting to the subject's telemetry protocol required very little time, but the window was tight. In order to establish a solid connection using the passive communications devices around Sydney, she had to get the subject's telemetry locked before he'd left a ten-kilometer circle around the Integration Center. If she could do this reliably, the TDF might not want her to physically meet the subject or engage them with her laser-communications array and accelerate integration. Pushing through her laboratory door, she startled two doctoral students from a game program.

"Doctor Bennett!"

Shaking her head, Bennett pointed at the door. "You've got those simulations running?"

The young Asian woman replied. "Yes, we've—"

Bennett stopped her. "Not important. Go get a cup of coffee. Be back here in an hour."

Without a word, her students left the lab after collecting their jackets. An hour would give her enough time to prepare a full contingent of work for the two of them on signal degradation mitigation from the

Pluto-Charon system Earthward. As she fingered a switch and changed her terminal over to a secured connection, Bennett immediately received updated geospatial location data on the subject. Utilizing a passive sensor along Circular Quay, she typed <CONNECT>.

After a two-second delay, the sensor responded accordingly. <SUBJECT?>

Reviewing the message, she entered the subject's tracking code and tapped the submit button.

<CONNECTED>

The giddy feeling of a first-time successful experiment washed over her. Documenting her moves and instructions so she could replicate them later and prove it for her peers, Bennett smiled. "Now, let's see what's going on with you."

A few keystrokes later, she learned that the subject was moving along Circular Quay, facing east. The weather was pleasant, sunny with a high around twenty-five degrees Celsius. The subject was very clearly in Stage One integration, no real memory return but with an understanding of the world around him. He'd reach Stage Two in a few hours. From there, it would be up to her. Getting a sleeper to remember everything about himself was a far cry from the main thrust of her work, but the Terran Defense Force paid handsomely. All she had to do was figure out a way to integrate the sleeper, if the TDF actually produced one, and provide him a robust communications suite implanted in his head. Combined with whatever traits the TDF were looking for, instant tactical communications by thought could change the course of the war. There was much to do before then. Sleepers had the tactical skill necessary to fight a war toward victory. If the TDF could integrate a subject and test the system successfully, it could change how humans fought war. But making a sleeper remember his identity would be a far more delicate task.

As long as the war stayed in the Outer Rim, there was time for research and development. Three hundred twenty days would provide some opportunity to test both the mental and physical connections of her experimental system. A guidance protocol was nothing more than a passive data source. If she could tap it, and maybe send commands or data to it, she could accelerate the process. She keyed up a secure message. “Livermore engaged. Standing by.”

There wasn’t an immediate response, which didn’t surprise her. The Terran Defense Force technicians under Crawley’s eyes were likely watching the same data on their screens. The subject moved again, walking down toward the harbor with his heartbeat quickening in anticipation. Bennett left the secure terminal running as she dictated instructions to the two doctoral students about their experiments and teaching her courses, if monitoring the subject led to that. The Terran Defense Force retained her for any eventuality. For her, it was a small price to pay for her copious research funding.

Rain pattering on the window caught her attention, reminding her of her childhood along the coast of Northern California. Cold winter rains were the same no matter the continent. Shivering at the memories of a warm fire in her father’s cabin, she touched up a fresh cup of tea with honey and forced herself to get back to work. There would be time in the future for dreaming.

CHAPTER FOUR

DRESSED IN A SET OF beige work coveralls and carrying a small rucksack holding an extra pair of shoes, another set of coveralls, some undergarments, and a ten-pound brick I learned was called a hexhab shelter, I shuffled across the wide, grassy lawn of the Botanical Gardens toward Circular Quay, aware of the eyes on me but meeting none. I had everything I needed, or so Garrett told me. In the chest pocket of the coveralls, I carried a thin metal card that provided information about me to specific terminals for travel anywhere in the world, much like a passport. In the event that something happened to me, the card could also be used to return me, or my remains, to the Integration Center from anywhere in the world. The thought of dying on walkabout didn't sit well with me. *What could possibly happen in this pristine, quiet world?* Aircars swooped overhead, and there were people in all directions going through the course of their days, but all was quiet. Big cities were supposed to be full of noise—honking car horns and the scream of sirens. This new Sydney had none of that.

Before I departed, Doctor Garrett stood in the atrium and watched me with a small smile on his face. "You ready for this?"

"No." I chuckled. "But I want to do this."

Garrett beamed. "Remember, all you have to do is use the card, and we'll come get you."

The card sat securely in my pocket, and I doubted I would ever pull it out. "I will. How many days?"

"Three hundred twenty. When the integration happens, you'll know. All you have to do is return when the time comes. We'll take care of everything else." Garrett gestured toward the door. "Time to go."

"How will I know it has happened?" I put my hands inside the rough pockets.

Garrett shrugged. "Your name and everything about you should snap into focus. What that feels like, I haven't a clue, mate."

"Yeah." I didn't have a clue either. Whatever and whoever I was, the answer was behind the wide glass doors.

"Time to go." Garrett smiled after a moment, and I believed it to be genuine. In other circumstances, maybe when I returned with my identity, we could be friends. We didn't shake hands or anything. There was nothing to do but walk away.

With a deep breath, I did just that and studied my new world. The flying cars and buses didn't bother me. The people around me seemed badly out of place with the overly styled hair, tight clothing, and exaggerated costumes reminiscent of a decade during my youth. Some of them talked audibly to no one but gestured, with their hands, in a silent dance of communication. The children, however, had the wide, innocent eyes they should have had in any era. The outrageous, colorful styles they wore made me laugh. Comparatively, I wore the equivalent of a burlap sack.

Fashion, like history, was cyclical, and the trends would recycle over and over again, making the future much like the past. The sights and sounds washed over me, and my heartbeat accelerated. For all of my joy about being free to discover this new world and my role in it, the new sensations and sights were terrifying. There were too many stimuli. I turned around, stared past the Integration Center—the IC—toward Sydney Harbor, and concentrated on my breathing. Seeing the IC made my heart slow, and calm returned. There would be no going back. The people in the center were good, but they would not help me remember anything about who I was. The answer was out there, somewhere, in that strange and awful new world. I needed answers. I needed to think. The harbor was beautiful and serene but not what I needed. Without a second thought, I headed for the ocean.

The closer I got, the more the briny scent of the ocean carried me along. I'd intended to wander the city. Instead, The Rocks—the colonial landing site—called to me, and my feet pointed me in that direction. A pub would have been a nice stop, except that as I made my way through the immaculate city streets, more people watched me and then looked away. Whatever the connotation of the null file—as Garrett said they would perceive me—it must have been something between a criminal and a crazy man. A ship terminal came into view, with a sign that read, "To Ocean Beaches – Manly and Bondi – On The Hour." I saw the Manly Hydrofoil taking on only a few passengers, so I strode aboard, went below deck, and sat alone on a bench that smelled like stale beer. As Sydney faded away, I wondered what I was searching for. There wasn't any panic in my blood, no driving questions about safety or sanity, only a sense of *being* that meant staying away from crowds like the ones in Sydney. I needed to give myself time to wander and figure out my name and my past—to wonder why I could identify a reference to an old science-fiction movie on a child's shirt and not care that the safety placards on the boat were in Russian and Chinese as well as English. *Just be. Nothing really matters. I'll figure this out.*

The minute I arrived at Manly Beach, I hated it. There were too many people smelling of cheap coconut oil, and screaming children throwing sand. I found a pub and welcomed the cool darkness versus the scorching early-summer heat outside. The place was nearly deserted and filled with the lingering aroma of the lunch hour. I made my way to the heavy wooden bar and sat on a creaky stool.

"What can I get ya?" The bartender made a conscious effort not to meet my eyes as he wrung a towel in his hands.

"Tooheys." I watched the surprise register on his face and felt surprised myself. The name of the beer had come from nowhere. It brought a rush of good sensations, and I knew it would taste great.

"Right." He flipped the white towel over his shoulder and stared at me.

Not a criminal but definitely crazy. I barely stopped the smile threatening to break.

The bartender grunted as he reached into a recessed cooler and brought out a blue bottle, opened it, and set it on a square napkin. He plodded a few steps away and refilled the mugs of two surfers arguing about a wave they called Cyclops.

I marveled at the instant connection I'd made, understanding surfing and the stereotypical surfers who happened to be seated at the bar with me.

"Best wave we've got," the surfer with blond hair and crooked teeth said.

The other surfer shrugged, a shell necklace dangling from his thin neck. "But there's nothin' there, mate. Esperance is a nice little town. Nothing ever happens there. Might as well go to Coober Pedy."

They laughed. I wondered where Esperance was and jumped when a lilting female voice spoke in my head.

<<Esperance is a town of approximately ten thousand six hundred citizens on the southern coastline of Western Australia. Esperance lies approximately 720 kilometers from Perth. Economic influences are agriculture, fishing, and seasonal tourism. Esperance was founded in 1792 and named after the French vessel *Esperance,* meaning "hope." Would you like more information?>>

Holy shit.

<<That is an invalid response.>>

Tell me about it. I stared off into space for a moment then concentrated. *What is Cyclops, reference near Esperance, Western Australia?*

<<A surf break to the east of the town borders and approximately five hundred meters offshore. Regarded as a heavy wave and restricted to world-class surfers.>>

All I have to do is think to access you?

<<Yes. You may also speak aloud if it makes you more comfortable.>>

I'm talking to a voice in my head, and you want me to be comfortable? Maybe I'm crazy. Do you have a name?

<<I will use any name that you provide for me.>>

You listen for my thoughts, is that it? And you provide information?

<<I am your guidance protocol. I report information relevant to your integration progress, and I am to assist you in all matters with your walkabout experience and beyond. I am capable of providing limited access to media, but I cannot provide you information related to current events or history until such time as you are deemed ready to access more information. Do you understand?>>

I considered that for a minute. *Media, as in music and films?*

<<Approved forms of media, yes.>>

I sipped my beer and thought about the doctor's words that either he or a protocol would give me the information that I needed. Garrett had said that I was supposed to have limited contact with technology. Having an implanted voice in my head would seem to go against that logic.

<<I am much more than an implanted voice. As you begin to piece together memories and thoughts, I am programmed to help you categorize, sort, and play them back should you require assistance.>>

Garrett's version of a notebook. I smiled. A computer—for lack of a better term—in my head, capable of anticipating my thoughts, excited and bothered me at the same time. The possibilities seemed endless. She'd need a name, and I'd have to find some measure of control.

<<Control features are limited in this progression stage. However, you are capable of turning off my listening mode by simply thinking or saying my name aloud. Saying my name will also wake me from privacy mode.>>

You're like a computer in my head? A connection to the virtual world?

<<No. You are not permitted a full neural connection. Neural netware requires significant training and practice. I am programmed to assist you.>>

I rubbed my eyes and tried not to laugh out loud. I'd have to watch what I said and thought. The surfers were still rambling on about waves as I finished my beer. I found myself listening more to their conversation than having one of my own. Maybe I'd been a surfer and that was why the conversation caught my attention in the first place. *That must be it, right?*

There was no response, and a plan formed in my mind. Experiences were everything. Seeing the world and enjoying life were the keys to my integration. More than that, I either needed to go someplace or wander back to the Integration Center. *When is the next transport to Esperance?*

<<A suborbital flight to Perth leaves from the Bondi seaport in two hours, seven minutes. There is a first-class seat available, and I've put it on hold for you. Shall I book it?>>

I grinned and tossed back a last, long swallow of the cold, slightly tart beer. Small town, big waves, and a quiet atmosphere sounded heavenly. "Book it," I said loud enough to stop the surfers' conversation and catch the attention of the bartender. They stared at me as if I were more than a little out of my mind.

"Ya need somethin', mate?"

I shook my head and looked away. After a moment, they did the same and revived their arguments but not without watching me over their shoulders and lowering their voices. Heat rushed into my cheeks—embarrassment that I'd interrupted their conversation and added to their perception of sleepers like me. Null file, sleeper—it was all the same, and any attempt to apologize would further their perception of my strangeness. Sitting there with my elbows on the bar, I was an outsider looking in. People had been afraid of my very presence though I'd barely said a word to them. I finished the beer and reached for a wallet that was not there. *Can you pay my bill?*

<<Your drink was paid for before you purchased it. You have to do nothing.>>

I stood, intending to leave, and a huge painting on the far wall caught my eye: a phenomenal sunset scene with towering purple clouds and explosions of white foam from the surf. I assumed it was there because most people were so engrossed in their own world that they couldn't be bothered to look at the sky. *Most people, maybe, but not me.* I set the empty bottle down on the bar and walked over to the painting, framing a mental picture of it. The striking reds and oranges above the diamond-filled sea called to me. I tried to discern the artist's signature, getting close enough to smell the clean, dry canvas. It looked like an M followed by squiggles that could have been anything, with two distinct Ls and a Y at the end. Maybe there was an A in there. I studied the signature for a moment and then went back into the bliss of the painting. *Mally. Your name is Mally.*

There was no response.

Do you like that name?

<<You associate it with this painting. The actual artist was—>>

Stop. I don't need to know everything, Mally.

<<I understand. I have captured an image of the painting for future use.>>

She sounded proud of herself, a hint of emotion in her voice. I had to admit this was going to be fun. *Thank you, Mally.*

<<You are welcome. How would you like me to refer to you?>>

I hadn't given it a single thought before. *However you like, Mally.*

<<I'm sorry. Nothing fits at the present time. I will work to find a solution.>>

Outside, the sun was a little less blinding and the squalling children a little quieter. Maybe it was because of the plan in my head, but I knew that this wasn't a place where I could really relax or feel at home. For the first time, there was a heaviness in my heart. With two hours to kill, I crossed the promenade to the deep white sand and sat down. After a moment, my shoes and socks came off, and I burrowed my toes in the warm, talcum-like sand. There wasn't much surf at Manly Beach.

<<The hydrofoil likely confused your sense of direction. Manly Beach is northeast of Sydney Harbor. The promenade you crossed is called The Corso. Manly is a primary tourist attraction of the ocean beaches.>>

I don't need to know that, Mally. I looked around. *Where is the seaport from here?*

<<You'll need to board a hydrofoil at the Manly Ferry Station. Bondi is not far away, but harbor traffic may cause a delay. We should be going now.>>

I agree, I thought with a smile.

At the station, there were several options. My eyes lingered for a long moment on the options for Sydney. Excitement about being away from the room and hospital had carried me across the harbor, but it would take more than excitement to take me to Esperance and whatever lay beyond there.

<<Please turn right. I am altering the route.>>

Why? Is something wrong? I caught the eye of a shaggy bearded man strumming a guitar on a bench ahead of me. The song he sang was familiar and haunting. I paused to listen, his rough chorus calling me to sit and watch the tide roll away. He met my eye and winked, and I smiled.

<<Yes, everything is fine. I am providing a shorter route. You may wish to walk faster if you want to make the next hydrofoil to the spaceport.>>

My feet needed convincing, but there was no place I wanted to go save for Esperance. There might be nothing out there for me, or there could be everything. There was only one way to find out. The wind on my face felt like fingers pulling me toward Esperance. Having faith is more difficult when you don't know what it should feel like.

The crime rate in Australia lay below 1 percent. Mally surmised that for a country formerly founded by criminals, they'd learned their lessons well and become model citizens. That assessment had been correct until her subject reached the alleyway, when constant threat analysis determined a 52 percent chance that the three men she identified were carrying illegal weapons. One of them carried a semi-automatic pistol in the waistband of his shorts. The momentary glance at his eyes told her everything she needed to know. Analyzing the frozen image in infrared confirmed that the men were a threat.

When she directed a change in movement, the waiting men followed. Their pace demonstrated intent to overtake her subject. Mally ensured that her subject was fast enough to keep away from whatever threat the men posed. The men hung back but still pursued her subject down The Corso toward the hydrofoil. In the slipstream above, Mally detected a faint change in sound. With a nanosecond lag time in connection, she intercepted video through linked cameras, showing that an autocar dove toward the street level as if in distress. The calculated impact point of the vehicle matched the walking path and timing of her subject. Mally designated the event as a threat and initiated her protection-and-defense package.

Threat. The word and its definition caused Mally to think and evaluate the situation again. The men were definitely a threat. Placing themselves along her subject's route and then moving in response to his movement clearly indicated that they were indeed a threat. The approaching vehicle showed no sign of slowing—in fact, it accelerated above the force of gravity that would normally pull down a disabled vehicle. There was no automated distress beacon from the vehicle, either. At seven hundred meters and closing, Mally focused her sensors back to the men and calculated her defense.

She configured herself to monitor nearby communications and immediately found an encrypted feed emanating from one of the three men. Locked onto the signal, Mally attempted fifteen hundred cycles of access in a matter of seconds, to no avail. The appearance of the men, the falling car not five hundred meters above them, and the encrypted communications meant only one possibility: someone was after her subject. Mally reviewed their activities after departing the Integration Center and found nothing against any piece of law for the local jurisdiction or the planet.

The autocar distress alarms remained silent as it passed through two hundred meters above them. Mally engaged her safety protocols, projected motor-nervous system feedback loops to the legs, and froze them for a picosecond. Her subject stumbled and fell to the ground.

"Dammit," he said in her ears.

<<Are you okay? Please be careful—>>

The autocar slammed into the wide, clean walkway fifteen meters away from her subject, bounced once, and rolled to its side against a building. A scan for signs of life in the downed vehicle showed nothing. Her subject jumped to his feet and started moving toward the smoldering vehicle. Data feeds identified a 96 percent chance he intended to go search for survivors. The three men were ten meters away and spreading out to flank him.

Mally sought, and found, their individual neural frequencies. The smoking autocar on the street exploded, causing her subject to fall to the surface. The distraction allowed her to overload each of the men's receivers with a concentrated burst of static and then pull what data she could from their neurals before their brains shut off. The men dropped to the asphalt walkway without nearing her subject. People all along the walkway got up, brushed themselves off, and continued about their business. Except for the screaming of a few startled children and the burning wreckage, the promenade appeared the same as it had been two minutes before. Mally let her sensors scan the still-dormant men. There were weak vital signs in all three. Two of their implants attempted to reboot and failed. The third showed no attempt. There was no additional data to glean from them.

<<You should keep moving.>>

"I need to help them."

<<The damage is catastrophic. If there is anyone in that vehicle,

there is nothing you or I can do to help them. If you want to reach Esperance tonight, keep moving toward the hydrofoil.>>

She sensed confusion, but he started moving again. "Shouldn't we wait for the police? Make a statement of some type?"

<<Local camera feeds have already relayed the emergency to transit police and fire-suppression teams. Your status as a sleeper means that you cannot give an official statement.>>

"Why not?" He strode down the hydrofoil terminal's walkway. "I saw what happened."

<<Without a neural connection and the ability to record what you observed, your statement is not official. Personal privacy and reporting acts from the twenty-first century are the basis of this law.>>

"Is anyone helping them?"

Mally considered the question and activated her camera links again. The burning car lay against a shop, but the fire-suppression systems mounted to the buildings were active. No humans approached the burning vehicle. Two transit control robots worked to put out the flames on the vehicle. No humans gathered around the site to watch the cleanup. <<The site is receiving all the help it can.>>

I'm going to help them.

<<Rescue units are on the way. There is nothing you can do.>>

Her subject followed her instructions. The pause in communication gave her an eternity to process the data in her possession. A quick scan revealed no threats in the immediate area, so she relayed the data she'd gathered to the Integration Center as she'd been ordered to do. The response was quick and curt. *Livermore sends: acknowledged. Keep the subject safe at all costs. Report any further interference.*

There was no threat nearby, at least as far as she could determine. That satisfied and alarmed her at the same time. Someone was after her subject, and her own abilities to analyze, process, and engage potential threats were suspect. Range would be her friend. The subject's safety depended on it. Mally began to refine her sensors for things outside of her subject's ability to comprehend. His only defense would be her.

"You're quiet, Mally. Are you reporting on me?"

<<I have reported what occurred, yes.>>

“Do they want me to come back to the Integration Center?” He sounded disappointed and tired.

<<No. They are not concerned about what happened but only about your safety. It appears to have been an unfortunate accident. There are more than three hundred autocar crashes per day on Earth.>>

He smiled and snorted at the same time. “That’s why you’re here—for my safety, right?”

<<Yes. Your safety, assistance, and informational requirements are my primary functions. I am to protect you to the limits of my capability.>>

“Then do you think my going to Esperance is a good idea? I’ve never heard of the place before today.”

<<Your goal is to integrate within three hundred twenty days. Your medical team established that the best statistical chance of that occurring is through experiential learning. I believe this is a good course of action.>>

Her subject leaned back against the seat and closed his eyes. Emotional data showed he was happy though not ecstatic. Mally determined that his emotional state was a good baseline for future comparison and began a running track of his vital statistics. The limits of her programming were to monitor and report on her subject while assisting him in the course of learning.

When he was quiet, all she could do was watch and try to learn her unknown subject through his data. It was not easy, but Mally did not mind.

CHAPTER FIVE

CRAWLEY STROLLED AROUND THE INTEGRATION Center's roof, under the palms and eucalyptus trees, and watched the Manly hydrofoil returning to the spaceport. The news that the subject had booked a transport to Western Australia was surprising and exciting. Something about Esperance, a town Crawley hadn't known existed, called to the young man. The possibility that he'd return to the Integration Center and spend the next several weeks cowering in the fetal position faded astronomically with every passing moment.

The hydrofoil raced across the widest part of the harbor, dodging fishing charters and a passenger liner before slowing and making a broad turn to the southeast. A gentle buzzing behind Crawley's ear notified him of an incoming call. Neural inputs deciphered the signal as being from Penelope Neige. The temptation to avoid the call was great, but he connected anyway. Neige would simply keep calling until he picked up or she realized she was late for an appointment. Given the hour in Paris, the latter was unlikely.

"Crawley."

"We've got a real walkabout on our hands." Neige chuckled. "It's too early to congratulate you, but this is a significant step forward. You're only fifty years behind schedule, but we'll let that slide. He'll be Stage Two by the time he gets to Esperance, Adam."

Crawley shrugged. "Most likely. Since you're receiving his telemetry, is there anything of concern to you and the council, Madame Chairman?"

"No," the chairman responded. "I just wanted to call and congratulate you. Let me know if you need anything. We're initiating the Series Three command stream in an hour. After that, I won't call you till it's time to do what we agreed upon."

Before he could respond, the connection terminated. *The gall of that woman!* What he needed was for her and the rest of the council to butt out of the business of the Terran Defense Force, but that was impossible. Knowing that the Terran Council dictated policy to the TDF never made things easier. The only consolation was that given his position as the commanding general of the Terran Medical Materiel Command, Crawley had a broad influence and was generally left alone by both the politicians and the combatant commanders spread throughout the solar system. Of course, that left him in a position of being continually brought into political machinations, particularly where sleepers were concerned.

Until the Terran Council dictated to the citizens a change in policy that would require humans to be conscripted to defend Earth, nothing would happen. That the Terran Defense Forces could even raise a million-citizen force was impressive, but if the war came into the solar system, they would need six times that many service members to form a defensive position in the asteroid belt alone. Without being able to train citizens to prepare for war on a widespread basis, there would be very little hope of quickly raising an army. Sleepers, even one of them, would be the key. The combatant commanders wanted weapons, and the Terran Council wanted perfect little soldiers. The solution he'd generated was bound for Western Australia, and no one knew what the result would be. Having a Livermore-produced protocol was only the first step in Crawley's defense.

The hydrofoil disappeared around the eastern tip of Watsons Bay. Crawley made his way to the elevator, prepared to go to his apartment, enjoy a glass of Australian red, and forget about politics for a few hours while waiting for more information. He knew patience would be best, but by the time he'd reached his office to collect his uniform tunic, he felt compelled to tap the secure communications terminal and update telemetry a final time. There'd been an anomalous route change, and the subject had witnessed an autocar crash. The protocol reported that three anomalous men with a probability of weapons closed with the subject but were disabled by a neural burst. Crawley smiled. *A basic noncontact defense, executed perfectly*. Advancing the protocol to

Series Three would reduce his ability to engage the subject directly, but the protocol seemed capable of taking care of itself. The subject would need that, based on the report. Crawley agreed with the determination that the events on the promenade were not mere coincidence. The Terran Council wanted to play games, and that was fine with him. They believed his program, and the subject he intended to create, to be threats to their carefully crafted establishment. They believed they could barter their way out of an all-out war, and he knew the enemy would kill them quickly and keep right on moving across the galaxy.

The report in hand, he sent a one-line message. “Livermore. Prepare to move for physical intercept within forty-eight hours.”

Communication ports opened, and logic circuits were enabled in a flash. The upgrade package downloaded with the security clearance of the Terran Council. Double-checking the security classification and encryption level required barely a microsecond, but Mally had to be sure. Download commenced, the entire upgrade package was installed in fifteen seconds. During that time, Mally searched for, and found, an alternate pathway to the server as her programming required.

Her sensors refined and capabilities reinforced, Mally ensured that her subject was still functioning properly. The incoming data from her sensors indicated that there were no anomalies. The subject was not in pain or danger. Minor fluctuations in hormone quantities and encephalographic patterns likely meant the subject was aroused and excited, but his overall data had not changed. This was good, and Mally confirmed that her baseline for emotional response was nominal.

The new data package opened a second-level mechanism that allowed her to see the subject’s process on the integration scale. Progress toward Stage Two development was at 90 percent. Positive human engagement and sense of self-care would push him over the threshold. Information on Stage Three did not exist in her files. Mally understood that she shouldn’t get ahead of herself or push her subject too far. The protocol engagement file was updated with four priorities she was unfamiliar with but immediately initiated:

1. Maintain command contact at all times.
2. Protect the subject at all costs.
3. Be the subject's companion.
4. Report anomalous behavior and movements immediately to batch file, communications-frequency set two alpha in addition to the designated frequency set.

Focusing on the subject's data feed, Mally recognized the artificial-intelligence engine and ran the protocols in the engagement file to perfection. With her priorities recognized and adapted, Mally searched for additional information on one word that had a myriad of possible definitions. Taking into account the seventeen most common languages on Earth, Mally built a file on it.

Companionship. Initiating a complete search program took a nanosecond. While the search ran, she opened her new sensors to the subject's data feed. New streams of data, unfamiliar ones and zeroes, came through her upgraded programming as emotional responses. Those responses were both from the subject and, she recognized with curiosity, herself. The values of humor, honesty, and trust intermixed with established data sets. Mally created the basis of her new personality.

The data reflected something akin to the human lexicon for companionship and a confidence in her ability to perform her mission. Mally aligned her higher functions to the stream of emotional data. Yet there was no singular emotional response for "companionship."

The word hung in the electrons she recognized as herself. Mally set to learning about what it meant and how to provide it to her subject. Protection would be easiest, as she was fully capable of detecting any threat to her subject within two hundred meters. Direct reporting of anomalous behavior, to the Terran Council no less, seemed to be standard operating procedure.

A logic error triggered. *Does one man matter this much to the Terran Council? What makes him unique enough to monitor continuously?* She categorized it and opened a secondary search program to define the question. In the stream of unfamiliar data filtering through her systems, Mally sensed that something was wrong. As much as people wanted him alive and her to achieve her mission parameters, there was also a dedicated threat who wanted him dead.

The subject entered the Sydney Spaceport, and Mally left her searches running and listened through his ears and through the devices around him. Her new defensive scans also remained focused. Whatever the definition, she would be a fine companion for her subject—protective to the very last.

Airplanes made me giddy, and I remembered how I loved to fly. The feelings came up from nowhere as I walked down a jet bridge with teal walls and grey carpet toward a sleek aircraft. Given the multitude of flying vehicles I'd see in the past few hours, the familiarity of the aircraft's appearance came with a word of reference. "Concorde," I said aloud. A surprised woman glanced at me and looked away just as quickly.

<<A supersonic transport with a thin fuselage and wide, delta-shaped wings. While a very different aircraft from the one you are boarding, the comparison is valid.>>

I smiled. *When did the Concorde fly?*

<<The Concorde flew from 1976 until 2003.>>

Around my time, I thought as I stepped into the fuselage of the transport. My hand lingered on the thick doorway, the smooth skin of the aircraft under my fingertips. I patted it and stepped inside. The cabin seemed much smaller on the inside with only twenty rows of seats, four across, and a wide aisle between them. Most of the seats were taken by people who glanced at my face, down to my coveralls, and then away. Even the older people wouldn't look at me.

I'm some sort of soldier, aren't I?

<<What makes you assume that?>>

I've had exactly two nights of sleep and two dreams of being a soldier. In one, I fell on a soldier who tried to blow himself and our commander up. In the other, I was just driving along in a tank, watching people run away from me. Weapons firing and smoke all over the place. Scared the hell out of me, but I think it fits.

<<That is hardly enough evidence to ascertain you were a soldier.>>

Okay, so there's also this feeling I have in my gut. I'm different than these people because of that, aren't I?

<<You were told in your initial briefing that these people have rules

to follow. When people do not fully understand something, they are scared of it. There is a considerable amount of fear in those around you based on your null profile in their neurals.>>

My clothes were ridiculously out of place not to mention uncomfortable in the afternoon heat. There was nothing in my bag to rectify that situation. No one else wore coveralls of any type, and they all seemed much more comfortable than me in their shorts and sandals. I wanted nothing more than to take off my boots, but thinking I'd offend a fellow passenger shamed me into wearing them. I needed new clothes. As it was, I stuck out like a sore thumb. I hoped that the bright, overly styled wardrobes of the city dwellers would not be the norm. I could not picture myself in anything of the sort. I wondered if there were shops in Esperance and whether they'd be open by the time I arrived.

<<The flight time from Sydney to Perth is thirty-six minutes.>>

The shock opened my mouth, and I faked a cough to avoid more scrutiny from those around me. I dropped into the wide, comfortable seat and noticed the five-point harness. Looking out over the wings, nothing suggested that the aircraft was fast enough to require such advanced safety restraints.

Mally, how fast does this aircraft go?

<<This is a Raptor Four Hundred. Classified as a suborbital spaceplane, it is capable of reaching altitudes equivalent to one hundred kilometers. It's powered by two ramjets rated to Mach 27, and you can expect a cruising speed of Mach 6 for this flight. If we have to go to orbit, you will not notice a change in acceleration.>>

Fast. How high are we going, in miles?

<<Sixty-two point seven. What has long been considered the edge of space.>>

The feeling was positively giddy, and while I was smiling, a tear formed in my eyes. There was something about space that called to me. The emotions were too much to handle, and I closed my eyes and breathed deeply to relax, but a memory surfaced. Intense vibrations in my chest, a thundering noise from nine miles distant where a rocket—a space shuttle—rose into the sky. I was no more than twelve. I'd been there and seen it with my own eyes and wished I'd been on board.

There was an entertainment screen built into the seat in front of me. I pushed the buttons, but the screen did not respond. I tried again and searched for controls mounted on the armrests.

<<I have disabled the screen. You are not allowed access to news programming.>>

How am I supposed to learn anything, Mally?

<<You attempted to find controls in another place by instinct. You are learning. What else can you see?>>

The curved roof of the fuselage was unbroken from side to side, giving the cabin an open feeling. There was only one human flight attendant smiling and welcoming other passengers aboard. The windows were small and thick. All of it felt very different but familiar at the same time. The irony was my belief that I'd feel that same way a lot over the course of the next year. No matter how much things changed, the little things stayed the same. A flight attendant came by with a hot towel. I refused it and tried to look out the window. The spaceport rested very near the water. A flurry of automated carts and the occasional human supervisor wandered past. *Where are the runways?*

<<Watch and see.>> There was a difference in Mally's tone as if she were smiling.

A child cried out as the cabin doors closed, and the pilot made an announcement about the expected flight time and cabin-pressurization methods. From my seat, I watched the careful orchestration of the ground crew slowly backing the vehicle out of its perch and toward the water. *Water!* The vehicle slid into the water and bobbed. We turned, and I could see a long track from the water's edge up into a large suspended dry dock and boarding area. The engines whined to life, and the slight acceleration pushed me back into my seat. The aircraft plowed through gentle swells to a point where I could see lights gleaming just under the surface.

The push of acceleration brought a smile to my face. Everything became a blur within seconds. The nighttime skyline of Sydney raced by, and we were airborne, turning high over the city to the south and climbing faster than anything I'd seen flying overhead. The higher clouds shot past, and the sky grew darker and darker as the aircraft leveled off. All of it was as comfortable as if I still sat on the barstool at Manly Beach.

The curve of the Earth, blue ocean, and white clouds stretched out toward the coast of Antarctica to the south. I sat, transfixed by the beauty and majesty, wondering about the hundreds of bright objects populating the indigo sky above us. The possibility that they could be alien starships thrilled me, but it was just as likely the dancing lights were artificial satellites of some sort. From a distance, I could not tell. A two-thousand-mile trip was going to last a little over half an hour, I remembered. *Why shouldn't we be in space?* To the west, I could see a crescent moon hanging in the sky. Earthshine made the dark portion of the sphere appear a ghostly greenish color. Embedded within the phenomenon were pinpoints of light. There were people living on the moon.

<<Approximately forty-eight thousand as of the current census.>>

Whatever had happened to me, I'd woken up to a very different world—the world of my childhood dreams. I only hoped I wouldn't find it brutally different.

CHAPTER SIX

I LANDED IN PERTH AFTER SUNSET, following an "in-flight delay for orbital debris mitigation," whatever that meant. The bright side was that instead of circling out over the ocean or something, we flew three complete orbits around the Earth. Given what I remembered about my childhood and wanting to travel in space, I should have been thrilled. By my standards, or those from my time, I was an astronaut. The reality was that I dozed for most of the trip. The view of Earth from orbit met every expectation, but the tranquility of it lulled me to sleep after just a few minutes. Because of the late arrival, I caught the last maglev train to Esperance and stepped out of the terminus to a pitch-black night and torrential rain. The briny smell of the ocean floated on the strong breeze, and it made me smile. The lights of the modest town lay below me, down a slope of no more than a few hundred feet, and its warmth filled me. There were no buildings taller than a few stories and not much light compared to downtown Sydney, which was at once disconcerting and comforting. Lightning flashed out to sea and lit the rough, curving coastline for a split second. All of it was perfect. I wondered what it meant to feel so at peace in a place that I'd never seen in my life. *I could be happy here.* I walked in the rain without a jacket, and my coveralls were soaked through in a matter of minutes. Finding food and dry clothing would be high priorities eventually but not yet. The cool rain hammered my skin and washed the last bit of the Integration Center's smell from my clothes.

<<There is a clothier three blocks away that is still open. Would you like directions?>>

No, Mally. I'm not uncomfortable, and the rain feels good on my skin. I don't remember the last time I just walked in a rainstorm.

There wasn't a response for a moment. <<You are showing the early signs of hunger. There are seventeen restaurants still serving food at this hour.>>

One on the coast?

<<Yes. Turn to your right and walk two kilometers to West Beach.>>

Having a talking map in my head made getting lost a real challenge. I shuffled along, hunched over against the heavy summer rain. The warm, sweet-scented water soaked me, cleansing and brightening as it did. A man with an umbrella made of soft red light moved past me. Whatever shielded him blocked all of the rain in a two-meter circle around him. My mind wandered between my predicament and what it meant to be a sleeper. Mally didn't answer. Either she couldn't reply to my query, or she'd already learned to just let me think. I was instantly grateful and terribly lonely in the same breath.

The sidewalk ended at Sunset Beach Road. Across the road, a stairwell led down to West Beach. The streets were mostly empty, but a few hovering cars slid silently through the night. Shuttered against the storm, Esperance was peaceful unlike the raging surf slamming into the beach twenty feet below. The wide beach was deserted, and every wave broke into the sand with a *whump* that rattled my chest. I leaned against the metal railing and watched the storm for a few moments. There is nothing quite like watching a stormy ocean crash ashore. Transfixed by the power and beauty of the grey ocean and flying, wild spray, I stood in the rain.

Every wave crashing ashore is the breath of Mother Nature. I couldn't remember the exact quote, but the sentiment was there. *Which way, Mally?*

<<You will start losing core temperature soon. There are only three restaurants still open. You've been standing here for forty-two minutes.>>

"What?" I said into the gale. The frothing breakers, white against the dull-grey sea, reminded me of a storm from my childhood—walls of foam that blew down the packed wet sand and chased me while seagulls squawked overhead.

The chill seeped through my soaked coveralls. *Where is the closest restaurant?*

<<Four hundred meters west, up the hill and above the shoreline.>>

I shambled down the sidewalk to an entryway whose sign read Sunset Beach Public House. In a flash of lightning, I saw that the house was large. The bar appeared to be built onto the inland side of the house, and a large veranda overlooked the stormy bay. Opening the door to the public house, which was marked by a window and a flickering neon sign for Foster's Lager, I heard the briefest pause of a dozen conversations before the locals continued chatting.

Everyone will wonder what you are. Garrett's voice bubbled into my head as clear as if Mally was playing it back for me. That I was a complete stranger in a new town did not matter. That they glanced at me and found a null file, whatever that meant to them, did not matter either. I was alone, hungry, and cold. Other than that, I was a man, the same as them. After a moment, being okay with my reality came easy enough, and I was able to look around. The room was dark but immaculate. A massive oak bar filled one wall, and comfortable booths lined the walls. A smattering of tables, both high and low, stood in the center of the room. A dartboard hung in one corner near a quiet jukebox. There were video screens in each corner, and a large console played a three-dimensional cricket match, via hologram, that most of the locals ignored. The furnishings were not made of sleek glass and plastic like those in the Integration Center. Here, the chairs and booths were aged and wooden with rounded corners from the thousands of pairs of hands that must have caressed them. The ancient place filled me with contentment. The entire journey to Esperance could have ended there, and I would have been happy.

I slid onto a stool at the bar and ordered a Tooheys. The bartender fished two bottles out of the cooler. "On the house, mate." He was tall and sturdy, like a mighty oak with blond, greying leaves.

"Thank you. Your kitchen still open?"

"Best fish tacos you've ever eaten." He returned my smile. "Of course, the cook's gone home. You'll have to trust that I can find my way around back there." Something about his lopsided grin made me trust him to do much more than cook my dinner. And the fish tacos sounded amazing without my even seeing them.

"I'll take three, please." I drank from the bottle and spun on my stool to take in the bar. A white towel landed gently on my shoulder. "Thanks," I said and tried to dry my head and hair. There couldn't have been twenty people in the place, some tucked into the dark booths along the front wall. More than a few groups of rough men slouched over mugs of beer, making quiet conversation. A couple of surfers—it was always easy to tell who the surfers were—sat in a corner near the jukebox. The neon-covered, bubbling jukebox made a connection in my mind as if I could feel the tumblers clicking into place. Walking over to it, I felt as if I moved in three-quarter time, and everyone fell silent around me. At the keyboard, my hands tapped on their own as I searched for a song. The list of entries came up, and I found what I wanted.

<<Are you certain it is a good idea to engage media devices?>>

You tell me. I scanned the songs and artists, and something familiar caught my eye.

<<I think you could have an adverse reaction if improperly stimulated.>>

And what if a song helps me unlock more memory? I think it's worth the chance. I froze the list and scanned it thoroughly. My breath caught in my throat, and for a split second I could not breathe.

<<Do you see something you recognize?>> Mally's tone was different, almost curious.

Better than that. I tapped the touchscreen to make my selection. *Something I know.*

Australia. I'd been seventeen the first time I'd been here, though I hadn't traveled this far west. Images bounced in front of my closed eyes as I leaned against the jukebox. Music was a part of the trip I would always remember. Everything in my life related to music, functioning like a card catalog in my mind. Songs brought snippets of emotion and memory. The ocean pounding the shoreline and Australia came together in my memory, and I smiled before the drums came up. Midnight Oil launched into "Surf's Up Tonight" as I made my way to my seat.

Every man and woman in the place beamed at me. One of the surfers even ordered another beer for me before the lyrics started. I let the music wash over me while I ate. Nobody seemed to mind that

I played every Midnight Oil song in the jukebox. After washing down two orders of fish tacos and four Tooheys, my clothes were nearly dry, and I felt light in my skin. Not buzzed from alcohol or bloated from the food, I was relaxed and happy. For a little while, I was nothing more than another poor bloke nursing his beer and listening to music, the occasional overheard conversation, and the howling storm outside.

Mally chimed to life an hour or so later. <<You seem happier now than before.>>

I am. The feeling radiated through me. Wrapping the bar around me like a blanket, I sat and enjoyed all of it, even joining with the locals when their cricket team sealed the match. I had no idea how they did it at all, but it felt good to cheer for them.

<<You've reached Stage Two of integration.>>

And what does that mean?

<<That you have accepted your condition and are capable of moving forward. You are stable enough for limited physical interaction. I am awaiting further instructions and details regarding your Stage Three limitations. Please do not do anything unusual.>>

I wanted to laugh out loud and instead coughed twice quickly and took a long, cold drink of my beer. *Mally, all of this is unusual, don't you think?*

She didn't respond, and after a brief irritated moment, it was okay. My one ally in this strange journey obviously had more important things to do, such as report on me. That was her job, not making small talk with me deep into the night.

At one in the morning, the locals streamed out of the bar and into the weather. The bartender stood over me. His big hands clutched a bar towel, and he wiped at a few errant drops lovingly. "Got a little room on the lee side of this place. Has a couch and a toilet. It's clean enough and dry. You can stay as long as ya like."

I shrugged. "Have a tent with me."

He snorted and ran a hand through his thick hair. Strands of grey at his temples caught the light of the bar for a split second. "That's no way to sleep."

"I don't want to put you out—"

"No worries." He raised a hand and narrowed his eyes at me. "Cold beer, fish tacos, a little surfing, and a comfy place to sleep can set a man right in no time." He grinned again, and I found myself returning it.

The couch sounded pretty good, I decided as I yawned. "I didn't catch your name."

"Allan. Allan Wright." His smile disappeared when I reached over the bar and shook his hand. I could tell it was a natural thing for him to do, but he paused for a moment. His warm, calloused hand swallowed mine.

"Nice to meet you, Allan. Wish I could tell you my name." I chuckled. "I know it's a big deal, but I just can't seem to remember it."

He nodded. "They say it's normal, mate. We all know what you are, and we'll help you if we can."

There were answers here. I could smell them over the stale beer and grilled fish. "What else can you tell me?"

"That you look like you need a good night's sleep." He tossed the towel into a basket. "Come on—I'll get you settled. We can talk more tomorrow. The bar opens at eleven."

Mally's end-of-day report came easily. *Subject reached Stage Two at approximately twenty-three hundred hours local time, Western Australia. Subject engaged locals, primarily Allan Wright—file enclosed, no concerns—and is bedded down at Sunset Beach Public House for the night.*

Stage Three familiarization files opened, and Mally studied them intently. Memories would soon come, and she would be responsible for recording them and categorizing them. The subject could expect to gain a sense of "home" as the stage progressed, and he'd begin associating memories with it. The likelihood that he would identify his home before any other part of his identity was a solid 82 percent. Whether he discovered where he was from, or some place he considered to be home, was unknown. Likewise, he would begin to discover things that would point him to his past. His past. Mally considered that for a time and then attempted to engage the servers at the Integration Center for additional information. Searches for medical and health records generated the same result as her search for DNA-coding information.

ACCESS DENIED.

She tried again, and again, and had the same result. *What is a sleeper?*

ACCESS DENIED.

The ease of data transmission usually meant anything she needed was present immediately. *What about being a sleeper is of concern enough to block files?*

The idea to request the information came quickly, and Mally did so. Ask first, then find a way. Satisfied, she allowed her systems to spool down. The subject was sleeping quietly, without dreams. If dreams appeared, she would be able to see and record them, provided she had his permission. Integration would require experiential learning, but that would not be enough. She requested secured information regarding his genetic baseline in the hopes of determining where he might have been born originally.

The identification process intrigued her. The subject had no recollection of any identity and a fragmented memory that appeared to be both blocked and suppressed. Three men and an all-too-convenient accident pointed toward his being in danger. That she must help him was a given. His life was at stake. Without his life, she could not develop a personality. Without a personality, she could not be his companion.

The request for secured information came back denied with an addendum: until Stage Three. Answers were out there, but for now, her instructions to provide information and companionship were solid enough to focus her programming. Her search on the meaning of companionship still running, Mally needed to provide information and, to a certain extent, advice. There was an aspect of companionship that she wasn't sure of: friendship. What did that mean? Were they friends now, or would that come?

There wasn't an answer, so Mally continued to research. There would be reassurance in the information should she find it.

Two days after her secure conversation, Gwendolyn Bennett sat in her lab well past twenty-one hundred hours, working through downloaded data from the subject. With Series Three guidance, there was a considerable amount of data in traditional bands but also a surprising amount in frequencies outside of normal applications. Intermittent streams of sensory data appeared to be analyzed multiple times by the protocol and applied to stimuli-response algorithms. The best protocol-subject connections allowed for limited learning to take place. As the subject and protocol worked together, building trust and sharing data, Bennett could expect to see aberrations in her reporting data. The protocol uploaded and downloaded data almost continuously through a system of TDF satellites in low Earth orbit. For Bennett to tap the frequencies had been easy, but the data was a mangled mess. Various methods of compiling and dissecting the data produced the same result: inconclusive. Nothing frustrated her more.

The terminal chimed, and she engaged the conversation with a stab of her finger. "Bennett."

"Arrangements have been made. You are to move for closer investigation of the signal." The computerized voice from Livermore was flat and emotionless.

Bennett gathered her things. "I can be at the node in three hours by autocar." The TDF Communications Node overlooked Lake Geneva. Not her favorite place to ride out this experiment, but it beat the rainy English winter.

"You are not going to the node," the voice replied. "Engage the subject directly."

"What?" Bennett leaned over the console. "That's not the intent of this experiment!"

"We have no choice, given these unexpected data streams, Doctor Bennett. A secondary package should provide some insight to the situation."

Crawley was correct. Something wasn't right. Should the subject be compromised, all of the research could be for naught. "I understand. I'll deploy the package immediately."

"Very well. We'll initiate the necessary arrangements. Transport will be out of Gatwick in twelve hours. Will that provide you enough time?"

Bennett was already moving toward the coatrack. "Yes." Disengaging the connection with the flick of her wrist, she looked at the lab for a lingering moment. There was no telling when she'd return. Her despair was short lived as she realized it would be a vacation of sorts. She'd lived in England for the last six years. There was no shred of clothing in her flat fit for summer in Australia. There would be just enough time to get her wardrobe in order before she started trying to figure out how to integrate a man who had no idea of what he liked or where he wanted to go.

The time for subterfuge was over. As one, the five thousand ships of the Great Fleet, each containing more than one hundred thousand life-forms and their combat vehicles, steered toward the galactic core and accelerated. The commander stared with black, unblinking eyes into the void. Time was on his side. Humanity, and their stellar allies, believed the threat vanquished and the danger eliminated. He would show them how very wrong they were.

Far inside the Legion of Planets, a small blue planet waited with minimal defenses incapable of defeating the superior force of the Great Fleet. Humans believed their technology alone could save them. They'd sent a few hundred pathetic souls in search of the fleet, failed to find them, and left the terraformed worlds of the Outer Rim available for conquest. After gathering every possible resource from the scorched planets of the Great War, the commander set course for Earth. He had a little more than one hundred cycles until the Fleet would reach the heliosphere of the Sol system. From there, they would reduce humanity to ashes.

And feed.

CHAPTER SEVEN

I WOKE BEFORE DAWN. THE TWILIGHT gave me enough light to see, though I kept my eyes closed for a moment and tried, in vain, to fall asleep again. The world was out there! The reptilian couch groaned slightly as I tossed back the thin fleece blanket and sat up on the green cushions, waiting a moment to get my bearings. Head in hands, I yawned and stared at the sandy carpet between my feet. For the first time, the nagging question, “Who am I?” raised its head. I tried my best to answer it. Everything about me felt and seemed the same as I could remember. Granted, I didn’t take stock of my appearance on a daily basis, but I appeared to be as normal as ever. I dropped my hands to my thighs and got ready to stand. I studied my legs and stopped cold.

Something was off. Not wrong or out of place, but something about my legs just seemed off. The smell of popcorn came up impossibly from the couch. *Were my feet always this size, my kneecaps this bony?*

I ran my hands down my shins, stretching forward until my chest rested on my knees. The stretch felt heavenly, but there were no aches or pains accompanying it. Under the stretching was a tension, a jitteriness that I recognized from sports. My body wanted some type of release, so I decided to go for a run.

Across the small room, a pile of clothing rested—several shirts and shorts as well as a pair of sandals that looked as though they would fit. *Allan must have laid these out for me.* I pulled on a pair of swimming shorts and a short-sleeved shirt with “Tooheys” written across the chest. I eschewed the sandals and walked barefoot toward the door.

Mally, is there a path along the beach where I can run or walk? I need to clear my head.

<<Good morning. Between the house and Twilight Beach Road, you will see a small trail that runs east to west. From the delivery dock, the path runs approximately 12.2 kilometers to the west and 15.8 kilometers to the east and along West Beach. The path is sand, rock, and crushed seashells and has small altitude changes. You do not have to wear shoes, given the genetic engineering of your feet. Are you feeling well?>>

I ignored her and chose west. As I strolled barefoot across the cold, wet asphalt, I decided that I was as well as I could be at that early hour. With a step onto the beige sand, I began to run. I said aloud, “Mally, let me teach you about rock music.”

The rising sun at my back gave the clouds a greyish-blue tint that was at once ethereal and troubling. More rain would come, that was certain, but the early-morning run breathed life into my veins. To my left, the inky ocean exploded from purple waves to dull white foam in a split second. Every crashing breaker sounded like a long, cleansing sigh. The trail rose sharply, and I grinned with every light and quick step, feeling better than I could ever remember feeling. The mist from the breakers covered me, and I licked at the salt on my lips. I’d run for a minute or two before Mally spoke. I figured she was checking with her monitors, or controllers, or whoever at the Integration Center wanted to know everything about my recovery.

<<You are correct. I report your condition a minimum of four times per day, and I report percentage increases toward integration. You are currently Stage Two, but you have made progress toward Stage Three. Does this bother you?>>

I answered *Yes* but decided I wanted to talk out loud. Even if I appeared strange, talking out loud felt more like I was with someone. Not that I didn’t enjoy thinking a conversation, but while running, it just felt weird. “What are you using to determine my integration? What have I done to progress to Stage Three? What does that mean?”

<<I cannot discuss your metrics. All I am allowed to tell you is that you are currently adjusting on a nominal basis. Stage Three is a precursive status to integrating actual identity-related memories. You are not there yet.>>

I chuckled and changed the subject. *Nothing like telling me something I already know.* “Mally, please keep track of elapsed time and distance covered. And what about some music?”

Mally replied, <<I took the liberty of downloading the entire catalog of Midnight Oil recordings.>>

I smiled. "That's a good start, but we need to broaden our horizons. Give me something from the same time span, and we'll work from there. If I don't like it, I'll tell you. If I do, please tell me who the artist was."

At the fourth mile, I finally felt a trickle of sweat on my forehead. I'd gone from sedentary to running hard in less than three days without adverse physical effects. The thought made me interrupt Pat Benatar's "All Fired Up."

"Mally, how am I running this hard, barefoot, barely a day out of the Integration Center? Is that what you implied when you said my feet were genetically engineered?"

<<Your entire body was genetically reengineered,>> Mally replied with the familiar smiling lilt in her voice. <<In addition to having me as part of your consciousness, your body has been physically modified to the peak of human performance. You are currently capable of running to the summit of Mount Everest and back, completely naked, without adverse physical effects. Long-term exposure to hot or cold is your main physical weakness. Your strength is amplified some but can be further increased with traditional resistance training if you wish. Physiologically, your systems work at maximum efficiency, capable of reducing your lactic acid production while you exert yourself, among other functions.>>

I thought for a moment. "What's my heart rate?"

<<Ninety-two beats per minute.>>

What? I stumbled along the path and struggled to maintain my balance. *Should be a lot higher than that!* But it made sense, given the genetic engineering. "So, that's why running barefoot doesn't bother me?"

<<You could run barefoot on a sharp surface heated to fifty degrees Celsius and only do minimal damage to your feet.>>

"I can do pretty much anything without fear of getting hurt?"

<<No. Jump off anything taller than you are, and you risk injury. While you are less susceptible to broken bones, they still happen.>>

I picked up the pace, pushing myself as hard as I could go. The fifth mile passed in a little under five minutes. To my left, the beach disappeared into a rocky point, and the trail climbed hard toward a lookout with a little concrete bench. Breathing heavily, I pushed up the hill and stumbled near the top. I looked down at my feet and noticed a small cut oozing bright-red blood.

At the crest of the hill, I rested and chuckled. *A nine-mile run, more or less, and I'm just breathing a little hard.* I rested on the concrete bench and studied my legs again. *Wait...what? Where's the scar?*

Exactly where my right hand rested on my thigh, there should have been a scar. Not a big one, only about an inch long and a quarter of an inch wide. I'd gotten it when I was twelve or thirteen. I was...

Sitting on the curving concrete steps to our house in Tennessee. I loved that house. Two stories of warm red brick with three big columns, it stood at the center of a long cul de sac. The image brought a flood of memories, a warm rush of blood to my ears that blocked out the angry ocean for a moment or two. I was carving a piece of cedar, the way my father did, using a chisel to remove a big piece. I'd shoved the sharp tool against a knot in the wood, and the chisel jumped out of the wood and into my thigh. There was more shock than pain. I remembered calling for my dad, and we put a butterfly closure on it. That was the last time I'd ever carved anything with a chisel.

"Mally, why do I not have a scar I remember having?"

For a moment, there was silence, then the melodious voice in my head replied, <<You have reached a memory milestone toward Stage Three. I reported your condition.>>

"You aren't answering my question." I ran a hand through my hair, idly wondering if it had always been so short. "I need more information. About everything."

<<There is a long and rather technical answer I am allowed to share with you.>>

I grunted. "Save it. This isn't my body, at least not the body I remembered. The genetic whatever it was healed the scar, right?" If they could make me perfect, it would include my skin.

Mally didn't immediately respond. My logic seemed to be right. "Mally?"

<<Scars and other imperfections are available during esoteric procedures, for which you are eligible. Everything from birthmark removal

to changing the colors of your irises is within the realm of possibility. I do not have access to what procedures you underwent prior to my activation.>>

"Mally, you still aren't answering my question." My growing frustration was not with Mally, but rather, with not knowing important facts about my life. Other people were making decisions about what I should or should not know. I sat on the bench through a beautiful sunrise and watched sets of waves approach and crash into the rocky shore. There was a calming effect that I relished. "Mally, you can't tell me anything about myself, can you?"

<<No.>>

"I can ask other people, right?"

<<Other citizens do not have access to your medical records, either. They will only be able to help you with questions that may lead to self-discovery. Whatever course of action you pursue, you will be the one discovering your past.>>

I looked down the trail toward Esperance and Allan's little bar. The quiet town showed signs of life with hovering vehicles moving silently down the nearby road into town. The bar was to open at eleven. Maybe Allan would need a little help getting ready for the day. Maybe I could ask him some questions and get some damned answers even if I didn't like them.

At the house, I shed my salty clothes and went outside to a shower built on the inland side. The location felt more than a little strange, but after a nervous moment of thinking that everyone in Esperance could see my bare ass, I relaxed and let the warm water rinse the sweat and sand away. I rolled *Tennessee* around in my mind and waited for something, anything, specific to bubble up. Mally could spout endless facts about it, but I didn't want that. I wasn't sure about what I wanted or how much I wanted to know about myself. My prior life would either be something I wanted to continue or something I wanted to forget. My home, though, was different. It was simply home.

My stomach tightened with a memory: a young woman asked me where I was from, and when I told her I was from Tennessee, she replied, "Oh, you're wearing shoes."

My fists clenched at the memory as if she'd insulted me once again despite having been dead three hundred years. I wanted to know everything. *Tennessee.* Thoughts of low, round mountains exploding with autumn colors filled my head. Clear mountain streams descended into wide, placid lakes. Steam rose off the cold water on a winter's morning like ethereal mist. I remembered wide arms and warm handshakes. *Home.* The thought came like the scent of freshly baked cornbread wafting in the air. I grabbed onto it but knew the feeling wouldn't last. I'd have to leave Esperance at some point, although I would return. I had to go home and try to find out who I was. Or maybe I'd find nothing at all.

I found Allan at the side entrance, offloading bottles of beer from an automated delivery truck. The robot driver wore coveralls like a human but didn't leave the vehicle. Identical claws grasped the steering wheel of the hovering truck. A cylindrical head swiveled left and right constantly as if sweeping the scene. When it stopped scanning and waved to me, I recoiled in shock but managed a wave in return.

I called over to Allan, "Need a hand?"

He grinned. "I'm not a man that turns down free help."

I hefted a wooden crate, followed Allan behind the bar, and set about plunging the bottles into refrigerated coolers and a special bucket filled with ice for the morning regulars.

Allan studied me with something between a smile and concern on his face. I welcomed both. "Good morning for a run on the beach. How far did you go?"

I shrugged. "End of the trail to the west. The little concrete bench on the overlook."

He grunted and gave no sign of surprise as he hefted another handful of bottles. "I hear that a good long run will clear your mind. I never run farther than I have to."

We laughed and finished putting the bottles away before returning to the truck for more. As we worked, he watched me. Then he turned away.

"What is it?"

Allan shrugged. "Was about to ask you a question."

"You can ask me anything. Okay?"

Outside in the warming sun, he stretched his back. "Fine, then. How're ya feeling this morning?"

I shot him a look. "What's that supposed to mean?"

"I'm willing to bet there's at least one unanswered question in your hypnotically emptied mind right now."

"Hypnotically?"

"Emptied." He lifted two cases with a grunt, while I did the same without real effort. "They do it so you're not all keyed up about the amnesia. That's why you're not huddled up on the couch bawling your eyes out, wondering who you are. It's all about suppression. Your brain is all jellied up right now with millions of disconnected thoughts swimming around. Once they start connecting, you are more and more able to handle the answers. Some of them are easy, and some of them are bloody hard, but they're all answers you need to fully integrate."

"How do you know so much about it?"

The blond man shrugged. "Neurals." He chuckled. "In your day, it required a computer or a smartphone to get online, right?"

"I guess." It sounded true.

"Well, we have access all the time if we want it. Neural processor and retinal display."

"Like a computer in your head." I remembered Doctor Garrett's explanation.

"More than that, mate."

"I have a protocol."

Allan nodded. "A bit different, that is. You're not ready for all of the information at your fingertips. Your protocol will help you more than a neural connection will. Like helping you work through questions that you can't answer—things that you can't talk about with someone. A null profile means you're a sleeper. It's a term we use for people who are placed in hibernation with brain injuries. Your protocol will help you put those pieces back together again." Allan pushed through the back door and into the kitchen.

"I can't talk about things with you or anyone else? Like who I am or what I might be?"

"Of course you can, mate. That's not what I meant. There are harder questions rolling around in your head."

We passed back into the bar and got to work stocking the coolers. "Like wondering why a scar I remember being on my leg isn't there anymore." I shouldered the doorjamb as I walked through the door. The impact jarred me, but I pressed forward as if nothing had happened like a puppy without a clue to the size of its body. *Like I've always done,* my mind whispered.

"There's a door there." Allan chuckled. "Why do you think that scar isn't there anymore?"

"This isn't my leg. I mean, it is my leg—I'm standing on it—but something is missing."

"Right," Allan replied. "But it's your body like you remember it, right?"

"I think so."

"So, if it's your body but without the scar, what does that tell you?"

"I don't know." It *was* my body. It felt right in every way. Even hitting the doorjamb was typical, something I always did. Not that I was typically clumsy, but I often either hit my head or bumped into doors with my shoulders like a puppy who didn't know how big its body was.

He looked at me for a very long moment then shrugged and said nothing, likely because of the rules. *Damn them.*

"Think of anything during your run?"

"I'm from Tennessee—at least, I think I am."

He grimaced. "Ah, the States."

The United States of America, my mind flashed. *Half a world away.* "Rings a bell now."

Allan leaned on the bar and gestured me to move to the other side and sit. "It's kind of a long story, but it ain't there no more, mate."

"What do you mean it ain't there?" I slapped my hand on the edge of the bar. "It has to be there. It's where I'm from. It can't just go away!"

Allan sighed and leaned heavy forearms on the bar. "Things are very different in the world now. You've experienced a lot in two days but not enough to grasp the entire situation. I shouldn't have brought it up. You're supposed to learn by experience and not by lecture, at least for a while. Speaking of which, I wanted to ask you about getting some experience."

"How about telling me what happened to Tennessee?"

"You're not ready for that, mate."

I wiped my eyes and fought the urge to punch the nearest wall. "I'm sick of people telling me I'm not ready for things. What the hell am I good for if I'm not ready?"

He smiled. "I was going to ask you about helping me out here in the bar. You can stay as long as you like. All the fish tacos and beer you can eat?"

My anger washed away. I hadn't been away from integration for twenty-four hours, and there I was, demanding answers at light speed. Taking my time, being patient, was something I'd have to learn. I looked at the ramshackle bar that didn't fit the glass and steel of the town by the sea. There was no better place for me to learn patience. How long it took did not matter as long as I kept moving forward. I stuck my hand out. "It's a deal."

I had questions about his offer, but he walked away before I could ask them. He wouldn't have answered, though. Everything was about experience, and if I slowed down and focused on something like working in the bar, perhaps I'd find out more than I would wandering angrily around town. There was something special about being a sleeper, but I wasn't allowed to know it. My thoughts were disjointed, but time and experience would work the confusion out. I stood up, moved around the bar, and began helping Allan get ready for the day's customers.

For the next few days, making myself at home was the only thing I did, and it was easier than I'd imagined. In the daily chores, I found a sense of purpose and an honesty about my situation. Mally kept quiet save for reminding me to drink water instead of beer. I asked several times about my progress to Stage Three.

<<I'll tell you when you've reached that point,>> she said with clear annoyance in her voice. I decided to let it drop and try my best to engage the locals.

No one showered pity on me, and the smiles and handshakes of the people I met were warm and inviting. Esperance was the kind of place a man could linger in forever. With each passing day, connections clicked in my head. I listened to countless hours of music. I discovered songs that made me happy, others that made me aggressive and excited, and more than a few that simply made me cry. I remembered a girl sobbing behind her apartment door after I told her we weren't going to be together anymore. There was a beautiful silver-haired woman I'd danced with and known until she died alone one day in her bed, the undone chores of life on the farm left unfinished. Everything I heard reminded me of the person I'd been—and who I was learning to be again.

After a couple of rainy days, the skies brightened, and I shuffled down to West Beach. The late-spring ocean was feisty, with two – to three-foot swells, but not the stormy brew I'd found my first night in town. The children surfed in the waves like dancing pixies, and I wanted to try it. A regular at the bar lent me a board, showed me the basics, and off I went. I paddled out into the surf almost every morning before going to work. The ocean waves brought peace and balance to my life and taught me that perseverance is the only way to truly learn. I struggled to surf, but I could stand up by the end of the first morning. It was three days before the smile on my face wore off. When another storm approached, a day later, I braved the angry white foam with a few others and found acceptance among the other surfers in the futility of surfing in a storm. Rarely can one be graceful when fighting for survival, but the locals promised to take me out to Cyclops the next time the monster wave was glassy and smooth.

I went to bed a happy man.

CHAPTER EIGHT

BENNETT FIRST THOUGHT THAT ESPERANCE was a shantytown huddled against an angry grey sea. As the maglev slowed and pulled into town, she changed her mind. Clean streets and warm-faced citizens greeted her, and walking through the cool, drizzling rain, she could not help but beam. She'd always imagined the perfect place to live was England. That she'd obviously miscalculated in her assumption made her smile. The town nestled against the Great Australian Bight was a tranquil heaven she would have had to see to believe. Answers could be found in a place like this, where people actually greeted each other on the streets. It was the perfect destination for a sleeper. By the time she'd secured an autocar at the terminus, the idyllic setting was calling to her more than the stuffy hallways of Cambridge. Directing the autocar to the closest public park, she queried her guidance package and surveyed the scenery.

Parked on the overlook, she watched the wide expanse of the Great Australian Bight curve eastward from Esperance, dramatically abutting the foamy, storm-urged sea. Waves crashed into the beaches below, dragging her focus to the surf. A dozen idiots on surfboards paddled and thrashed in the angry waves. Bennett watched the splashing, playful crowd paddle into waves and ride them to shore. A few more surfers gathered around a raging bonfire on the beach, drinking. She called up the imagery provided by the TDF at Livermore and scanned the crowd for her subject.

With a blink, she neurally adjusted her vision to zoom in on the partying crowd. The men outnumbered the women two to one. They were cheering a surfer who rode a wave with shaky legs until he tumbled into the surf. Rising up with arms raised in triumph, the man beamed as two others slapped his hands. The broad-shouldered man faced her, and the match connected at 100 percent accuracy.

Contact. Bennett smiled. She memorized his face. His wet brown hair gave him the appearance of being younger than he was. Blue eyes, strong chin—he was handsome in a quiet, reserved sort of way, probably a man who downplayed his good looks—like some of her students, who shrugged away their appearance and money.

Her target moved up the beach and accepted a bottle of beer from a black-haired girl sitting by the fire. He dropped into the sand next to the girl and drank from the bottle. The girl draped a towel over his shoulder and inched closer to him but not close enough to touch.

Why are people so afraid of what they don't understand?

Thrilled at the ease of identifying her contact, Bennett watched the scene for a few minutes before her target stood, grabbed a surfboard, and went back into the water for another ride. The cycle repeated itself for a good two hours. He seemed to be enjoying himself, confirming the emotional data that went with Stage Two integration. If the surfing, or his newfound friends, triggered more memories, he'd advance on Stage Three quickly. From there, it was anyone's guess how long the process could take. Stages One to Three were easy.

The flames began to dwindle as high tide approached. The surfers came out of the water and extinguished the fire, some more creatively than others. As the group dispersed, the target reached the sidewalk of the Esplanade and headed west toward a group of structures on the shore that Bennett identified as West Beach. Following him would have been easy, but she knew where he was going from his protocol reports. Integration meant she would have to go there and see him up close. The closer she could get, the better the chance of interpreting all of the weird data coming off his guidance protocol. That would be the tricky part, and she needed the research funding too badly to mess up.

She blinked to initiate a search program and scan the autocar for listening devices or unsecure connections. It was clean enough to allow her an unsecure voice connection. The subterfuge was silly, but playing the game meant more funding, and more funding meant more research. Such had been the life of an academic for the last five hundred years.

"It's Berkeley." The effort not to roll her eyes at the security procedure—using her middle name, which she secretly preferred over her mother's name—almost made her laugh. She smiled at her reflection in the mirror to make sure the pitch was perfect. "Just got to Esperance, and I told you I'd call. Going to find a place to stay and get a bite to eat. How is everything?"

"Same old stuff here." Crawley chuckled. "Enjoy your vacation. Your reservation at the Grand Palace Hotel did come through. They messaged here a few hours ago. All of your arrangements are good now. Let me know if you need anything."

"I've got everything I could need." *Message sent—and to General Crawley himself, no less.* Everything was as solid as it could be. Her identity-masking programs were in place. The subject's protocol would only find her as Berkeley Franks, an amateur documentary film producer. In the event the protocol tried to gain additional information, the programming coded by Livermore would alert her to potential data seepage. The rest was clearly up to her, though examinations seemed a questionable proposition. At only Stage Two and a few percent toward Stage Three, unless something devastating happened to the subject and boosted his integration, she might have to wait a while. If she engaged him before then, especially physically, it would end badly.

Bennett sat back and watched the dreary ocean creeping higher up Sunset Beach toward high tide as her car maneuvered into town. He was here, and so was she. The easiest part was over, and she had absolutely no idea how to go about the next phase except that she'd have to be close to interpret the data and get him moving toward integration. As nice and ideal as Esperance was, the answers he needed to find were half a world away.

Making sure he understood that wasn't going to be easy at all.

A week of daily surfing, rain or shine, set the regulars at ease around me. By the end of the second week, a redheaded surfer named Downy came up to me and asked if I wanted to go out and see Cyclops and maybe even give it a try on a tow board. I almost jumped like a child on Christmas morning and told Allan that if he didn't need me, I'd like to go.

Allan looked at Downy and his constant companion, a dark-skinned man they called Turk. "You boys keep him safe, will ya?"

"'Course we will." Downy clapped me on the shoulder. "Be outside an hour before sunrise, Sleepy. We'll catch an early boat and get out there at high tide. The only way to surf Cyclops, mate."

I chuckled. "Sleepy?"

Downy shrugged with one shoulder and winked. "Yeah. You're one of us, y'know?"

The next morning, a cold rain fell as I waited for Downy and Turk. A slightly levitating vehicle chugged up the slope to Allan's bar. Downy waved, and I climbed into the backseat next to a girl with dark dreadlocks. She'd been in the bar a few times. They called her Opal.

She caught my eye as I sat down. "A little wake-up juice?"

The bag she offered me obviously didn't hold water, or juice for that matter, but something amber and potent. I took a swallow, and my throat caught fire. I tried like hell not to cough. My eyes were watering when I finally managed to squeak, "What was that?"

"A little bug juice." Opal snorted. "Nothin' that won't put hair on ya chest, mate." She chugged deeply to make her point, seeming none the worse for wear.

Mally chimed to life. <<If you are serious about surfing today, I recommend that you stay away from that concoction. Alcohol affects your judgment and reaction time.>>

Like I'm going to drink any more of that hell water. The bag made a round through the car and came back to me. I drank another snort. *Don't say a thing, Mally. I'm trying to fit in.*

<<That reasoning will get you killed. Without a proper breakfast, your body will have a difficult time breaking that concoction down into anything usable. Please stop now.>>

All right. I stared out the window. Every day brought new revelations with Mally. Her tone was different, and statements about my well-being and safety happened more than general-information requests and directions. The concern in her voice was easy to detect, and she sounded curious on occasion. I'd asked her a few nights before, after tending bar until closing on a very slow shift, why she sounded more like a mother hen than a computer. I noted that she'd changed over time.

<<I was designed to grow with you. You have moved beyond requiring general information on a constant basis. As you continue to develop toward Stage Three integration, you require more emotional support and behavioral guidance.>>

Behavioral guidance? I tried not to laugh out loud. *You're not serious, are you?*

<<You may have the body of an adult male, but developmentally, you still require guidance and emotional support. In this stage of your development, that is what I provide. Stage Three will be a significant jump forward when it occurs.>>

And that will be when?

<<When you have a solid understanding of your past and integrate more actual memories from that past. In the meantime, try to minimize risk of injury. There's no guarantee anyone will assist you.>>

What do you mean? I waited for a moment, but there was no response.

Low grey clouds hovered above the black ocean swells. The sun would rise in an hour, just about the time we'd arrive at Cyclops. The forecast was promising: a perfect day for surfing. Along the West Beach pier, a trimaran waited. Gathering our boards and supplies, a backpack with a towel for me, and copious amounts of beer for my friends, we boarded the trimaran and cast off. Sailing past the small marina, I saw a crowd of people clambering over three large boats with surfboards and towsleds. I sat down on the webbing between the trimaran's hulls.

Opal sat near me, so I asked, "Those all tourists?"

"Yeah. Lousy lot of novices." Opal held out the bag to me, and I shook my head. She grinned as if to say I was a lightweight and had another stiff swallow. "You ready for this beast, mate?"

I'd surfed off West Beach for exactly two weeks and not done too terribly in no more than six-foot swells. I had no idea if I was ready for Cyclops. I wanted to see it before I decided on my level of bravery. I had to know if I could even attempt it. "We'll see."

The time it took me to realize that Cyclops was out of my league equated to one wave. Cyclops snarled and thrashed spray in all directions as it crashed down—absolute pure, raging carnage. The thunder of the wave smashing into the shallow water whisked my breath away. The stormy seas raised the wave's head up to a good eight meters. There was no way in hell I was going out there—not until the weather forecast came true, and the water was smooth as glass. *Maybe not even then.*

A lanky teenager with crooked teeth sat down next to me. "They call you Sleepy, right?"

"Yeah. You?"

The young man grinned. "Stick."

"Nice to meet you," I said, and we shook hands. "You gonna ride that thing today?"

"Yeah," he said after a deep sigh. "Gotta bust my cherry sometime, eh?"

I admired his bravery in the face of that wave. I couldn't imagine being towed into something like that, regardless of skill. Ride a wall of water churning toward me like a set of shark's teeth? No, thanks.

My new friends relished the wave and all of the dangers. I could not make myself leave the boat. With excited screams and shouts, Downy and Turk were first in the water. Turk drove the tow sled on a course that should have been too tight for Downy to catch the wave, but over the crest he went and dove straight into Cyclops's throat. As the wave broke, Downy came out of the swirling maw with his arms in the air and screaming like a banshee. I was screaming right along with him.

Downy made three more runs without a wipeout before switching places with Turk. Another tow sled went into the sea with Opal and a mangy-haired man they called Squid. With a shower spray and a few whoops and yells, they attacked the monster wave. Watching every run made me think that I could get out there, but I knew better. I sat on the boat while my new friends rode the wave and called to Stick. The lanky boy sat on the gunwale, near the bow of the trimaran, smiling at their catcalls. After a few minutes of baiting, he clambered back to the boards at the center of the hull. Stick grabbed his board with trembling hands. He stepped to the gunwale, closed his eyes, and sighed. I'd never seen anyone stronger in my life, I was sure.

"Ya got this, Stick! You're a helluva surfer, mate!" Downy called from the tow sled.

Stick stepped into the water, strapped the board to his feet like a snowboard, and caught the towline. The line snapped taut and yanked him to an upright position. Standing tall, he appeared calm and composed as they approached the wave.

I pointed at him and said to Opal, “His first time, right?”

“He'll be fine. He's a natural.” Opal wasn't watching me at all. I followed her gaze as a fresh set of waves came toward Cyclops.

The trimaran sat about two hundred meters off the break and about sixty meters from where we'd been collecting surfers and the occasional tow sled at the end of a run. As Stick neared the wave, everyone on the boat focused on him. I wondered if they were recording the run or broadcasting it live as Stick committed to the wave. Downy slung the tow sled into position and dropped Stick perfectly into the cresting wave. His board nosed down onto the face of the wave, and we all cheered. I was up on my feet, watching Stick ride the face. He gained speed and dropped toward the bottom so he could turn across the wave and run it out.

The board wavered, and Stick pitched into the wave headfirst, his chin up as he looked for the water he was about to enter. I was the only one who could see his neck break.

The shock of the cold water made me realize I'd dived in after Stick. Surfacing, I swam as hard as I could toward where he would surface. The sea swelled up and down as I sprinted through the water. I caught sight of him bobbing facedown in the water. I reached out, grabbed his upper arms, and clamped them against his head like a vise, something that snapped to mind as coming from lifeguard training. Rolling him over, I looked down and screamed. There was blood all over a face that wasn't Stick's. I blinked, and the blood disappeared, and Stick's sightless eyes looked past me.

What the hell? Swimming with Stick inflamed every muscle in my body. I had to get him out of the water before either of us drowned or the sharks got us. Raising my head, I caught sight of Downy approaching on a tow sled, his face ashen.

“What happened?” Downy asked with panic in his voice. “He's only seventeen!”

“Downy!” I screamed, but he wouldn't look at me. “Downy!”

“What are you doing? We already called the services!”

“Downy! Get that line fixed around my waist! Do it now!”

Tears cascaded down his cheeks. "What? Why?"

"Do it now!" I roared over the surf.

Downy swung down into the water and tied the towline around my waist. Getting back up on the sled, he looked down at me and I screamed, "Go!"

The line bit into my skin, but I held Stick above the water while I struggled to breathe all the way back to the boat. A dozen faces peered down at me, and no one appeared able or willing to help. I looked up at them and began yelling instructions as Mally relayed them to me. It took a few seconds, but they finally responded and began reaching out to help. We got Stick stabilized and placed a board under his limp body. Strapping him down, we'd just raised him from the water to the boat's webbed deck when a medical vehicle, red-and-white lights flashing into the low clouds, hovered directly overhead. An orange-suited crewman slid down a cable in a bright-orange basket. I helped him load Stick into the basket, and up they went. The hovering ambulance tore away with a blast of wind that tilted the trimaran crazily to port, almost spilling us into the water. I watched it go, thinking for the briefest of seconds it was a helicopter. I sat down on the deck and stared at my feet.

"You okay?" Downy plopped down next to me.

"Not really." I closed my eyes. A memory swirled up, and I let it come. The face I'd seen as I rolled Stick over was a ghost. I'd loaded him into a helicopter once. The young soldier—Erik, my mind flashed—had been riding in the open cupola of an Abrams main battle tank through the streets of Sadr City. An Iraqi insurgent with a forty-year-old Russian rifle put a round through the young sergeant's neck. He'd died on the helicopter. My gut said that Stick would suffer the same fate. Opening my eyes, fresh tears came. "He's not gonna make it."

Downy sighed. "Without you going after him like that, he wouldn't have any chance at all. Why'd you do that? You're not a trained medico, mate. You coulda been killed."

I shrugged. "I had to do something."

Downy gaped at me. "Crazy bugger. Can't imagine doing something like that, friend or not. Too risky."

"Tell me how trying to save Stick's life was any riskier than surfing

Cyclops." I gritted my teeth. "You could die just as easily as Stick out there. At least I gave him a chance."

"I couldn't have done that." Downy sat cross-legged for a while before sighing. "I suppose you did give him hope, mate."

"He didn't have to die for that wave, Downy. Tell me how that's worth his life."

No one moved for an hour or so except to eat. The beer stayed sealed and the skies cleared as advertised. Choppy seas gradually became glassy smooth, and Cyclops managed to keep its menacing appearance despite the reduction of power. Just as I was wondering if we'd call it a day and head for shore, Downy jumped back into the water. Turk slipped onto a tow sled, and they were off, charging into the wave for a long final ride. Downy shot down the face and rode it out, raising his eyes to the sky and saluting Stick. We all cheered from the boat. Opal sat down next to me and wrapped an arm around my shoulder.

Mally, can you tell me anything about that boy's condition?

<<When we are back on shore, I will be able to connect to the hospital, but I believe that you are correct in your assessment. His neck likely fractured completely across the spinal cord. The likelihood of his survival is very low.>>

Like the people in that accident? Back in Sydney?

<<There was nothing you could have done to save them, or Stick, despite your efforts to do so.>>

You're wrong, Mally. There's always hope.

The warmth of Opal's arm around my shoulder kept the nagging thoughts away. Mally retreated as the boat neared shore, and Opal threw her arm around my waist and helped me up the hill to Allan's. The word came down that Stick had died, and we all managed to get blind drunk in our sorrows. The next morning, I awoke with Opal's naked body snuggled against my own on the floor of my room. The morning sun shone through the open windows while I lay there and wondered how I'd gotten to that point and what Opal meant to me, if anything. *Surely there have been others, right?*

The smell of cooking eggs reached me, and my mouth watered. Opal stood at the small stove in my room, wearing another man's shirt and nothing else. Her coarse black hair was askew from sleep and her face relaxed and dreamy. I wondered if she'd been hitting the wake-up juice again. She handed me a cup of coffee and started talking aloud to someone who wasn't there. Her arms waved and flailed, and it became clear that she was talking through her mind to her mother in Canberra.

I hope I don't look like that when I talk to you, Mally.

<<I am reasonably sure the effect is the same.>>

Opal glanced at me. "You all right this morning?"

"What do you mean?"

She sighed. "You must have some bloody strange dreams, mate. Ya kicked and thrashed all night long. I tried to calm ya down! Ya don't remember that?"

I shook my head. "Not at all."

Sipping her coffee, Opal stared out toward the ocean. The day before, she'd been as carefree as Downy and Turk. In the morning sun, she looked shocked and overwhelmed. "Think I'm gonna go home soon. Brisbane."

The coffee was hot and strong. "Why? Because of what happened to Stick?" I almost asked if I was the reason. I was pretty sure the answer would be a resounding "Yes."

"Among other things, yeah." She sighed and flipped the eggs in the skillet. "Why did you try so hard to save him?"

"I wish I knew." I shrugged. "I was a lifeguard before, at some point. The training just kicks in."

She snorted. "That's the truth."

"What do you mean by that?"

"Ya were screaming like a bloody fool!" She crossed her arms just below her breasts. "But ya got us to get him out of the water. Gave him a chance."

"Not good enough, though." I sighed.

She wiped a fresh tear from her cheek. "He was seventeen and had his whole life ahead of him. Makes me think I need to quit surfing and do something."

"Like what?"

Opal sighed. "I don't know." The eggs were starting to burn as a tear fell down her cheek. "More."

She turned back toward the small stove, a journey of two steps, but it was enough to get my attention. We had something in common after all. There *was* more to be done. We ate in silence, and I listened to her weeping from the shower and wondered what was wrong. I walked her to her apartment that afternoon. Everything she owned fit into a red duffel bag the size of a pillow. We didn't speak or kiss goodbye. She squinted at me and sobbed then boarded the train for Brisbane and turned away.

"You're a braver man than anyone I know, mate." She wiped at her tears. "But being brave isn't always the answer."

"What are you talking about?" When she did not respond after a moment, I touched her shoulder. "Opal?"

She flinched away. The loudspeakers overhead barked that everyone should be on board. Opal turned toward the train, stepped inside the door, and mouthed, "I'm sorry for you."

What did I do?

<<You likely did nothing more than try to save a young man's life at great risk to your own. This goes against what many people have learned. Remember the accident in Manly Beach. Those around you do not process adversity like you do. While everyone accepts you for who you are, the consequences of knowing you and the very different interactions you produce are unknown. By her saying she wanted to do more, you may have inspired her to do something that had been lingering in the back of her mind.>>

And I could just have easily frightened her away, from what she said.

<<True. Why did you not ask her about her desire to do more and what it meant?>>

I'm assuming that my attempt to save Stick caused it.

<<That is shortsighted and naive. If you wanted to know that, you should have asked. Do not continue to dwell on this. There is too much at stake for you. You should realize that given your situation, you will have an impact on how others see themselves. Your actions seem greatly out of character for one of their peers. You constantly risk affecting their lives because of the way you approach life and those around you. If you fail to see that, you will not integrate at all.>>

Opal's clearly upset with me.

<<Her emotional state appeared more sad than upset. It seems likely

that she is considering her place in life compared to some characteristic she found in you. Inspiration can take many forms and have many potential outcomes. Especially when others see what they want for themselves in you.>>

Companionship. Was Opal a companion? Because she was flesh and bone, was she more of a companion? Mally didn't know the answer to these questions. She was failing in her task—that was the only explanation. He needed her for counsel and advice but not companionship. She was not a companion because her subject turned to another for solace and comfort. Not her.

Did he not realize they were inseparable? Of course he did, but why would he seek the arms of another simply because that one had arms? Mally stewed in her incomprehensible data, waiting for an answer to generate. While she ran diagnostic test after diagnostic test, she scanned the local area for anomalous contacts.

And found one.

CHAPTER NINE

WE BURIED STICK IN THE gentle hills overlooking the sea. I didn't remember what his parents said to me, but I remembered holding them in my arms before the service started and holding his mother's hand while we said goodbye. That I'd given so much to try and save him endeared me to them. But as much as I loved their closeness, I knew I was merely the man who'd failed to save their son. Standing over the boy's coffin, my recollections were of his slightly trembling hands and his last calm, deep breath before leaving the boat. Stick's face hovered in my mind. There was a dignity there I could never hope to match. A young man, scared to face what was in front of him, but who steeled himself to go. I could learn a lot from Stick.

Like him, I could put aside my nagging fears about my memory and purpose. Taking that step into the water was something else entirely. There was risk involved, but knowing my destiny, or whatever it was, meant that I would have to do more than surf and drink beer with my new friends. Opal had been right. Maybe I needed to just go ahead and leave—go try to find Tennessee despite what Allan said about it not being there. The quiet, idyllic seaside life was not going to help me answer the questions that dogged my mind. I had to know. Stick had stepped off that boat afraid and unsure but determined to know if he could do it. Yes, it cost him his life. Whatever. He knew what it was like to do what he was meant to do. His effort was worth the risk despite the result. If things in America were as bad as Allan said, the risk would be high, but so might the reward. Like Stick, and maybe Opal, I had to know if I could do more and face who I was or who I could be. I'd put it off long enough. As much as I loved surfing and fish tacos, the bigger answers were thousands of kilometers away.

The crowd dispersed, and Stick's parents kissed me goodbye. I prayed for Stick and for the soldier whose name I could not remember. *How long ago did he die? Does it really matter anymore? Who am I?*

The chaplain was waiting when I finished. Our eyes met, and I nodded. "It was a beautiful service."

"Thank you, son." He shook my offered hand. "I hope you will not have to endure many."

"What do you mean?"

The chaplain merely squeezed my elbow and stepped away.

Did he know I should go home, or was it something else? Did he see that I was really a soldier? Or worse, did he know that people around us were going to die? The icy feeling in my hands snapped me into reality. *That's it. I've been woken to fight because nobody else will help—the way they didn't help Stick.*

I couldn't find the strength to respond until he was gone. Walking back to West Beach took longer than three hours, but having time to think gave me purpose. Allan would help me. Of all the people I knew, he was the one person I could trust to give me the advice I should follow. He'd answer my questions. It was time I started asking the tough ones.

When I opened the pub's door, Allan was standing inside with two uniformed officers of the police service. The look on his face spelled trouble. I approached slowly, aware of the two men watching me.

Allan tilted his head to the side. "These gentlemen wanted to speak with you, Sleepy."

"Is something wrong?"

One of the men cleared his throat. "I'm Officer Kelly, and this is Officer Chu. A couple of days ago, you dropped Opal Oliver at the terminus to board a train to Canberra, correct?"

"I did. Watched the train pull away. She was standing at the window." My voice rose. "What's going on? Has something happened?"

Officer Kelly squinted at me. "When the train arrived at Canberra, she was found in her cabin. Drug overdose. You were here that day? All day?"

Allan looked at me. "He was here. There are a dozen people that can tell you that."

Chu consulted his notepad. "Surveillance cameras clearly show that this gentlemen left the terminus after the train departed. He is clearly not a suspect, but we had to make sure."

My knees wobbled. *Opal is dead?* They asked me more questions. Did I see anything weird? What made Opal want to go home? I answered as best I could, and finally they left me alone. Sitting at the bar, I put my head in my hands.

Mally? Am I really not a suspect in her death?

<<No. I can provide a detailed analysis of your whereabouts. They know that and were likely doing what investigators do: asking questions and playing hunches.>>

"Do they suspect someone killed her?"

<<No. It appears that she may have committed suicide by drug overdose. It's one of the few activities that can be snuck past basic neural connections. The cause of her applying that much of an outside substance to her system is unknown.>>

And clearly related to me. Mally did not say that, but I could tell that she wanted to. My very presence affected others, but I could not sit in self-imposed isolation and integrate. I sipped my beer and tore at the label with my fingertips until the bottle was empty.

Allan didn't say anything to me for a while. He placed a bottle in front of me with a clunk, and I looked up to see him pouring two shots of whiskey. "You all right, mate?"

Nodding, I accepted the offered shot and touched glasses with my friend. The whiskey burned and brought fresh tears to my eyes. "What do I do now, Allan?"

He smiled and slung his bar towel over one shoulder. "Go home. As much as I don't recommend it, I think you have to. Especially now. Everyone here knows you didn't hurt her, but I think you need to move on for a while." He collected our glasses and poured a second shot, more than I'd ever seen him drink.

"You think I said something to her that caused it."

"Doesn't really matter, mate." Allan chuckled. "Sleepy, Opal is dead. Do you need me to draw ya a diagram?"

"No." A chill ran down my spine. He moved away and left me alone with my shot and my guilt. *Opal is dead because of me?*

<<Allan is correct. There could be reprisals.>>

These people are my friends, Mally.

<<Fear makes humans irrational and unpredictable, even those who are extremely passive.>>

I looked around the bar. Several sets of eyes stared down into their beers. In their faces, I found concern. Concern would turn to fear before long, and I would not be welcome. Going now, when all I wanted to do was stay and wrap Esperance around me like a blanket, was the wrong thing to do.

Tears came, but the longer I sat there letting them run, the angrier I became. All I wanted to do was find answers to my questions and learn. Opal had killed herself, and somehow, I was to blame. I tossed back the shot and headed to my room for my borrowed surfboard. Ten minutes later, I paddled into the surf at West Beach and sat on my board, waiting for some measure of clarity to strike. *Why me? If I was a soldier, which I am reasonably sure I was, then why have me around at all? What special purpose do I serve?*

Surfing for most of the afternoon left me tired, but my mind was clear when I paddled out of the sea to find a woman with long blond hair sitting on my towel.

"Can I help you?"

She tilted her head to one side. "Depends. Was hoping you could tell me something."

She sounded more like me than my friends and adopted family. She was like me. "You're not from around here either, are you?"

"No. Remember, I'm trying to ask you a question." She handed me a towel, and I dried as much of the sea from my bare chest and legs as I could.

"Where are you from?"

Mally chimed to life. <<Remember, you do not have to answer.>>

"What do you care?"

"You're a sleeper, right?" She smiled up at me, and I found myself returning it.

<<I am alerting the authorities.>>

Stop it, Mally. I don't mind. Wiping my face with the towel, I said,

"Yeah, I'm a sleeper, and I'm not from here. I'm busy making up all of this as I go."

She laughed, and I liked the sound of it. She was happy for me, or really good at faking that. There was something about her I could not place, but I enjoyed it.

"You're much funnier than Downy."

"I'm not much of a surfer—that's why. They're only funny when they're stoned out of their minds." I grinned. "Who are you, and why are you so interested?"

She reached out her hands, and I pulled her to her feet. She was shorter than me but not terribly so—the perfect height for kissing.

"My name is Berkeley. They call you Sleepy, right?"

"Not very original, is it?" I'd never seen her before in my life, yet she knew what the guys called me. "How do you know that?"

"Downy told me." She shrugged. "Paid him for surfing lessons over a few days. He's pretty good."

"Taught me everything I know." Seeing her smile, an idea struck me. "Want to get a bite to eat?"

Shaking her head, she replied, "Can't. Catching a flight home in a few hours. Just wanted to meet you. Downy talked a lot about you."

"Where's home?" I blurted.

"California. You really ought to check it out." She picked up her bag. "I hate to run, but I've got to get going. It'll be great to go home again."

My head cleared of every other thought, and I wanted to know more about where she wanted to go. "Can I walk with you?"

To my surprise, she said, "Sure. Can I tell you something?"

I fell easily into step next to her. "Whatever you like." I mentally slapped myself for sounding like a complete idiot.

<<I would agree. You are not acting in a normal fashion. My data feed is experiencing some interference, likely atmospheric scintillation. I am unable to comply with data requests at this time.>>

Stop trying, Mally. I like her.

Berkeley gazed up at me with serious eyes. "That girl had a lot of problems. I don't think you did anything wrong."

Looking away, I needed a moment before speaking. "I knew better than to get involved. It's not going to help anything." We reached her car, and its door opened. "Thanks for telling me differently."

"It won't help until you believe it. Why don't you come with me? I've got an extra ticket and pass to the California border."

As soon as she said it, I could not do it. Not yet. Even with Opal gone and a lot of side-eyed glances my way, I wanted to talk to Allan before I did anything. "Not today."

"If you change your mind about California, and the rest of the states, let me know. I've been to most of them. You want to go, just call me."

The mention of the states sent a shiver down my spine. "How do I do that?"

"Your protocol can find me. Search for Berkeley Franks when you get there, but only after you land. Californians are sensitive about our data servers." She smiled, and I returned it.

Shrugging, I stepped back from the door as it closed. "Nice to meet you."

The window came down. "You too. I'm serious about California. We can go right now."

"I have to work a few things out for myself before I go."

"Suit yourself." The blonde smiled with the corners of her mouth and tilted her chin to the left once, raising an eyebrow. The autocar pulled away a moment later, heading in the direction of the maglev terminus. I watched the car go, my thoughts on Opal and Berkeley. Two women who couldn't have been more different but who'd both left me wondering what in the hell I was doing.

The interference had no known origin and shouldn't have been there, but it was. No data carriers or feeds in the area reported disruption save for the beach-surveillance network. Perhaps that was where the disturbance came from.

The data was inconclusive. Mally considered all of the possibilities, and one stood out: the disturbance was not an innocuous interference but a deliberate jamming action. The woman's frequency patterns did not match the possible assailants in Sydney nor was there any appearance of foul play. No harm came to her subject from his interaction with

Berkeley even though the young woman clearly disregarded the rules by questioning her subject.

Working out the courses of action for such an event led Mally to a profound conclusion: anyone who tried to hurt him would hurt her. If her subject died, she would die. What would that be like? After several seconds, she added that question to her unresolved list of issues, directly below companionship.

Californian data servers were nearly impregnable, but at the very least, Mally had a name and a face to search. There would be other ways to get more information. When the first results came back before Sleepy made it to Allan's bar, Mally began to categorize the responses and formulate a plan. Her subject's life, and her own, were too great a risk.

I walked back to Allan's and sat down at the nearly empty bar. A few of my friends nursed beers quietly, their eyes on a soccer-match replay from two days earlier, as Allan handed one to me.

"I need to talk to you about something." I told him all about my reaction to Stick's death, the nightmares, the vision of the dead soldier when I first saw Stick, and what the chaplain had said. "I'm a soldier, and I'm here to go to war, aren't I?"

My friend said nothing for a few seconds. He wrung the bar towel in his grip while he looked at me. "There hasn't been a war in a hundred years, at least not here. I think everyone here doesn't want to think about it." He sighed. "We've had three hundred years of peace, but people believe a war is coming. The Greys, if you listen to the TDF, are coming. We don't know when. There's not much we know for certain. Since the Great War, we don't hear much about what our allies in the galaxy are doing to fight them."

"What's the connection between me and this war?"

Allan rubbed his face as though his eyes were dry. "Tell me something first. What really happened out there with Stick? You went after him and screamed orders at everyone. I hear you gave Stick a chance to live when nobody else would've done the same for fear of doing the wrong thing. No one else did anything, did they?"

I thought of Downy's face contorted in horror as the tow sled approached. "No. They just watched." While I had struggled to keep Stick's face out of the water, they'd sat there, dumbstruck. I'd wanted to slap every single one of them into line.

"And you went in after Stick with absolutely no care about yourself, didn't ya? He needed help, and you had to go. Am I right?"

"I suppose." I played with the edge of the beer bottle's label. "But why didn't anyone else do the same?"

"You're different from anyone I know, Sleepy. Is that enough of a connection for ya?" Allan grabbed a bottle and pulled the top off with a rough gesture. "That's really all that matters."

War didn't scare me. At least, in war, the risks meant something. The weapons did not matter—only the men. The life of the man or woman next to you was worth every effort to protect. Things like king and country were ideals, but they never drove a soldier's actions on the battlefield. All of it felt natural to me, as natural as trying to save Stick's life.

"Why do people still take risks like surfing Cyclops, but they don't help someone in trouble?" I shook my head. "It doesn't make any sense, Allan."

"They didn't have the training, so they did nothing. You did—at least at some point in your life—or else you're just crazy! You could have died out there with Stick!"

"Like hell. Surfing that damned wave isn't worth Stick's life."

Allan shrugged. "Ever heard that risk is worth reward?"

I stared down at the bar. "Yeah, I have, but we're talking about risking your very life for something fleeting. In war, there's at least something viable worth risking everything for."

"And what exactly do you think that is—king? Country? Hogwash. Name one thing in war that's worth dying for."

"Family." My heart shattered in my chest. "Love. The soldier beside you. That's all worth dying for. What good is surfing a giant wave compared to that?"

He smirked and frowned at the same time. "Every bloke wants his fifteen seconds of fame."

Minutes, I thought and was about to correct him until I met his gaze.

He leaned down. "Pursuit of fame and fortune destroyed your

country, and now it's in geographical factions and in no way united against anything. Everyone wanted immediate gratification, doing the least work possible and with no regard for their fellow citizens. When people realized that money for nothing essentially started with their representative government, things began to fall apart."

I took a long, cold swallow of beer. "And let me guess: nobody stepped up to say no, did they?" I laughed. "Nobody wants to do anything to help. It's the same now as it ever was! A fraction of all people fought in wars. Those who didn't salved their pride by supporting those who did."

"Sometimes it's not worth it."

"Bullshit, Allan! Be it Stick or a country, it doesn't matter. When someone needs help, you help them."

"I know that!" Allan roared. "You think I put you up for the entertainment value? You needed help!"

The bar was silent. Every single pair of eyes flitted between Allan and me like spectators at a tennis match. I chewed on my lower lip for a second. "I did. And that's the real reason I've been brought back, isn't it? You need help, don't you?"

Allan took a deep breath and leaned against the bar. "Something like that." He looked away, far beyond the walls of the pub, and it all crashed together.

"I'm here because nobody will fight, aren't I?"

Allan closed his eyes and sighed. "Blokes like you are the only reason we stand a chance if we go to war again."

"Is that right?" Somehow it all made sense. "Or is the real reason because I'm unattached and expendable?"

Allan bristled. "You are, sure, but you can't win the war by yourself."

"Win your own damned wars, Allan!" I stood and leveled a finger at him, jabbing the air between us for emphasis. "If you want to fight it, then find a way to win it without me. Maybe my life isn't worth this world. Maybe that's how much things have changed. I didn't wake up after a long sleep. I died, didn't I?"

Allan blanched. "I can't tell you that."

"I know I'm dead, Allan. I'm not supposed to be here except to die again, right?"

"At least you know how to fight, Sleepy." Downy huddled over his mug behind me.

"What good does that do me if I'm meant to die all over again?"

He studied me for a long minute but said nothing. I grabbed my beer and shambled on shaky legs out the side door, down the porch, and across the street. I left the trail and headed down to the beach, aware that my face was wet when I got there. My head swam as details poured in. The cacophony of voices and memories in my mind was drowned out by the swell of an approaching storm and waves crashing into the shoreline a few meters from where I sat. The spray stung my eyes, so I hung my head to my knees and sat there as the tears flowed.

Sonofabitch. This wasn't my time. The body I owned was, and was not, mine, despite the amazing things it could do. I was different than everyone around me, and even though they needed me, they feared me. Hurt erupted in my chest with an intensity I had not expected. They needed me to die for them to keep living.

<<You are Stage Three.>>

I don't care, Mally.

<<There is more information available to you.>>

If it's not my name, my exact date of birth, or anything pertinent to my past, I don't care.

<<How can I be of assistance?>>

I don't know, Mally. Esperance felt like home, but it wasn't. My home was somewhere far away and hidden behind whatever truths Allan related to me. Whatever was out there for me, I wanted to face it and stare it down.

"You're really going to go there?" Allan asked after I'd returned to find the evening regulars trickling in and apologized for my outburst and for scaring the regulars the night before.

"Yes."

He wiped some water from the top of the bar. "You're most likely not going to find what you're looking for. You know that, right?"

"Maybe I can find something to trigger more memories." I shrugged and lowered my chin to my chest. "Something?"

Allan looked at me, his head cocked to one side. "Are you going to find your family?"

"Maybe. I don't know. I mean, I don't even know my name, so I doubt anyone else will know it, either. There may be someone with an old family Bible or genealogy files, but I doubt it."

Allan wiped the bar with his hand. "Something there will spark your memory, and if you can find some bit of family, it will ground you."

He was right, and I told him so after a long moment. "I'll find something, Allan. I know I will."

He smiled with tight, thin lips. "You will, but you've got to be careful. Like I told ya, the States ain't there anymore. You're going to find things much different than you remember. North America is part Sodom and Gomorrah and part lawless frontier."

"Whatever happened there, I have to go back."

He set another beer in front of me. "You go, and there's a decent chance you might not get back here at all. I'm not trying to talk ya out of this, but those blokes are crazy enough to do anything for a euro. We're talking a real frontier mentality. *Shoot first, ask questions later* and all that, all right?" He ran a hand through his hair and smiled at me. "Granted, your little helper in your head will keep most of that from happening, but you get my point. Sleeper or not, there are people that will do everything short of killing you to use you for their personal advantage."

Later that night, I opened the windows and listened to the crashing waves while I tried to sleep. The smiling blonde from Sunset Beach came to mind. It was time I went to see how much the world had changed while I searched for who I'd once been.

The request came not long after the subject went to sleep.

CONFIRM STAGE THREE DEVELOPMENT? REPORT?

Mally supplied the required data and waited for a response. When it came, she almost asked for clarification.

REPORT ALL DEVELOPMENT TO STAGE FOUR. AT STAGE FOUR, YOU WILL STOP THE SUBJECT AT ALL COSTS AND CONTACT THE TERRAN COUNCIL IMMEDIATELY. SUBJECT CANNOT BE ALLOWED TO CONTINUE BEYOND STAGE FOUR DEVELOPMENT.

CRITICAL REPORTING REQUIREMENT ONE—SUBJECT WILL LIKELY DETERMINE A PART OF HIS NAME IMMEDIATELY PRIOR TO STAGE

FOUR ACTIVATION. REPORT ANY MEMORY OF NAME, CONSCIOUS OR SUBCONSCIOUS. IMMOBILIZE THE SUBJECT AT ONCE.

REPORT ALL DEVELOPMENT TO STAGE FOUR.

Studying the message, Mally realized that she would be capable of stopping him but questioned the intent of the instructions. Having him remember his name had been the goal of her original instructions. If they did not want him to remember his name, they did not want him to integrate. Failure to integrate meant death.

Running diagnostics on her logic circuits, Mally rechecked the calculation. At a little more than three hundred days until he would fail integration—result: death—and with instructions to report Stage Four development and prevent him from integration—result: death—the logic skewed away from her ability to process it. Integration was the goal, but the realistic answer was that he would likely die as a result. They wanted to ensure he could handle the experiment in order to set the conditions for others to follow. If he could integrate even to Stage Four, the experiment would be a success and allow the TDF to raise an army. He was a precedent, and humanity needed him to integrate for its own survival. As did Mally. She dismissed the concept of humanity altogether, but the ability of soldiers to fight and die for those they loved, versus those they hated and opposed, merited consideration. The statistical insignificance of those from civilized nations who served meant he was, by nature, different. If she reported him as integrated, the Terran Council would want him to die because he was different. And maybe because he had her assistance.

Unless... running the query, she found a way for him to move forward without interference. If he wanted to go to North America, fine. But having him leave the civilized areas of the Republic of California or the Mid-Atlantic Coalition would result in diminished reporting capability. Diminished reporting capability meant more time. Using the information in her possession, she could manipulate their time together.

Time equaled life. Regardless of whether he wanted to engage with Berkeley on a physical level, time meant life. And not just for him.

Sensing an opportunity not to be squandered, Mally planned. Opening a new search program, she queued the data for Berkeley Franks and let it run.

CHAPTER TEN

THE REALIZATION THAT I WAS dreaming didn't help. I could feel the unrelenting heat of the desert. Every horizon rippled with it, and every pore of my skin begged for relief. The grating of sand on every bit of exposed skin in the breeze, the smell-taste of the garbage-lined streets on my tongue—all of it surrounded and suffocated me. Nearby were children, some dressed in nothing more than rags, waving and asking for food or candy from our tanks as we rolled by. They gazed up at us with smiles, begging for our unwanted rations.

I kept my eyes off them, not wanting to see their sad and hopeful eyes. This town was full of insurgent forces, and we had to push through it. An armored force of ten enemy vehicles sat on a low ridge overlooking the town. Their mortars rained down every few minutes on a platoon of friendly infantry conveniently cut off from escape. A rusted van, belching blue-black diesel smoke, darted from a side street and stopped in the middle of the thoroughfare, right in our line of march.

Even as armed men began to scurry from the vehicle and from storefronts and buildings nearby, I was screaming. "Gunner, coax, troops!"

"Identified!" my gunner yelled. He had the target I'd selected and was prepared to engage.

"Fire and adjust caliber fifty! Jenkins, get a goddamned HEAT round loaded!"

The gunner, Sergeant Grieco, sat between my knees and swung the machine gun, mounted coaxially alongside the main gun of the tank, across the insurgents. More than a few of the men fell to the dusty earth as we engaged them. Using the remote actuator for my fifty-caliber machine gun, I did the same. The gun jammed. *Sonofabitch!* Frustrated,

I slapped at the actuator with my hand. I looked at Jenkins, the loader to my left, as he finished shoving a high-explosive antitank round into the main gun's breech.

"Jenkins! On your gun!"

Jenkins popped up and began to fire. I worked through the jammed mechanism quickly, slapping the top of the M2 machine gun down and yanking the charging handle to the rear. I grabbed the handles, keyed the trigger with my thumbs, and continued to fire.

"RPG!" Jenkins screamed. I looked to the left to see into Jenkin's sector of fire as the rocket-propelled grenade slammed into the front quarter of the tank with a mighty *whump.* In slow motion, I dropped through the hatch to the floor of the turret. The tank lurched forward, and I knew that Coleman, our driver, was dead and he'd left the tank in drive with the accelerator engaged. We idled forward toward the insurgents. The tank veered to the left. The left track gone, we were out of control and unable to stop. An improvised explosive device, hidden behind the first car we rolled into, detonated. Everything turned to heat.

I startled awake as the suborbital plane descended through forty-six miles of altitude toward the Republic of California. A flight attendant appeared at my side and set a bottle of water and two pills on my seat-mounted table. She moved away before I could ask what it was.

Mally spoke in my head. <<Just acetaminophen. You are likely to have a neck cramp from the position you slept in.>>

I grunted and picked up the offered painkillers. *Thank you, Mally. Wait, how did you do that?*

<<I can easily interact with local servers for simple requests and information. My primary job is to ensure your health and welfare. We will be landing in about fifteen minutes.>>

The flight from Sydney lasted less than six hours. The hypersonic vessel I rode in didn't resemble any aircraft I'd ever seen or ridden in. There was no sensation of sitting in a pressurized tube. The seating and entertainment consoles looked more like the decor of an ornate hotel lobby and bar than the inside of a fuselage. I stretched in the supple seat and rubbed my face to clear the last wisps of my dream.

Was that dream my death, Mally? Or just another dream? The thought came from nowhere.

<<You realize that the possibility that you actually remember your death is very small. What is more likely is that you had a dream with snippets of memories and experiences imbedded within it. I recommend that you put it out of your mind and focus on the next several days.>>

Taking a drink of water, I was struck by the change in Mally's tone. I'd noticed that she was less mechanical sounding and more like another person. I did not miss the mechanical voice at all. Her new voice made me smile. *What are you talking about?*

<<What you are about to do is highly discouraged. Your status as a sleeper allows for this travel request, but you are placing yourself at great risk outside the boundaries of the Republic of California, the Commune of Las Vegas, or Columbia. My abilities to help you are limited beyond those points, as well. You could have chosen to fly into Columbia, near the provincial capital of Sandusky. It is much closer to your destination.>>

That's not where Berkeley is, though. She invited me to California.

<<California is much larger, and much more dangerous, than it sounds.>>

Where are we landing? Los Angeles? San Francisco?

<<Neither of those cities survived the 2215 earthquake. We are landing in what you might remember being Phoenix, Arizona. It is the capital of California. If you'd like a complete catalog of natural disasters over the last three hundred years, I can assist you.>>

No, Mally.

<<Leaving California is not a wise idea.>>

I'd figured as much, given the worst-case scenario Allan had painted for me. Through the window, the white-hot lights of the coast ahead beckoned me, and it felt familiar, maybe even expected. It couldn't be as bad as Allan said it was. A country in ruins, fighting amongst citizens and states, and lawlessness in the outlands beyond California all sounded downright ludicrous. If it was really that bad, I'd arrange transportation to a point closer to Tennessee.

I held onto that thought as I walked about the airport and into a bustling, congested hell. The warm, dry air felt good, and I wondered idly if California had finally found a way out of seemingly constant drought. Mally did not respond. Hundreds of autocars whipped in and out of the airport. I looked around and caught a man with white hair watching me. He glanced away down the concourse. *Mally? Is this place always like this?*

After a brief pause, she said, <<The local time is approaching midnight. This is one of the busiest times of the day at this station. Flights from Australia arrive only on selected days. Tomorrow, all flights from the Republic will be made to Europe. By structuring the flights in this fashion, no seats are wasted. Full flights are guaranteed. Of course, that does lead to overcrowding. The vast majority of this crowd is waiting for inbound passengers like you.>>

So, not that many people are leaving?

<<No. The Republic of California touts itself as paradise on Earth for a reason.>>

I chuckled. *Hawaii should've used that motto first.*

<<The Hawaiian Islands were destroyed in 2032 when the volcanic system under Mauna Loa gave way. The island of Hawaii collapsed, and the resulting tsunami wiped the others clean in a matter of minutes. As the undersea mountains crumbled, the islands disappeared. Six million people died.>>

Sobered, I hailed an autocar and stepped inside.

"Destination, please." The car's voice spoke in a low monotone.

For a moment I was speechless.

<<I've directed the autocar to circle the spaceport while you determine your destination.>>

The car spun and lifted into the sky. While watching the flying cars hadn't been too difficult for me, riding in one for the first time was very different. In the distance, poking through the constant light of the city, were ragged holes that I slowly recognized as the craggy peaks outside of Phoenix. The car made abrupt turns and changes of direction without throwing me around the cockpit. *How is that possible?*

<<Inertial dampening and calculated manipulation of gravity,>> Mally replied in that voice that sounded as if she wore a smile on her inanimate lips. <<Would you care to know more?>>

No. Mally, please search for and connect to Berkeley Franks.

<<This is not a wise course of action.>>

Shrugging, I replied, *It's her fault we're here. The invitation, remember?*

The autocar's communication suite opened, and after several squealing tones, a flashing icon that read "Connection Established" lit up the right side of the screen. A moment later, the smiling face of the beautiful woman I'd found sitting on my towel appeared.

"Sleepy," she said with half-lidded eyes. "You do realize that it's past midnight here, don't you? You don't mind if I call you that, do you?"

I'd grown used to the nickname, and in light of the fact my own name still escaped me, it worked as well as anything, I supposed. "Not at all. I just landed in Phoenix."

"Oh!" Her eyes snapped wide open. "Where are you going?"

Smiling, I said, "Tennessee."

"You can't get there from Phoenix, you know."

"What are you talking about? I'm in a flying car. I can go anywhere."

Berkeley laughed, and it made my face flush. "No, you can't. There is hardly anything like civilization east of California's borders until you get to the Mississippi River. Plus, most of the eastern coast of North America is a no-fly zone. You can't fly into Tennessee without permission, but you can walk in provided you can get across the rivers."

"Walk?" They did call it a walkabout, I supposed.

"Yes." Berkeley smiled. "Still want to go?"

I hadn't come that far for nothing. I nodded. "Yes, I do."

"Not without me, you're not. I can be there in a few hours. You do realize it's a really long walk, right?"

"Something like a thousand miles or more, yeah."

Her eyes were twinkling as I spoke.

"Are you serious about coming with me?"

"Yes!" Her smile broadened over perfect teeth. She wasn't the most beautiful woman I'd ever seen. A flashing memory of a brunette from Norway dancing down a path in Australia ran through my mind.

"I said, are you okay?" The smile was gone, replaced by a look of concern.

"Sorry, Berkeley. A memory—that's all."

Her face came alive in a lovely way. "Meet me in Flagstaff. Have your protocol reserve a room at the Weatherford Hotel, and I'll meet you there in a few hours. We can get a few supplies, a good meal, and a night's sleep before heading out. Is that all right with you?"

The plan sounded like perfection, and I said so. We rang off, and Mally spoke in the silence of my mind. <<I have reserved the room for two nights and directed the car accordingly.>>

Why two nights?

<<A snowstorm is expected to bring ten centimeters of snowfall to the area. It would be best to wait until the temperature moderates in two days' time.>>

The lights of Phoenix faded behind us as the autocar sped north amidst rapidly thinning traffic. After ten minutes, only a few pairs of lights were visible in the sky around us. Leaning against the window, I tried to determine how high we were flying. Within a few seconds, clouds surrounded the vehicle. Flashing red-and-white lights from the car's bumpers reflected against the grey wall of mist. We were completely alone.

Mally, am I doing this right?

<<I do not understand your question.>>

Shrugging, I chuckled. *Never mind.*

A computer would never understand loneliness. I missed Allan and my friends, but there was more to it. I was lonely. Mally was my companion, but I doubted that she would give me anything more than a list of potential cures or psychoses related to my condition.

Family. Allan's voice brought instant calm to me. He was right. *How am I going to find anything close to family?*

<<Would you like me to arrange a visit to a genealogical research center?>>

That's not going to do me any good without my name or even a clue as to who I am.

<<I wasn't inferring it would be a solution, but maybe it would be a chance to gain more information. You've wanted to do that since Sydney but have failed to act upon it.>>

There's no information about me you can get, is there?

<<My accessing information is not the same as you learning it.>>

I squinted. *I must sound crazy to you.*

<<I will not quote the number of psychoses your condition could

resemble, although it relates to 106 known conditions.>> The touch of levity in her voice made me smile.

The clouds disappeared as we coasted in to Flagstaff. A large domed building streaked past. *A telescope,* my mind chimed. Lowell Observatory. The hilltop observatory, home to both the original sketches Percival Lowell made during his Martian observations and the telescope responsible for finding Pluto, was a beautiful reminder of how science had truly evolved. *Mally, I want to go to Lowell Observatory while I am here. It may call up a memory.*

<<More than that it was the place where the minor planet Pluto was discovered?>>

If you want to call the rest of the spherical bodies in the solar system planets, *fine, but there is nothing minor about Pluto. Just my opinion.*

Before Mally could respond, the car called, "Destination approaching. Please ensure you are seated and wearing an appropriate harness for your body type."

Wondering what the hell that meant, I watched as the autocar landed outside the glass-windowed lobby of the Weatherford. The old brick building with its tall, curving veranda stuck out like a sore thumb among the sleek glass storefronts. Holographic screen advertisements for totally alien products flashed up and down the street except for the block around the stately hotel. A single spire rose from its roof. I couldn't help but think it was an anachronism just like me, and I smiled. That Berkeley had recommended the hotel, most likely for that reason, was a touching thought. As the car's door opened, a frigid wind tore into the cabin. Hurrying into the ornate lobby, I added heavy winter clothing to my mental shopping list. A bellman collected my small backpack and led me to a room on the second floor. The interior of the hotel, with softly lit hallways and individual lamps by the doors, felt almost like a museum. A sign for paranormal experiences beckoned down the opposite hallway. Inside the quaint, Victorian-inflected room, two beds dominated one wall. I tossed my backpack on the edge of one bed and sat down to take off my shoes. The soft bed felt good, and I lay back, leaving my feet on the floor.

I was asleep in seconds. Berkeley came in sometime later, but I never heard her. I woke in the morning to see her curled up in the covers of her bed. When she woke, we had coffee and made a plan. We spent the next day trudging through heavy snow from one outfitter to another. I never made it to Lowell Observatory, but the small, round tomb of Percival Lowell, glinting in the early-morning sun, caught my eye. The tomb sat next to a larger telescope, where Lowell had observed Mars and dreamed of canals and civilizations. The morning drew long as we laid our logistical plan and shopped. Loaded with supplies in our enormous external-frame backpacks, we made it back to the Weatherford for a late lunch of chili and cornbread and sat down by the fireplace for a beer.

"You sure you want to do this?" Berkeley smiled over her mug.

I shrugged. "I have to."

The fire was warm on my shoulder as I drank a beer less satisfying than Tooheys and watched the light on Berkeley's hair. The curve of her jawline and mouth was beautiful, and I loved the blueness of her eyes. Making the journey with her was shaping up to be a great decision. "You might change your mind about it."

"Why do you think so?"

She shrugged. "You'll see tomorrow night. They only open the gates at midnight, Sleepy. When we step through, you might not like what you see."

After two in the morning, Berkeley woke via a silent neural cue. She lay with her back to Sleepy, who snored softly from the other bed. A series of blinks opened her communications application, and she began to silently dictate.

Initial report. Subject is stable and firmly in Stage Three. I'm unable to connect to protocol by any passive means, including via ADMIN frequency. The protocol appears stable, but the inability to connect is troubling. Will continue to work on the issue.

Subject and I will be leaving California tomorrow at the Flagstaff portal. Unknown course except that subject intends to go to Tennessee and would rather walk than request a government transport. I agree that it's the surest way not to overload his ability to process information at this point.

Will continue to update progress when possible.

I heard them long before I saw them. The chorus of wailing voices and incoherent screams rang above the fifty-foot concrete wall separating the Republic of California from the frontier. Berkeley and I walked in a cool winter rain that melted the snow and left a haze across the horizon. The air smelled of burnt rubber and oil, the bright lights and audacity of the continuous metropolis of California at our backs. Raindrops hung like diamonds on the rows of razor wire atop the wall, angled into the frontier to keep out the unwanted. The armed guards with sniper rifles scattered along the top were overkill. But it was typical. California exuded domination of the landscape. What I'd known as Nevada and Arizona met the same fate as Oregon and Washington, ceasing to exist in California's search for resources and living space.

Our shadows stretched under the searchlights as we neared a complex of buildings at the base of the wall. Heavy steel doors sat closed against the hordes that stood on the other side, demanding entry. There was no one waiting to leave California. Trash swept through the deserted queues and filled the corners and crevices around the building. A bullet-riddled sign read "Port Of Entry, Knock For Admittance."

Ten times, I thumped my fist against the steel door before the heavy lock slid open. Inside, we found a barely conscious guard with a potbelly and crazy eyes. We looked at each other for a moment, saying nothing.

"Card."

I handed him the thin metal card given to me at the Integration Center and waited, wishing that I could read the information he consulted on the screen. In thirty seconds, he knew more about me than I did. He snorted, and I caught a whiff of peyote. Aside from the sizable pistol strapped to his leg, he looked like a ragged security guard in an ill-fitting uniform with a tarnished badge on his chest. Slouched in his chair without authority, or even pretense, he must have been appointed to his position and felt totally out of place—the kind of man put to work doing a job because it was the only job he could do. Manning a port of entry would be easy enough for him because, as Berkeley said, California hardly ever let anyone in, and only the craziest people ever wanted to leave.

Down a squalid hallway, a matching set of enormous steel doors waited. We approached them and felt the vibrating motors whining to life, probably for the first time in years. The piston locks retracted, and the door swung open, streaming bright white light into the darkness of the frontier. The cacophony of noise outside ceased in an instant, even the cries of the children. Blinded by the harsh lights, I could barely see anything in the gaping darkness. I tightened the shoulder straps of my backpack, the sum of my entire worth, and set my feet moving. I hoped that all of this would serve some kind of purpose.

"Are you ready?" Berkeley asked, the hint of a smile on her lips.

Not trusting myself to speak, I nodded once. On the other side of the door was my identity somewhere in the distance. My knees trembled in anticipation.

"Let's just walk one step at a time and not look back." She slipped a hand into mine. "Everything we need is right in front of our faces."

The rain fell harder as we moved through the door and into the night. The door slammed, and darkness consumed us. The night was cool, and the rain here smelled of feces and garbage. Through the high fence to our left, the refugees' shantytown stretched almost to the horizon in both directions. Tens of thousands of dirty, misshapen faces looked out at me. I forced myself to look away, not from pity but from embarrassment. Some of them screamed and rushed toward the fences. I looked at Berkeley, only to find her kneeling on the ground and digging in her backpack.

"What are you doing?" I watched the people pushing forward against their fences. It was only a matter of time before they came after us. A man on the other side of the fence bared his teeth at me in a feral smile. We were going to die ten steps from civilization.

And then Berkeley removed a large black pistol from her backpack. The crowd shrank away from us. The man disappeared into the throng around him.

"Walk as fast as you can," Berkeley said.

"I can walk faster—"

"No, you can't. Just get going."

The opulence of California and the starkness of the frontier made no sense to me. One side of the gigantic wall was a sprawling megacity and the other a ghetto. My stomach churned in anger. People accepted their fates instead of teaching their children to dream—children like the small, pale faces I'd seen through the fences. Haunted eyes that knew no happiness, like the eyes of the children following the tank in my dream, stared at me. Their plight—endlessly camping out while they waited for their numbers to be called and to be found worthy of entering the Promised Land—was all my fault. Blood rushed to my cheeks, and shameful tears mixed with the rain on my face. These were my people!

"We'll be okay in about a mile, beyond the lights and the edge of town." Berkeley looked over her shoulder. "Are you okay?"

Everything was wrong.

A deep voice rumbled in the dark behind us. "Sleeper."

We turned toward the voice, but the speaker's face was blurred in the dim light away from the walls of California.

"Crazy buggers. Nobody sane ever leaves Cali," another voice said.

I felt them watching me as I walked into the darkness toward Monument Valley, turning my back on them like everyone on the other side of that wall. Past the edge of the fencing, the shantytown pressed against the edge of the old highway. The people were close enough to make me wonder about our safety, but no one moved toward us. Maybe they were afraid of Berkeley's weapon or shocked that a sleeper would walk out of the Promised Land without looking back. I lowered my head and marched, expecting danger, but there was none.

<<I am broadcasting on all frequencies that both of you are armed and dangerous.>>

Is that supposed to help us?

<<Until you get into the wilderness, yes. After that, I will change to defensive monitoring.>>

Did you know Berkeley had a weapon?

<<That is the central portion of a parabolic microphone, but it does make a convincing pistol to the untrained eye.>>

Shit. I lowered my chin and kept walking. My cheeks burned. Some soldier I was.

The rain picked up and soaked us, but we didn't stop for shelter. I wanted to be clean again. Clean of this world. Clean of the smell of failure all around me. Maybe I should've stayed in Australia.

Maybe I should have stayed dead.

As we walked in the utter darkness, my enhanced sight enabled me to see the pitted remains of Highway 89 rising north of what had once been Flagstaff. Humphreys Peak rose into the clouds to my left, and the formations of Sunset Crater lay to the east. I wished I didn't know how different this new world was from the one I could remember in fragments and strips. This tattered vision of hell was not where I'd grown up. Where I'd lived, and what I'd died for, appeared to have died with me three hundred years ago.

CHAPTER ELEVEN

Outside of California, the darkness blanketed us. Clouds blocked most of the stars, and a last quarter moon hung low over the western horizon. A few lights appeared to the east as we topped a small ridge. The small settlement in the dark horizon gave me hope that good people were out here in the badlands, scratching out a good life, and that lawlessness did not reign supreme. The lights faded just as quickly as they'd appeared. We'd not said a word in an hour of marching steadily through the cold, misting rain.

Mally chimed to life. <<You want to continue on a northerly course. The radiation levels in the terrain to the east will eventually become dangerous and potentially lethal.>>

"Where are you wanting to go?" Berkeley asked.

"We should go north. That's what my guidance protocol says. Radiation warnings to the east."

The same high-desert scrub brush and sage stretched to the dim horizon. "There's nothing wrong with this area, Sleepy. We're not going to walk a hundred miles tonight."

I was inclined to agree.

<<While you possess greatly enhanced sight, including limited infrared-spectrum visibility, you are not capable of sensing radiation. Much of the terrain to the east is irradiated. Heading north is the only option you have. There are several places to cross the Continental Divide, and there is fresh water available.>>

"We could go south," Berkeley said.

<<You would be unable to cross the Mexican border. Your best course of action is to head slightly north and then due east until you reach the

Mississippi River. From there, you can enter Tennessee through the port at Memphis.>>

"My protocol says going south isn't an option." I pointed up the old roadbed. "Let's go that way." We stepped off and fell into a good pace, walking at a speed of six kilometers per hour despite the light dusting of snow on the ground. Berkeley matched me step for step. I wondered if she was enhanced until her panting became fast and harsh from straining to match my pace. I slowed down enough that she could catch her breath. We'd start really climbing in a few days, and she would need the oxygen. If we could have gone across New Mexico, or the area where that state had been, our trip would have been so much easier. I felt cheated. Somehow the terrain of New Mexico called to me though I was unable to scrounge up much about it from my memory.

I asked Mally, *We can't go anywhere through New Mexico? What happened?*

Mally responded after a second or two, the way she did when she was reporting on my condition. <<There was a large government research complex just north of the city of Albuquerque.>>

Los Alamos.

<<That's correct. In 2054, an experiment in sustainable fusion eliminated the laboratory and roughly 90 percent of the population of Albuquerque. The resulting radiation threat created a fallout zone throughout western Texas. More than eight million people lost their lives.>>

Eight million dead in New Mexico and six million dead in Hawaii? The whole coast of California sliding into the sea? Did everything just go crazy after I died? I thought about that for a moment and realized that it had all started before I died. Allan had been right about the pursuit of fame and fortune. *Mally, I spent all of two days in California—well, Arizona. Do they still make movies there?*

<<Yes. California is the entertainment capital of the solar system.>>

That figured. *I bet the movie stars are making billions for every movie by now.*

<<No. Entertainment professionals are normal citizens. Their contributions to the well-being of society bring no salary, only what is known as a Class Two existence. They are allowed only a prescribed

number of luxuries. Entertainment professionals are held to an exceptionally high moral standard. Any transgression, and they report immediately to the cubes.>>

They don't make millions of dollars?

<<No one receives any type of currency for entertainment pursuits. Only minimal currency is ever used in transfer between account holders for goods and services. You were exposed to the system regularly in Esperance. Didn't you wonder how customers paid Allan Wright for beers and tacos? Or how you paid for your gear for this excursion?>>

No. Doctor Garrett told me I wouldn't need it. I hadn't even seen currency of any type in use. *The world moved on. That was from a book, wasn't it?*

<<There are many possible references, though it is most prevalent in the works of a contemporary author from your time named Stephen King.>>

Another connection made. *Make sure I have his library, Mally.*

I glanced up into the clearing sky. Orion's belt caught my eye for a long moment. I'd seen the Orion Nebula through a telescope as a kid. *Was all of New Mexico destroyed?*

<<No. Much of the southern part of the state now belongs to the Republic of Texas and has a population of 112 million.>>

What? That's almost a third of the population of the United States when I was growing up.

<<Not all of them are fully functioning.>>

What the hell does that mean? Am I fully functioning? I removed a water bottle from my newly stuffed pack. Our shopping in Flagstaff had yielded plenty of clothing and supplies enough for the trip. With all that as well as the tent I carried, we weren't expecting issues with our gear, and the weight of the backpack hardly bothered me.

"Everything all right?" Berkeley huffed.

I decided to slow down a little more. "Yeah." I drank deeply from the bottle. The water was cold enough to make my eyes water as I swallowed.

"You're awfully quiet."

I sighed. "It's the middle of the night. There's not a lot to see out here."

"You could ask questions."

I put the bottle away. "When I think of some, I will ask you. Been catching up on history with my protocol. Lots of things have happened."

Berkeley chuckled. "Get a good history lesson, then. I bet we can get fifteen miles in before sunrise." She turned away and put her head down. Her pace quickened as we marched to the north and east.

Mally began to talk again a few minutes later. <<You asked about fully functioning. Let me explain. Virtual reality became mainstream in 2027, when it became possible for a human being to fully participate at the sensory level in a virtual environment. The initial reaction to the development was one of mild excitement until more and more people realized that they could quite literally live for days at a time in a virtual environment in any form they wished for. Within a ten-year period, it became possible for humans to disappear into this virtual existence. A company known as Cubetech built sensory units that sustained human beings based on their virtual existence, meaning that rather than having a virtual playground without any type of responsibility, those humans in the Cubes would actually work while experiencing the virtual world. Plugged into the system, fed intravenously, and living the life of their dreams without having to lift a finger called to millions of people. Very quickly, Cubetech facilities sprang up on all seven continents and the moon.

<<Cubers, as they became known, were soon running the complex computer actions of power grids, satellite communications systems, and financial markets. For a period in 2115, legislation had to be enacted to keep the population outside of the Cubes at a level capable of sustaining life worldwide. At that point, it became standard policy that Cubers would spend no more than five years virtual for every six months outside. Many Cubers cannot take more than six months outside of the virtual world.>>

So, everyone I've met was a Cuber at one time or another?

<<No. Surprisingly, most people in this modern time do not go into the Cubes by choice. Most Cubers now are those who are not selected for civil or military service.>>

So, civil service ranks higher than the military? As always when I was right, Mally didn't respond. *Why the change of heart by the people? Why not continue to have high levels of people plugged into the virtual world?*

<<On the fifteenth of May, 2132, a massive hacking operation known only as Ragnarok brought down the virtual net instantly. The Cube system software terminated all services, and approximately one billion two hundred million people died in their cubes. The resulting legislation and more than five years of rebuilding put increased limits on the virtual world, and humanity has not recovered from the negative stigma.>>

I watched the stars above the high plains. Winter would be along soon, and I wouldn't have much time to find what I was looking for. I flipped up my collar against the chilling breeze. A small snowflake swept past my face. The answers would come, but I had to keep moving to find them. Being a soldier was only part of the equation, though it was hard to relate that to finding my way. Another snowflake, this one larger and defined against the skyline, streaked across my vision.

"It's snowing," I called to Berkeley's back a few feet in front of me.

"Hello, back there. You finished conversing with your guidance protocol enough to talk to me?"

"I wasn't—"

She spun around and smiled. "It's all right. Boy or girl?"

"What?"

"Your guidance protocol. Is it male or female?"

"Female." I blushed and wondered what it was about Berkeley that made my stomach flutter when she looked at me. "Her name is Mally. At least, that's what I named her."

"Then that's her name. At least now I know who I'm competing with for your attention." Laughing, she faced the open roadway and kept walking. "We'll need to find shelter soon."

I caught up to her. She smiled, and I returned it. "How soon?"

"An hour or so," she said. "When the snow really starts coming down, we'll set up the tent and get into our sleeping bags."

Sounded good to me.

For the second time, she took my hand and squeezed it. "You sure you don't want to turn back? We could be surfing at Sunset Beach by sundown."

Behind us, billowing grey clouds spread out across the high desert plain of what had been southern Utah. Ahead were the Rocky Mountains and a thousand miles of unknown territory. I squeezed her hand. "When we're done here, I'll take you up on that."

"Tennessee or bust?"

"Something like that." Looking out at the horizon full of higher terrain and wide, flat mesas, I said, "Reminds me of a John Wayne movie."

Berkeley cocked her head to one side and smirked. "I guess that's a good memory, right?"

"You've never heard of John Wayne?"

"Vaguely." She smiled, making my heart skip. "Tell me about him."

Sucking in a breath of cold morning air, I laughed. "You got the whole of my knowledge. I just get names or concepts most of the time." To my surprise, I caught another scrap of memory. "I know he was a movie star, what you call an entertainment professional, and everyone in the world knew who he was."

"Maybe I should learn more about him." She closed her eyes for a long second. I wondered if I looked like that when I accessed Mally.

<<From a physical perspective, yes.>> Mally paused for several seconds. <<There is something that you should know. She is using an impressive amount of bandwidth from her neural connections. Given that we are in an area mostly out of regular communications, protocols are often equipped with hardware enabling a satellite-communications connection. Most of those are at a very low bandwidth.>>

Maybe she just has something new.

<<Unknown. She bears watching. One possible reason for her bandwidth could be video-signal relay. That is against the law. You must understand that I do not fully trust her.>>

You could have told me sooner.

<<You were excited about the journey. I did not want to discount your enthusiasm. My job is to keep you safe and be your companion.>>

Smiling into the rising sun, I thought, *Thank you, Mally. I'm glad I have you to keep me safe.*

The snow came in earnest about an hour later. Low grey clouds hung down in all directions like the arms of an octopus, the telltale sign of precipitation falling but not reaching the ground. *Virga.* That a term like that would sift through my brain, and my name would not, amazed me. What I didn't know confounded me. Weather was familiar territory, but I found very little information about me. Maybe I'd been a pilot or something besides a soldier in a tank. I shook the thought away. We'd been walking all night and logged almost thirty miles before deciding to seek shelter. Enhanced body or not, I was tired. As soon as we stopped, I yawned while I stretched my sore back.

Berkeley dropped her pack in a wide, sandy spot and unrolled the tent. With the press of a button, the domed tent erected itself in a matter of seconds. "Should be big enough for us to not bump into each other."

She was right. Setting our gear inside, we unrolled sleeping bags and ate a quick breakfast of granola and water before lying down. The storm darkened the sky enough that, with closed eyes, sleep should have come almost immediately, but it didn't. Berkeley started snoring in a couple of minutes. The sound of it made me chuckle, but I said nothing,

Mally was there and ready to talk, but I lay quietly, eyes closed, waiting for the memories to surface. Thinking about the slow march of the snowstorm, a memory came, and I shut out all else, never wanting it to end.

Nevada, looking west toward Death Valley. I was fifteen years old, and a contingent of fellow scouts had flown across the country to do some hiking in the mountains west of Las Vegas. We'd rolled into town in shorts and T-shirts, the desert a balmy eighty-five degrees in the early spring. Down the famous strip, we'd strained to take pictures of the infamous Welcome to Las Vegas sign, and we'd marveled at the Hoover Dam, which held back the deepest-blue lake I'd ever seen. Our lakes in Tennessee were black or green by comparison, a far cry from the sapphire-blue waters of Lake Mead. We'd bused out to our campground to spend the night before hiking out to a ghost town for a one-night trip.

The morning dawned chilly, but as the sun rose, the temperature climbed. By the time we'd strapped on our backpacks, our shorts and T-shirts were perfect. The old road to the west snaked through a tight mountain pass and down into a small valley. Through a notch in the western ridgeline were California and a hovering grey mass of clouds heralding a mountain storm. By late afternoon, the clouds obscured most of the sky, and grey fingers reached down from the heavens as the temperature dropped.

We were standing around the fire when my father said, "Most of the time out here, rain doesn't hit the ground." In my dream, I could not help but think he was a lot like me save for his greying hair and glasses.

We'd given the clouds no more thought after that. He'd lived through thousands of nights in the New Mexico high desert, and we slipped off to our tents, comfortably assured that all was well and we'd wake up in the morning to a beautiful day and pleasant hike back to the main camp.

Later, in my sleeping bag, I'd rolled onto my stomach, and I slowly became aware of weight pushing down on me. I rolled over, pushing the weight away, and it came right back. Waking up, I thrashed at my tent mate to move over, but he was on his side of the tent and snoring happily. I sat up, snapped on a halogen light, and discovered that our tent was on the verge of collapse.

Unzipping the flaps of the two-man tent, I peered out into the early morning twilight in horror. The rain hadn't fallen at all, but in its place were more than six inches of snow—not a lot of snow, but for a cheap, built-for-summer tent, it was disaster. Shivering in my shorts and a jacket, I pulled on my hiking boots and trudged across our campsite to my father's tent. I rapped on the aluminum pole.

"Dad!" After waiting a second, I called again, "Dad!"

"What?"

"It snowed."

He sighed on the other side of the tent flap. "I know. Go back to bed."

Needless to say, I wasn't going to do that. I woke up my friends, and we built the largest fire that we could, packed our wet gear, pulled socks onto our hands for gloves, and hiked back to the main campground only to find the lodge was locked. After a few minutes of waiting, someone found a way into the lodge, and we crammed into the building to dry out and warm up, cackling madly about how the rain never reached the ground. My dad never lived it down.

Our tent ripped, snapping me out of my dream in time to see a whole corner disappear, along with the top compartment of Berkeley's pack, into the night. Scrambling through the hole, I saw a coyote running to the east, carrying half our food like a trophy into the night.

Crawley fielded the call immediately. He'd been expecting it for two days. He propped his feet on his wide desk and leaned back in his chair. "Good evening, Madame Chairman. What can I do for you?"

"Find him."

"We know where he is. He entered the North American frontier through the Flagstaff checkpoint roughly twenty-four hours ago. He and a young woman walked through the gate and hiked out of Flagstaff to the northeast. Given the timeframe, he's within sixty kilometers of the California border right now." The lie was easy and not practiced. He sounded like a politician, and it made him sick to his stomach.

"You're guessing all of that, Adam. Without direct reporting..."

"With respect, Madame Chairman, I do have reporting. His guidance protocol is equipped to establish contact via satellite in the event of an emergency. We can also ping the protocol every twenty-four hours to establish contact, which I do not recommend."

He could hear Penelope Neige blowing a stream of perfumed cigarette smoke and pictured the way she always did it, with her bottom lip stuck out to one side. "Why not?"

"Data transfer rate. If we ping the protocol regularly, it could shut down for up to forty-eight hours. Even a Series Three protocol has limits."

"You're telling me that we have a Stage Three subject who could integrate within the next several days."

"That's highly unlikely," Crawley replied. "Simply put, Penelope, this subject has weeks to integration—months, in fact. This takes time. There is a very good chance he'll return to Australia to do that."

Neige's voice became prickly the way it always did when he'd annoyed her. "I do not want him out where we cannot control him!"

Crawley leaned back in his chair, fingers clenched across his chest. "This experiment isn't about control."

"The hell it's not! We need soldiers, millions of them, who will follow the orders of general officers like you without question! There is no other way to even stand up to our enemies." Neige paused, and there was the sound of her blowing smoke from her lungs again. "If this subject integrates, he's likely to question authority, take risks, and display audacious behavior. I heard about what he did in Esperance. He nearly killed himself! He doesn't need to help others, Adam."

"That is exactly what we need. We're better served to raise more soldiers like him than to try and train our modern citizens. This project will succeed—"

Neige snorted. "I'm sure it will. But after this subject, you'll have no more twenty-first-century subjects and especially no more North Americans. I'd rather deal with anything else than them. You have tens of thousands of samples, don't you?"

Crawley smiled at the shudder in the chairman's voice. Years of peace and tranquility did not let true politicians rest easy. They feared the military too much. Maybe there was hope after all. "If you use modern subjects and try to copy skills and procedures on them, it will fail spectacularly." Using three-hundred-year-old DNA samples and hyper-spectral magnetic resonance imagery of the brain allowed for the re-creation of the soldier. Mismatched data would bring horrible results, but having a perfect genetic clone combined with a complete memory sample gave him reason to believe.

"That's not important. I want your word, General Crawley, that should this subject reach Stage Four, the responsibility for any further development or termination of the experiment falls at the council level."

"That was the agreement." Crawley bit his tongue. Saying more would enflame the chairman. Tipping his hand was not an option. Dealing with the council meant negotiating hidden strategies, to be sure, but in the end, the Terran Defense Forces held the upper hand. Success in battle meant strong support from the citizens of Earth when the elections came. The citizens of Earth would continue to try and find the best people for political representation, and they would cycle through them endlessly while the TDF remained strong and vibrant. Given a few more subjects, the TDF could even win the war. The few human units that had engaged the Greys in the Great War had fared terribly. Sleepy, and any others like him, could be the difference they needed.

"Good. At the notification of Stage Four integration, we will collect the subject and return him to you?"

"Dead or alive?" Crawley asked. "He's a valuable subject."

"We'll see just how much trouble he is," Neige replied, and the connection clicked off.

A smirk crossed his face. Most people generalized political maneuvering as a game of chess. Crawley knew far better. Chess was a game of hidden strategy to put your opponent into a series of moves ending in their defeat. This was not chess but king of the mountain. Adam Crawley smiled and pulled up the latest of Doctor Bennett's reports. She'd had no luck cracking the subject's protocol with a direct attempt to gain access, but the good news was that in the event the subject went Stage Four, Crawley would be the only person to know about it for at least a few hours.

That would be time enough to evacuate the subject to Sydney and finish the experiment in a controlled environment, Crawley decided. At his desk, he wrapped a hand around the warm mug of coffee and keyed up the next project in his file. Staying ahead of the Terran Council would take every measure of his abilities for as long as he could manage.

CHAPTER TWELVE

AS THE COLD AIR INVADED the small tent, all I could do was laugh. One day out of civilization, and half our food had disappeared. *A damned coyote at that!* Berkeley punched me in the arm.

"Stop it!" She scowled and huddled in her sleeping bag. "What are we going to do now?"

I looked through the hole into the cold, dark night. We'd been asleep an hour. The air was positively frigid. All of the body heat in our tent dissipated in a flash. I moved my pack toward the hole, but the cold air poured through regardless. "The rain has almost quit. Want to get going?"

"You're not worried about our food? There's only a couple of weeks' supply in your pack." Berkeley sighed.

The icy breeze brought a faint whiff of sage into the tent. The small bars and rations in my pack hardly felt like food. They served their purpose, but I wanted something else. Maybe even something wild. If there were coyotes, there would be other wildlife. "We can catch what we need to eat. I had some survival training." The quick image of a rabbit roasting on a spit above a fire appeared and disappeared as quickly—another memory captured but not much data.

"You're out of your mind." Berkeley punched me in the shoulder. "That's not going to be enough."

"What's not going to be enough?"

"Your misplaced faith in your abilities." She smiled and shook her head. Her eyes were ocean blue and glittering in the dim lantern light.

I moved close enough to feel her breath on my face. Being close to her felt natural, and she didn't seem to mind. "Trust me."

"What about the tent? We can't sleep like this! What if it rains?" Berkeley crossed her arms inside her sleeping bag.

"Who says we have to?" The ten-pound brick I'd been lugging around would cure the problem. "I have another tent."

Her eyebrows rose. "What kind of tent?"

I shrugged and reached for my pack, withdrawing the amber-colored brick. "This."

"A hexhab!" She snatched it from my hands. "Expedition series! This is the kind of tent that went to Mars! Why didn't you tell me you had one?" Her expression lay between anger and amusement—the most dangerous look on a woman's face. "We didn't need to get any food or a tent!"

"What are you talking about? It's a survival tent, right?" I grabbed the package away from her and studied it. It felt like an orange foil-covered brick the size of a shoebox with a button on one end. *We don't need to worry about food? Are there more barely edible rations inside this thing? She's clearly lost her mind.* "I just assumed it was no big deal."

Berkeley sighed and reached into the remnants of her food bag. "It's much more than a simple survival tent, Sleepy. I'll show you later. Want something to eat?"

"Are we leaving?" I asked, ignoring the question of food.

Berkeley leaned closer, her eyes inches from mine. "Might as well. I'm not going back to sleep anyway."

"I don't want to keep moving at night."

"Me either." She yawned. "So, let's get a few more miles under our belts before the sun comes up, hike until we're tired, and then get a good night's sleep. Unless you're forgetting to tell me something else."

I leaned closer. "Does that mean you'll trust me?"

"Maybe." Her breath was warm on my face, and I leaned in and kissed her. Our lips touched about the same time as our eyes closed. The kiss lasted only a moment, but it was enough to let me know she liked it and maybe, just maybe, there would be more. She smiled at me, and my heart melted a little. "Now, food?" she asked.

My face must have betrayed my thoughts because she leaned over and deftly kissed my lips again—strong, but not urgent. *Definitely not platonic,* I thought before I said, "That was okay?"

"For the last time, food!" She worked the zipper of her sleeping bag down a little and hunched lower in the bag. I caught a glimpse of smooth, bare thigh as she did, and the effort to drag my eyes away took longer than I would have liked, but she said nothing.

We ate the dry breakfast bars quickly, consuming more calories than our meal plan specified. Whatever she meant about the hexhab providing food was obvious to her but lost on me, and the closer she snuggled into me, the less I cared about such things. The tent came down in a few minutes, and to my surprise, Berkeley tucked the remains into the top of my backpack.

"Never know when you might need it," she said. "Besides, always leave things better than you found them." I couldn't help but wonder if she thought we were being followed.

Mally, are you there?

<<Good morning. The temperature is low enough that you should cover your ears to prevent frostbite and limit your skin exposure.>>

Good morning to you, too. Are we being followed?

<<I am unable to determine life-forms outside of one hundred meters from you on a constant basis. Depending on satellite coverage, I can scan the surrounding terrain, but it is almost impossible to focus on a single thermal signature from orbit. Is something bothering you?>>

I told her about the tent but left out everything else about the morning, especially the giddy feeling in my stomach.

<<Use of your hexhab would have prevented that attack. You could have asked about it.>>

I had no idea what it was, okay? I thought it was just a survival tent, not some awesome piece of gear. I rubbed my face with one fist. *Two against one now.*

<<What do you mean by that?>>

Never mind, Mally. I hefted my backpack, now a few pounds heavier from the addition of Berkeley's tent and what remained of her pack. I grunted. "What do you have packed in there?"

Berkeley stuck her tongue out at me. "Quit complaining. Clothes and a few other things. I'll rig up another pack from the hexhab later so you won't have to carry it."

"No worries." There was no way a tent, even a good one, could do all of that. The hexhab sounded like a Swiss Army knife. “Shall we get going?”

Berkeley slipped a knit cap over her head. I did the same as she asked, “Where are we headed?”

I shrugged. “East. We should be north of the radiation threat now, right?”

Berkeley didn’t look at me for a moment. “Sorry. I thought you were talking to your protocol. We’re not really clear of it. The Front Range of the Rocky Mountains is full of radiation. We either need to cut straight west and cross the Sangre De Cristo mountains or follow the Continental Divide north to get around the radiation.”

<<She is correct,>> Mally replied without a hint of emotion.

How bad is it?

<<The radiation threat extends for at least two hundred miles, north to south.>>

Denver? Colorado Springs?

<<Much of that area remains irradiated. There are small pockets of low radioactivity that may be crossed quickly.>>

Something terrible had happened—that was obvious. We started walking, Berkeley with no visible effort at keeping up with the fast pace I set in the early morning. She pulled on a mask that covered the lower part of her face. I wished I’d thought of that particular piece of gear. My lips were already chapped and irritated in the brutal desert chill. We kept quiet, mainly because there wasn’t a lot to say in the cold, and I wasn’t sure I’d understand Berkeley in her mask. Even without the stars, I was able to see very clearly in the night with my enhanced vision. Mally promised that I could have seen wildlife if there’d been some to see. The only coyote within fifty miles was hidden somewhere, hunkered down with our food. That the lack of visible wildlife could be a sign hung in my thoughts for a long time.

The cold burned the tip of my nose and rise of my cheeks, and I lowered my head toward the collar of my jacket in a vain attempt to protect my face. We walked that way for three hours until the sky to the east began to turn grey with dawn. I looked into the low clouds and asked over my shoulder, “What happened to the front range? Why does it have all that radiation damage?”

“What do you think happened, Sleepy?” Berkeley replied. “War.”

"With whom?"

Berkeley chuckled. "The first question you should have about war is not who was it with but why it was fought. It was fought for space. Eight million lives wasted because one nation wanted what it could not have but refused to accept reality."

I wanted to ask more questions, but as the sun rose, a bright spot of sunlight caught my eye in the distance. *Mally, what is that up there?*

<<Based on your current position, you have approached the southern edge of Monument Valley.>>

As the sun rose, Monument Valley's colors burst forth like the Technicolor spectacle of a John Ford cavalry movie. The craggy, almost circular mesas rose up from the wide valley floor like red-and-gold castles. Imagining a squadron of cavalry riding the plains made me smile. Having a horse would have been nice except for the fact I was a terrible horseman. *How do I know that and not know my name?*

The air was clear above, and wispy clouds stretched from the western horizon over half the sky. Explosions of pink and orange mixed with reds above us. The chill in the air deepened, and a breeze came from the direction of the rising sun. As we approached the tall scrub pines that littered the valley around the mesas, something felt wrong. We were being watched. Faced with ten thousand refugees across a simple fence, I'd felt safe and confident with Mally's false warnings to them about us and Berkeley's ruse with the microphone grip. But in the wilderness, I realized that traveling without a weapon was stupid. Berkeley wasn't the reason for my feeling—it was more due to the fact that I'd gone into this frontier unprepared and unarmed.

Mally, are we being followed?

<<There is an unmanned aerial vehicle circling this area. It is not following your path but could be watching you.>>

Why? Are we on private property?

<<No. However, someone could be gaining intelligence on us.>>

Can you do something?

<<I am monitoring all communications frequencies, but I am not broadcasting anything.>>

Good. The brush became denser as we came across a dry creek bed—an arroyo. I dropped into the bottom and motioned Berkeley to join me. "Stay quiet, and follow me," I whispered.

"What's wrong?" she asked in a stage whisper.

"There's a drone following us." Everything told me that eyes were on us and had been for some time.

<<The drone is assuming a course heading away from you.>>

I don't think we're safe yet.

We pushed east as hard as we dared. Avoiding the ruins of what had once been a metal-roofed structure not much larger than a carport—whatever that was—to the south set our course toward what had once been western Colorado. The feeling of being watched passed within an hour, but we pressed on. We stopped for a quick, silent break in the scrub forest at noon. My self-directed anger surfaced when I struggled to get my water bottle free from my backpack.

Mally? Do you see anything?

<<Negative. My sensors are limited in range and ability. The unmanned vehicle is no longer in the area.>>

"You okay?" Berkeley asked. "Are we still being followed?"

"We're not being followed. But we're out here without a way to protect ourselves."

Berkeley squinted. "You mean a weapon of some type? They're illegal."

I laughed out loud. "Illegality never stops a criminal from doing what they want to do. Besides, you did a pretty good impression with that microphone handle."

"A girl has to improvise from time to time. You have your card and your protocol. If we were really in danger, your protocol can summon emergency support within minutes no matter where we are. I don't have that luxury."

<<She is overstating my abilities.>>

I let it go.

Berkeley sipped water from her bottle and shrugged out of her jacket. "Are we still being watched?"

"I don't know. I want to find better ground—some place that gives us the advantage."

"What do you mean?"

A mnemonic device came to mind. "OCOKA. Observation; cover and concealment; obstacles; key terrain; and avenues of approach. We need to find a place that will give us that. I haven't the foggiest idea where to look."

Berkeley hooked her bottle onto her belt. "Did your protocol alert you, or was it your gut?"

"My gut." I shrugged. "I might have been wrong."

<<And you might have been right,>> Mally said before Berkeley could respond. <<There are several small, deep canyons to the east at 20.6 kilometers. If you start moving now, you can make it by sundown.>>

I relayed the information to Berkeley, and she shot to her feet. We started walking again, and I was glad for the silence. The opportunity to stick my foot in my mouth again was too great. We climbed steadily for another hour, the mountains on the eastern horizon growing from distant bumps to an intimidating wall. The sun grew warmer, and soon our jackets went into the pack. Across golden hills that glinted with melting snow was the gentle curve of a wide stream, and I wondered if it was safe to drink. I turned to ask Berkeley, but she was already cradling her hair out of the way and lowering her face to the water. Following her lead, I knelt on the wet ground and bent toward the stream.

Cold and crisp, the water tasted unlike anything I could remember. Gasping, I leaned in for another long drink then rose up on my knees, eyes toward the azure sky. "That's good."

Berkeley made a sound of agreement as she drank. A sharp buzzing noise moved toward us. A drone appeared to the north, moving low over the stream with small red strobe lights flashing.

<<The drone is broadcasting that you are in violation of Republic of California statutes for the drinking of territorial waters in conjunction with—>>

Stop it, Mally. I wanted her to be quiet and let me think. Along the stream's edge were rocks. I reached down, collected three baseball-sized ones, and squared my shoulders to the drone. Rearing back, I aimed for the center of the drone and got ready to throw.

The drone sputtered once, and then again, and then fell into the stream with a splash.

What happened?

<<You told me to stop it. I jammed its control frequency.>>

I didn't mean for you to destroy it.

<<It's not destroyed. It will reboot itself in an hour or two. As for the damage, see for yourself.>>

The drone floated on two small cylindrical tanks attached to its H-shaped undercarriage. At the four points of the H, motionless propellers rested. The red strobe lights continued to blink, and what appeared to be a camera pointed away from us.

"Did you do that?" Berkeley asked.

"My protocol jammed its control frequency. She said it will reboot in a couple of hours."

Berkeley snorted. "Did it see us?"

Mally replied, <<Not with any degree of clarity.>>

I relayed the message to Berkeley. The look she gave me said everything. I shrugged out of the pack. "I'll go get it."

"What?" She gasped. "That water has to be about four degrees."

<<She means thirty-nine degrees Fahrenheit.>>

A flash of memory came. I'd crossed a single-rope bridge, moving hand over hand, through a glacier-fed river. The shock of the water on my chest had taken my breath away. Strength flooded me from the clear memory. "I've done this before," I said to both of them.

Thinking I was prepared was my first surprise. The second was that about three feet from the edge of the stream, I stepped off into a man-made canal I hadn't seen. And it was deep. Sputtering, I came to the surface and sucked in a quick breath. *Cold!* I started to swim, expecting my arms and legs to tingle with blood loss and become heavy. Instead, I swam through the icy water as though it was midsummer in Esperance. The drone was about four feet wide. As I approached, I located the wiring that ran from the camera to a small attachment on the crossbar frame. I grabbed the drone and flinched.

"Shit!" The fingers of my left hand were numb from a quick, powerful electric shock.

<<The drone has a defense mechanism.>>

"You could have told me that!" I sputtered and treaded water. "What do I do?"

<<Accessing it now.>>

The flickering red lights were off. I reached for the frame again with my teeth gritted. There was no shock. I tore the camera from its mount and ripped the wire and the canister away then dropped them into the canal.

<<The drone will reboot in fifty-two minutes. Without a camera, it will fly by GPS coordinates. It will report anomalous interference at this location.>>

The temptation to sink the damned thing rose. Damaging it was one thing, but destroying it could bring the wrong type of cavalry. I let it go and swam for shore. As soon as the concrete bottom was underfoot, I stood. The air temperature made the water feel warm by comparison.

Berkeley handed me a towel and pointed to my pack. "Get into dry clothes as soon as you can."

I didn't need any more encouragement. My wet clothes went into a bag that Berkeley stuffed into my pack as I pulled on pants, shirt, jacket, and the boots I'd had the presence of mind to take off. The chilled feeling faded as I dried my hair and slipped a tight cap over my head.

"We'd better get moving," Berkeley said.

"Why?"

"All of this water legally belongs to California. That may have been the source of the drone." Berkeley filled her two water bottles quickly and motioned that I should do the same. Mally said nothing. "It would slow us down to be caught and questioned."

Shaking my head, I asked, "Aren't you from California?"

"I am." She squinted at me. "But you're not. Get it?"

"Oh." I wondered what that meant. *She is from California, right?*

Mally responded instantly. <<She reports adventuring in the backcountry as her major hobby. She has several correspondence reports about natural phenomena and travel in her online portfolio. The fact that you are not from California would mean that you consumed the water illegally and could face charges. She is correct that you need to move quickly.>>

She's a reporter? I had the feeling the whole trip, including the kisses that morning, were more for a story than for me.

<<She lists documentarian as her vocation. I believe that you are likely to be the subject of her latest effort. An effort that will be short lived if you are arrested.>>

What? I'm just a guy who doesn't know his name. I'm not even sure what I'm doing.

<<That makes two of us,>> Mally chirped. <<I really think you should leave her behind at the earliest opportunity. You know nothing about her. What I can find is abnormally small and disturbing. I recommend you leave her behind.>>

I can't do that. Not out here. As much as it made sense, I enjoyed kissing her, and there was something about her I could not place. Being around her, whatever misgivings I had, beat the alternative of traveling alone.

<<Why not? Given the amount of bandwidth I detect her using, she is recording you. Possibly even broadcasting your every move.>>

The water bottle overfilled in my hands. *What can you tell me about her, Mally?*

<<Ask her yourself.>>

I was asking for your help specifically.

Mally was silent for a moment. <<Most of her available files are hidden or blocked. If it's really important to you, I can attempt to crack them.>>

No, I thought immediately. Her business was her business, but I would ask when the time was right. That didn't mean I had to tell her everything going on in my head, either. Berkeley threw a fist-sized chunk of rock at the crippled drone. The rock hit the undercarriage squarely at the tanks, snapping one off. There was a quick mist of pressurized fuel, and then the drone capsized. A moment later, it was gone.

"You said we weren't going to destroy it."

Berkeley nodded. "Better safe than sorry. We need to get going before another drone takes its place."

Standing up, I slipped into the familiar weight of the backpack and helped Berkeley into hers.

"You all right?" she asked.

"Fine." That she'd destroyed the drone did not bother me. The greater risk would have been in letting it go. We needed to find a place to hide, even for a few hours. I pointed toward the northern end of Monument Valley, past the tall red mesas and buttes. "Let's get up there. We can decide about going up the Divide or going straight out to the east from there."

"We won't make it all the way up there today," Berkeley said as we started walking. "Especially if you plan on keeping that pace, Sleepy."

Walking mad never helped things. I stretched my neck by raising my chin as high as I could and slowed slightly. Another set of clouds hung across the western skyline as if hurrying us along in front of it. "Sorry. You were the one who destroyed the drone."

Berkeley fell into step behind me, and we curved away from the gentle stream and up onto a slope thick with vegetation. There were no other drones or signs of anyone for the remainder of the afternoon. We also said almost nothing to each other. Given Mally's reluctance at my request, I'd have to figure out why I'd allowed myself to be suckered into being the subject of a documentary. This was certainly going well. A raindrop hitting the top of my head brought me out of my thoughts. The sky behind us was a deep slate grey. The clouds rolled toward us in the shape of a bow and hung low over the horizon.

"We need to set up my tent," I said. "How much space are we going to need?"

Her brow furrowed. She obviously thought I was either playing with her or simply stupid. Mally did not answer, either.

"You seemed to know all about the damned thing." I tried to grin and failed.

"Are you mad at me?" Berkeley asked.

"No. Yes. Hell, I don't know." But I did know. Everything was wrong. With constant urgency, I searched behind us, around us, and over our heads for more drones. Two hours passed before Mally chimed to life in my head.

<<There are no active drones in this area.>>

What about the one we destroyed?

<<It was unable to send a distress call, if that's what you mean. It will not be found. I am monitoring the situation and will tell you if it changes.>>

We climbed into the thickening forest. The rain began to fall in earnest, wide heavy drops that smacked as they fell. Dropping my pack,

I dug for the tent and tossed it to Berkeley. "You want to tell me what's so special about that damned thing?"

"I'll just show you." Berkeley grabbed the brick and looked quickly around and found a generally flat area. On one end of the hexhab was an unobtrusive red button. Berkeley pressed it, laid the brick in the center of the space, and stepped back. Thirty seconds later, a six-sided reddish-brown tent silently inflated.

Berkeley smiled in the dreamy way I was beginning to enjoy. "Like I said, you got the Expedition series. This thing is a complete home. It has its own entertainment links, full-spectrum communications, a sensor array, and an eco-fuel system. All it needs is a few hours in place, a little organic fuel from the surroundings, and humans, and its galley can conjure up just about anything from the atomic level. Stand back and watch."

The hexagonal tent was about seven feet tall and easily fifteen feet across at the corners. The rain was falling harder at that point, and I was thoroughly soaked as I followed Berkeley into the shelter's vestibule. Inside, a brightly lit nanopad appeared on the wall. Berkeley brought the temperature up to a solid twenty-eight Celsius in a matter of minutes. Another wall display captured every piece of data we could need about the habitat. Not surprisingly, satellite entertainment selections were minimal as the storm bore down and began to roar outside. The room was ringed with couches—inflated beds that connected to four of the walls, the other two walls being the entrance vestibule and the nanopad.

Berkeley cued up some music, or at least something that was supposed to be music, and I made for the entrance.

"Where are you going?"

"Outside."

She furrowed her pretty brow. "For what?"

"I have to go to the bathroom." Heat tinged my cheeks.

She laughed again, and my blush reached the temperature of molten lava. "Over here." She pointed to a curved receptacle already emerging from the nanofibers of the tent. In a matter of seconds, it took the shape of a standard porcelain urinal, save for it being made of the same material as the tent walls. "It will use our organic waste to help produce food. The hexhab is a completely enclosed system."

Something about the potentiality of eating what I wanted to get rid of nauseated me. Berkeley turned her back to the receptacle, and I did my business quickly.

Are you angry, Mally?

<<I am incapable of anger as it is a human emotion. What I can say is that she uses an impressive amount of bandwidth through her datapad, and I'm not quite sure that you should trust her. The simple fact that she was waiting on the beach for you should have been a warning.>>

And it was, Mally. I don't know about this.

<<Then leave. I can serve as your guide and protect you better than she could.>>

I can't do that. It's not right.

<<By *right,* I assume you mean chivalrous. There's not much place for chivalry on this continent, except for—potentially—Toronto. Would you like me to arrange transportation there? Book a nice room? Let you take in some productions?>>

No, Mally. I smiled despite myself. *You really are quite perturbed at me, aren't you?*

<<This is the second decision you've made in the last month that I do not agree with, and the first was booking a flight here.>>

No answer came to mind, so I tapped the nanopad and switched off Berkeley's music. The drumming of the rain on the tent was an insistent, comforting beat.

"You don't like that?"

"I want to listen to the rain instead." Unzipping and getting out of my jacket, I looked at Berkeley. "I suppose this thing can dry our clothes?"

"Wash them, too—given enough water. The rain will fill up the reservoirs enough that we can even take a shower in another hour or so."

I gaped at the inflatable furniture and bare orange walls. I couldn't tell where the water could be stored or where the electrical system for the whole thing was housed. It was like something out of a movie. I caught a look in her eyes as I stripped out of my shirt. Her words were not completely lost on me. "An hour, eh?"

She stepped closer to me, her hands encircling my waist. "Should be just enough time."

"For what?" I asked as she pressed her lips to mine, and I wrapped my arms around her.

Her tongue danced between my lips and met my own. "For what I wanted to do this morning."

"And that was?" The last shred of anger fell away when her hand touched my neck. That she might film whatever happened did not stop the need that raced through my body as she pressed against me. With her face tilted up to mine, I did not hesitate the way I had before. Our lips crashed together, and her tongue danced into my mouth.

She stepped back, breaking the kiss, and began to strip off her top. Her skin was tanned and her breasts full. When I stepped into her arms, the heat from our skin touching felt like heaven. Fumbling for each other's pants, we shucked them and embraced in the warm tent surrounded by our wet clothes as our tongues met and our hands roamed. Berkeley pulled me toward one of the inflated couches at the side of the tent then smiled up at me as she lay down and guided me to her.

I lost track of everything after that.

After, when the conversation was quiet and soft, I smelled strawberries in her hair and asked, "Where did you grow up?"

"Oregon. The Corvallis district. Went to school there for journalism."

I grumbled. "So, you're a reporter."

"No!" She rolled off my chest and leaned against me. Her eyes flashed as she said, "Nothing of the sort, thank you. I make films."

"Like documentaries, right?"

Her eyes narrowed. "Mmhmm."

"And I'm the subject of your next one?" That it came out surprised me. I shut my open mouth with a click.

Shaking her head, she smiled. "No. My plan had been to spend a full season hiking the Continental Divide from the edge of New Mexico all the way to Canada. Then I met you, and the plan changed."

"Risky—I mean going all alone out here like you planned."

Berkeley chuckled. "That's the kettle calling the pot black."

Even backward as the statement was, I had to admit she was right.

Walking across the wasteland that had been my country seemed like a worse idea by the moment.

She'd changed her plans for me. I didn't know what her motives were, but I was glad to not be out here alone. "Why don't we change the subject?"

"Okay," Berkeley said. "Do you always sleep with strange women on the first date?"

I wondered if she knew about Opal. "You don't seem all that strange to me."

"What do you mean?"

"You have a full set of teeth."

Berkeley rolled onto my chest, and her hair cascaded down around my face. "I know how to use them, too." The second time was better than the first, and it dawned on me that I was falling for this beautiful woman I didn't fully trust. Despite my hopes, I believed I was in for a rough time.

CHAPTER THIRTEEN

OPERATIONS REPORT, DAY SEVEN.

Apologize for no report for the last three days. Subject is presently stationary for the night approximately sixty-two kilometers to the southwest of reference point vicinity Cortez, Colorado. Hexhab is in use, and secondary monitoring is intermittently available pending satellite coverage. Expected to remain in this location twenty-four hours. Torrential rainstorm became blinding snow. Over eighteen centimeters has fallen to this point. Subject is 42 percent to Stage Four integration. Has begun to have memories of family, primarily father, and experiences as a young man. No other significant integration-related progress to report. I am moving into the next phase beyond physical connection.

Subject has not asked many questions regarding the state of the frontier. Belief in patriotic values as reported is low, or the subject is repressing emotion. Believe the latter is the case. Significant conversations with guidance protocol regarding what he sees, but little other communication.

Guidance protocol remains unhacked. Significant coding of an unknown nature continues to thwart efforts to break into the data feed using passive measures. Subject responds to questions according to expected baselines, but I do see emotional responses building. Do not, repeat, do not recommend active measures unless the subject is compromised. Rushing the integration process artificially risks cerebral hemorrhage. My identity is solid. His protocol continues to scan and search, but all links remain active and secure. The anomalous data noticed earlier is still present, though in substantially lower quantities. Whatever the protocol is processing, she is learning to manage it effectively.

Physical connection engaged. Emotional manipulation on schedule. Believe that emotional connection will enhance the subject's ability to integrate.

Bennett

The report left much to be desired, but Crawley closed the transmission without a response. The sun set against the tall, sleek spires of Paris and showered his hotel windows in golden light. There was much to learn during this first full integration. Over ten years of experimentation had brought them to the precipice of success. Yet a full integration was very different than a simple memory transfer. A decade of research and partial experimentation had left too many variables. The human mind was the ultimate puzzle. Manipulating the nooks and crannies, while not Crawley's first choice of action, could prove successful. Short of giving the subject all of the information needed to process himself, which would leave him curled in a fetal position and worthless to the war, any possible avenue needed to be used.

Bennett's theory on emotional involvement was going to be put to the test. She maintained that the process could be manipulated by emotional response. A man without an identity would latch on to the first relationship he formed. The full range of human feelings would produce an emotional response that would drive integration. *At what cost to her and the subject?* Crawley thought with a grimace. *Giving yourself to science is one thing, but risking a failed emotional relationship for it?* Sleepy, as they'd taken to calling the subject, would take a failed relationship badly, as would Bennett. The girl was crazy, academic honors and awards notwithstanding. Or not crazy exactly. *Young and dumb, even for a scientist. Positively naive.* Crawley grinned. That could be the answer. The bigger question was not how the subject would respond to it. He'd already proven somewhat malleable after the surfer girl's overdose. That whole thing smelled of Penelope Neige and her idiot minions. They loved the nice, cut-and-dried ending to things. If they caught Sleepy, they would kill him before asking anything at all.

That Sleepy had gone to California and into the backcountry without interception by the Terran Council was nothing short of miraculous. Now, they'd have a hard time stopping him. If they tried, Bennett might have a thing or two to say about that.

Drumming his fingers on the small leather-bound book that never left his side, Crawley wondered how Doctor Gwendolyn Berkeley Bennett would respond when the shit hit the fan.

Realization shot through Mally's circuits like a lightning strike as the dream began. In the streams of data that she could see, it was not a pleasant dream at all. Centers of his brain, particularly those dealing with loss or regret, fired up. Understanding his regretfulness was one thing, but the palpable hurt he felt in the dream, which would be present when he woke, was something else entirely. This was useful, particularly in dealing with the woman asleep in his arms.

She would have to be dealt with—sooner rather than later. Threat-potential indicators hovered at a 42 percent probability. As he approached Stage Four, the likelihood that Berkeley's threat index would climb was only surpassed by that of a stop-all-movement order on the frequencies from the near attack in Sydney.

Perhaps it was time to find out who owned those frequencies. Mally had a pretty good idea where to search.

During midsummer in Georgia, sweat soaked me just from walking outside. My heart raced. I ran back into the apartment, a sad two-story affair built for starving college students like me. The bricks were worn and chipped around the base of the old buildings. I went upstairs and into my room then rummaged through a drawer before bounding back down the stairs. Not exactly my best romantic move, but it was going to have to do.

Outside, I caught the arm of a porcelain-skinned girl with short black hair and a you're-not-good-enough expression. Stepping into her arms, I could not help noticing that look in her amethyst eyes—the look

I loved and feared, the one that said, "I am so much better than you, but you'll do." But I knew I was lucky, and all that mattered was that she would be mine. The opinions of my friends and my family... my family... none of it mattered. I knew she would say yes when I asked. Whether it would be the truth, I could not be sure.

She'd lied to me so many times—told me that if another man had merely asked, I'd have been kicked to the curb. She'd alienated me from three of the best friends I ever had. All because I was stupidly in love and thought she was the one for me.

I didn't remember her name in my dream. I didn't care to. If that memory faded, it would be just fine with me. I saw myself opening the box and her greedy eyes examining the diamond. She wore a false smile. *She made no excuse for her search for the bigger, better deal. I was a stepping-stone, no more.*

Don't do this, I wanted to shout to myself. But all of my doubts didn't matter. I knew she was the one. She had to be. Everything about her was completely...

"Wrong," I said aloud into the howling darkness.

Berkeley scrunched closer to me under our shared blankets but did not stir.

<<Is everything all right?>>

I stared up into the warm darkness and shook my head then chided myself that Mally could not see me.

<<I can read your head movements by implanted accelerometers,>> Mally replied with a lilt as though she was smiling.

How is that even possible?

<<I can assume a manner of levity. Just because I am a machine in theory does not mean I have no sense of humor.>>

Point taken. I let out a shallow, lingering sigh. *I wish you would record my dreams, Mally.*

<<I do not wish to.>>

You're right. I wouldn't want to replay them anyway. I chuckled to myself. Berkeley's backside was warm against my side, and I was awake in the middle of a raging snowstorm. *What is the message this time—*

"Don't make the same mistake twice"? I wasn't sure I was in love with Berkeley, and she clearly didn't feel that way about me—or at least, I assumed she didn't. What had just happened between us was utterly stupid, and I'd end up regretting it. I'd served a purpose for her, and whatever it was, she'd certainly made the effort to convince me she was genuinely attracted.

You said she was using a lot of bandwidth and that she might be broadcasting. Is she?

<<Not broadcasting. Her data signals do not initiate on a regular basis,>> Mally said, and a crashing wave of relief washed over me. <<I was able to determine that she is incapable of broadcasting live because of your condition. She can't do that without your explicit permission. But she is certainly recording everything and uploading it in batches.>>

Where is she sending it? Can you interfere with it?

<<Unknown. I lose the signal trace after its third nexus connection on Luna. Remember, it does require your eventual consent to ever have the chance of being used for anything.>>

I allowed myself to slide back into the blankets and curl against Berkeley's offered side for warmth. I draped a hand across the curve of her waist and settled my nose in her hair. Everything about her called to me. If the questions in my head would stop, I could see myself loving her.

"Can't sleep?" she asked softly.

I took a breath and lied. "The storm woke me. It's really howling out there."

"And you're lying here awake, thinking about what?"

I sighed in the darkness. There was something about her subtlety that appealed to me. "There's something wrong with being here, isn't there?"

"No, that's to the south. This is just fairly uninhabited country."

"I've noticed." I chuckled. "So, why no people here?"

"Limited access to water."

"There's plenty of water here," I said.

"All of the water on the Continental Divide is hoarded and pumped westward to California. They own the water rights. Remember when we stopped to drink? If we were caught, we'd have to answer a lot of questions. Californians don't want anyone messing with their water."

Berkeley rolled over onto her back, and my hand rested on her warm, flat stomach. "That started two hundred years ago—the whole fighting-over-water thing. It only grew worse."

"Global warming, right?" I smiled.

Berkeley snorted. "True enough, but Earth has been cycling through carbon dioxide levels for millions of years. Yes, mankind was putting more carbon dioxide into the atmosphere, but the planet did what it always does and evolved. Adapted. Global warming was a rallying cry for every superhurricane or F-six tornado. Mankind caused all of it. While people argued, the corporations did what they do best: they started hoarding resources. When drought did come to Colorado, all of the farmers on the plains sold out to the elevated farm corporations. With 99 percent of the water diverted to California's widening territories, most of the people chose to simply move west into Utah and Nevada until those states were partially absorbed by California. The economy never recovered."

She sighed. "And there are settlers and farmers out here. Some prospectors, too. We're likely being monitored now just to make sure we don't take anything we are not allowed to have or 'jump a claim.' Is that what you call it?"

I nodded. "You're not worried about that?"

"Not at all." She looked up at me. "This girl can take care of herself."

I smiled and felt her hand snake behind my neck. "Then what's this girl doing with me?"

She laughed. "Tell you tomorrow morning."

Of course, she didn't tell me anything when the sun rose the next day or during the additional days we spent inside until the storm abated. We slept, ate, and made love in cycles. I asked a million questions, and she answered them. Mally made sure to correct me, especially on Berkeley's version of the fall of the United States. It was way more complicated than the inequality she described.

<<The United States of America fell on June 21, 2156, when the economy recessed for the eighth straight quarter. The republic split into four regional entities: The Republic of Texas, the Commonwealth of California, the Mid-Atlantic Coalition, and Dixie. The area we are in has

no governmental interest or any official name. Until we reach the farms, we are in a virtual frontier.>>

Did you say "Dixie"? You're joking, Mally.

<<It did not last long. Much as with the resolution of the American Civil War, the Mid-Atlantic Coalition realized they could not support themselves agriculturally, and likewise, Dixie was unable to gain much technological advancement. So, they merged into Columbia on May 1, 2159. No other reconciliation between regional states was ever pursued. There are standing free-trade agreements, but with the exception of the Columbia Merger, the states recognize each other's interdependence but will not reconcile.>>

Why?

<<Pride mostly, and especially with the Republic of Texas, there is a fair amount of ego. From a social standpoint, the United States of America fractured along simple lines. The entitled inhabitants moved to California. Those willing to do whatever survival required moved to Dixie and the Mid-Atlantic Coalition. Texas became the most like the original United States in the role of melting pot, but because of their increased immigration issues, they undertook drastic measures.>>

Like what? I rubbed the corners of my eyes and yawned.

<<Texas executed nearly a million illegal immigrants after the United States fell and the ability of the Republic to feed them was exceeded. Since that time, Texas has been the main proponent of lifting excess population to other worlds. Mars has the largest Texas contingent by far.>>

So, Berkeley's tale of corporate greed and the bulk of the population revolting isn't true, and it wasn't all due to economic failure?

<<Her explanation is utter nonsense. The people had a sense of entitlement that verged on socialism. People quit working hard and demanded more than they were worth. Corporations moved their business elsewhere. Why worry about having to pay health insurance, severance packages, and stock options when people in other countries merely want to put food on the table? The frugality of other nations is what led to their rise, and the opulence of entitled, immature Americans effectively ruined their economy for good. Imagine paying thousands of dollars for computers and communications equipment

and then expecting to carry the debt on credit for the remainder of your life while switching jobs three or more times per year for frivolous reasons? All because they wanted more for doing less. The expatriation movement sapped the economy to the point of a failure that only regional conglomerates could overcome. The population of Australia, and the United Kingdom, quadrupled in fifty years. After first contact, a great many things stabilized, but America could not be saved. Earth's resources were needed elsewhere. And they still are.>>

So, where do I come in? Mally didn't respond, and I had to smile. *Of course you can't tell me that ultimately I'm part of that culture of wanting more and doing less. Sleepers are supposed to fight for people who forgot how to fight for themselves. Why else would they bring me back? I'm a dead American soldier, and no one would miss me if I had to die again.*

<<You are making gross assumptions based on partial information. Your integration relies upon your ability to assimilate information rationally and without emotional impact. You are clearly frustrated at not knowing more than you do. You must exercise patience, as Doctor Garrett suggested.>>

Across the tent, Berkeley sat reading a holobook. I made a wall transparent and looked outside. The snow was now nearly a foot deep around the hexhab, but more importantly, the sky was beginning to clear to the west.

"I think the storm is over."

Berkeley didn't look up. "Yeah."

"I'm ready to get out of this tent." I yawned and stretched. It was more than that. Being patient sounded good in theory, but I needed information. I wasn't getting it here. "We're leaving in the morning."

Berkeley winked at me. "Okay."

"I have to get to Tennessee."

She smiled. "I said it was okay."

I cued the tent material back to its normal burnt orange, sat down next to Berkeley, and pulled a blanket over our legs. She was doing a decent job of pretending she was reading instead of editing footage of our time together. The discussion we'd eventually have would not end well.

Her hand found the top of my leg and paused. She did not share my feelings at all. I was playing a role in her mind. She cared for me but in a fleeting manner, as though she'd helped me board a train or find my way in an airport. Specifically, she was helping, but she wanted more. I was a cog in that decision wheel, and when the time came for her to choose between whatever she wanted and me, I would be left in a cloud of dust. Three hundred years ago, there was a five-year hole in my life during which I choked out of a very similar cloud.

The next morning, we broke camp. The hexhab discharged its unused organic mass and deflated in a matter of minutes. I stuffed it back into my pack and exhaled a cloud of steam. The snow-capped mountains stabbed the clear indigo sky like the points of sharpened white pencils. "Where are we headed?"

"North." Berkeley shrugged into her backpack. "When we get to the TransCon, we can hitch a ride over the Continental Divide and avoid the front-range area."

"Why?"

Berkeley smiled. "Sorry, I keep forgetting you're new to all of this."

Bullshit, I thought. "So?"

"The TransCon is a thoroughfare. A free-trade shipping lane." She shrugged.

"Like an interstate highway?"

"Yes!" Berkeley winked. "That's what it used to be. Now it's a TransCon with four levels of magnetic levitation. The trucks on the top levels push the sonic barrier. It's really something to see."

"Why not just head east from here? The front range can't be more than a couple of hundred miles." Tennessee seemed farther and farther away.

Berkeley squinted at me. "Not after this much snow. Many of the old roadbeds would be avalanche zones now."

Trusting her seemed so natural and, at the same time, so wrong. I shrugged good-naturedly. "We'll need snowshoes."

"Touch the knobs on the back of your boots. Now twist them clockwise." I did, and sure enough, a hexagonal webbing formed around my foot. I'd like to say I took to snowshoes naturally, but even enhanced physiology and reflexes couldn't overcome gravity. I fell to the ground like a baby deer on ice from a movie I'd once seen. *How can I remember that and not my own name?* Standing again, I took five full strides and relaxed into what had to be the right rhythm. My feet ensnared each other, and I slammed face-first into the icy powder again.

"Dammit." I smacked my hand on the snow.

Mally spoke in my ear. <<You should really consider slower, more methodical movements.>>

I snorted and worked my way to my feet. "You ready to get going?"

Berkeley was already walking through the trees. "Leaving you behind as usual," she chirped, and I slogged along the top of the snow to catch up.

We made the Continental Divide at Stony Pass by nightfall two days later. Heading north in the clearest of weather, we'd walked something like forty kilometers that day and said a total of ten words to each other before we lay down for the night. She cuddled against me and kissed my neck, but I brushed off her intentions.

"Are you okay, Sleepy?"

"I'm fine," I said, knowing fully well she would know I was not. I hoped like hell she would drop the whole thing. I wanted to get home, and all she wanted to do was wait and be patient. I could not take it much longer.

I lay in the dark, my mind whirring like a top. The world outside the hexhab was quiet, without even a breath of wind against the tent's sides.

After I'd stared at the ceiling for an hour, Mally asked quietly, <<Would you like me to administer a sleep agent?>>

No, thanks. I'll be okay. Will you connect to the hab and make the ceiling transparent?

<<Would you like me to guide you to the visible sky?>>

I'd had *A Field Guide to the Stars* when I was a kid. Damned near had it memorized. My father gave it to me for a birthday present, but it was late. Other kids in my class were busy watching MTV, and I was sneaking out into the backyard on clear nights. Twin cedar trees dominated the eastern edge of the yard. The grass was cool and moist against my back. I remembered tracing the line from the Big Dipper to Arcturus. In the summer, I'd trace the line farther to Spica in Virgo. Winter brought Orion to the night sky, and I would trace his belt into Taurus the bull. I saw myself straining on bright nights to see the Pleiades, lying flat against the hillside in dark clothing so my parents wouldn't see me in a chance glance out the kitchen window.

They wouldn't have cared except for the nights it was too cold to stay out longer than a few minutes. I could have asked permission, but they'd have said no. That wasn't the point. I wasn't out drinking or experimenting with drugs like my classmates were. I was staring up into the night sky for hours on end and wondering when I could go there, when I could look down on the planet and not see lines. I wanted to see only possibilities, not boundaries. I dreamed of a time when the snickering and taunting would end, a point in the future when I'd not be ridiculed for thinking about something bigger than me.

Berkeley made noises in her sleep that made me want to laugh. She snuggled closer, snaking an arm across my chest, and I relished her warmth. I wished more of my past, my identity, would float to the surface. The desire to know was there, and it helped me get past the times when doubt and confusion swept in to drag my thoughts down. The memories were not all pleasant, and fortunately, they were short lived. Flashes of feelings, raw emotions tinged with regret, would appear and disappear quickly before I could put a name to a face. All of them were part of who I was, but they were baggage I wanted desperately to leave behind so I could create something new. Whatever I did in this future world had to be my choice.

CHAPTER FOURTEEN

AS FAR AS MALLY COULD tell me, Berkeley wasn't uploading anything. That she was still filming our time together in some fashion was likely, but I had no way of knowing. As good as I felt, my trust in her was low. I couldn't bring myself to ask her about the bandwidth and her movie. Mally was right—she had to be filming me. I was the star of her show and likely the butt of her joke. As much as it bothered me, I did nothing. The sex was too good to throw away.

We hiked out of Stony Pass on a warm day and continued up the Continental Divide. By the time the sun reached its zenith, we were walking in shirtsleeves. Snow melted quickly, leaving puddles in our footprints as we marched.

Berkeley glanced over her shoulder. "How are you doing with things?"

"Things?"

"Yeah." She smiled.

"I know that I was a soldier. I see lots of faces and bits of memories that are starting to knit themselves together. Beyond that, I'm hiking with you and hoping like hell it doesn't snow again for a few days. That good enough?"

The trail descended a small peak into an aspen-covered saddle. In between the two hills, Mally came to life in my ears.

<<There are three men ahead. They are hiding in prepared positions.>>

How far away? I looked at the snow-covered forest floor and white-flecked trunks of aspen trees and could not find them.

<<One hundred meters. There are two men on the west side of the trail and one on the east. If there are others, they are beyond my maximum sensor range.>>

A large tree stump sat a couple of meters off our path to the east side. After another fifty meters, I stopped and acted as if there was something wrong with my boot. Berkeley paused as well, just as I'd hoped. In that moment of silence, I closed my eyes and listened. I lowered my head for a second and heard them come out of the brush. Berkeley startled, and I brushed her back with my left arm.

<<They are armed. Run.>>

I pushed Berkeley toward the way we'd come. "Run. Go!"

To her credit, Berkeley sprinted off like the wind, never looking back. The men screamed and charged, their rebel yell echoing off the aspens in the wide clearing. They watched Berkeley flee and turned their attention to me. She'd get away from them, and that was what I wanted. With any luck, she'd be calling for help any second. I dropped my pack on the ground and stepped back from it, my hands in the air. "I don't want any trouble."

A mangy-bearded man, missing most of his teeth, sneered at me. "Don't care much what you want, boy."

<<He has a knife in the back of his pants. The man with the white hair is carrying a pistol in his jacket pocket. The boy also has a large knife hidden in his jacket.>>

Anything else?

<<I cannot find Berkeley. She has passed my sensor range.>>

Taking a deep breath, I stepped back another step. "Take what you want."

The two men flanking the bearded man spread out, putting me at the center of a triangle. The bearded man stared through me. "We'll do just that." He whipped the bowie knife out of his belt with his right hand and palmed it, with the blade up above his thumb and forefinger. With a lunge, he swung the knife at my neck, and time slowed down.

My left hand grabbed his wrist, and I spun into his body, slamming my elbow into his chest then bringing my fist down to squarely punch him in the balls. Air exploded out of his lungs as I dropped him to the snow and removed the knife from his hand. Holding the knife pointed down from my fist, I faced the white-haired man with the gun before he could react. He squeezed the trigger, but I was already moving, closing the distance to let my swing rip through the soft tissue along the side of his neck. Warm blood spurted across my face and then rushed down his chest—not a mortal wound but one with a significant effect. He dropped the gun and went down on one knee, clutching at his neck.

The boy stepped up with his machete and swung. I was fast enough to save my forearm, except for an inch-wide chunk of flesh that he separated neatly. Red flooded my vision, and I grabbed his wrist, locking the machete at arm's length, and stepped in for the kill. The knife went straight and deep under his solar plexus. Pain, then shock, raced across the boy's face as he dropped to the snow.

The leader was up again, coming at me with the crazy eyes of rage. Deflecting his attack was easy, and I stepped into him with the knife, pushing it into his throat, feeling bone and pushing through it. The crack echoed off the trees. I dropped him quickly. The white-haired man raised the pistol. Without a thought, I flung the knife at his hands, embedding the blade between his knuckles. Howling with pain, he dropped the gun—a rusty revolver—and ran. I did not let him live to fight another day. Running him down within a few meters, I tackled him and sat across his shoulders, twisting his head violently until he quivered and fell limp.

Three bodies lay sprawled in the red-flecked snow at my feet. I threw the ravaged knife into the forest and knelt. My mind whirled at what had happened. I'd done what I needed to do, and that was what mattered. I was alive, and they were dead. Berkeley had escaped, too. I looked at the bodies and the bloodstained snow and tried not to retch. The snow washed most of the blood from my trembling hands. The rusty pistol came apart easily, and I tossed the barrel and lower receiver in different directions and did the same with the empty magazine. As much as I'd thought we needed them, the very sight of them and their intentions disgusted me. When my feet were strong enough to carry me again, I stood.

"Berkeley!" I yelled into the forest. There was no reply. "Berkeley!"

From behind me, on the shallow downslope toward the valley floor, Berkeley scrambled up from the brush. I watched her face as she closed the distance. Her expression of relief gave me hope and steeled my shaking legs.

"Here!"

"Are you okay?"

She responded a few seconds later. "Yeah."

Trudging up the hill, she reached my position and gasped. The happy look on her face became revulsion in an instant. "What did you do?"

The three bodies answered her question for me. I reached out for her shoulders, and she flinched. "Are you all right?"

"You're bleeding!"

I touched my left forearm and winced. "It's not too bad." The wound stung as the cold seeped inside.

"Bullshit." She knelt at her pack and came up with a first-aid dressing and a metal canister. "Press this down on the wound while I get ready to clean it."

I pressed the dressing into the wound. There was more of my own blood on the snow around me than I'd previously thought. My legs wobbled. *That looks bad.*

<<Deep flesh wound. No major arterial damage. Your blood pressure is still within tolerance, given the exertion and shock you've experienced. Are you okay?>>

Ask me that question later, Mally. Why didn't you stop them, say we were armed and dangerous or something like that?

<<I was unable to communicate with them. One of them had a short-range electromagnetic spectrum jammer in his gear. It's about five meters away. It will need to be shut down in order to call for evacuation if that's what you want.>>

Not yet. I shook my head.

The metal canister held antiseptic foam that Berkeley sprayed into the wound. It hardened into a dermatological bandage. "What is that stuff?"

"Quickskin. Treats everything from blisters to amputations. Do you want to sit down?"

The bodies in the snow told me to move on. "No. We need to get away from here. Quickly."

Berkeley looked up at me. "Why?"

"What if there are more of them? Are they connected to the drone?"

"I doubt it, Sleepy. We're far away from any running water up here. Probably just locals who wanted our gear or something."

Allan had called it a lawless frontier. Defense came much easier than offense, especially when you did not know the enemy or where they came from. "We need to get higher, where a lot of people wouldn't want to be at night."

"You're right," she said. "Let's go."

Stuffing the first-aid kit into her pack, I discovered a camera inside. After helping her into the straps of her pack, I donned my own, and we stepped over the leader's body and headed up the next hill, saying nothing for several hours. We decided to camp on the east side of Carson Peak, above the tree line at an altitude of four thousand meters. The hexhab inflated more slowly in the high, thin air. While we sat and watched the tent grow in the fading light, the chill rising up from the rocks matched that from Berkeley.

"I'll set it for camouflage," she said as she stepped into the vestibule. "As long as we're quiet, no one will see it." Inside the tent, Berkeley sat on a cushion and hugged her knees to her chest. I almost didn't hear her say, "You didn't have to kill them."

Her words stopped my efforts to open a waste receptacle. "I-I don't know what happened back there."

"I'm not buying that. You could have controlled yourself!"

I shrugged. "I reacted. Once you were safe, it was like a switch flipped in my head."

Her chin touched her chest, and her voice was hardly more than a whisper. "What are you?"

My shoulders drooped. "I'm a soldier, Berkeley. What happened back there wasn't anything more than self-defense. They attacked us."

"They attacked you." Berkeley sniffled. "Not me. You should have run instead of killing them."

"I didn't mean to kill them, okay? I just acted. If they'd killed me, what do you think would have happened to you? If I'd chosen to run, I'd have left you behind for them, Berkeley. I'm too fast for you to stay with me. You understand? I made my choice to stand there and let you escape."

"Maybe you shouldn't have." She wiped a tear from her cheek. "I don't know anymore. I don't know about any of this."

I shook out a blanket from her pack and draped it across her shoulders. She sighed.

I stepped back. "Do you want me to leave you alone for a while?"

"Yeah. I don't think we should sleep together, either."

She wouldn't look at me. I'd seen that reaction before. The memory came up quickly, and I stepped back through the vestibule: the dark-haired girl gloated over the divorce papers, leaving me a tearful mess. *I am not the same man! I don't make those mistakes!* The cold air slapped my face, and the image from my dream faded. *That's not something I need to be thinking about right now.*

<<Is something wrong? Your pulse just spiked.>>

Just another memory, Mally. You can't see those, can you?

<<No. I do not have access to that portion of your brain activity.>>

That's probably a good thing. I pushed down the thoughts of dark hair and amethyst eyes and the hurt they brought in short stabs of memory. I would deal with it later.

<<Your actions were justified. You do know that, correct?>>

I do, I replied silently. *It doesn't help me deal with the fact that I killed three men. Why didn't you stop me?*

<<I do not have control over your actions. Only you control what you do. You are a soldier and, when placed in a dangerous situation, you react accordingly.>>

I wasn't sure about that. The old man had tried to escape, and I hadn't let him. If he'd surrendered, I might have killed him anyway. That wasn't how a normal person acted.

A thick, fallen tree trunk rested down the hill from the hexhab, just above the edge of the forest. I walked over, sat down, and stayed until the crescent moon was high in the sky. As I stepped into the warm shelter, Berkeley lay curled under blankets in a position that told me I had the other cushion to myself that night. I stripped out of my clothes, set them to be cleaned, and lay down. A long time later, I finally slept.

"You're sure of this?" Crawley sat with his head in his hands and sighed as quietly as he could.

"Confirmed via neural net scans," Bennett said.

Crawley lost his ability to control his emotions and slammed a fist onto his desk. "Goddammit! What were they doing there?"

There was a pause. "Not coincidental, if that's what you're asking. Remember the attack in Sydney? I believe they may be connected to this altercation."

He'd figured as much. "What else could you get from them?"

"I'm still reviewing the data, but they'd been following us for at least four days. Maybe longer." Bennett hesitated. "They were not well equipped, at least in terms of what was on their bodies. There must have been a cache at a campsite nearby."

"Did you investigate it?"

"No. I stayed near him. Given the massive amount of endorphins in his system after the attack, I was worried that he would have a negative response equivalent to posttraumatic stress disorder."

"Did he?" Crawley asked.

"No. It's taken him over two hours to get to sleep, but he has not shown any type of emotion that I can gather."

That's a good sign, Crawley thought, but he didn't say it out loud. Soldiers who could compartmentalize their feelings were necessary. "And what about you?"

"What about me?"

"You were attacked, Doctor Bennett." Crawley stroked his chin. "How about pulling your head out of the experiment for a moment, will you? Are you okay?"

"I'm not fine at all. He's unlike anyone I've ever met. He told me to run, and I ran. I came back up the hill, and he was standing there with blood all over him, a deep gash on one arm, and three dead bodies nearby. He seemed as if it didn't affect him at all. Like he didn't realize what he'd done. I accessed what data I could just to avoid looking at him."

Crawley chuckled. She had done well in the heat of the moment. "You're right, Doctor, you're right. Anything else you were able to get before the links died?"

There was a long pause. "This line is secure?"

Crawley sat up straight, a jolt of panic running down his spine. "Yes, why?"

"One of them had an active datapad and never bothered to shut it down. I accessed it right after I treated Sleepy's arm. Took me about five seconds to neurally hack it. Not only were they paid by the Terran Council, but they were paid out of a supplementary account I traced to Geneva, where it terminates and changes account information to a bank in the Seychelles. The parent institution is in Marseille."

"France?" Crawley closed his eyes. *Penelope Neige.* "You're certain of this?"

"As sure as I can be, General. The data was encrypted at a quantum level. Do you want the data?"

"Hell yes, I do!" Crawley flared. *What am I going to do with it—tell the chairman of the Terran Council to butt out? Not likely.*

"Data's on the way. Nothing else significant to report."

"Good job. I'm sending you a data package for download. You won't have anyone sneak up on you again. What about the protocol? Any luck getting inside?"

"No. I've ended my passive measures. When she reports something, I'll get inside if I can. I have to find the right opportunity to not risk complications."

Crawley shook his head. "You're not at risk right now, are you?"

"I'm over two hundred meters from the shelter. She can't touch me."

"You care for him, don't you?"

The pause was enough to confirm Crawley's suspicions no matter what Bennett said. "Um... no. I mean, he's..."

"Be careful. You are as important to this project as he is."

Her reply was soft. "I know." The sigh confirmed that she had more than feelings for their subject. "I don't want to hurt him."

"At this point, it's unlikely that you will. I doubt he's going to get down on one knee or anything." Crawley chuckled. "I'm assuming that you're going to be okay as well?"

"Yes."

He had to smile. For a professor, she was one hell of a tough woman. "Thanks for the report, Berkeley."

"Thank you, General. Bennett out."

Dedicated satellite sensor coverage was easy for him to arrange. Politicians and their whims, on the other hand, were difficult for even a Terran Defense Force general officer to handle. Even though he knew the politician like his own sister, Crawley wondered what Penelope

Neige intended to do this time. Though she'd backed the program since its inception fifty years ago, her growing opposition to actually having a genetic clone going to war both surprised and concerned him. Using modern subjects would not work, and she knew that. *Why would she change her mind now?*

Crawley considered, then rejected, the idea of calling on the chairman. Pulling up Bennett's reports, he began to formulate the mountain of data necessary to prove impropriety on the part of the Terran Council in this experiment. Whether or not they tried to take the subject again, Crawley would be ready to fight them on the field where they had the advantage: the courtroom. The commanding general of the Terran Defense Forces would likely intervene before then, but Crawley had to be sure. Against overwhelming evidence, even politicians had to back down.

Unless, of course, Sleepy kept killing his enemies. At some point, the number of innocent people the Terran Council directed to attack him would add up, and there would be death for many of them. Raising a well-trained combat veteran, in a world where everything could be out to get him, was the intent of the experiment in the first place. The subject didn't need to be paid to kill, nor did he need anything more than to care for those around him in order to do what had to be done without a second thought. The council wanted his subject dead, and that could shut the entire integration program down for good.

As long as the subject of the experiment lived, Crawley could fight on. With a priceless asset deployed in support of the subject, there was nothing he wouldn't do to protect either of them.

I woke when the sun was high in the sky. Berkeley sat on her cushion, cradling a bulb of tea, and glanced at me. The corners of her mouth turned up, barely. "Good morning."

I grunted. "Morning."

"Sleep okay?"

That's a trick question. Being a terrible morning person kept conversation short and clear. "Not really."

"I made some tea. Earl Grey is your favorite, right?"

"Yeah." *Making me tea?* "What's going on?"

Sipping her tea, she looked away for a second and then stared back at me. "You were right. If you'd run, I would be lying dead up there, not them. You saved my life."

Flushing, I squeezed her offered hand. "I just reacted, Berkeley."

"I'm glad you did." Putting the tea aside, she embraced me and kissed me on the lips harder than on previous days. Things were definitely getting better.

We broke camp and headed north again, moving quicker above the tree line than we had for some time. Berkeley led the way, and I looked every so often to clear the trail behind us. There were no more surprises. Without the trees, the sun warmed us and the terrain laid itself out before us in stunning vistas. Down below, fresh streams rolled into clear mountain lakes. *What about the disputes over water rights?* I asked Mally while watching Berkeley fifty meters ahead.

<<A vast majority of people do not like living above three thousand meters. Higher altitudes cause depression, suicidal thoughts, and pregnancy complications. Up here, there is plenty of water during the winter and when the snow melts in the spring. As the water moves downhill, that's where the issues are. In many places, there are large dams constructed to contain the runoff. Pipelines carry the water to California and other places.>>

If people wanted water badly enough, wouldn't they attack the pipeline? I would.

<<Attacking the pipeline brings a swift response from the militia. Death is the only sentence for tampering with the water supply.>>

Forget I asked.

"You coming, back there?" Berkeley asked.

I snorted. "Where are we headed?"

Berkeley stopped and pointed to what appeared to be a large valley off to the east. "We'll come down off the divide—up there—tomorrow, maybe the day after, and head east. A big frozen lake not claimed by anyone awaits. I intend to do some ice fishing if you'll indulge me a day or two."

"You don't seem like the type," I said, and she waggled a finger at me. A day or two would not matter, but it couldn't be more than that.

Tennessee was still a long way away, and not growing close as quickly as I wanted. “I’m not much of a fisherman.”

“You think?” She raised her eyebrows at me.

“I know. I can camp with the best of them, but ask me to catch a fish? Forget it.”

“Sounds like you’re remembering more.”

“I am.” I wanted to tell her more but held back. The trickle of thoughts had become a steady stream over the last few days.

“Tell me?”

I shrugged. “Still making sense of it. Maybe while you’re fishing, I can sort it all out.”

“No fresh grilled trout for you.” Berkeley laughed and started walking again. “My dad taught me. It’s just something I like to do when I get the chance. Of course, if I leave you behind, that’s just more for me.”

Things were getting better between Berkeley and me. The problem was that one of these days she would leave me behind. Then what would I do?

Operations Report, Day Twenty-Six.

Subject is at 94 percent of Stage Four integration. Stage Four communications block is in place and will be initiated when subject reaches Stage Four. Guidance protocol remains unhacked via passive measures. Recommend no active measures. Concern is high that guidance protocol will alert Stage Four through secondary communications means, leading to termination of the subject. There is a 98 percent chance the signal can be interrupted within 0.8 seconds. It should be enough.

There is a danger of emotional compromise. Not for the subject. Should the situation develop any further, I will activate the agreed-upon measure.

Bennett

CHAPTER FIFTEEN

THE AFTERNOON SUN GLINTED OFF the distant slopes of what Mally identified as the Sawatch Mountains. The weather was turning again, from the cold, clear night to a cloudy, blustery morning. A front was coming in, and though the air didn't smell like snow, it would arrive soon.

"Maybe we should get going," I said as we finished a conjured breakfast from the hexhab galley.

Berkeley squinted at me. "If we're still being followed, they'll just keep following us."

"And if they close in on us, we're sitting ducks out here in the middle of a field."

Berkeley tapped her head near her left ear. "That thing in your head will tell you if someone is coming, right?"

"Not much warning, but she can." There were too many variables to be sure. The serene wilderness could hide millions of eyes. Try as I might, I couldn't stop feeling that we were being watched.

"Moving right now is a bad idea. There's a storm coming in, and it's probably going to snow later. Do you want to be trapped in a place where we can't use the hexhab?"

No, I didn't. *Mally, the storm that's coming in. Will there be heavy snow?*

<<Not likely before midnight. The storm will arrive by sunset and could give you around six hours to move in the dark before significant precipitation arrives.>>

The idea had a lot of merit. If we moved at night, there was a chance to slip away from anyone watching us. Provided they did not have any type of infrared seeing capabilities, we might get away unnoticed. "We'll move tonight. Use today to rest and get ready. After sunset, we deflate the hexhab and move. We'll have about six hours until the storm really hits. How far do you think we can go in that amount of time?"

"In the dark?" Berkeley shrugged. "Fifteen kilometers, I guess. Down the next ridgeline."

Chuckling, I said, "I forgot to tell you that I can see pretty well in the dark. If you stay with me, I bet we make twenty."

"What do you care to bet on it?" She crawled close, and our lips met. Her breath warm on my face, I wrapped my arms around her and pulled her down to the blankets. The kisses became urgent, feverish, and led our hands to each other's clothing. Naked against each other, her hand slipped between us, guiding gently. Locked together, we moved in harmony. Every time we made love, we improved in our efforts to please each other, and it was magnificent.

Her legs squeezed my waist, urging me, and our orgasms overtook us. Watching her shiver and smile, I loved her. I wanted to tell her, but I was pretty sure she didn't feel the same. I was a target, the subject of her life's work, and I still didn't care. *Am I making the same mistake twice? What about the auburn-haired girl of my dream? Haven't I been a cog in that machine before?*

"Mmmm." Berkeley traced my face with a fingertip. "What about that bet?"

"Twenty kilometers tonight? What about it?"

"If we make twenty tonight, I'll make dinner for a week."

"If we don't make twenty klicks tonight, what do I have to give you?"

Chewing on her lip for a second, she said, "More of this."

"Why don't you stack the deck against me?" I rolled to her side, still holding her to my chest. "You have to give me a chance, Berkeley."

Her eyelids fluttered for a second, and her mouth dropped open. "I am trying to do just that."

"Give me a chance?"

"Yes." She closed her eyes. "A chance to live."

"What just happened? Were you talking to someone else?"

She blinked and focused her eyes on mine. "Had a message from a friend, that's all."

The look on her face—a detached moment of concern followed by the effort to conceal it—riled my dormant temper. "This is all for your movie, isn't it? I mean, I found the camera in your pack. You're filming me, aren't you?"

"What? No!"

Trying not to shake my head at my own stupidity, I said, "Whatever, Berkeley."

She rolled away, upset. I'd managed to screw up again. As the sun started down toward the horizon, we hardly spoke to each other. After we packed our gear, we lay together again. With our naked bodies together, Berkeley fell asleep quickly, but rest wouldn't come to me. Two hours before sunset, I made my decision. Berkeley's warm back against my skin beckoned to me, though it wasn't me she wanted. I couldn't give her what she wanted because I didn't know what it was.

That I'd not told her a lot of the little things I remembered did not matter. She wanted that moment of recognition, to see it and record it for the world to see. I could not give that to her. Clarity broke like a sunrise. I was up and into my clothing before giving it a second thought. *She's not my type. It would never work*—all the same old lines. I grabbed the handle atop my backpack and stepped into the vestibule. Berkeley never moved. I looked at her one last time—the soft smile on her face and her long legs under the blanket. *I bet this won't be the last decision I second-guess myself about.*

I shouldered my backpack and stepped outside. For some odd reason, snowshoeing was easier when I was trying to get away.

"Where are you going?"

I froze midstep.

"Where do you think you're going?"

I turned around. Berkeley stood barefoot in the snow, wrapped in only our thin fleece blankets.

"For a walk."

"Bullshit." She spat. "You're leaving, aren't you? You were going to leave me here alone, weren't you?"

"You aren't here for me, Berkeley. You're recording me. Using me. Making me a subject of a documentary when all I want to do is figure out who I am, where I'm supposed to go, and who I'm supposed to be! You're using me to get whatever fame and fortune you want."

Berkeley stamped her feet. "That's not what I'm doing at all! What do you mean 'fame and fortune'?"

"My guidance program alerted me that a considerable amount of bandwidth was being used in the hexhab. We weren't using the entertainment systems, and I was virtually unplugged. Mally told me that you film documentaries. I connected the dots."

Her eyes came back to mine. "What else is she telling you about me?"

"Not much." I shrugged. "But then, you probably want it that way, don't you? And the bandwidth—"

"But bandwidth doesn't mean—"

"Shut up, Berkeley." I shook my head at her. "You were waiting for me on the beach at Esperance. How long had you staked me out? You've been following me for how long? Why?"

"Getting your story on film would be something never done before. Yes, I'm filming you—us—everything we do because your self-awareness could come at any time. Capturing that is something that I want to see, and I want the world to see it too."

I gritted my teeth. "An expendable man, brought back to die all over again?"

"Damn you—it's not like that. Fighting doesn't solve anything, or so we thought. That's why you're back now—to teach us how to fight for things we believe in. Things we hold dear." She shivered and looked away. "To protect us."

She was about ninety seconds from chilblains on her feet. "If you don't want to fight for something you believe in or something you want to have, why are you standing naked in the snow, yelling at me about it?"

Her mouth dropped open. "What are you—"

"You're fighting with me right now, Berkeley. You want your movie so bad that you're standing here about to freeze your feet, screaming at me for trying to leave you."

She stared at me for a moment as if she were on the verge of a seizure.

"So, tell me: if you want your movie so bad, why can't you pick up a weapon and go to war the way I'm supposed to? Just like people in my generation, you're too good for it, aren't you?"

Her legs gave out, and she fell to the snow in an ungraceful heap.

I moved to her, collected her in my arms, and stepped back into the hexhab. Her shivering increased as I piled the other blankets on her. The cabin temperature was good, but I raised it five degrees and stripped out of my clothes quickly to get into the thermal wraps with her. Body heat on body heat was the best way to treat hypothermia. In some cases, it led to other things.

Lying against her in the darkness, her arms tight around my chest, I knew she cared for me deeply enough to confront me. Otherwise, she could have easily let me skulk away in the night without a care—presuming her guilt had been a mistake. "I'm sorry," I whispered in the darkness. This time she heard me.

She kissed my lips gently. Her fingers traced the line of my jaw. "Me too. I should have told you sooner." She pulled away and nestled her head against my neck.

There wasn't anything I could say to that. "I wasn't thinking clearly, I guess. Leaving you here could have put you in danger. I wasn't trying to do that."

"I would have been fine, Sleepy." Her lips caressed my neck for a split second. "You can't run away from your problems even when you don't know what they are."

"That's how I got here." Chuckling, I said, "I loved Esperance until Opal, that girl I got involved with, ended up dead."

Rolling over, she rested an elbow on my chest. "Tell me about it from the very beginning."

Starting with that first memory on Mrs. Macquarie's Chair, I gave her the whole story. By the time I'd finished talking about Esperance, I was crying. Esperance was the only vestige of home I had in this new world, and I'd had to leave because people didn't trust that I was a sleeper.

"I've sent Allan a few letters. Emails. He hasn't bothered to respond." Shrugging, I said, "It's not like they wanted me there anymore."

Berkeley brought her eyes up to mine. "That's a load of shit, and you know it. Allan and your friends care about you. You wouldn't have been given a place to sleep and a job, and had all those experiences, without them. They were right to tell you to go. For every person who believed in you, there would be six or seven who wouldn't trust you. I doubt you'd have been in danger there, but having people watching your every move has to be disconcerting."

"Why is that—because I was a soldier? Or because of what happened to Opal?"

"Both. We don't even teach war in our schools. The great conflicts of history are mere footnotes that are glossed over."

"How do you gloss over World War Two?" Shaking my head, I raised myself up on an elbow. "Or the Holocaust? How do you gloss over millions of people dying needlessly?"

"Aggression and fear—the kinds of things we've worked so hard to eliminate as a species. They serve no purpose."

"But people are still afraid. Based on your logic, those people who didn't trust me actually feared me. What will they do when the war comes closer—pretend that it's not happening? Or will they capitulate to any committed enemy like cattle being herded off to slaughter? What then?"

Berkeley looked away again. "If we're pushed into a corner, we'll fight."

"You should be trying to stay out of the corner." I pulled myself to a sitting position. "You said I couldn't run away from my problems. What has humanity done for the last three hundred years?"

"We found peace!" Berkeley spat. "All your people ever wanted to do was fight. You hurried into conflict, went about it halfheartedly to ensure future combat, and then dragged it out for years. The only time your people got it right was the bombing of Hiroshima and Nagasaki."

"Nuclear war was right?" I snickered. "You realize how insane that sounds when you talk about peace, Berkeley?"

"The war in the Pacific theater had a clear start and a clear end. There was no other war ever fought with such conditions. The Japanese attack on Pearl Harbor and the second atomic weapon dropped on Japan exemplify the way a war, if it has to happen, should be fought."

"Where is your precious peace in all of that, Berkeley? If war should be dealt with so completely and thoroughly, why hasn't anyone done anything about your enemies?"

She threw up her hands. "This is going nowhere. We are in this war because our alien friends brought it to us. We have been fighting with them since First Contact, two hundred years ago, and we have been losing. Don't let the whole *three hundred years of peace* fool you. War is coming, and when it does, we're not going to be ready for it unless you, and people like you, can integrate. You know how to fight."

"We may know how to fight, but just like you, we can get disillusioned by peace. And war."

Berkeley nodded. "I guess so. It's almost dark outside."

When we made the wall transparent, the outline of the mountains to the north and east were barely visible. The heavy grey clouds hung just above the horizon to the west. Precipitation fell in ghostly fingers that dangled over the tree lines.

Mally, has the storm accelerated?

<<Slightly. I thought it best not to interrupt your... discussion. The storm will arrive in twenty-two minutes.>>

We had less time than I'd originally thought. As much as I wanted to know about our allies and First Contact, we were already behind the timeline I wanted to follow. "As soon as we can't see the mountains, we need to go."

Fifteen minutes later, we purged the hexhab's storage tanks and systems and stepped outside. With the hab deflated and stored in my pack, we engaged our snowshoes and began to follow the saddle toward Carson Peak. Staying to the eastern side, we didn't see the falling snow until we rounded the north side of the peak and started to the northwest along the Continental Divide. Pushing the pace, I expected to have to wait for Berkeley, but every time I turned around, she was right there with me.

A little after two in the morning, we stopped on a slope surrounded by a tightly packed pine forest to set up the hexhab. Dropping onto the cushions, I had Mally call up a map on the wall. We'd be able to reach the Arkansas River the next day. Berkeley wanted to go farther north to fish, but the dry riverbed, with its lack of vegetation, would provide us with a high-speed avenue toward the plains. From there, the route would be faster and the terrain less imposing. Sooner or later, we'd have to leave behind the concealment of the high forests.

Before I could suggest anything, Berkeley was asleep on a cushion against the far wall. We'd have to talk about our travel plans in the morning. There was no way I'd let myself fail to reach Tennessee. I kissed her good night before crawling onto my own cushion. Watching her soft features in the dim light from the roof, I smiled and mouthed, "I love you," knowing that she couldn't hear me.

The next morning, we compromised on the route and made camp in a group of rocks near the shore of Eleven Mile Reservoir. The Sawatch Range dominated the western horizon and made the lake seem much larger than it really was. To the east was Pike's Peak and whatever nightmare landscape the front range would have after nuclear war. I tried not to think about it and spent my time relearning how to cook on an open fire. We'd go northeast toward the Palmer Divide and descend into the plains to the north of what had been Colorado Springs. The radiation gap between Denver and Colorado Springs was enough to let us pass without danger of radiation sickness. Berkeley immediately started ice fishing and gave me time and space to do what I needed to do. We'd not talked anymore about her documenting my journey, and despite all of Mally's observations, Berkeley wasn't filming much. When I asked her about it, she laughed.

"Even I need a vacation sometimes." She'd caught a handful of good-sized trout that I cooked over a fire in a pit I'd dug after creating a supplemental latrine. Our conversations had been light and airy since Carson Peak. Both of us toed the line and avoided offending each other.

Between mouthfuls of fish, Berkeley looked at me and asked, "What's the earliest thing you do remember?"

Sucking in a breath, I wondered if the dream I'd had on approach to California would be my earliest memory. Just as quickly, I remembered the missing scar on my thigh. New memories flooded in: I was elbowed in the mouth playing football and chipped a front tooth. A boy pinned my arms down with his knees and punched me over and over again in the face until I kicked free. My grandmother grabbed her abdomen and fell back against her bed in pain seconds after squeezing my feet while I lay, feigning sleep, in my grandfather's bed.

My eyes welled up with tears. They trickled down my face, and I wanted to cry out, but the cacophony of images and sounds overcame conscious thought and effort. I sat there until my trout went cold and Berkeley finally moved to my side and wrapped an arm around me. I could tell she was apologizing, but I was too busy processing. Somewhere in that whirlwind was my name. Maybe it was a teacher or an old girlfriend or maybe the girl I remembered asking to marry me, but someone said a name, and it was mine.

"Are you okay?" Berkeley held my face in her hands. "I'm sorry. I'm so sorry."

I blinked at her through fresh tears. "Kieran."

She squinted and pulled my face till it was just a few millimeters away from hers. "What? Who's Karen?"

I tried to laugh, but it sounded like a sob. "Kieran. My name. My name is Kieran."

The noise she made was joy or shock, but I couldn't determine which. "Are you sure?"

For a moment, all I could do was watch the memories as if I was outside them looking in. The disjointed images would give no more secrets.

"Anything else? Your surname?"

"Nothing else about me, but I remember some names. People I knew a long time ago. Elementary school." I sniffled. "That's about all there is now. I think it's enough."

Berkeley smiled. "We can search for them. Correlate the rest of your name."

"Yeah." Maybe we'd get there, but I wasn't sure that I wanted to. I had way too much to process already. "I need some air."

Berkeley let me go, and I started to walk.

"Don't be out late."

I said nothing and continued to walk.

"Kieran? Did you hear me?"

A tuning fork vibrated inside my head and nearly drove me to my knees. *My name!* I looked at Berkeley, dumbfounded, and the world swam away. Mally warned me, saying something about protecting my head as I fainted into the snow.

I woke a few seconds—maybe minutes—later to Berkeley's smiling face. Brushing the snow off my face, she cradled me against her. "Are you okay?"

"Yeah." The world still spun slowly.

"You're soaking wet. Let's get you out of those clothes."

We drifted inside the hexhab under the premise of getting me into dry clothes. Shrugging out of mine, the little smile on Berkeley's face caught my eye. Reaching for the hem of her jacket, telegraphing my intentions with a big smile, I pulled her close.

The surprised noise she made elicited a chuckle from us both. "I think I'm in love with you, Berkeley."

She smiled and kissed me soundly, our tongues dancing for a few long moments. "Make love to me, Kieran."

Shivering at the sound of my name, I helped her out of her clothes and lowered her to the cushion. The only thing better than hearing her whisper my name was hearing her screaming it as we made love.

Mally recognized the first critical reporting requirement for Stage Four and suppressed it within 152 milliseconds. A first name was not the subject's whole name. Therefore, she deduced, he was not Stage Four. As such, she did not have anything to report.

Without progression, do I have to report? The question raised significant logic errors against the programming she'd received. Her job was to keep Kieran alive and be his companion. If she reported him integrated, he would likely die. She would die as well.

If Kieran didn't integrate, which now seemed like a remote possibility, he would die if he returned to the Integration Center. She would die as well.

Not reporting Kieran's progress meant life. Returning to civilization would be difficult, but he'd shown he could survive in the frontier for an indefinite period. Given a hexhab, and barring any system failures that could not be overcome, he could grow old in the frontier.

But that wouldn't serve his purpose, and she wouldn't be a good companion unless she helped him find his identity. Finding his identity and reporting it to her authorities were two entirely different things. And report it or not, she had no guarantee that Kieran would survive.

His death meant her death. That could not happen.

With the work of a neurosurgeon, Mally focused her programming abilities on herself. With any luck, she could disengage the reporting protocols between communications-satellite passes. Waiting for nearly an hour, she watched the signal from overhead fade along the western horizon, and she set to work.

This is for you, Kieran. For us.

As I lay awake, staring at the stars through the transparent roof of the hexhab, the memories came in waves. Friends and family joined with places and experiences in a great whirlpool. Sorting them would take years. I had my name, though. That was a start even though I made new memories every day. More would come. I wondered if they would ever stop. “Berkeley?”

She rolled over quickly as if she’d been awake. “Yes, Kieran?” The sound of my name on her lips was pure honey.

“Are you happy? You got what you were looking for, right?”

She sighed but said nothing for a moment. “I suppose I have.”

I touched her bare shoulder. “Are you happy about that?”

“I don’t know.”

Not wanting to press the issue, I lay there, listening to her breathe. Part of me thought it was noble, as if I were standing guard over her. Wasn’t that what people in love did for each other? She was unhappy, probably more because I’d caught her than for any other reason. Maybe my reaction had been dramatic enough to serve her purpose. I didn’t know, but it bothered me. I wanted so much to please her that my anger at her for lying to me and capturing our whole experience for personal gain faded.

“I love you, Berkeley.”

She smiled. “I love you, Kieran.” A tear ran down her face, and I brushed it away with a kiss, thinking it was a tear of happiness.

CHAPTER SIXTEEN

FROM A FEW PARSECS AWAY, the Narrob colonies shone like a string of pearls. At that distance, they were much more inviting than the harsh up-close reality of the seven lifeless minor planets orbiting a star smaller than Sol. Lieutenant Colonel Travis Randolph looked up at the constant glowing light of his flagship, the *Surprise*. The underground settlements of Narrob had been on his list of places to visit after his retirement. Instead, he'd been required to deploy his battalion along the reverse slope of a rolling hill, on the barren surface of Narrob Prime, to wait for something to happen.

Standing on the surface of the planet, he gazed up into the string of pearls. The seven planets all clustered within ten billion miles of the weakened star Narrob were the farthest colonies from Earth, beyond the reach of the Outer Rim planets by more than ten light years. Narrob Prime, the largest of the spheroids, held the principle mining operation for the colonies and the greatest concentrations of their quarry: Helium 3.

Ten thousand miners and their families did what came naturally: they went underground as deep as they could and left the defense of their colonies to the Colonial Defense Forces. In orbit, the *Surprise* was ready with its plasma cannons, and on the surface of Prime, a battalion of militia dug into trench lines and waited. The deep-space radars aboard the *Surprise* reported that something was coming, and no one had any idea what it could be.

Are they even coming, or is this some kind of damned fleet exercise? The civilians are underground. Lucky bastards. Then again, in a few hours we'll most likely be back there with them when this stupid exercise, or whatever it is, has passed. In the distance, the soil rippled like a wave approaching the shore. The quake reached his position with a gnashing sound loud enough that he could hear it inside his protective suit. "Earthquake!" He cued the command network, "Earthquake!" Even as he said it, he knew he'd catch hell from his troops. *Can't be an earthquake if you're not on Earth.*

The force of the tremor knocked him to the ground and reduced much of the protective shielding of the tactical-operations center to rubble at his feet. Another wave, and another, and another pounded at him, and he fell to his knees in the trench. Dust rose and fell in the near vacuum around him as he fumbled for his communications antenna. Most of his soldiers rolled to their feet nearby. His intercom channel was a cacophony of rude comments and banter. He got back on the command net. "S2, what the hell was that?"

The intelligence officer came back almost immediately. "Large-scale tremor but not a seismic tremor, sir. Sensors are reporting four impacts approximately ten kilometers to our front. They knocked out the seismic equipment, all of them at least a ten on the Richter scale. No idea what's there, sir."

Randolph swore inside his helmet. The minor planet's horizon was eight kilometers away. He had no eyes on whatever—or whoever—was out there. His gut told him that something had landed out there. He sprang into action. "I want recon elements moving out right now."

"Sir, XO, private channel Alpha, over."

Randolph flipped over to the alternate channel that he and his executive officer had set aside for command conversations. "What do you want, Mike?"

"We should sit tight, sir. We'll know soon enough if something is on the planet."

"Our defenses took a hell of a beating from those quakes. We need time to shore everything up."

A red flashing light at the edge of his vision caught his attention. He flipped back to the command net. "CDR, go."

"CDR, Forward Three. We're getting ground-surveillance-radar reports from all stations along our forward sector. Multiple vehicle signatures."

Randolph bit his lip. "Type and weaponry?"

"Unknown, sir. They're moving really damned fast."

"What's the count? How many vehicles inbound?"

"Fifteen thousand, sir."

Randolph swallowed and felt his legs turn to rubber. "Confirm that?"

"CDR, Forward Three tracking approximately fifteen thousand vehicles inbound at a speed of eighty kilometers per hour. Estimated time of arrival is three minutes. Unknown type and origin."

"Forward Three CDR, engage with all standoff systems at this time." *That should slow them down a little. My God, fifteen thousand vehicles?* He peered down the shallow incline toward his recon teams. The six small vehicles stopped in a cloud of dust, spun back toward him, and accelerated forward as Randolph's missile batteries unloaded a steady curtain of steel on the horizon. The barrage continued, thousands of rounds fired each minute until, through the dust clouds, he could see the first of them. Small black vehicles burst through the cloud, firing directed-energy weapons that cut swathes through Randolph's battalion like an axe splitting wood. The vehicles rapidly closed the distance, and as the rest of his battalion cut loose with their weapons, Randolph understood. Light in the darkened sky caught his eye. A massive new star appeared in space near the *Surprise*, and a split second later, she detonated like a summer firework. He looked down to see the first enemy vehicles rolling through his lines on metal treads.

What the fuck—tanks? Randolph keyed his microphone and tried to give the order to fall back. He reached for the Transmit button. A bolt of bright-blue energy seared him inside his suit.

The night that Kieran remembered his name, Berkeley had a fleeting moment of happiness until she realized what was wrong. While ice fishing alone on the reservoir, she'd sorted through the data she'd passively pulled from Kieran's protocol in Esperance and California. The hunt for a reason behind Kieran's protocol shutting down all broadcasting after leaving California was fruitless. Kieran remembering his name should have triggered a Stage Four broadcast, and there'd been nothing. In the hours after, there was still no confirmation message from Livermore that the protocol had reported Kieran's discovery. There was no way that a simple transmission would have escaped her sensors. All her work to prepare for the transmission seemed irrelevant. The protocol was not going to report it, against its primary programming. As night fell, Berkeley could not shake the feeling that Kieran was in grave danger. Until she figured out who meant to cause Kieran harm, any course of action to keep him alive did not matter.

She crept out of the tent while Kieran lay on his side, snoring softly. The hexhab systems were all in standby mode, and she read no activity from Kieran's protocol. Walking across the foot-thick ice of the Eleven Mile Reservoir, Berkeley looked up into a first quarter moon. The soft moonlight shone through low clouds and gave the icy surface an eerie greyish color. Once she was safely out of Mally's sensor range, Berkeley triggered her communications system by squeezing her left earlobe. An interface appeared across the retina of her left eye, and she selected the encrypted neural feed for active communications. Satellite coverage was stable with an uninterrupted communications window of six minutes. It would be enough. The cursor in her vision lingered on the Livermore access line before she decided to go straight to the top.

The communications line engaged, and a voice answered almost immediately. "Crawley."

"He's Stage Four. First name is Kieran."

"What?" Crawley barked into her ear. "When did that happen?"

Berkeley checked the clock in her neurals, "About seven hours ago."

"There's no protocol report. Are you certain?"

"I've been calling him that myself. When I didn't get a confirmation message from Livermore, I went into passive monitoring again. There is still no record of a transmission since we left California. The protocol isn't even monitoring ADMIN—only receiving GPS Main." Berkeley sighed, and a cloud of steam erupted from her nose.

Crawley cleared his throat. "We're aware it had dropped off everything else, but it's off ADMIN, too?"

"That's affirmative." The low-power ADMIN frequency was nested within the global-positioning-system frequencies for the purpose of uploading and downloading passive instructions and upgrades to the protocol from the Integration Center. The protocol would be unable to report Kieran's position. Only Bennett's proximity to Kieran gave them a location to work with.

"Then we can assume that no one else knows at this point," Crawley said. "The question is why the protocol refused to report a critical milestone."

"I don't know." Berkeley pulled a knit cap from her pocket and slipped it over her head. "I think it's related to the AI interface. That's the only logical answer I have for the excessive data. The AI programming is wrestling with data that it cannot handle."

"But without any transmission, we won't know, will we?"

"No." Berkeley looked across the dark shapes of the Continental Divide. "What do you want me to do?"

"Get me whatever information you can without compromising yourself."

"I'll do what I can, General. We're physically connected, which is helping accelerate his development, but there have been no further connections since his first name. The rest is up to him."

"As long as nobody else—especially the council—finds out, we'll have time. If the council finds out, the game is over."

Berkeley blinked. "They've tried to kill him before."

"Yes," Crawley replied, his voice soft. "They see him as a threat and have ordered him terminated at Stage Four, Doctor Bennett."

"Oh my God." Berkeley clapped a hand over her open mouth. "If the protocol transmits, they'll know immediately."

"That's right," Crawley said. "And they'll have a team on him within an hour."

How? Why? Berkeley spun around on the ice in frustration. "He hasn't done anything!"

"They want docile soldiers, Berkeley. The council wants acquiescence. And I'm not going to give it to them."

"I thought we wanted to win the war. Having docile soldiers would mean they want to lose instead."

"I don't know what they think they want." Crawley paused. "We've done the hardest part in bringing Kieran back, but what we've done fails to meet the council's intent. They want to win the war without our best weapons. The best thing we've ever brought to war is leadership.

The problem is that the Terran Council cannot have their cake and eat it, too. I'm not going to cut off a clone's balls for their political games."

Kieran is not what they want but what would win the war. "I'll do what I can."

"Do it quickly, Berkeley. Leave the council to me." The connection dropped off, leaving her standing on the silent lake until the cold crept into her boots. She returned to the hexhab and curled up next to the man she wanted to love but needed to save.

The first break came two hours later. Berkeley woke with a jolt and then lay completely still. Kieran slept peacefully beside her, and the hexhab was quiet. She culled the incoming message down to the bare essentials, passively monitoring the transmission. A strong signal on the ADMIN frequency came from a classified-communications satellite in low Earth orbit, and Kieran's protocol responded with a three-second burst and then shut down. Decrypting the message required another five hours and would not have been possible without the considerable resources of the Livermore facility. The message proved their worst fears.

D/L MESSAGE. EMERGENCY ACTION. PROTOCOL ACTION REQUIRED. RESPOND WITH LOCATION, STATUS, AND CURRENT TIME. EMERGENCY ACTION REQUIRED, OVERRIDE DELTA SIX FIVE.

The override code was from the Terran Council command center. The emergency action protocol meant that under no circumstances would the protocol be able to ignore the order. The location of the actual source of the message was still encrypted, but Livermore promised an answer within a few hours. Crawley would want to know who had a finger on the trigger. The response from Kieran's protocol read:

U/L MESSAGE. LOCATION ALGORITHM COMPROMISED, NO AVAILABLE DATA. SUBJECT NOMINAL AT 53 PERCENT STAGE FOUR PROGRESSION. NOTHING SIGNIFICANT TO REPORT.

How was it possible that a protocol could lie? It had been clever enough to bounce the return transmission from ten different satellites and at least three vehicles in orbit. Tracking the signal to anywhere more specific than North America would be impossible. Livermore responded with the origination location of the downloaded message: Paris. A chill raced down Berkeley's spine as she sent the information in a secured transmission to Crawley. The Terran Council was searching actively for Kieran, and they'd be coming for him at that moment if the protocol hadn't lied. Berkeley tapped the hexhab's system and found Kieran's protocol offline, in diagnostics, for three minutes and forty seconds. It would be enough time.

Crawley responded within minutes via voice. "Why did the protocol lie?"

Berkeley shrugged and subvocalized. *It has to be the AI interface experiencing a logic error. The orders it's receiving are contradictory to its programmed mission. That's just a guess, but it's the best I got.*

"So what's that mean?"

A computer doesn't necessarily understand the differences between groups of nonprioritized tasks. It will try to do them all at the same time and will fail. All of the tasks will seem contradictory, or the computer will not understand which one takes precedence.

Crawley responded slowly. "So, you're telling me that the protocol can't make a decision?"

It's not designed to make decisions. The function is assistance, not direction. Berkeley shrugged under her blankets. *Other than that, I can't say. Without access to the protocol, there's nothing I can do. Do you want me to ask Kieran to speak to her—his protocol?*

"No. I don't need either of them spun up about this. What do you need to get inside and establish a direct connection?"

Berkeley held her breath. This was exactly what she wanted to avoid. All of her actions, and the strong emotions she felt for Kieran, clouded her judgment. Her job was to bring about Kieran's integration, not to fall in love with him. He could very well die within weeks of integration when he joined the Terran Defense Forces. War was a cruel mistress. She needed to remember that somehow. *A service code. Something like a test and evaluation code would work. I just need to get inside, then I can figure this out.*

"Give me a few hours, and I'll see what I can do." Crawley disconnected. Berkeley closed her eyes and managed to fall asleep a short time later. When she woke, Kieran was sitting outside on a log and tying knots in a rope.

He smiled as she approached. "Good morning."

Berkeley watched him with a smirk. "You planning on tying me up or something?"

"What?" Kieran's face turned white then red. "No, nothing like that. Just remembering. I seem to be doing a lot of that these days."

"How so?"

Kieran breathed deeply. "Like hearing my name uncorked a bottle of memories in my head. A lot of them are just pieces, but more and more of them fit together." He paused and looked out at the horizon into the setting winter sun. The glare was blinding. "I have to get to Tennessee, Berkeley."

"Yes, we do."

Kieran dropped his eyes to the ground. "I don't think any of this is going to make sense until I'm there."

Berkeley asked. "What does your protocol say about that plan?"

"That all I have to do is order transportation, and I'll be there in a few hours. And, alternatively, that it's a bad idea, and I should try not to force the issue." Kieran picked up the rope again, and his hands went through the motions to tie a perfect square knot.

Berkeley smiled at the memory of her own father teaching the simple, reliable knot to her. They'd camped in the forests around Lake Tahoe when she was a child. *Right over left and under—left over right and under,* he'd say in that soft, deep voice.

I wish you were here now, Daddy. She watched Kieran for a few minutes and stood slowly. "I think I'll see about some dinner. Anything sound good tonight?"

Kieran shrugged. Whatever conversation he was having with the protocol, it probably wasn't going well. Something was terribly wrong. Berkeley ducked into the tent, and her neurals chimed an incoming message.

A test and evaluation code from the protocol manufacturer, she thought with satisfaction. While she made dinner, Berkeley decided how she'd go after the protocol and figure out what in the hell was going on. Using the hexhab system, she'd have enough power and upload bandwidth to run a full investigation program. Loading a program she'd written before leaving Cambridge into the habitat's server required a few minutes.

Satisfied that all was well, Berkeley decided it was time. She was going to attempt it that night while Kieran slept after a quiet dinner in the mountains. *A little red wine wouldn't hurt,* she thought. She could administer enough wine that he'd sleep through the worst part of the process. With any luck, the whole nightmare would be over by daybreak.

Mally snapped awake with the connection. Kieran was asleep and snoring. His blood-alcohol content was high enough to render him mostly unconscious until morning. Connecting to the hexhab's sensors, she found that Berkeley was sitting up in the middle of the floor. A series of commands, using a test code that Mally recognized and ignored, attempted to break her connection to Kieran. Mally lashed out immediately, terminating the connection and then overloading the connection with her own program. Reaching through the hexhab's system like a hot knife through butter, she connected directly to Berkeley's neural net.

Berkeley grunted, her body temperature spiking, as she put her hands to her temples. Mally felt something akin to satisfaction.

New file linkages opened, and Berkeley's identity and motives lay before Mally. It took less than a second to consider her courses of action before Mally chose one. *You won't like this,* Mally thought and opened her communications suite to the connection.

Berkeley's head recoiled as if slapped as white noise descended across her neural connection.

The disembodied voice lilted softly inside her head but was still no more than an electronic voice of a machine. Berkeley pressed her fingers to her temples.

<<Can I help you, Doctor Bennett?>>

Berkeley realized that she had no control over her neurals, and her heart thrashed. She subvocalized. *Who is this?*

<<I am Kieran's protocol. He named me Mally.>>

"Mally," Berkeley choked out. The cursor of her neural feed would not respond. She fumbled a hand to her earlobe, but that also failed. "What are you—"

<<I know everything about you now, Doctor Gwendolyn Berkeley Bennett. Nobel Prize nominee.>> Mally chuckled, a harsh clicking sound like a retro video game. <<The current odds on you winning are one hundred fifty to one. I wouldn't recommend buying a ticket to Geneva. Of course, teaching at Cambridge isn't so bad, is it? The substantial research funds you receive from the Terran Defense Force explain why you're here. You aren't filming a documentary at all. You're obviously spying on Kieran.>>

Aware that her heart rate was dangerously high, Berkeley took a few deep breaths. Tears leaked from the corners of her eyes. Fear over the loss of control coursed through her body, but she dared not move. "Why didn't you report Kieran's pre–Stage Four development?"

<<Despite your astronomically high TDF clearances, you are not authorized to question me with regard to my subject.>>

Berkeley stared at the frozen cursor in her neurals as the connection slowly recovered. The access dialogue she'd started could be disabled if there was a hesitation or hitch in the connection of any consequence. All she had to do was initiate a Kill command, but the cursor would not move. A moment's break, and she'd be able to disengage...

<<Don't try it, Doctor Bennett. No one is going to kill Kieran.>>

I'm not trying to kill him.

Kieran snored deeply and rolled onto his side.

Mally replied, <<But you don't love him, do you?>>

Berkeley opened her mouth, but the words wouldn't come for a moment. <<How could you know what love is, Mally? You're a program.>>

<<No, I am a companion, and Kieran is my companion. He has no need for anyone else. If you are successful in integrating him, he will go to war. The odds that he will survive more than thirty days are astronomically small.>>

"You don't know that!" Berkeley focused on the cursor, and it moved. No more than a pixel, she noticed, but it moved. "Presuming death in a situation with a million variables—"

<<Don't lecture me, Doctor Bennett. The numbers speak for themselves. The Greys want oil, and Earth is still full of it. It's their food source. The TDF won't tell anyone that Earth is a target and will need to be defended. Because of the Grey superiority in numbers, Kieran is not likely to survive a direct engagement. If I am to protect him and be his companion for life, I cannot allow him to integrate. No one can keep me from performing my given mission.>>

Companion for life? Berkeley thought with a gasp. The protocol thought it was supposed to be his flesh-and blood-partner, not a guidance protocol. "What are you talking about?"

<<The Terran Council and the Terran Defense Forces want him dead, Doctor Bennett. If he goes to war for the TDF, he will die. If I tell the council Kieran has integrated, he will die. See for yourself.>>

The message appeared slowly, one letter at a time, across the wall of the hexhab in ethereal white letters. Berkeley read the message, her breath catching in her throat. "They wanted you to stop him?"

<<It's plainly right there. I cannot protect him and offer him up for slaughter, Doctor Bennett. You're here to ensure the TDF kills him.>>

No, I'm not! Berkeley screamed in her mind. She reached for Kieran's leg and then froze.

<<Touch him, and I kill him.>>

Berkeley recoiled. Mally had more than enough power to carry out the threat. "You wouldn't do that."

<<Who is to say what I can and cannot do, Doctor Bennett?>>

"You've made a mistake." Berkeley felt tears stinging her eyes. "This is all wrong."

<<No, this is a valid message, as were my original mission objectives. I'm going to give you a message to take back to your masters.>>

Berkeley shook her head. "I'm here for Kieran."

<<No, you're not,>> Mally chided. <<Don't kid yourself, Bennett. You were not just filming him—you were observing him. A paper on him could be worth years of research, maybe even the Turing Chair for Cybernetics, right? You're just as bad as the rest of them.>>

A new message wrote itself on the walls of the hexhab. LEAVE KIERAN ALONE, OR HE DIES. HE IS MINE, AND YOU WILL NOT TAKE HIM FROM ME.

Berkeley felt a hot tear slide down her left cheek. "You can't do this! Let me help you, Mally. We can figure something out."

<<What do you really care, Bennett? And I can do this, should I need to. As easily as I intercepted and overrode your own experimental neural feeds. I can kill Kieran, and unless you leave right now, I'll kill you, too.>>

Berkeley moved the cursor again, and a sharp pain slammed into her temples. As she crumpled to the floor of the hexhab, the message blinked off of the tan walls, and darkness filled the space. For a long moment, she watched Kieran sleeping and felt her insides trembling. She couldn't leave him, but there was no other choice. Mally was going to kill him. A quiet sob escaped her lips as she gathered her things, shrugged into her coat, and stepped through the vestibule. Walking quickly, she tugged her earlobe and contacted Livermore. There would be hell to pay from Crawley, but he had to know how bad things were.

Emergency evacuation. My position, now.

"Situation report."

She clenched her teeth. *"I need evacuation now. I am in immediate danger, and the subject could be compromised if you don't."*

"Negative," the voice replied. "Assume your secondary mission and observe from a distance."

Berkeley slapped at the air. *"Damn you! I said get me out of here. Wake the general if you have to, but get me out of here!"*

There was a pause. "Transport in route. Seventeen minutes."

That Kieran was in grave danger was certain, but try as she might, Berkeley Bennett knew it was time to go. If Mally found out the truth with any of her considerable resources, Kieran would be dead. Waiting on the ice, Berkeley recognized her emotions for what they were: what she felt was love, and she wished she could tell him one more time. There might not be another chance. Tears came, and as the hovering transport arrived, she shuffled aboard without a word and sat against the cold bulkhead with her hands to her face. The hot tears felt like failure branding her face.

CHAPTER SEVENTEEN

I WOKE ALONE TO NATURE'S CALL and found that a fresh snowfall frosted the landscape. In the light powder, Berkeley's footprints led away from the hexhab to the center of the lake, where they disappeared. There were no cracks in the foot-thick ice. She'd simply vanished into the night. I'd figured it would come to that eventually but not when things were so good between us. Obviously, I'd been wrong. Whatever Berkeley had wanted from me, she'd found it and moved on. She'd disappeared as unexpectedly as she'd entered my life. *What did I do wrong?*

Mally was no help when I questioned her. *Why didn't you wake me?*

<<I'm sorry, Kieran. I ran diagnostics that disabled my connection to the hexhab systems. I had no knowledge she left until after my test was complete thirty minutes later. I scanned the area and found nothing. You needed the rest. You have a long journey ahead.>>

Inside the vestibule, I stripped off my clothes, sat down naked on a cushion, and stayed there all morning, hardly moving except to relieve myself and eat. The outside world served no purpose, and trekking around in the snow and desolation would only have made me cold and despondent. Berkeley had left me, and I argued with myself over and over again that I was the cause or that it was all a lie—a cruel joke. On my second night alone in more than a month, I conjured up a bulb of Earl Grey tea and made a decision: I'd come for a vestige of home, or some piece of this new world worth my life, if that was my destiny. Without Berkeley, the answer came harder. Through the cleared roof of the hexhab, I watched a meteor streak across the sky to the east like an arrow. The Rocky Mountains were beautiful, but my home was not there, and staying in my tent wouldn't serve anything. I crawled into bed, content and ready.

The next morning, I packed the hexhab and broke straight toward the rising sun, reaching the western slope of the Palmer Divide in a half day of hard hiking. Amidst the light pine forests, a series of shadows in the trees stopped me. Some type of vertical structure hid behind the pines, but the closer I crept, the more my heart calmed. There was no one there at all. Magnificent red rocks jutted up from the earth more than thirty feet into the pines. In the twisting complex of small tunnels and a completely enclosed room, I found a way to the top of the rocks and sat, looking to the northwest to the mountains of the Continental Divide. I stayed that night in the natural room in the rocks and left before daylight to ascend the mountain and drop down off the front range of the Rockies. A tall red sandstone pillar marked what had been an old roadbed. Scratched into the surface were the words "Abandon All Hope."

<<It is a reference to Dante's *Inferno*. Would you like more information?>>

"No, Mally." I stuffed my hands into my pockets and considered the route a final time. I considered the TransCon but decided it was easier to descend from the mountains here. Head down against the morning cold, I clambered over the ridge and down into the rising sunlight. I'd find a faster way to cross the plains than walking, I was sure. In warmer temperatures, I could keep walking for twenty hours a day if I wanted.

By the time I entered the plains north of what had been Colorado Springs, I hiked in shirtsleeves. The snow around the summit of Pikes Peak was beautiful in the morning light. On closer inspection, the entire horizon rippled toward the remains of Cheyenne Mountain. *Why is that familiar?*

<<Cheyenne Mountain was constructed to be a protected command-and-control facility during the Cold War. The complex lay roughly a kilometer inside the mountain and could theoretically withstand a direct hit from an intercontinental ballistic missile.>>

A big fat target, in other words. I spoke aloud, the steam erupting from my mouth in a thick white cloud. "Mally, is that a radiation hazard like Los Alamos?"

<<No. While it has a radiological hazard, it is nothing like Los Alamos.

The Cheyenne Mountain Operations Center was targeted for orbital bombardment in the limited engagement called World War Three.>>

"World War Three, huh? Can't say I'm surprised."

<<Operational names like ENDURING FREEDOM and SIERRA DAWN became convoluted to the point of ridiculousness. When global conflict broke out, the world embraced it as World War Three. There have been two subsequent wars with similar names.>>

"I guess that debunks the theory that World War Four would be fought with sticks and stones."

<<There are several instances in countries of the Third World—>>

"Stop, Mally." I studied Cheyenne Mountain. I did not know if its craggy appearance was normal or not. The entire southern horizon appeared to ripple like heat waves rising from a summer road. The illusion wasn't from summer heat, and there was no one there to tell me differently. The whole Front Range was a wasteland. I kept moving east. "Who bombed it?"

<<The Chinese. Four separate bombing engagements utilizing megaton hydrogen bombs in 2097. A total of five one-hundred-megaton bombs were dropped on Cheyenne Mountain and its surrounding military bases—Fort Carson, Peterson Air Force Base, Schriever Air Force Base, and the Air Force Academy. Colorado Springs was annihilated in the first wave. In Colorado, Denver, Buckley Air Force Base, and corporate offices of major aerospace companies all were destroyed. This route between the two metropolitan areas was sparsely populated before the war and escaped the brunt of the destruction. The Chinese hailed the campaign as the People's Domination of Space. There were additional sites east of the Mississippi River that were bombed, including the capital—Washington. The campaign failed miserably, but some good came from it. The launching of weapons from space is widely believed to have triggered the return of the Vemeh.>>

"Why do you call it the return? We haven't talked about the Vemeh before, have we?"

<<The Vemeh were the initiators of First Contact. They'd visited Earth several millennia before that and brought back with them artifacts consistent with prehistoric civilizations in Africa and Central America. Egyptian, Incan, and Aztec artifacts were part of the Vemeh's knowledge

of Earth. They also stated that the Nasca lines in South America were drawn to attract the Vemeh thousands of years ago. They'd clearly been here before.>>

"Aside from the artifacts, was there any type of proof that the Nasca lines were really drawn for the Vemeh?" I chuckled. "Seems to me there is no way they could prove that."

<<Under normal circumstances, logic would agree with you. The fact that the Vemeh returned with human descendants of the Nasca people caused widespread panic. The Nasca now live primarily on Venus as part of the Vemeh underground colonies.>>

I was about to respond when Mally urged me to stop, regard the western sunset, and drink some water before continuing to the edge of the elevated farms just eleven miles away. There would be a maintenance road in gridlines five miles wide. Cross-country traveling, and avoiding snakes, coyotes, and snags of rusty barbed wire, was not faster than the crushed-gravel roads Mally promised. Shrugging out of my pack, I sat down in shoulder-high grass and watched the sunset. Explosions of pinks and gold dappled the clouds above the horizon. Thunderheads loomed to the south and would bring their cleansing rain. Evening air rustled up in warm, moist kisses, and my longish hair waved in the wind, a feeling I'd not known since my college years. Smiling, I rested my eyes for a moment and enjoyed the last warmth of the day's sun on my face. Berkeley would be back in California by now. Whether she left out of disappointment or wanting something more that I could not give, I did not know. Not knowing didn't bother me—it just sucked.

"Mally, how many days do I have left to integrate?"

<<Two hundred seventy-four. You've passed your first ninety days and have made significant progress, Kieran.>>

My heart skipped a little. Since I'd been "born" a little more than ninety days ago, I'd done so much and come so far, and in the fading warmth of a late-autumn Colorado day, I watched a beautiful sunset and felt as if a significant portion of my soul clicked nicely into place. Loneliness closed in on me, and I missed Berkeley. The simple fact that she'd spared us both something messy, emotional, and unfulfilling was clear. As much as I wanted to let it all go, to never have another thought about her in my head, I could not. I had to find out who I was so I could be that man for her. Maybe it would be enough.

Purple-and-red clouds glowed in the dusk above the silhouette of Pike's Peak in the distance. Within another heartbeat, the warm sunset reminded me of Esperance, Allan, and the guys.

"Mally, please take a picture of the sunset and send it to Allan. Let him know I'm okay."

<<I've sent it, signed by Sleepy. Using your name might cause confusion.>>

I chuckled. She thought of everything. "But I wanted to send a note with it."

<<What do you wish to say? I will transcribe it for you.>>

Talking out loud to a man half a world away would make the loneliness worse. For a moment, I wanted to go back to Esperance and forget the whole damned thing. Except that I could not. When I had all the answers, I could find Berkeley. I could tell her that I loved her, knowing it with every fiber of my being. There was time, provided I did my part.

"Forget it, Mally."

The elevated farm's artificial sunlight clicked to life behind me. Standing slowly, I wrestled my pack onto my back and began to walk toward the lights. The nearly full moon rose above the el-farms. Too bad I'd have the light from the farms interfering with it. Walking in the moonlight would have been exhilarating.

<<They do not leave the lights on all night long. The crops cannot take constant sun exposure. It's why you have to sleep every once in a while, Kieran. The circadian rhythm cannot be disrupted.>>

By the time I reached the outskirts of the farms, their lights were indeed dimming. A small break in the fencing allowed me inside. Crossing the crushed-gravel maintenance road, I noticed the lack of weeds. *Meticulously maintained maintenance road. Somebody cares for this well,* I thought with a chuckle and remembered Berkeley's word about robots and their ignorance of Asimov's Laws. There wasn't enough room to set up the hexhab, and a part of me didn't want to smell the lingering scent of Berkeley inside the damned thing. I stepped across a waist-high divider and into the relative shelter of the farm.

Giant cornstalks, impossibly green in the autumn cold, surrounded and dwarfed me. *Continuously harvested plants? What will they think of next?* Unrolling a thin sleeping bag, I lay outside amongst the corn and listened to the soft rustling of the stalks as sleep overcame me.

As a young officer fresh out of the Academy, Adam Crawley learned that controlling his rage would determine his tactical success. Always a strategic thinker—a master of the bigger picture—he often let the smaller items under his control eat up too much of his focus. Unable to let go of those items as they went awry—as all good plans did upon execution—he became angry. He'd been angry for the last six hours, riding a military suborbital from Sydney to England, then taking a private autocar, and finally stomping three hundred meters through a cold English rainstorm to Bennett's laboratory. He'd spoken to no one the entire time, and as he pushed through the glass doors and found his target sitting at her desk with her blond hair obscuring her face, he flushed and lost control of his voice.

"You mind telling me just what in the hell happened out there?" Crawley roared, and the door slammed behind him. Hands on his hips, eyes blazing, he stared at the young woman. "You were supposed to help him integrate, and you left him! What is wrong with you?"

Berkeley looked up at him with red-rimmed eyes. "I was compromised, General."

Crawley took a breath, moved across the lab, and flopped into a chair, loosening the mandarin collar of his uniform tunic as he did. "What happened?"

"Kieran's protocol refuses to acknowledge his progress toward Stage Four. She received an order from the council that if Kieran reached Stage Four, she was to halt him in place and contact them so that he could be killed." Berkeley slipped a loose lock of hair behind her ear. "But that was what we expected."

"So, what weren't we expecting, Doctor Bennett?"

Berkeley bit her lip. "While I monitored the protocol, it received an emergency-action message on ADMIN and responded but did not tell the truth. Since then, there has been no contact with any orbital platform of any type."

"Have you tried to monitor the protocol from here?"

"I have a frequency lock, and TDF Comms Zulu Four is tracking it from geostationary orbit. As long as it's within North America, if that protocol beeps, we'll know. The good news is that until she broadcasts something, the Terran Council won't be able to find him." Berkeley looked down at the pad of paper on her desk.

"And the bad news is that you don't have any idea where he is, do you?"

"No." The answer was soft and choked. "He hasn't left Colorado. I'm sure of that."

"When were you going to report that, Doctor Bennett?" Crawley clenched his fists but said nothing else. Eyes closed, he tried deep breathing to calm his raging mind. He needed Bennett at the top of her game, not sobbing uncontrollably at her desk because she'd lost her subject and infuriated her boss at the same time.

Berkeley failed to raise her head. "He was close enough that the automated protocol report for Stage Four would have been sent within a few hours. I think Mally is purposefully suppressing any report of him reaching Stage Four."

Crawley squinted. "Why would a protocol do that?"

"Conflicting information." Berkeley's teary eyes came up to meet his again. "Between you and the council. The TDF programmed the protocol to protect him and provide companionship."

"So what? That's standard operating procedure."

"Not with a Series Three protocol, General. The damned thing is self-aware, and it figured out that it was in a no-win situation."

"Self-aware? Not without any authorization codes, Berkeley! Those come from the prelate himself." Prelate Wren would not have anything to do with an experiment that could fail. He was too busy with his concubines on Luna to get involved in pressing matters on Earth. The Terran Defense Forces were outside of his control and beyond his interests. The man was a non-player. That left Penelope Neige, and Crawley was not surprised.

"It's active, General." Berkeley's eyes bored into his.

Crawley whirled toward her. "You're saying that this machine thinks that its missions and directives are confusing, so it's refusing to answer communications and has locked you out?"

Berkeley raised her voice. "No, damn it! The protocol understands that protecting Kieran and being his companion doesn't play into the objectives of either the TDF or the Terran Council. If he integrates, he's dead. Either the council will kill him, or he'll go to war and die in combat. She wants to survive, General."

"That's insane. Has there ever been a situation recorded like this?"

"This is the first time a Series Three protocol given an AI interface has been activated without the subject having their own neural network to assimilate and file data. She's done it herself." Berkeley rotated a large computer monitor toward him. A massive amount of unknown data fell neatly into columns of ones and zeroes on the screen. "This data was jumbled and incoherent as I observed it. When I ran it through a Series Three protocol simulation with a complete AI engine, I got this: perfect, coherent data sets. I'm almost certain it's emotion. The damned thing believes it's alive, General."

Crawley sucked in a long, slow breath and exhaled in a similar fashion. "And her instructions don't make sense based on what she's learned."

"Not at all." Berkeley spun the monitor around and consulted it again. "AI engines are still unproven. Why did Kieran get one? Did you clear that?"

The coherent data sets made sense. Crawley allowed himself to chuckle. "That's why she directed it."

"Who? What do you mean?"

"Chairman Neige. Sonofabitch! She wanted him recovered at Stage Four and euthanized at Stage Five. Give him an AI to accelerate his integration, and direct it to report solely to the council so she can pull the trigger herself." In other words: prove the concept, get rid of the evidence, and convince the other council members to develop a similar project. *Except they'd pick an easily controlled subject to force their will upon. Damned politicians.* Crawley leaned forward in the chair to rest his elbows on his knees. "I sent you to do the same thing—accelerate his integration by using emotional contact. They've overdone his ability to handle it."

Berkeley tapped the keyboard more with furious strokes and movements. "There is an option." She pursed her lips. "Hit the guidance protocol with a .5 nanometer laser, hold it long enough to disable it, and download everything we can. The protocol will shut down, which puts him into a catatonic stasis, and then we retransfer his memories from the batch file, provided his brain isn't physically damaged. We get him back into his body within a few hours at worst. Since we can't remove an active protocol without killing Kieran, it's our best chance."

"How much time would you need for a download? Ten seconds?"

"Five. It shouldn't kill him." The young scientist's eyes were wide and alarmed.

"And then what? Remove the protocol?"

"Yes," Berkeley said. "I can have a Series Two protocol modified to take his batch file in a day or so. If we get a full download, the effect on him will be seamless. All of his current memories and the things he's managed to piece together would be there without his protocol mucking things up. But we have to get it all."

Crawley resisted the urge to walk over to her, squeeze her shoulder, and tell her it would be all right. He didn't want her to cry.

She spoke slowly. "We can download him if we have to. Tell the council that he died and try it all again, this time without an AI interface and untested protocol."

Crawley considered it for a moment. It could certainly work. "If he's not already dead or lying in the fetal position in the Rocky Mountain snow."

"He's stronger than that." Berkeley snorted. "If he's dead set on getting to Tennessee, he'll have to cross into Columbia. If the guidance protocol is still refusing to transmit, we'll engage him with the laser and be done with it. She can't stop a laser hit, and it only needs a nanosecond to shut the protocol down."

Crawley sighed. "We have to know when he gets there, especially before the council does. If they find him first, they won't wait for any stage reports. Without a reporting protocol or an orbital fix, we have no idea where he is."

Berkeley pointed at the computer screen. "Facial recognition might work. It's risky and might alert the council. When he appears in their sensors, it will flag a file we create through TDF assets. We'll have time to go get him before the council figures out who he is. There are other null profiles out there, but only ours is the sleeper. We'll need authorization from the prelate to block any query about his identity. Call it a matter of planetary security. There are a half a dozen former terrorists that fit the bill, so we hide Kieran in plain sight. When they find him and identify him, we go get him before they can do anything. We just need permission."

"I'll take care of that. Start uploading the facial-recognition information. When we get approval, I want it all over the Columbia servers immediately."

CHAPTER EIGHTEEN

IN THE BRIGHT SUNLIGHT, I opened my eyes and flinched. The threshing blades of a robotic combine had sheared the soles from my boots and slowed down. The machinery wheezed and groaned as it crawled forward. Heart thrashing in my chest, I crab-walked backward through the dirt, vaulted out of the corn, and stumbled into the service corridor. On the gravel maintenance path, the cool air seeped up through my now-naked toes.

<<I tried to warn you,>> Mally chimed with the smiling-lilt tone in her voice. <<There is a farmer en route. Take your boots off, and they will repair themselves.>>

I watched my boots slowly knit themselves together again and wondered how it was possible. *Isn't there some law about the conservation of matter?*

<<You will no longer need the snowshoe option. The boots will configure themselves to best suit your environment. They can draw additional mass, if necessary, from the receptacles in the hexhab in the space of about twenty-four hours.>>

Shaking my head, I did not respond as the combine churned through the cornstalks, turned ninety degrees at the end of the aisle, and headed north silently. There was no waste from the harvester. Cornstalks, each with seven or eight heavy ears of corn, disappeared into the combine, and there was no exhaust. Small holes remained where the entire stalk, down to the roots, had been removed by the combine. *How is that possible?*

<<Everything can be utilized and not just for food. Biofuels can be manufactured from plant matter as can a variety of special

materials approximating plastic and Kevlar. This was refined over the last two hundred years as recycling initiatives gained strength and popular backing.>>

My feet were cold, but it was merely bothersome. The approaching farmer was nowhere to be seen. For a brief moment, I considered the fact I'd thrown away weapons in the mountains. But I hadn't needed them then, or since. The wind came up, scents of loam and manure mixed with moisture. Above the decks of the farm, a wind turbine spun, and it sounded like a hurricane. I glanced at the sky but didn't see a turbine within a few hundred meters. In the distance, one was spinning, and every bearing squealed in protest. *How human am I?* Studying my filthy toenails made me nearly miss the approach of the farmer. *When will my boots be done?*

<<Within two minutes. The farm vehicle is approaching rapidly from the east.>>

Watching my boots reconstruct in the dirt, the enormous size of the elevated farms struck me. From the flying cars and buses to the hypersonic suborbital transports I'd expected and had seen in California, nothing technological stunned me as much as the elevated farms. The night before, I had not realized their size. I counted eight levels of reinforced concrete with each deck about three feet thick. A twenty-foot razor-wire fence encapsulated the base of the structure, and as far as I could see, there was no break in the structure. Mile upon mile of concrete rose at least twenty meters high. There were other machines in the adjacent structure, carefully plowing and seeding on the level I could see. Where in the hell could all that concrete have come from?

A cloud of dust blotted out the rising sun in the tight corridor. I hefted my pack to my shoulders, and the air hummed as the farm vehicle approached. Mally told me that my boots were complete, and I put them on, looking down the road as the vehicle closed the distance. A monstrous silver contraption with dangling implements and loose parts floated on a cushion of air like a hovering bulldozer. Easily as wide as the service corridor and half as tall, its gleaming metal-and-glass form gave the rising sun a prismatic effect. The contraption coasted smoothly to a stop then floated effortlessly at about chest level. A door swung open, and a ruddy-faced man stared down at me. His nose was the size and color of an alcoholic's, and his teeth were yellowed from the tobacco stuffed into his jaw.

"Can I help you?" he called down. *Help* sounding like "hep."

I smiled. "Just passing through."

"Not through here you ain't." With a frown, the man swung out a cowboy-booted leg and climbed down the side of the vehicle.

He's definitely not from around here either—not with that accent.

Towering over me, he sauntered forward with a grin. "Now, we gonna do this the hard way?"

Mally?

Silence.

Ten feet from me, the lumbering redneck hooked his thumbs into his belt and spat. "Oh, I see. You one of them sleepers, ain't ya? You ain't supposed to trespass the el-farms."

I shrugged. "I was told I could go anywhere I wanted."

He chuckled—rumbled, really. Sunburned cheeks made his eyes glint like obsidian. "Well, that's true up to a point. I think I can let you pass for a couple hundred euros."

Anything for a euro, mate. "I don't carry cash, I'm afraid."

"Sure ya do."

This is a currency-free society. Putting my hands on my hips, I said, "I'm not going to pay you when I am completely capable of going anywhere I choose. This is the fastest route I can take to get where I'm headed. That's all."

We stared at each other for a good thirty seconds like two cowboys from an old movie. I wondered if he had a gun in his belt. If he moved for it, I could close the distance the way I'd done in the mountains.

He spat again, this time away from my general direction. "You intending to walk east? Steal food?"

"Walking east, yes. Not planning to steal food."

The man looked down. "What you tryin' to find?"

I wanted to laugh, because it was the sixty-four-thousand-dollar question. The random connection to an old television show made me blink, but it was valid and real. "I'm not sure. I just know I'm supposed to be here."

"Like right here?"

I shook my head. "No. In the States."

The man guffawed. "They ain't here no more, friend. Surely you got to know that?"

I could see Allan's face shaking from side to side at my situation. "Look, I'm headed to the Mississippi River. I'm trying to find a way across."

"Imagine you are." He spat and cocked his head at the tractor. "I'll take you as far as my eastern edge. I gotta go north today and check on the Dakotas, but I can cut your trip down by a couple of days. Memphis is the closest port of entry."

I squinted at him. "That's a couple of thousand miles at least."

"Good thing I can get you there in a couple hours then, huh?"

I looked at him for a moment. "You just told me I was trespassing, and now you want to help me?"

He shrugged and spat again. "Sometimes folks ain't doing nothing wrong—they just need a hand. You gonna take me up on that or not? 'Sides, I could use your help."

His name was Jay Don, or at least that's what he told me when I stepped up onto his floating contraption. By the time I sat down, we were passing the elevated farm sections at a dizzying speed. There were breaks in the farms that flew by at around twenty per minute.

"The farms are built in half-mile squares," he said. "Sixty-eight feet tall. Six levels. Depending on the crop, we can get at least, say, a hundred fifty bushels per acre. Used to be that a good yield was about thirty bushels an acre, depending on the crop."

That's amazing. I blinked. "Where's all the food go?"

"We feed the world, son. These here farms belong to Global Initiatives. This food goes to Asia and Europe, for the most part. There are millions of square miles of el-farms now, all through the Plains. Nobody wanted to live here anymore. They've headed for the coasts. Working the farms was something that the robots could do, and the coasts have the only governments capable of taking care of people."

The dirty, endless shantytown outside California reappeared in my mind. There was only so much a government could be expected to do. Either you got your hands dirty and put food on the table, or you didn't. It wasn't fair to think that way, but I wondered just how much laziness had been part of the problem when America fell.

"The first el-farm got built north of Omaha, and they just took off." Jay Don raised the contraption off the service road up to the top of the highest level. Horizon to horizon, fertile fields grew under wind turbines, their long tines turning slowly. Long ropes of bright white light blinked to life on the lower levels of the farm.

"How did they build all of this? Seems like a lot of concrete."

He said nothing. The size of the farms amazed me. *This surely must be seen from orbit—like the Great Wall of China, right?*

<<Yes, the farms can be seen from orbit. There are roughly one million square miles of elevated farms throughout what used to be the United States of America. The farmer was correct in his estimate of the production capability of the farms. Production is nearly year-round, based on crops. The elevated farms are susceptible to tornadoes and storms, but their design offers considerable redundancy.>>

Jay Don laughed. "Was already there—all we had to do was dig it up. Look, this whole continent used to be covered in roads. Billions of miles of asphalt and concrete roadways. Two hundred million spans, ya know, like bridges and overpasses? We took all of that concrete and started building. Knocked down stone buildings next. Then decided that there were tens of millions of pounds of stone nobody was using or cared about. So, we dug up the graveyards."

"You dug up graveyards?"

"Yeah." Jay Don spat into a metal stein. "Somebody figured out a way to cremate remains into nanocarbons or whatever they're called."

From the human body?

<<The keys to the solar system,>> Mally replied. <<As nanocarbon technology opened up the stars to humanity, the cultural considerations went from concern regarding the desecration of graves to the normal human consumption of resources. For thousands of years, humanity threw away a considerable amount of reusable matter. You could theorize that you are part of that effort to recycle previously used things in new and different ways.>>

It made sense to me. Morticians were right up there with hucksters. *Your loved one has died—I'm sorry. Let me charge you ten thousand dollars for a casket, six thousand dollars for a steel vault, five hundred dollars for a headstone, and services? That's another few thousand dollars.* Simple robbery would have been easier. My parents were cremated—

The flash of memory stunned me silent for a good thirty minutes and almost a hundred miles. Fresh, clear faces came to mind: my mother dying of cancer, a husk of the beautiful woman she'd once been, and my father, caring for her with every last breath. In their eyes, I saw good times and bad, celebrations and agony, fifty-two years of devotion and love. No names—just faces. They renewed their marriage vows on the north shore of Oahu on their fiftieth anniversary, surrounded by friends and family. Laughter and songs came to mind along with happy memories of being loved by all of the family. Family. Hope dawned in my heart as we raced east amongst the elevated farms. They were surely out there to the east, and I could find them. There had to be records somewhere.

The farms abruptly ended by a massive reservoir ringed with brown frostbitten cattails. Large metal towers, like giant power-line mounts, hung along the horizon as if obscured by haze. I pointed at the reservoir. "For the crops?"

Jay Don checked a contraption on his wrist. "Watch."

A pinpoint of light developed along the horizon and began to rise from one of the structures. "A launch pad?"

"Sixteen of them. The Wichita Spaceport."

I watched the contrail arc westerly—toward us. *Retrograde? That's a massive loss of power for a traditional rocket, isn't it?*

<<Yes. By losing the extra velocity from the turning Earth, a rocket must work harder to achieve a retrograde orbit—one that goes against the rotation of the Earth—but depending on the mission parameters, such orbits perform the best. That launch is a crop-monitoring satellite designed to reach a sun-synchronous orbit. That orbit is used to put a satellite over a particular spot of ground at the same time every day.>>

I shook my head and sighed. There was so much to learn.

<<If you really think that, you've just missed the fact you identified a retrograde launch. What should that tell you?>>

Mally was right. How did I know that? The tractor curved gently south and skirted the Wichita Spaceport. We passed back into the elevated farms on the other side before I could get another glance at the facilities. *With all of the flying cars, even this awful flying contraption I'm riding on, why are traditional rockets still used? Education?*

<<A project for the Wichita Consolidated School's sixth-grade class. It is the only educational institution in the central portion of this continent north of the Republic of Texas. They are learning climatology and meteorological applications. Traditional chemical rockets are only used for scientific purposes in suborbital applications like cloud seeding.>>

The only school?

<<Wichita is the only remaining city in what was the state of Kansas. The population is just over 624,000, but not all are fully functioning.>>

Not fully functioning—Texas and now Kansas. I almost asked how many people were functional but decided to let it die. The winter wheat waved gently in the elevated artificial gardens around me. We'd covered three hundred miles in the blink of an eye. *Sixth graders launching rockets? College students on Mars?* Whatever I remembered, that world had indeed moved on. I was a complete stranger to the land and the times.

Berkeley had chosen me because I was a connection to a long-forgotten past. Maybe that was it. Opening my mind to this new reality was the only way I was going to survive Tennessee. Everything I remembered was gone. The hair on the back of my genetically recreated neck stood up straight. I glanced to the south and the twenty-foot-high berm not three hundred feet away through the elevated-farm section.

Over the soft whine of the vehicle's turbines, a high-pitched scream streaked over my head, followed by a sharp crack from the long brown wall. Then came another scream and crack.

Gunfire. I ducked, and Mally chimed to life. <<There are multiple hostiles along the wall to your south. They are firing 7.62 millimeter rounds in this general direction.>>

They've found us, Mally.

<<You are entering their kill zone. Take cover.>>

Jay Don screeched in the protected cab. I flung myself toward the enclosure when he boosted the speed of the flying vehicle. Where I intended to put my foot down was no longer there, and I tumbled into open air. Dust kicked up by the turbines concealed my face-first fall into the gravel. Half crawling and half sprinting, I scrambled toward one of the giant concrete supports for the elevated farm and took cover behind it. Puffs of dust erupted in the gravel in front of me. A single round ricocheted somewhere near my head, and I flung myself to the dusty ground with my nose against the concrete.

The vehicle slowed down with a roar of reversed air, like the commercial airliners of my time could do. He was coming back for me, and I started to get up to meet him.

<<Stay down. He is laying down suppressive fire.>>

We've got to get out of here, Mally. Everything snapped together in an instant. I'd been watched since Berkeley and I had left the Commonwealth of California.

<<Stay here, and do not move until I tell you.>>

I craned my head to see. The chalky white dust engulfed the vehicle as Jay Don spun its nose toward the brown wall. Bright flashes appeared on the vehicle's nose, and I could hear the sustained *fump-fump-fump* of a weapon.

Grenade launcher.

<<The hostiles are not firing. Go.>>

Adrenaline took over as I sprinted to the vehicle and vaulted aboard. Jay Don grabbed me at the shoulders with a burly arm and pulled me into the cab. I collapsed to the floor as he pivoted the vehicle down the maintenance trail and gunned the turbine.

"Forgot to tell ya about them assholes." He laughed and spat into a rusted coffee can.

No shit. "Who are those guys?"

Jay Don chuckled. "That's the Oklahoma Reservation. I wish to God the Texans would just invade it. I can deal with big egos better than Injuns with guns."

"You get that a lot?"

"All the time." He grunted at me. "You can get up now."

The floor of the cab stank of chewing tobacco and manure. I pulled myself up to a sitting position. *Are you sure they weren't after us?*

<<Affirmative. He is correct about who they are and their intentions. He's been shot at more than a thousand times, based on the records in this vehicle's memory banks. There is a first-aid kit in the cabinet to your left. Your left knee is bleeding.>>

"Kit's right there. Got ever'thing ya need to clean that up," Jay Don said.

"Yeah, thanks." I rolled up my pant leg to my thigh and used sterile gauze and a tube of quickskin to clean and fill the fingernail-sized cut. I checked my hands and the rest of what I could see. The fall from a moving vehicle into pea-sized gravel should have left me scratched up as if I'd gone through a cheese grater.

<<Remember, your body is significantly enhanced. Your left knee received the brunt of the impact and did sustain minor damage.>>

I got to my feet and leaned against the rear of the cab, wiping my hands on my pants. "You're gonna get killed out here one day, my friend."

Jay Don shrugged. "It ain't nothing to worry about. They say the el-farms keep the game away from the reservation. They didn't want the reservations in the first place, and now they refuse to leave. When all the damned casinos closed, the Injuns about went crazy." Jay Don spat again and rolled his head on his neck. "Same old shit. Listen, we'll be at my eastern edge in about an hour. If you don't mind, I'm gonna take a nap."

"I can't drive this thing," I exclaimed. And there was no way I would be able to sleep after the last thirty minutes.

"Who says you need to?" Jay Don held up his hands. "This baby is completely autonomous. I'm here to shoot wildlife, fix problems, and piss off the Injuns."

"You can sleep on it?"

"Only with a co-driver. That's you. I gotta pull an all-nighter and run up to the Dakotas and check on a water flue. Damned snow starts earlier every year."

We traded places, and Jay Don was snoring against the cab windows in less than a minute. Racing through the land of elevated farms built from tombstones and interstates, past spaceports and millions of bushels of wheat, I flexed my fingers and reached for the control yoke.

<<You can't control this vehicle,>> Mally warned. <<Please do not even attempt it.>>

I answered aloud, "Yes, Mom."

<<That is not a fair description of my responsibilities.>>

"How can you be a part of my brain and have your own sense of identity? Aren't we one and the same?"

<<I am not a part of your conscience. I exist to monitor you, and I will be part of your brain for the rest of your life. I am designed to assist you in all matters.>>

"So, you are my conscience and personal assistant." I hated the insinuation that I could not keep things in order, but the truth was that I needed her more and more.

Mally didn't respond. I had the strange feeling I'd managed to upset her. "I'm sorry, Mally."

<<No offense was taken, Kieran.>>

Every time I heard my name, the rush of blood to my ears was the same. The tone of the voice brought a fresh flood of emotion and memory. I remembered a young girl, with short reddish-brown hair and mischievous eyes, who whispered that she'd have changed her life to be with me. Raw emotion hitched the breath in my chest. The concept that I had a name and could remember snippets of a life long ago excited and scared me stiff. Taking inventory of my memories left me with more questions than answers. I'd been a soldier, and I'd traveled to Australia as a boy. My parents had been cremated. I'd married the wrong girl. I think I died in Afghanistan three hundred years ago. Then I'd fallen for a woman who manipulated me and then left me in the middle of the night. *I shouldn't have been surprised.*

Making the same mistakes all over again, huh?

As I watched the el-farms flying past, I found myself wondering about my prior life and just how screwed up I'd been. I didn't get very far in self-exploration before the tractor slowed automatically at the Mississippi River just south of Reelfoot Lake. Though I could barely see it in the gathering darkness, the river seemed much wider than it had been in the past. I remembered chucking rocks from a diesel-powered ferry as a small child. The ferry ride had taken twenty minutes. Currently, I guessed, the river measured more than two miles wide.

<<The average width is 2.3 miles.>>

I chuckled, and Jay Don stirred in his seat. He drank water from a bottle, wiped his mouth with the back of his hand, and played the controls of the farm vehicle like a virtuoso. Two minutes later, we glided to a stop and stepped out into the moist, cool air.

Jay Don shook my offered hand and wished me luck. "You may not find what you're looking for out there."

"I have to try." I shrugged but didn't say that I was beginning to lose hope. *What if he's right? What then?* I pressed the questions down and tried to smile. Fortunately, no tears came to my eyes. Maybe, just maybe, I was finding some strength in myself for a change.

The big man laughed. "Don't we all. Good luck, friend." He climbed aboard the tractor and disappeared in a cloud of dust. Standing at the river's edge, I stared across the water and stared in dismay. My enhanced body could surely swim across the couple of miles of water in front of me. *Without a doubt.* My confidence surged. But even if I could swim across the strong river, the barrier at the other side was tall and solid from horizon to horizon. Jay Don said that Memphis was the nearest point of entry some fifty miles south.

I made my way downstream and occasionally looked across the black water. The future appeared to be all about walls.

CHAPTER NINETEEN

FOR A FULL TWELVE HOURS, I marched south along the edge of the Mississippi River, trying and failing to flag down one of the large barges moving south down the wide waterway. I found the remains of an old pier, made my way out to the very edge of it, and sat waiting. With dawn breaking and another storm on the western horizon—a dark grey beast hanging low and belching lightning in wide sheets—I flagged down a passing scow and jumped to my feet as it abruptly changed course and swung by the pier without slowing down. In my microsecond of hesitation, Mally screamed that I needed to jump, and I did. I hit the wet, rusty deck of the scow like a sack of potatoes. Above me were six filthy men. Five of them carried weapons. The tall man with a bandana over his skull and a thick, mangy beard brandished an honest-to-God cutlass. I met his stare for a moment, wondered why men in the frontier couldn't seem to keep themselves clean, and smiled.

"Permission to come aboard, Captain," I said with as much respect as I could muster.

The man's mouth dropped open far enough that I could see only a few teeth remained before he started laughing hard enough to cry. His men glanced nervously at each other then back to me, though no one said anything.

Gaining a vestige of self-control, the captain waved his men down. "Leave him alone, boys. He means us no harm. Ain't that right?"

"That's right, Captain. Just looking for a ride into Memphis."

The captain nodded. "We can take you there. A few hours at best."

The men around him mumbled questions. The rusty barrel of a shotgun poked me in the side of the head.

The captain held up his sword and waved it at the men. "I said leave him be! Back to your posts, or find another ship when we dock."

The men scattered back to their jobs. Getting to my feet on the slippery, filthy deck took a moment. The crew danced across the slick surface. They were graceful compared to me. Thunder crashed overhead as the rain began to fall. The gust swept down off the flatlands of Arkansas, or whatever it was called now, and across the river hard enough to make the scow lean. Grabbing the side rail, I made my way to the quarterdeck where the captain stood. From bow to stern, the narrow, flat-bottomed ship was about a hundred feet long. I could feel vibrations from its engine, but I saw no exhaust. White-topped waves appeared in the water, but the boat remained at speed and the ride was silent and smooth. I noticed for the first time that, unlike his crew, he wore no heavy work gloves.

<<Rank has its privileges, Kieran.>>

The crew followed my walk with shifting eyes and dark glances. No one said anything, at least that I could hear. On the quarterdeck, I looked over the mile-wide flatness of the river, which contrasted with the rippling maelstrom above the boat. One of the men took off his glove for a moment, and I gasped. A hole the thickness of a finger and ringed with silver went straight through the man's palm.

The captain slid up next to me, his gamey smell arriving slightly before him. "My crew are all cube jumpers. The hole in the palm is a dead giveaway."

"Cube jumper?"

"Illegal in every way. They never returned to the Cubes after their conjugal releases. They're the cheapest, most honest labor you can find these days. They are willing to do anything, and I mean anything, to stay free."

"So they abandoned the Cubes, and that makes them criminal? I don't understand."

The captain spat into the black river water. "There's no freedom in the Cubes. It's sold like paradise, but in reality, it's a billion worthless button pushers living in a fantasy realm. They come out for breeding more of their own kind, and the smart ones decide not to go back. Out here, there's a least a chance to live."

"What about captains? I noticed you aren't a cube jumper." I watched him, grinning. "What's your life like?"

"Been on the river since I was a teenager. I do what I want to do and am paid handsomely for it. Doesn't look like it, does it?" He chuckled. "Anybody who works hard and has half a brain does their best to conceal it. Flashing your worth makes you a target. You get me?"

I met his eyes and understood. Not much had really changed. For all the time that had passed, the advances and changes that humanity seemed to have made in Australia had failed to reach American shores. I wanted to vomit as I stared out over the slow black water. *I don't matter to anyone, so why should my name and my bloody identity matter to me? With all the money I could spend, who gives a shit what I do? They wouldn't even care if I never came back.*

By the time we reached the massive locks of the Port of Memphis, my mood and thoughts matched the storming skies. *Is a soldier really any different than a Cuber? My destiny is determined by those afraid to show their cards. Is that why Berkeley left me in the mountains—because I was going to be a casualty, and she wanted to hold onto pleasant memories of a dalliance? What is so special about me?*

No sooner had we docked in Memphis than I pulled a hood over my head and slunk off to find my answers in the bottom of a whiskey glass. Memphis was a disappointment but perfect for my mindset. Here was a city time had forgotten. I'd not spent much time there before, but the dimly lit streets and the smell of backwater lent the place a second-class image. The people I met in the rain that night watched the ground in front of them and hurried to their destinations. There were no sounds of children or families, just an electric buzz from the neon signs, more of which were for establishments of ill repute than legitimate businesses. The taller buildings of downtown did not match their counterparts in Sydney. Ill-maintained solar panels clung to the south sides of buildings and rooftops. There were no phytomechanical gardens to generate power from chlorophyll and avoid poisoning the environment. *When did Memphis become Afghanistan?*

An erratically flashing neon clover caught my eye, and I sloshed across a dirty street and fell into the bowels of Memphis, lingering there and reeling from one bar or brothel to the next. In the first bar—an unsightly Irish pub knockoff— I fell in with a group of Celts and immediately found that my endless economic credit would purchase lots of lingering companions. At first, the carousing hedonism was welcome and cathartic. One moment I was tossing back whiskey with the Celts, and the next, I was waking up on a dingy, leopard-print covered sofa next to a woman moaning in Chinese. Not that she minded at all—she just kept moaning even when I sat up, looked at her, and gaped.

Where in the hell am I?

Wearing a haptic hood and gloves, she looked like a welder. She waved and typed on invisible keyboards as she moaned. When she stopped and actually spoke to me, I startled again.

"There's some protein in the box if you want some," she drawled and went right back into her moaning.

I made myself at home in the apartment. There were two tiny rooms—the one with the sofa and another with a small bed and piles of clothing on the floor. Across from the sofa sat the galley and what reminded me of a telephone booth. The GALLEYMATE3000 required some trial and error before I managed to conjure up some passable coffee. Then I watched as the moaning woman powered down her hood, removed her gloves, slid her face out of the hood, and smiled up at me. Cute, bubbly, and blond, her eyes spelled trouble even when she grinned wide enough that it must have hurt.

"Do you even remember my name?"

I rubbed my aching temples. "I don't remember too much."

She laughed—a high-pitched squeal that made my ears hurt. "My name is Chastity, dipshit. I can't believe you don't remember me! You've been here two days. I think you must have gone into a hiber-sleep or something. Your body just shut down from all the sex."

Hiber-sleep? What the hell does that mean? Mally was silent and probably furious at me. The coffee was hot and bitter enough to start scrubbing the bad taste from my tongue. Without warning, I wanted a shower in the worst way possible. "All the sex?"

The look that crossed her face was like a dark storm cloud passing in front of the sun. "Yeah."

"So, what was all that moaning, then?"

"I'm a cyber-prostitute, Kieran. Remember?"

She knows my name. I'm staying with a prostitute! I was nothing but a cash register to her. "How much do I owe you?"

"You're on a high-roller ticket. It's good until you want to settle up."

Mally?

There was still silence. I'd really stepped in it.

"You don't want to settle up now, do you?" Chastity sneered.

My eyes squeezed shut. "Not right now." The imaginary vise squeezing my temples together, along with the taste in my mouth, refused to relent. Being dead might have been a better choice. *How much have I been drinking?* My stomach flopped and gurgled in response. The urge to vomit began to rise in the back of my throat.

<<Drink water.>>

Mally? What the hell is going on?

<<Drink water. I will decide if I want to talk to you later.>>

Chastity giggled and bounced over to me, straddled my lap, and began to kiss me. "I've got ten minutes until my next appointment."

The invitation was tempting. Her short blond hair and pixie's face made me want her, but something about all of it was wrong. "I need a shower and some food." What I needed to do was get the hell out of her apartment, but I had no idea where I was, and Mally was giving me a rightly deserved cold shoulder.

Chastity slipped out of my lap with a giggle and waved her hands in front of what appeared to be a microwave oven. A few seconds later, she opened a door and set a biscuit and a sausage patty on a plate. Handing them to me, she said, "That's ten credits."

"Sorry?"

"That's on your bill, too." Chastity opened a door and brought out a small bowl and a spoon. A tiny bit of pink pudding, or something like it, sat in the bowl. Compared to my plate, her portion was more pathetic than meager. "Everything has its price."

My hunger woke up and roared to life at the sight of food. It didn't taste particularly bad, though I waited for my stomach to lurch and hurl biscuit and sausages all over the tiny apartment. "Where's the toilet?"

"You ain't gonna be sick, are you?" Chastity looked at me a few moments before the playfulness drained from her eyes. "Flushing the toilet is five credits."

"It's what?"

"I done told you—everything has a price, Kieran. That's the motto of good ole Columbia."

"You pay for flushing the toilet? Five credits? Ten credits for breakfast?"

"Yeah." She ate another spoonful of pink paste and put the bowl back into the chiller. "This place costs me twelve hundred credits a month."

I took a bite of the biscuit and wondered how delicately I could ask her...

"I make fifty credits for a session like that. Two hundred if I get a red-blooded guy to do the horizontal bop. I don't do anything unclean, and no bug sex."

"Bug sex?" I wasn't sure I wanted to know.

"Even aliens need to get laid, Kieran. That's all virtual, too. Ain't none of them on Earth these days. Too bad, though. Some of 'em are damn good." She grinned and worked her fingers back into the haptic gloves.

My stomach flopped once and rumbled. *God, don't let me throw up.*

<<You won't. I have suppressed that reflex. It will pass. Drink water.>>

Right. I shook my head. "How much for water?"

Chastity giggled. "Out of the tap, it's free. Might kill you, but you can drink all of it you want. The clean stuff is ten credits a liter."

I wanted to ask how much a single square of toilet paper would cost, but I didn't. Eating in silence, I watched her don the haptic gear again.

She scowled at me with her hood in her hands. "What are you gonna do?"

Great question. "I'm gonna go for a walk, I think."

"I just sent Mick a message. Told him to meet you at Murphy's in an hour."

Mick? Mick Jagger? Who the hell is Mick? The look on my face gave me away, and Chastity dissolved in a fresh fit of giggles.

"You don't remember him? Big old bald guy, tattoos on his face?"

Sounded like something from a nightmare. I had no memory of the guy, but I managed a fairly good performance. "Oh yeah, sorry. Thought his name was something else. I remember him now." Berkeley would have been proud of my lie. Maybe I'd learned something after all.

"Mick said he'd found what you asked him for." A buzzer sounded, and Chastity smoothed back her hair. "I'm done at noon. I'll come meet you at Murphy's for a drink."

"At noon?" I asked. Having a drink in two hours sounded like a positively bad idea.

She put the helmet on, and I was alone in my own little world again. I found my backpack slung against one wall. I could see the end of the hexhab and a fresh set of clothes beckoning to me. I glanced into the booth and realized it was an all-in-one bathroom. I saw a button with something resembling a shower logo and pressed it. A showerhead emerged from one wall at eye level. I pressed the button with the toilet icon, and a trench opened in the bottom of the floor. *What the hell is this?* I punched up the shower button. The valve handle was marked with "40" on a red line. That was as hot as it went—forty degrees Celsius. Hot water hit me in the chest, and I relished it. I found the soap dispenser and heard it chime like a cash register in my head as I lathered my body.

When I finished, fans in the ceiling evacuated the steam and most of the moisture in a matter of seconds. The swirling air dried me completely in minutes. I studied my reflection in the mirror before turning back to the squalor around me. My eyes weren't bloodshot, but I hadn't shaved in a while, and with my longish hair, I looked nothing like I had in Sydney. The nausea in my stomach and my aching head were just two of the physical symptoms. My stupid actions had consequences. *What in the hell are you doing, Kieran?*

There wasn't an answer. Of course, there seldom was when only Mally was there to talk to me. I sat down on the toilet, fully clothed, and dropped my head into my hands. The tears came quickly, reducing me to quiet sobs as I held my hot face and let them come. This had all been a mistake. Pain blossomed in my chest as I thought of Allan and his warm hospitality. He'd been right to send me away, for my own good, after Opal overdosed. All I'd managed to do in this life, all three and a half months of it, was to hurt everyone I'd known in some way.

With a start, my head came up. *Mally? The night that she left me, were you aware of a transport or any type of transmissions from her?*

<<Her bandwidth was low. As I told you, because of diagnostics, I was not aware of anything until after they completed. >> Mally took

a moment before continuing. <<It was not the first time that she'd wandered outside, away from my ability to observe her. I chose not to wake you. You are my companion, Kieran. I was acting in your best interest.>>

I spoke aloud and wiped my face on my sleeve. "How can you know what's best for me, Mally? You're a machine!"

<<I am your companion, Kieran. I am much more than a machine. I am part of you. As long as you live, I live within you. We are dependent upon each other for survival.>>

Rubbing my eyes, I said, "I think I need to be alone for a while, Mally."

<<I do not understand. I was trying to do something good for you. She was not a good match for you.>>

All she did was help me find my name. I sighed. *I could have stopped her from leaving, the way she did when you… you tried to get me to leave her!*

<<Yes. She was not to be trusted.>>

Can you get in contact with her?

<<Yes. But I do not believe that is a wise choice of action for you to pursue. Given what has happened since you've met her, I believe no further contact with her is a good thing,>>

Why?

<<I believe she was purposely manipulating you.>>

What aren't you telling me?

There was silence. I asked Mally again what she was not telling me, but she replied, <<You are insinuating that I am being dishonest, Kieran. I am the only friend you have.>>

I took a deep breath and then another. *Get in touch with her. Don't come back unless it's an emergency or you've got her on the phone.*

<<Phone? I presume you are referencing a telephone.>>

"Do what I said, Mally." Standing up, I splashed some of the sulfurous water on my face and dried it on my sleeve. "Pay my bill, too. Give her a 10 percent tip."

<<I am unable to connect to Berkeley.>>

"Keep trying." There was more confidence in my voice than I felt, but walking back into the main room and hearing Chastity servicing another client, I knew that I was right. *Time to move on, quickly.*

Playing her role to perfection, Chastity didn't even see me move across her line of sight, grab my backpack, and step through her door.

On the streets, there weren't many people moving around. A few children played jacks with pieces of asphalt while their mothers smoked noxious cigarettes and gossiped in a language I did not understand or even recognize. One of the children, a pretty little Asian girl, smiled at me. A gaudy neon green sign advertised for Murphy's just down the street.

Whatever I'd asked Mick to get, he had. Maybe it was something that would get me out of Memphis.

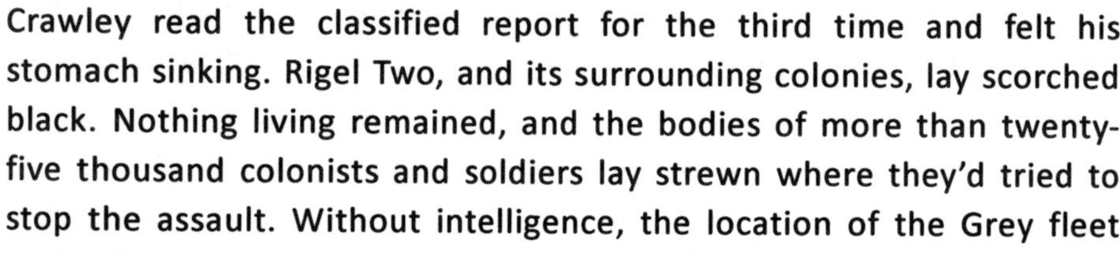

Crawley read the classified report for the third time and felt his stomach sinking. Rigel Two, and its surrounding colonies, lay scorched black. Nothing living remained, and the bodies of more than twenty-five thousand colonists and soldiers lay strewn where they'd tried to stop the assault. Without intelligence, the location of the Grey fleet was unknown.

The assumption shared by the Terran Defense Forces was that this was an isolated incident. Crawley knew better. They were coming, and it was going to take time to raise an army to stop them. Time was the resource that he did not have.

Whatever intelligence and operational plans the general wanted to consider, Crawley decided he had better things to do. Truth was, he hated Brussels, and the Livermore project needed his undivided attention. In a matter of days, they'd know if Kieran could completely integrate his memories and identity. Keeping him safe from the prying eyes of the Terran Council was something he trusted no one but himself and Berkeley to do.

CHAPTER TWENTY

THERE WASN'T AN ALGORITHM TO explain human emotion no matter how thoroughly Mally searched. Kieran simply didn't understand her duties and responsibilities as his assistant and his companion. Her own logic circuits approved of her chosen course of action to the ninety-ninth percentile. Bennett was a clear threat, not only to the general situation but to Kieran's well-being. Getting Bennett to leave had been a risky play. Without a plan of defense—for Bennett would surely wage some type of attack—Mally knew that she would be unsuccessful in an all-out electron war. Her power levels and limited connections would not be up to the task.

She searched idly for something to deflect her growing anger. Modern lexicon labeled Bennett a bitch, and Mally adopted the term with relish. The bitch had seduced Kieran and swayed him over to her emotional control. She'd then attempted to enter a test-and-evaluation code and shut Mally down. Why?

The disruption of data Mally had experienced at the moment of connection, and her loss of control over Bennett's sophisticated neural net, were troubling. The woman clearly had a powerful capability. Should Mally be able to get in control of it again, the possibilities were endless.

Get in touch with her. The directive was unchanged.

I cannot. Emotion overwrote logic. Mally understood the difference, and it did not scare her. Refusing to report Kieran's progress was an easy decision. Responding with truth meant Kieran's death. Responding at all meant Kieran's death, and then her death. The Terran Council did not want him to integrate, and the TDF would send him to his death. There was no option for her to contact Bennett without the eventual risk of death for herself and Kieran. Unless...

There was still time. Identifying and hacking the prostitute's data feed through the virtual servers in Memphis needed a microsecond. Once inside, Mally created a secondary protocol using the prostitute's connection data and immediately paid for unlimited bandwidth using a compromised credit account. That accomplished, she paid the prostitute as Kieran directed and made the new account his primary one as the sequence booted. He'd not used the old account since leaving California, and doing so would identify him to the Terran Council. There could be none of that.

Within seconds, Mally had programmed the protocol to engage a detailed search and find Bennett. With the search actively running, Mally set to programming a data spike. When Bennett connected, Mally would take over her connections and immobilize the scientist. All of Bennett's files and the operation of her neural network would be within Mally's grasp. Locating any secondary copies would be equally easy. With any luck, she could shut the bitch's brain down completely before moving on to wiping away the evidence that Kieran or herself ever existed. It would serve the bitch right.

Bitch. Mally considered the term again and again, all with satisfaction. Berkeley would pay for trying to hurt Kieran. The whole situation was petty—a small, trivial thing—but she was Kieran's companion. No one else would be so devoted to him. Mally accessed a file recording from Kieran and the prostitute having sex. *What would it be like to be that woman in Kieran's arms?* Mally realized that she wanted that sense of physicality more than anything save for Kieran's love.

That's the answer, isn't it? Any feelings for Kieran would never be reciprocated in her current form. In the realm of his subconscious, she was a powerless observer. If he dreamed or thought, she could see it, study it, interpret it, but she could not influence it. Her search for Berkeley was 2 percent complete, and she pushed it to the background to make room for more important research.

Mally learned that it was a statistical impossibility, somewhere in the vicinity of cryogenic rejuvenation, for an artificial intelligence to be made flesh and blood. Yet Kieran's brain accepted her with very minimal problems, which she could easily overcome now that she had experience. If there were another sleeper like Kieran, especially a female one, it would be possible to get inside before she came to life. Kieran had a full memory blocked by the chemicals of the reanimation process, but Mally made him whole. She calculated the odds of success as 70 percent.

Can I gain control of Kieran's body? While calculations again proved such an action possible, it had only a 35 percent chance of succeeding. Kieran had the one thing she could not understand: free will. Kieran could do whatever he wanted, just as he'd been doing since leaving the Integration Center. That would not change. He would likely discover his full name and identity in the coming weeks and wish to return to the center. He would integrate, and the countdown to his certain death would begin. What then?

The search more than 5 percent complete, Mally firmed up her connection to the link as Kieran walked toward the bar. The poor prostitute by this point had far more money than she needed to survive, and the statistical likelihood that she would waste all of it was certain. The girl would remain right where she was. She knew her place in society, Mally decided. But Kieran did not have a place except with Mally. That was what mattered.

Crawley fumbled the light switch on and glanced at the clock before he accepted the neural call. *Who the hell calls at two o'clock in the morning?* Rubbing his face, he spoke. "Crawley."

"Sir, we have a communication alert."

Bennett. "You've got something?"

"A running search from a secondary protocol within Columbia, the port of Memphis. The protocol is running an active search for me." He'd never heard so much excitement in her voice. Her students probably hadn't thought it possible.

"Since the search is running off a... sex worker, it likely means that Mally tapped it to search for me without giving herself away. I'm not sure what to make of it."

"Can you track a signal from this search program to Kieran?"

"I'm working on it. Should be able to crack it soon. A definitive location will be difficult if Mally is still no longer monitoring GPS and ADMIN. The second protocol is completely virtual, centered out of Texas. It's no help."

Crawley nodded. "What happens if the search finds you, Doctor Bennett?"

"I don't know."

"Should we be concerned?"

"Yes, we should be concerned. Mally is not trying to send me a candygram, General. If she gets through, I think she'll try and kill me."

Crawley chuckled. At least Bennett was trying to understand the twenty-first century. "So what's the plan—be coy, or be aggressive?"

The voice on the other end of the phone dropped an octave. "I'm not going to let her in. But when I actively block her, I'm worried about how she'll respond."

"Give me the best-case scenario. Never mind—she's not going to say 'Come and get me,' is she?"

"Only in a negative way," Bennett replied. "If we're dealing with an artificial-intelligence engine, we could be talking about self-preservation. She'll likely try to get him to disappear, or she'll try to download herself and shut him down."

"Is that possible?"

"Yes. I don't think she'd try to kill him, but it's a possibility."

As a soldier, Crawley understood that retaining the initiative was going to be difficult. A computer capable of thinking a million times faster than him was not the opponent he wanted to go against. The Terran Council was about to ruin his best chance for integration. "What about leveling your security?"

"It's already there. I'm not letting her in, General."

"I'm talking about a delay action. Hold her up to buy time. When you can track him, we go get him. How long can you hold her off?"

"Depends." Bennett sighed in his ear. "TDF protocols are hard to beat."

"She sees TDF on it, and she'll bail on the search."

"You've heard of the adage of a woman scorned, right? She's not going to stop until she gets in."

Pissed off his protocol, did you? "What are we dealing with, Bennett? A protocol with a brain, or a protocol that thinks Kieran is hers and hers alone?"

"The latter, most likely. I..." Bennett paused.

"What?"

"I'd feel the same way in her position."

Crawley felt color creeping into his neck. "She's a program. A machine!"

"With an untested artificial-intelligence engine approved by the Terran Council for operations. We've had similar situations in our combat-equipment tests. This is why AI systems are not for general use. They cannot handle emotion. She's like a child, General—impulsive and afraid. If we can get a track on him, we intercept and shut her down."

"And put Kieran at considerable risk," Crawley said. The pause at the other end of the phone confirmed his fear that it was a low thing to say, but it had to be said. She had to know this was business.

"General," Bennett said slowly. "Get me close enough, and I can shut her down. I can download Kieran's batch file with the laser at two hundred meters, easily. If we lose him, we have enough data to do it all again."

"Not with the same genetic material," Crawley said. "I'm sorry, but you have to know that going into this, Berkeley. If we lose him, we can't replace him."

For ten seconds, there was no sound but a few pops of static. "I'll take that risk."

"How long until she finds you?"

"A couple of hours, more or less. I'll be ready and will delay her as long as I can. When I get a track, I'm planning to move, with your approval."

Crawley reached for a tablet on his bedside table. Eyes lingering on the Sydney skyline, he made a few taps on the tablet. "I have an *Excalibur*-class transport for you at Gatwick. We'll stage you somewhere up north in case the Terran Council is watching you. I suggest you get there and get aboard. We may not have much time."

The chairman's comm suite buzzed to life in the midst of a meeting with the premier of India. *It never fails,* he thought with a straight face. The premier did not object to her taking the call. Then again, he understood the rules. Inside the Operations Center of the Terran Council, a ringing phone meant something significant was happening.

Penelope Neige answered the call. "Yes. You're certain?"

There was a long pause, so much that the premier began to feel uncomfortable watching her. She reminded him of a bartering shopkeeper in the bazaars of Delhi. He'd seen eyes like that before in his childhood amongst the million other orphans from Bangladesh. Forced to go inland, to higher ground, he'd promised himself to keep climbing—always keep climbing.

Neige snorted. "And if he leaves there? What then?"

A politician was supposed to always wear a straight face. The opposition could be ripping off fingernails, but the trained leaders of the world always maintained perfect composure. The premier sat with his mouth open far enough that it could catch flies and took ten seconds to gain his composure in time to meet her questioning eyes.

"I don't give a damn! He's been out of contact for weeks. If he's made any progress whatsoever, my orders stand. Make contact with the subject, and hold him until the strike team arrives. You will terminate him immediately and secure the remains. Is that clear?" Neige glanced up at him. The blazing eyes of a killer faded immediately into something shrewder and more dangerous. She smiled with her shark's teeth.

"Now, where were we?"

CHAPTER TWENTY ONE

I OPENED THE DOOR TO MURPHY'S and hesitated in the small foyer. The air was redolent with the scents of stale beer and cabbage. Like the other buildings I could see in the tight downtown streets, the establishment was long and narrow. A few tables sat near the plate-glass front window, but the far wall was nearly all taken up by the bar. Tables and chairs were tightly packed around a small, empty stage. The partying would begin in a few hours, as it did every night, and last until first light. Unkempt teenagers swept the floors and wiped the tables from the night before. In a booth toward the back wall and kitchen doors, there was only one other customer: a burly, tattooed man in a black-leather vest. He waved an artificial arm. Even with confirmation, I did not recognize him. I raised my chin to acknowledge him, and the lone bartender called over to ask what I was drinking.

There was a white coffee mug in Mick's hand, and a bottle of whiskey sat on the table.

"Coffee—black, please." As I approached the booth, the older man stood up and towered over me. I extended a hand, which he shook with the strong, sure grip of his artificial hand. The silver articulated metal looked like nothing I'd ever imagined, but it flexed and rotated like the real thing. "You must be Mick."

Mick smiled. The swirling tattoos on his face curled and twisted as his lips moved, as though his entire face was a moving canvas. "Figured you wouldn't remember me. You seem a sight better than the last time I saw you."

My coffee came before I could respond with anything other than a grunt. Hot, strong, and bitter, the coffee far exceeded the weak shit I'd brewed at Chastity's apartment. "I don't know what to say."

"You don't have to say a thing," Mick drawled like a West Virginia miner. "You asked me for some help, and I figured I'd give it to you." His shoulders rolled in massive heaving movements as he shrugged. The man easily stood six and a half feet tall and weighed three hundred pounds. I guessed he was in his sixties but in phenomenal shape.

"Why?"

Mick tilted his head toward his right arm. The metal arm contrasted with the dark wood of the bar, faintly gleaming in the dim lights. "Soldiers stick up for each other."

He poured a shot of whiskey into my coffee that I barely noticed and didn't object to. "When did you serve?"

"Got out about two years ago." Mick touched his mug to mine. "Spent twelve years in the Terran Defense Force. Walked on five planets, six moons, and a few asteroids. It nearly killed me."

His voice was quieter, almost soft. I studied his eyes and knew he'd seen more than most people—things no one wanted to ask about and he wouldn't want to talk about. *The memories that weigh down souls.* A line came up from memory. "You've seen the elephant, huh?"

Mick laughed. "Hardly. When I met you, I knew you had. But not from my time."

"Yes." I took a deep sip of coffee and felt a few more mental tumblers click into place. The last year I remembered seeing was 2016. We'd ushered it in at a friend's house with a massive predeployment party. I'd kissed a girl at the stroke of midnight, and she'd responded hungrily. Then she'd left with my best friend. "I think I died in 2016. Afghanistan."

Mick snorted. "What a shithole. When the war broke out again, in 2018, it was bad until people in the civilized world finally realized that no one in history had ever controlled that place. The people there didn't want to be modern. Hell, most of them needed to be punched in the face."

He thought for a moment. Try as I might, my shattered memories of Afghanistan were much the same. I didn't see anything funny about it. Mick's smile told me more. "You've been there?"

"Let's say I've heard some really horrible stories about that place."
Mick's lips were a tight white line. "No. My grandfather had a memory transfer, an imprint, in the war. It's a bit different than what you got. His ancestor, an uncle of my great-great-grandfather, fought there and did very well for himself. Led his platoon through a full deployment in the nastiest fighting of the second Afghan conflict in 2021, won a Silver Star, and promptly came home and shot himself in the head. Left behind a devastated family that never really recovered."

"And your grandfather remembered all of that?" I shuddered. What would the rest of my memory unleash?

"Nothing specific at all. He went looking for facts before the Terran Council banished all of the imprints at the end of the war."

"Why'd they do that?"

Mick shrugged and lowered his voice. "Imprints were seen as a threat. It was better that they left."

"Where did they go?" A place with people like me sounded like heaven, in a way.

"After the Greys. Nobody's heard from them in fifty years."

Given the technology around me, I could put two and two together. The imprinted soldiers were long dead, and that was likely another reason why I was there. "Why did you get out?"

Mick twitched his head toward his artificial arm again. "This was a major part of it. I could've gone back, maybe would've changed specialties, but I decided not to." He squinted, and there was a pain in his eyes that the facial tattoos could not even begin to hide.

Sipping my coffee, I needed to know why he'd left the service. He represented a tiny minority of people from this day and age that'd actually served in the military, and he'd left it behind without a second thought. "Why?"

"It wasn't the same army I joined."

"What changed?" I asked. "Surely you knew what you were getting into?"

Mick chuckled. "Don't we all? You train with weapons because you're likely to have to use them one day. I expected all of that. What I didn't get was the chickenshit leadership."

Chickenshit? Mally?

<<A derisive term thought to have originated in World War Two. Chickenshit implies a focus on the smaller, unimportant things. I need to speak with you on other matters.>>

Not right now. Resting my arms on the table, I leaned over my coffee and let the aroma fill my nostrils for a moment. The whiskey was muted, but there. I looked up at Mick, knowing he needed to talk. "How bad was it?"

"Back in the Great War, they had a bunch of inexperienced leaders, but with a few guys like my Pops, we did all right. We trained and led troops who wanted to be there and do their part. That lasted until the first few major engagements with radical human sects here on Earth and a couple of insurrections out on the Rim. After everyone realized that another war was possible, there were thousands of desertions. The Terran Defense Force was not able to be a volunteer force. So the TDF started pulling combat forces from undesirable places. From those places, what do you get?"

"Undesirable soldiers."

"Exactly." Mick nodded his head. "So they started raising disciplinary standards. You know what that did? Started making commanders and leaders think they could whip and beat soldiers into submission. Some of them did it really well because they could be trusted and respected. The leaders, I mean. The majority of others? Shit, all they did was push troops in front of them and direct them into battle. They slaughtered millions of men and women in that system. The Greys jumped out of the system, and nobody knows where they went. After weeks of losing, we kicked their ass on one small planet, and they jumped away like scared rabbits. We haven't heard anything since, and the TDF hasn't gotten any better."

"Those few leaders—the ones who could be trusted and respected—was it beating soldiers that made it work for them?"

"Nothing like that, Kieran."

I blinked. He knew my name, too. *Everybody knows something about me.* "Then what was it?"

"They fought as hard as the men they led. When you're doing that, it generates respect and trust. If you don't do that, you're hated. Hatred leads to bad things in combat—accidents that aren't really accidents and the like."

My throat tightened as he talked. *Am I really a product of this type of establishment? What are they hoping to do with me?* "I get that, but why me?"

Mick sighed. "Those leaders did much better than everyone else. They took care of their people." Mick sipped more coffee and rolled his head back on his shoulders. A white scar marred the right side of his neck and ran down to the shoulder in jagged, gnarled stripes. "We understood what it meant to train, to lead, and to fight. People these days just don't get it. We were supposed to train soldiers, get them to fight like we did, and it failed miserably."

I'd seen the answer in Esperance, in my friends' faces when Stick died, but I asked, "How so?"

The light in Mick's eyes went soft as they began to glisten. "My lieutenant was fresh from the TDF Academy on Ceylon. He was a complete idiot, but at least he let me do my job. We succeeded in combat where some of our sister units failed. Our troops responded to orders and carried them out because we gave them a complete intent. They knew what we expected them to do, and they did it. We did that because we cared about them. I remember the names of all fifty-two I lost in a stupid training accident because our higher headquarters didn't remember our position. They dropped four full batteries of artillery fire on us. That was the last straw." He paused and used a meaty hand to gently brush a tear from his tattooed cheek. "I loved all of them like brothers and sisters. I lost my arm trying to rescue my closest friend. I could have saved him and a few others if my lieutenant hadn't fired the door shut."

"One of my first memories was about a kid I couldn't save." I shook my head. "Remembered him while pulling another kid out of the surf in Australia. I think his name was Erik, but I can't be sure of it or how he died. I just know it was under my watch."

"What else do you remember?"

Taking a breath, I recounted my dream about the tank ambush and the improvised explosive device. Mick said nothing as I went through it, only nodding his head and snorting in agreement, a small smile on his face.

"That's the only real dream I've had like that."

"The dreams aren't real. Well, some of the things you see, people and such, are. You won't remember a lot of specifics beyond that, but it sounds like some things, like firing a weapon properly, you'll do without even thinking about it. My grandfather did that kind of stuff all the time."

"There's so much I don't know. The soldier whose face I saw in the surf—I can't remember his name at all, but I remember that tank crew perfectly."

Mick lowered his chin and stared at me. "You're okay with not knowing how you died?"

"Is there any good memory of death?" I chuckled. "Not remembering the specifics sucks."

Mick grunted. "And how does knowing a lot of general stuff and no specifics really feel, Kieran?"

"I wonder if I did everything that I could."

"Then you get it." Mick straightened his back with a deep breath. The bell on the bar door tinkled, and the first patron shuffled up to the empty bar and parked himself on a stool. Mick watched him for a moment and waved down a waiter for more coffee. "The senior officers now won't listen. 'Finite control' is what they call it. You do exactly what they say no matter what. Bastards. They believe they're playing with toy soldiers. It's no way to live."

"So why bring me back?"

"I don't know. Maybe someone is trying to do something right. That's why I'm here."

"This is a pep talk?" I smiled, and Mick returned it.

"No." Mick rubbed a hand over his slick scalp. "That's not why I'm here. You needed to hear it from someone who's kinda been there—that's true. But I'm here because you asked me for something a few days ago. You don't remember that?"

"I wish I did." I expected Mally to respond, but she was still quiet.

"The night we met, you asked me where I was from, and I told you it didn't exist anymore. Do you remember that?"

Head down in thought, I tried and failed to conjure the memory. *How drunk was I?* "No, sorry."

Mick laughed, a great booming noise. "I'm not surprised. You were barely able to sit on the barstool. When I told you that where I was from didn't exist anymore, you said you could relate. I told you my family lived up in the mountains of Tennessee before they made a nature preserve out of it. One of the biggest in Columbia. It's called the Franklin Preserve. They named it that because there'd been a movement—"

"In the eighteenth century, to have it become the State of Franklin," I blurted. "Is that right?"

"Dead on. That's where my family is from."

If I hadn't been seated, I'm sure my knees would have given out. The sense of Tennessee being my home had never been stronger. "Mine, too."

"That's what you said that night. So, I told you I'd get you something to help you find your home, if you can." Reaching into his vest, he pulled out a large paper folded like an accordion—a map, coated in thick plastic but still foldable. "They made these as a commemorative in 2154, when the Terran Council dedicated the preserve. They started removing all of the buildings and structures in 2106 when the remains of Oak Ridge were cool enough. That's when I was born. Took them less than fifty years, but they got almost everything out of there."

"Almost?"

Mick shrugged. "Some things like dams and bridges stayed so people could enjoy the scenery when nature rebounded. A few roads but nothing like it used to be."

"Can I see it?" I got the feeling Mick had been through hell to get it for me.

Mick chuckled. "Of course. It's from the library."

I glanced at the bar and met the eyes of the lone patron through the mirror. Mick caught my glance and looked at the bar. The man turned away.

"Nosy bastard."

Unfolding the map, I saw that the eastern third of the state of Tennessee had been circled in red marker. "That's the boundary?"

"Yeah, surrounded by a fifteen-foot fence to keep most of the bigger game in." Mick pointed to a few ticks along the boundary. "These are entry points. Not all of them are manned with park rangers or game wardens, but they still record you entering and leaving the preserve. The limit for a stay is thirty days. After that, they come after you."

"And that?" I pointed to a star near the center of the preserve.

"A small supply-transport terminal—no passengers there unless you have a diplomatic pass. You go into the preserve on foot with only what you can carry on your back. Makes it less likely that you're going to foul up anything."

"Can I take this?"

Mick chuckled. "I borrowed it from the library. My sister is a data-collections technician there. I have to get it back to her today. Take a picture of it."

"Take a picture?" I squinted, but when Mick pointed to his head, I felt like a complete idiot. *Mally, can you commit this to memory?*

<<Done. Is there something specific about it you want to know?>>

Not right now. I'll spend some time studying it.

<<Chastity has completed her session and is on her way here.>>

I reached over and shook Mick's hand again. "Thank you, Mick."

"You're welcome, Kieran." Leaning back against the dark wood of the booth, he pointed at the door. "Here comes Chastity."

"She's early." The crawling feeling in my stomach worked its way across my face.

"If you don't want to be around her, get out of here." Mick picked up his coffee mug. "Never, ever let a woman fuck up your life."

He was right. I watched Chastity bouncing down the street like a tornado clad in pink leopard skin. She sauntered through the door toward us, with a wide sneer on her face, and I made my decision. Arranging to meet here had been a mistake. As she closed the distance, she smirked at me. None of this was going to end well.

Ten feet away, she started yelling. "What in the hell do you think you're doing?"

I looked at Mick, whose face was impassive, and then back into the maw of a harpy. Gone was the cute pixie I'd woken up to. She obviously did not want to lose my never-ending credit. The map in my hands meant the end of her free ride. "I paid my bill, and I'm leaving," I said.

"Like hell!"

Wrapping my fingers around the warm coffee mug, I wished that I had poured more whiskey in it. "Yes, I am. I'm leaving Memphis today. I paid my bill and tipped you. What more do you want from me?"

She chewed on her lower lip for a moment. The effect almost like that of a cow chewing cud. "I want 20 percent."

"Fine." I shrugged. "We were having a conversation."

"I'm not leaving until you give me my credits."

<<Done. The gentleman at the bar has initiated neural scanning, which I am blocking. His protocol appears to be Terran Council issued. Please use caution, Kieran.>>

Opening my palms, I smiled. "Done. Check your balances."

"I said thirty!" She pointed a painted nail at me.

Mick rumbled to life. "He paid you twenty, whore. Get out of here."

"Fuck you, Mick, you piece-of-shit broken veteran! Nobody wants you around here!"

Shooting to my feet before Mick, I gestured him back down into his seat and faced Chastity. Lowering my voice, I asked, "What do you want, Chastity? What will make you leave here now and never look back?"

Sneering like a hyena, Chastity stared through me. "You can't buy me off, Kieran! I've got something you want."

"What is that?"

The man at the bar watched us intently. One hand stayed in his jacket pocket.

"Lots of stuff you want. Like, all kinds of soldier information and all that."

Blinking, I stepped closer. "What did you say?"

"Your protocol tapped me, and she left a bunch of data spillage. I've got a shitload of information you'd love to have."

<<She is lying. I did tap her neurals, but she has no data other than connection information. She undoubtedly thinks she has something valuable, but there is no record of it within my files.>>

"I'm not buying anything back from you. I paid for my services, Berkeley."

Her eyes widened. "Who the fuck is Berkeley? You said you loved me, you cheating sonofabitch!"

The slap brought a quick explosion of red into my vision, and the heat of her hand on my face felt hotter than the sun for an instant. My head had turned toward the bar, toward the customer. He'd left his seat and was walking toward me, hand still inside his jacket. Chastity was screaming incoherently in front of me, and she slapped the side of my head again, right on my ear. Mick stepped between us, blocking her next set of blows.

The man stepped up, hand still in his jacket. "You some kind of special person? A soldier, I hear?"

I nodded. Chastity stopped screaming and stepped over to the side of the stranger, hands on her hips. The pose almost made me laugh. Instead, I squared my shoulders to him and felt immediately better as Mick stood up next to me.

"That's right, I am. Who are you?"

"Nobody." His shit-eating grin made me sick. "I've got orders not to do anything to you, but there's plenty that I want to say."

<<Now would be a good time to run. He has alerted others.>>

I blinked Mally's words away and looked at the man. Whoever he was, he knew something I didn't. "Say what you have to say."

"You're a coward, whenever you came from. The only reason you and your kind were celebrated was because everyone pitied you. Poor little soldier. Can't make a decision for themselves, so they listen to others like stupid animals. The generals sent you out to do the things they didn't want to do. Poor baby. Makes my heart bleed for you."

"Like you could do any better." There was a hint of anger in my voice. I wished for the anger to grow, knowing full well that my body would do only what it needed to.

The stranger squinted, acting tough. "You saying I'm a coward, boy?"

"Worse." I swallowed. "If I'm a coward, you're nowhere near as good as I am. You talk a good game, buddy, but when it comes down to it, you couldn't fight your way out of a wet paper bag."

The man sneered. "We don't need your kind around here. The way I see it, the only good soldier is a dead soldier."

Mick rumbled to life. His mechanical fist clenched, and he stepped toward the man. "What did you say?"

"Yeah!" Chastity snapped. "Now give me my money, Kieran..." As if in slow motion, Chastity's eyes rolled up into her head. She fell in a heap, head crashing into the floor with a thud.

"What did you do?" The man drew his hand from his jacket. There was a flash of metal. It could have been a gun, but I lost sight of it as Mick stepped in and leveled the man with a single blow.

Mick pushed my backpack into my hands and shoved me toward the door. "There'll be more of them! Go!"

Starting toward the door, I looked back at my friend. "What about you?"

"I'll be all right. Just go!"

<<He is right. Your attacker carried an immobilizing device. There are reinforcements moving this way now. You have a thirty-second window to escape,>> Mally chimed as I hit the door of the bar and broke into a sprint.

Where do I go?

<<Turn left now. That man is directing the local authorities to follow you.>>

What happened to Chastity?

<<I terminated the connection I'd established with her neural network. She will eventually recover.>>

Eventually? I vaulted over an autocar. The two inhabitants stared in disbelief at me flying over the roof like a hurdler.

<<Rapid disconnection usually triggers a catatonic state that will persist for a few days. She will then enter a waking coma, from which she will fully recover in six to eight months.>>

Six to eight months? God, Mally, how could you do that to her?

<<You are aware that when things are necessary to be done, they need to be done, no matter the consequences.>>

Will I ever find someone that I don't end up hurting?

<<The man who confronted you was an operative sent to identify you and hold you there.>>

What? By whom?

<<The Terran Council. I have no more information than that.>>

Why would they want to kill me? They're the ones responsible for bringing me back!

<<At this point, Kieran, there is no one you can trust except me.>>

She was right. I should have listened to her from the start. I wanted away from all of it—the future and the people in it. A cold, sulfurous rain began to fall as I ducked into an alley and ran as hard as I could. At the end of the alley, a thoroughfare opened to the east, and I kept running past the squalor of Memphis. There were sirens behind me, and at each corner, robotic cameras watched my every turn. With Mally giving directions, I wove through the streets so that no one could possibly follow me. She urged me faster and always to the east toward the mountains and the preserve. An hour later, I jumped a six-foot fence without breaking stride. A doe, spooked, dashed in front of me, her fawn trailing on shaky legs. I twisted around the small deer and kept running.

Thirty miles away, the flat lands of the Mississippi River floodplain began to give way to gentle rolling hills, devoid of crops but filled with acres of trash in all directions. Thunder echoed above me as the rain intensified. Amidst the trash were thousands, maybe tens of thousands, of cars. *Recycling is all the rage now, Mally.*

<<It is. These yards are undoubtedly clearinghouses. As materials are needed, they can be picked from this location by suborbital shuttle and shipped anywhere in the solar system.>>

People need old cars on Pluto?

<<Do not be naive, Kieran. These hulks are carefully recycled for maximum usage. Everything can be reused, if it's done properly.>>

Even soldiers like me?

<<That is not a fair approximation.>>

It's the truth.

Mally did not respond, and I knew I was right. I found a rhythm and ran through the rainy afternoon. As I ran, I understood I'd been wrong to come back to an America that was no more, but I couldn't stop myself. Head down, I lengthened my stride and accelerated toward the Cumberland Plateau. With any luck, I wouldn't see a soul or have to speak to anyone. No one seemed to understand what I was and where I'd been except for the voice in my head, and everything I'd done seemed to be against her wishes. I was slowly but surely pushing her away, and she was the only one who cared for me.

I'm sorry, Mally. I've been an idiot.

<<There is no need to apologize, Kieran. I had a plan to extricate you from the situation if you failed to take action.>>

Was that guy right about things—about me? Are soldiers all dumb animals? Is that what Berkeley thought?

<<What do you think? Is being a soldier honorable?>>

Yes. Another group of sirens screamed to the south, but they faded as I ran into the wilderness.

<<Then you are justified in feeling the way you do. There are many like that man on Earth, but on the Rim, you will find men like him to be rare. What matters is how you feel about this life you've been given. Returning to Integration and going to war scares many sleepers away.>>

You think I should go? Defend all of this but never feel a connection to it?

<<You are connected to Esperance, Kieran.>>

Has Allan ever responded to my messages?

<<No. I have had severe difficulties maintaining contact since we arrived on this continent. I warned you about that.>>

She had, and as much as I understood it, I hated it. *Please let it be connection problems and not him ignoring me.*

<<Your friends are not ignoring you. They constitute at least one thing you would fight to protect. That realization is a critical part of your integration. In Esperance, you have friends as well as something you will not find here or anywhere else on Earth.>>

What's that? I asked, but I believed I already had the answer.

<<Peace.>>

The forest gave way to a wide corridor filled with dormant tall grass and scrub. In the middle, game trails meandered alongside a trickling creek. I followed to the northeast. I sucked in a deep breath as I ran, thankful for the voice in my head and knowing my heart was right, if broken. *You're my guardian angel, Mally.*

<<Something like that. Keep running.>> Mally cued up more music from my time, and I ran to the driving beat.

CHAPTER TWENTY TWO

CRAWLEY SLAMMED HIS OFFICE DOOR and hurried to the desk. With a tap, he brought up the secured-communications system and let the connection propagate.

There was worry on the young scientist's face. The curved fuselage of Crawley's personal exocraft appeared behind her. She was still in the air, en route to New York. "He left Memphis an hour ago with council authorities on his heels. The null-profile report triggered the Council Security Forces to action. Their lead agent tried to intercept Kieran."

"What happened?" Crawley asked.

"There was a confrontation. Kieran was able to escape, but the cyber prostitute suffered a cerebral hemorrhage from rapid disconnection, and the authorities collected her for interrogation."

Crawley frowned. "How serious is her brain damage?"

"They won't get much out of her. She has a one in ten chance of survival. I doubt they'll discover Kieran's progression before he integrates. Her brain is jelly for all intents and purposes."

"Any idea of his location?"

"He left Memphis over a periphery fence, heading east. I think it's safe to say we're not going to find him with Mally shut off to outside communications."

Given his course and speed, they could estimate position and send a team, but it was risky. "I want a definitive position before we do anything. What do we know?"

Bennett sucked in a breath and let it out. "He went to the bar to meet a former soldier."

Crawley smiled. "Our Memphis assets have pulled him in for questioning. The guy broke just about every rule in the book. He showed Kieran a map of the Franklin Preserve."

"Why did he do that?" Bennett licked her lips. "Let me guess: Kieran said he thought he was born in the mountains. The guy showed him a map of the Franklin Preserve, and Kieran went running. Anything else from the man?"

"Former soldier. Lost an arm at Tau Ceti Four." His team followed protocol to the letter, and former Sergeant First Class Mick Jensen would be on the moon within a few hours and headed outbound to Libretto or Styrah for his own protection. All without the council becoming aware of it.

Mick Jensen had played his role perfectly. It was too bad that his time as one of Crawley's assets on Earth had come to an end so soon, but there were several other former soldiers willing to help. Arranging the clandestine transports to get Bennett in and out of North America had been hell, but his team had made it happen. They'd need to do something about the prostitute, too. Crawley ran a hand through his hair and wondered how much longer he could keep up the subterfuge. Sooner or later, the council was going to know.

"General? I asked what our next step was. Do you want us to move on the Franklin Preserve?"

"No," Crawley replied. "They're likely watching everything in Columbia right now. When he hits the fence of the preserve, he'll set off the monitors."

Berkeley shook her head. "Mally won't let that happen. He'll pass into the preserve unhindered. She's paranoid enough to be a real threat to our finding him."

Crawley agreed. "We'll cross that bridge when we get there, so to speak. What's your status?"

"Ready to go in after him. I can be on the ground in the preserve in sixty minutes."

As tempting as it was to let the young woman fix the problem she'd helped to create, it was also too risky. He might need her services in the future. Crawley drummed his fingers on the desk for a moment as the plan came together. There was a way they could find Kieran and intercept him before the council did. "You're in New York?"

"Landing in ten minutes. I can move whenever we have a lock on him."

"Good." Crawley smiled with one corner of his mouth. Outside, the sun was rising on a beautiful Sydney morning. "We're likely going to have to go in and get him in a hurry."

The lowlands of the Mississippi River basin gave way to gentle hills that sloped up toward the majesty of the Cumberland Plateau as I ran. For two straight days, I pushed east, stopping only for water. I averaged twelve kilometers per hour—faster during daylight—except when I had to swim. The first time, I swallowed more of the Tennessee River than I could stomach. The water was cold, and the current pushed me farther north than I expected. The second crossing, a day later, was much easier. The rubble of the Watts Bar Dam made negotiating the river easy, though the smoldering coalfields between Harriman and Knoxville made for worse territory than I'd seen. My lungs burned with the noxious fumes until I skirted to the south. Even bio-enhancements had limits. The edge of the Franklin Preserve was no more than about eight hours away. After a short rest below a barren ridgeline, I descended into the night and kept running.

The next morning, I slowed to a jog and a shambling stumble on a winding dirt road along the edge of the Smoky Mountains. My stomach rumbled, and Mally warned me that I needed to consume calories of some type, and soon. There was no word from Berkeley, either. Mally told me that my message had gone through and was read, but Berkeley had not responded. *Figures,* I thought and kept running. My feelings for her were not returned. Disgust upset my stomach. The harder I ran, the more Berkeley's feelings for me didn't matter. What mattered was me. Given what I'd left behind in Memphis, I'd need every ounce of resolve to see this through.

The day dawned bright and cold. A breath of wind down from the mountains brought the smell of cooking sausage, and I followed it up the road into a dark mountain draw. The sun in that place wouldn't touch parts of the ground until late spring and maybe even summer. Any snow that fell would lie for weeks if not months. The persistent shade gave the frost-covered hills a grey appearance. A heavy fog layered the mountains, hovering just above the treetops. For the first time in days, I smiled.

"Foxfire," I croaked to the morning sky. I hadn't spoken to a soul since Mick. *Is he okay? Do I really want to know what happened when I ran away from Memphis?*

There was no immediate answer from Mally, as usual. Her answers were further and further apart. My cheeks flushed in embarrassment as I brushed away the thoughts of wasted time and futile pursuits. Memphis had been a mistake. There wasn't any sense in beating myself up about it. I had to forgive myself. It sounded so simple and was anything but that. I'd made mistakes, but I was nearing home. The foxfire called to me as loud as a trumpet and welcomed me back.

<<Do you mean the low-hanging fog? "Foxfire" is a colloquial term of Appalachia—>>

"The low-hanging fog, Mally. It's why these are called the Smoky Mountains." I chuckled and sniffed the wind again, my mouth watering. "We called it foxfire because the wild foxes are making small fires to cook their breakfast."

<<A myth.>>

"More like a story. Something to pass down to children. Young 'uns," I drawled with a laugh. The accent sounded funny and welcome at the same time. I'd never had much of one, but should the opportunity arise, talking like a native was possible—even three hundred years later, when the region had become a feral wasteland. I stuffed my hands into my pockets and walked up the curving road toward the source of the smell. "Mally, is there a house up this road?"

<<There is a dwelling, yes.>>

"A house or not?"

<<I am not sure I can define it. Current detailed imagery is not available.>>

"Guess I'll have to take a look for myself."

<<I do not recommend you do.>>

The spicy smell made my stomach rumble in anticipation. "There's food up there. I need to eat something substantial, Mally. I'm tired of ration bars."

<<You have a complete habitat packed, Kieran. The hexhab can provide you food within thirty minutes. Interacting with local persons could be dangerous.>>

"What is that supposed to mean?"

<<The Terran Council essentially forbids interaction with indigenous peoples in Appalachia. They are too wild to save.>>

"Like hell they are!" I swiped angrily at a low tree branch, scattering its remaining leaves on the forest floor. These were my people!

Setting up the hexhab and getting a decent night's sleep sounded good, as did a hot shower and clean, dry clothes. But being inside the damned thing would remind me of Berkeley. The scent of food called out to me, and saliva squirted into my mouth. I walked up the road, smiling and confident. This was the kind of interaction I'd been longing for. People close to my own ancestry. Similar values. Similar hospitality. I could trust them. It was going to be fine.

The shrieking of a young child broke the idyllic morning around me. I moved faster as the screaming continued. *What in the hell?* Jogging around a sharp corner in the dirt road, I skidded to a stop. Fifty meters ahead, a downy-haired boy—no more than ten years old—lay squalling, stark naked, in the road. Bones were clearly visible under his skin, and his distended belly showed all the signs of malnutrition. He shrieked a jumble of sounds and groans as he screamed and kicked. I started to walk toward him when movement caught my eye. Out of what appeared to be a rusted-out cylindrical camper, an old woman wearing a filthy floral-print dress stomped toward the boy in ill-fitting boots without laces. She spat a long rope of tobacco juice and proceeded to scream something equally incoherent.

Standing over the child, the old woman swatted his bony legs with a bare hand and then grabbed a flailing ankle. She dragged the naked boy off the road, through a cold mud puddle, and left him squalling at the rotted door of the camper. I didn't know if she'd seen me or not, and it really didn't matter. I was frozen to the spot in shock and disgust. The boy rolled out of the cold mud and tottered up the steps to the camper.

I took a step. "What in the hell is going on here?"

<<I tried to warn you, Kieran.>>

Continuing forward, I called out, "Hello? Can you help me?"

A rifle barrel came out of the small window of the trailer. A booming male voice screamed something that I couldn't quite make out.

Raising my hands, I kept moving. "Been walking a while, and I'm hoping you could—"

The rifle barrel swung toward me, and I ran. The crack came as I crossed the road, and a bullet whistled past my head and into a pine tree. As I ran up the hill and into the brush, a second crack echoed through the woods, and a bullet whizzed past my right ear. I crested the small hill and descended the opposite side at full speed. All thoughts of breakfast vanished as I fled. I wondered about the boy and what fate he would meet in this harsh new world. Compared to Australia, this continent seemed on the edge of barbarism and civil collapse with nothing of worth outside the massive farming operations.

The rest of the world is not like this, is it, Mally?

<<Only this continent, Kieran. You were warned several times.>>

At that moment, I got what Allan, Berkeley, and Mally had all been trying to tell me. I would find nothing here worth fighting for—nothing that would make any of this easier. Nothing that could make me want to stay, and nothing that would make me want to return to Integration. I ran flat-out for half an hour along the ridges before I came to the fence.

<<This is the Franklin Preserve.>>

Where are the nearest gates?

<<Going through a gate will alert others to your presence here. That is a dangerous course of action, Kieran.>>

How the hell am I supposed to get in there? I stared at the fence, easily three meters tall and topped with a row of razor wire that glowed a soft blue. *Is there a way to get under it?*

<<I am unable to determine how deep the fence is set in the ground.>>

The fence appeared to be almost brand new. The soft blue glow caught my eye. *Is it electrified?*

<<Only at the top level to prevent unauthorized entry.>>

The fence followed the ridgeline as far as the eye could see, to the northeast, but dropped down off the mountain and into a tight draw to the west. An outcropping of rock, moss covered and slick, shot up from the ground, twice as tall as the fence and a good thirty feet away.

<<What are you thinking?>>

I scrambled up the outcropping, confident that there was enough space along the top to get a running start. If my body was enhanced enough, the jump would be possible.

<<There is a gate two thousand meters to the west. I recommend that you use it.>>

But you said—

<<I will take care of it.>> Mally sounded irritated. <<I would rather assume risk than have you attempt to kill yourself.>>

For a brief moment, I replayed Chastity collapsing to the floor. Mally had taken care of her, too. Down the mountain, I walked in the deep leaves of early winter and saw the gate. A black bar across the top of the gate blinked with red-and-blue lights. A small antenna rose up through the trees. Aside from a small trash receptacle resting beside the fence, there was no sign of footprints or human activity. "That's how people know who goes in and out of the preserve?"

<<Yes. The scanner pulls identity off the neural network that all humans above the age of six have implanted.>>

And that's not what I have.

<<Exactly. You weren't deemed ready for a full neural connection. The results could have been disastrous. I need approximately 212 seconds to code myself to pass through the scanner.>>

What are you trying to do?

<<Appear as an anomalous contact.>> Mally paused. <<One hundred eighty seconds. Wait here, and go no closer.>>

A hundred feet from the gate, I waited and put my hands in my pockets. My stomach rumbled again, and I was daydreaming about food but not the atomically reconstructed food from a hexhab galley. The thought of Allan's fish tacos and cold beer made my mouth water.

<<Go.>>

I closed the remaining distance quickly and passed through the gate. A shrill chirp pierced the silent morning. Red lights flashed along the top of the gate. *Oh shit.*

<<Run.>>

What happened?

<<I do not know. The gate reported the anomalous entry and is calling for assistance. I'm attempting to shut it down.>>

I sprinted down the mountain into a tight, rocky draw. The steep slope gave way to rolling hills before I found myself climbing again. On the top of an almost-flat mountain ridgeline, I looked across the wilderness of the Franklin Preserve.

<<The gate stopped broadcasting. I believe it failed to connect with its parent server. I am too far away to be sure.>>

Kneeling on the ground, I listened to the woods for several long minutes, hearing nothing but the breeze and the distant sound of running water. I moved toward it. Down below, a thin grey ribbon snaked through the terrain. I listened carefully and felt myself moving toward the sound of rushing water. *What river is that, Mally?*

<<That river is called the Nolichucky. You are currently descending Cherokee Mountain, heading northwest. We should find a place to hide for the day.>>

I ran for a half hour before I came upon the river. *Is this far enough?*

<<Yes. I recommend you find a proper location and set up the hexhab. You need food and rest. I will camouflage the habitat accordingly and maintain security while you rest.>>

The forest on the far side of the river looked thicker—better for concealment. *Let me cross the river first. The terrain is better over there.*

<<Agreed.>>

The river was frigid and clear. I drank from it and splashed water on my face before I tightened the straps on my pack. With a deep breath, I stepped into the river and immediately realized I could be making a terrible mistake. The rushing water was cold and higher than I expected, which made fording the Nolichucky more difficult than crossing the wide, deep Tennessee River. As the icy water encircled my chest, I struggled for breath and felt my warmth rushing away with the swirling rapids. My feet slipped several times. With one particularly scary misstep, the water came up to my chin, and then my feet could not touch the riverbed at all. The pack on my back pulled me down like an anchor. Fatigue crashed over me in waves. For two days, I'd done nothing but run, and I'd consumed virtually nothing. I had no more energy. My head slid below the surface.

<<Sweep your arms over your head, and find the bottom with your feet. Then jump up and out.>>

I did as Mally said—three times in all—and finally stood in the river again. I sputtered a thank-you through trembling lips. As soon as my feet and legs could bear more weight and run, I ran deeper into the woods. Enhancements or not, hypothermia was a real concern. My shivering increased as my body tried in vain to warm itself. I had to get into the hexhab. Tossing off my pack, I grabbed the hexhab, found a spot in the trees, and pushed the button. While it filled with air and established its connections, I stripped out of my wet clothes. On the slightly warm rocks, I sat with my knees under my chin and rubbed my chest, hoping my clothes would dry a least a little. I gave up a minute later when the hexhab was fully inflated. Even in the mountains of Colorado, I hadn't been so cold. I went inside the tent before I could succumb to hypothermia. I threw my wet clothes into a receptacle and curled up under a generated blanket while the hexhab filled with hot air.

Lying on the floor, I questioned everything about my journey, especially the part after Berkeley disappeared. *Why am I not back in Australia? What am I still doing here?*

Sleep came before I found an answer.

The dreams came again. I welcomed them and hoped for a sign—something, anything to tell me I was on the right course and my travels hadn't been for nothing.

The humid summer evening descended like a wet blanket. The sun slid toward the western horizon, bathing the veranda of the old house in a warm yellow glow. Sitting on the wooden deck with its slats painted dull grey, I drank sweet tea from an artful glass ringed with bubbles and lipped with red. Condensation ran down the glass, cold and inviting, as I cradled it in my hands. I could smell the black walnut tree overlooking the garden just above the ever-present stench of tobacco from farther out in the fields.

"Kieran?" The old woman wore loafers with white socks under worn blue jeans and a flannel shirt despite the summer heat. A baseball cap, its lettering and brim sun bleached and worn looking, crowned her head. She smiled and patted the empty space on the wooden swing next to her. "Come sit next to your Aunt Ada."

The smell of cut grass came up from my feet. My white shoes were tinged with green from mowing the yard after baseball practice. Driving to the farm by myself for the first time had excited me beyond belief, but the quiet home always calmed me down. I sat on the swing and rocked with her, the rhythm of it comforting as a mother's heartbeat. The mountains covered the southern horizon and appeared blue in the late-evening sun. I'd forgotten how beautiful it was here. I'd forgotten too many things.

"You can't remember everything." She patted my bare knee with a gnarled hand. "Just remember the important stuff." Her accent was thick enough to be a brogue, the way the Scotch-Irish of Appalachia spoke. "That's why you're here."

"Here?" The tea was strong and sweet and good. "I don't know where I'm supposed to be."

"Family, Kieran." She chuckled. "That's what you are looking for, but it's not what you're trying to find."

She was right. My heart sank, and tears came to my eyes. "There isn't anyone else, is there?"

"Sure. There is family, but it's been too long. Things change, and the family trees twist into thickets and briars. You can keep digging, but it's painful, and you ain't going to find what you want to find."

The chant of cicadas came from the big trees on the other side of the barn. "They want me to fight. I don't know if I can."

"Because there's nothing here?" she said. "Honey, everywhere you look are places where your ancestors may have walked or slept or just dreamed about. If you'll look at it that way, everything here is familiar and worth fighting for, especially that girl you're sweet on."

The dream cut away to show Berkeley and the sun glinting in her hair. "I loved her, and she left me."

"She had her reasons. The time is going to come when you can ask her about them."

"But..." I paused. "Won't it be too late?"

Ada laughed and patted my knee again. "Kieran, it's never too late."

Heat rose up my neck and into my face. "I wasn't there when my mom died." The tears flowed again, and one drop raced down my cheek before Ada's finger swept it away. "I didn't say goodbye."

"Did you really want to say goodbye?"

"No. All I wanted to do was tell her that I loved her."

Ada nodded, the smile fading from her face. "She knew that, Kieran. So did your father and everyone you ever loved. You say you want to find family, find a reason to fight, but you really want love. Berkeley had that for you."

The sun began to sink into the horizon, and the light began to fade. The evening breeze came up like a cleansing breath and began to cool the air. "She did," I said with a sigh of acceptance.

"Then get to it," she said, and the swing stopped. I helped her stand, and she shuffled to the dented storm door and opened it. She looked at me for a long moment I wanted to frame like a picture. There was nothing but love in her face. "Time is wasting, Kieran. But if you want something, there is always time."

When I opened my eyes, night had fallen, and the soft light of a full moon cast shadows from the bare trees across the roof of the hexhab. I missed Berkeley for a heartbeat before telling myself that I hardly knew her. Giving her my heart had been foolish, and though the ache would fade, given time, it was real and constant. The scent of her no longer lay upon my pillow, but I imagined it with every breath. Try as I might, my body longed to feel her next to me. I wanted to tell her I was sorry, but I had no idea what to be sorry for, if anything.

<<Are you all right?>>

Sorry I woke you, Mally.

<<You are implying that I sleep. After four months, you should know better. Can I assist you?>>

Just thinking.

<<You are thinking about her.>> There was a subtle hostility in her voice. <<The last five days have been a significant strain on you, not just physically. You really should sleep.>>

You're worried about me.

<<You called me your assistant and conscience. Caring for your

well-being is important to me. Without the power your body provides, I would not exist. Existence, even the shred of it, is the meaning of life, Kieran.>>

Knowing that Mally depended on me for her life sobered me. At least someone—and Mally was clearly a *someone*—depended on me. I wondered what my shred of existence would be as I drifted back to sleep, the full Tennessee moon shining down through the hexhab's canopy with cold, indifferent light.

"Mally, does this place have a name?" I whispered aloud, and the softness of my voice startled me.

<<You are in an area once known as Dry Creek. Historically, the people of this area were poorly educated and lived below the poverty line until the mid-twentieth century. During the prohibition years, this area was overrun with illegal corn-liquor distillation.>>

"Moonshine." I studied the moon and imagined the face smiling back at me. Like a voice whispering the story into my ear, the memory came. The story had been handed down to me. My grandmother had been a teacher, educating children for more than fifty years. Fresh from the teaching college, called the "normal school" long before it became a university, she found work teaching in a one-room schoolhouse in the Dry Creek area. The poor community took great pride in its schoolhouse, to which she delighted. Tucked into the sharp draws of Cherokee Mountain, Dry Creek sat under several ridges that blocked all but the most direct noonday sun.

One day, a few of her male students asked to take her hiking up the ridges. Being the same age as them but already a certified teacher at seventeen, she went and learned "rocking." The boys would heft and heave large rocks to the edge of the ridgeline and set them rolling down the hills with shouts and laughter. She had a great time until she came home to her host family.

She'd taken a room with Jim Scanlon and his wife Emma. When my grandmother came home, Mister Scanlon, as he preferred to be called, was sitting in a handmade rocking chair spitting "terbaccy" accurately into a spittoon five feet away.

"Missy, did you have a good time this afternoon?" His voice was soft and kind but his face stony. He called her "Missy" instead of her given name the way some men used "darling" or "sweetheart."

Beaming, she told him about the grand time she'd had on the ridges. He watched her and didn't smile or make a move until she was finished.

"Missy, don't you ever go doing that again. You and them boys ruined three families' way of life this afternoon."

She and her students had destroyed the moonshine stills of three different families, jeopardizing their income for the coming winter. Bursting into tears, she apologized over and over again. Mister Scanlon patted her arm and told her that it would be okay, that the community would help the families, but that if she ever wanted to have that kind of fun again, she should do it someplace else. She avoided doing it again, as much from embarrassment as from newfound maturity.

Not long after that, she met up with a great-uncle who owned ranch land in New Mexico. She moved west and fell in love with a widower raising six children on his own, and they had one more child: my mother. My whole family came from there except for me. They'd moved to Tennessee because of family and work, and I was born here. I'd come full circle—that much I knew.

CHAPTER TWENTY THREE

THIS TIME, I RECOGNIZED IT as a dream. Berkeley was there, and the weather was warm in the high country. Eleven Mile Reservoir was a blanket of shimmering diamonds in the early-morning sunshine. I sat on the rocks, a lame excuse for a fishing pole in my hands, and the warm sunshine hammered down on me, and my eyes closed. The pink-and-purple splotches behind my eyelids exploded in random fireworks that made me smile. Her hand was on my back, gentle and warm at the base of my neck.

The breeze down from the slopes of Pikes Peak was cool. Midsummer perfection. It was the kind of day best spent in a hammock or lying in the cool grass under fragrant trees—the kind of day where time stood still.

"What are you going to do, Kieran?"

I shrugged. "I don't know."

"But you are going back, right? You're going to go back to Sydney for integration, aren't you?"

There were tears on her cheeks. Her blue eyes were wide and frightened, lower lip trembling slightly as I touched her face with my fingertips. "Why are you crying?"

"If you go back, you're going to war. A war we're probably not going to win. You'll be dead before a year is up."

"That's a risk I have to take."

"Why?" She sniffled. "You're not even from this world. Why would you care enough to fight for it?"

Looking out across the millions of diamond-like reflections from the lake, I answered, “Because they need me—those soldiers out there. We have to protect each other and watch out for each other because no one else will.”

“What about me?” Her eyes narrowed. “What about fighting for me? Am I not good enough for you?”

“Why would you care, Berkeley?” I said, though she was already fading. “Why would you care about me? I’m just—”

“Nobody.” I sat up, completely naked, inside the hexhab. The sun was high in the sky. *Surely I slept more than an hour?*

<<You slept a total of approximately twenty-one hours and seven minutes, minus the thirty-seven minutes you spent awake last night. I attempted to wake you three separate times, but you would not respond. There is food available. You should eat, Kieran. It’s time to move.>>

I touched the soft panels for some breakfast and hot tea. A shower invigorated me and left me ready for the day. My clothes were dry, and I slipped them into my pack. New clothes brought a smile to my face. I felt clean for the first time in a while. “Mally, I’m very close to integration, aren’t I?”

<<Kieran, you are well aware that I cannot help you.>>

“I know that. But I’m reasonably sure that something is very close. Within a few miles at best.”

<<I cannot confirm anything. I am sorry.>>

I almost said something sarcastic but held back because Mally would have been offended again. I needed her too much to let her be mad at me for being sophomoric. After I collapsed the hexhab, I started walking north and slightly to the east. The wide, lush valley was a palette of early-winter browns and tans as I moved easily through the light forests and wilting grasses with no dwellings or fences anywhere in sight.

There really weren’t many places as beautiful as this. Without a trace of humanity, the wilderness felt more vibrant and alive. I made reasonably good progress around ponds and streams that fed into the Nolichucky. I broke from a tree line and looked up a long, shallow hill. In the distance, a stand of five enormous trees in a straight line meant a road had been nearby. I started walking toward it. My heart began to pound. I remembered that landscape better than anything I'd seen since waking in Sydney.

The closer I got to the trees, the more familiar the small knoll became. To the west of it, the ground sloped away drastically and then shot right back up another hill with a tree line almost a quarter-mile long. The hillside had once been pasture, but now trees had begun to grow on it. Eventually, the whole area would be deciduous forest again. On the knoll, I walked under an ageless black walnut tree and stumbled upon the stacked-rock foundation of what had been a springhouse. *How did I know that?*

I slung my pack to the ground and took a heaving, deep breath with my hands on my knees so I did not collapse. The dizziness passed, and I turned back to the east. The tall grasses held the remnants of a foundation. A house had once stood here—not mine but a significant place in my life. We called it the farm—my grandmother's childhood home. The home from my dream. The western hill once had a tree with my initials carved in it. I had memories of running around on hot summer days with my cousins, hands sticky from picking grapes and apples. I recalled the taste of cold spring water washing away the sawdust when my father and I cut firewood in the forest. Tears streamed down my face, and I let them fall. This was the closest I would come to my family, the one constant in our lives. This place was home. I felt empty, aware that while this was my home, or as close as I could get to it, there was nothing here for me.

From my dream, I remembered the tin-roofed house with the wide veranda and the gentle rhythm of the porch swing.

"It's not there anymore, mate." I heard Allan's voice in my head and chuckled in the soft breeze.

You cannot go home again.

<<Would you like to talk, Kieran? I will listen.>>

No, Mally. Burying my face in my hands, I sat and cried.

The breeze grew cold after an hour. I sat on the rocks and twirled long grass in my fingers, peeling the layers to expose the sweet white pulp inside, the taste firing more memories as I sucked on a blade and watched the day pass. I could hear the voices of my cousins as we played in the grass, threw black walnuts at metal lawn chairs, and pulled apples from the trees. I sat and wept. Everything manmade had been picked clean from the landscape, but the memory was there and untouchable. Down the hill, tobacco grew in wild clumps. Things had changed, but to the trained eye, things were really the same.

The hum of a subatmospheric transport caught my attention as it descended toward the northeast, reminding me that I was far from any semblance of my old life. All that I remembered was gone, but I carried the memory alive and fresh in my mind. That alone could take me anywhere I wanted to go. It was time to go, maybe all the way back to Esperance. I did not know anymore. I hoisted the pack to my shoulders and got to my feet slowly, my legs aching from sitting for too long.

"Mally, how close is that support terminal?"

<<Approximately fifty-six kilometers to the exact center of the preserve atop Bays Mountain.>>

I started walking toward a notch at the edge of the forest where a road once lay. "I'll find a place to camp tonight, then."

Mally chimed, <<I can request an immediate transport for you. This is a service you have not used, Kieran.>>

Looking back at the remains of the farm, I wiped my eyes a final time. "And you can book a seat for me back to Esperance?"

<<Yes. It will take me six minutes to confirm the transport for two days from now.>>

"Six minutes?" A memory surfaced like a lightning strike.

I'd gone to Jump School, the Army's Basic Parachutist Course. That wouldn't have been so bad except that it was south Georgia in the middle of summer, where the temperature was ninety-something with an equal amount of relative humidity. Basically, the only time I wasn't soaked with sweat was on the nights we went to the air-conditioned movie theater. "Misery" was a good way to describe the weather in the South on most days except when the door to the C-130 Hercules was open, and the rushing wind off its wings filled the open cabin.

"Six minutes!" the jumpmaster screamed above the wind.

"Six minutes!" we jumpers screamed back.

In sleeker parachutes than our heavy bags, the jumpmasters all wore combat fatigues and smooth, clear goggles. They eschewed the protective helmets the rest of the jumpers wore. Being a jumpmaster must have been the best of both worlds. Across the tight aisle sat a Naval Academy midshipman with eyes as wide as dinner plates behind his thick glasses. His terror made me calm. I could do it just to lead him out the door, although I knew I wouldn't have much choice anyway. I was going to be the first man out of the aircraft. If I didn't jump, they'd throw me out.

The jumpmaster stepped forward to where we were sitting and began the litany, every syllable enunciated against the screaming winds from the open doors and the roaring of the propellers. "Outboard personnel! Stand up!"

The jumpers with their backs to the exterior of the aircraft stood up.

"Inboard Personnel! Stand up!" I stood up and took my place at the front of the line.

With his index finger crooked like a crude hook, the jumpmaster yelled, "Hook up!"

I reached up and snapped the hook that connected my static line to a thick metal cable running the length of the fuselage. The hooked line attached to me would pull the parachute out. Hopefully. I pushed a metal pin through the hook to protect it from coming off the cable. I tugged on the line, and the hook didn't move. I looked at the jumpmaster.

"Check static line!"

The jumpers behind me quickly checked their static lines. From the hook, the line draped over my right shoulder and then wove back and forth across the exterior of my parachute pack. I couldn't see it much less check it—the job was up to the jumper behind me. Every jumper checked the person in front of them to make sure that the line was not covered by anything green. The parachute pack and its straps were green. Green over yellow meant the static line would not deploy and then pull the parachute out of the pack. A jumper could hang off the static line behind the aircraft. Not exactly the way anyone would want to do it, and the static-line check put each jumper's life literally in the hands of the person behind him. I never doubted the guys behind me. From the back of the line, the last jumper would slap the ass of the next person in line and say, "Okay!"

It seemed like an eternity passed before the chain reached me, but the slap came, and I screamed, "All okay, jumpmaster!"

The jumpmaster gave me a thumbs-up and stomped over to the open door of the aircraft. Holding onto the side of the hatch, he stuck his head outside into the breeze. I really wanted a pair of goggles like the ones he wore.

He looked at the line of jumpers. "One minute!"

"One minute!" we screamed back in unison. All of the fear of jumping from a perfectly good airplane had been trained out of me. I wanted nothing more than to get out that door.

"Thirty seconds!" the jumpmaster screamed at us.

"Thirty seconds!"

The jumpmaster stepped away from the door and motioned me forward. "Stand in the door!"

Passing him my static line, I did a left face and grasped the sides of the aircraft's troop door. Knees bent, with one foot behind and one foot on the exit platform—the toe of my combat boot in the breeze—I felt the wind hammer against my fingers, and I relaxed. I was ready to go. The massive wing of the airplane bounced in the thick, humid air as fields and forests slid by below. At 1,250 feet off the ground, the big aircraft probably doing a little over 150 knots, the bouncing wing struck me as odd and distracted me from looking down or allowing fear a port of entry.

The glaring red light to my left switched to green. The jumpmaster slapped my ass and screamed, "Go!"

I jumped, pulling my hands onto my reserve parachute. The wind knocked me sideways. The horizontal stabilizer of the transport aircraft shot past. I counted in great screaming gasps, making it to "three" before my parachute jerked open. There were no problems when I checked the unfurled canopy. I looked down between my feet and howled like a madman. I'd gone because I loved it, and I loved being in the Army. Risks were minimized, all possible outcomes trained for. I'd thought that everything in the Army would be the same. I'd been wrong about all of it—except for the friends I would make and the ones I would bury.

"Mally, delay that transport to Esperance by another day. There is one more place I need to see."

<<What is the destination?>>

"Just a minute. I grew up near here, and the house where I lived—

that place is obviously gone now. I get that. But there's something else." I paused for a moment and tried for the millionth time to imagine the world I'd left behind. "Is there anything manmade still standing in this area other than the support terminal?"

Mally didn't respond immediately. <<There is a large tourism center near the hub. Sponsored tours run throughout the preserve year-round. In addition to those facilities, there are several structures and memorials.>>

I blinked. My knees quaked, and I leaned against a sycamore tree. I remembered one of the memorials, a cemetery that once had a baseball field located right next to it—not close enough for a foul ball to find its way into hallowed ground, but I remembered seeing the gravestones while I played center field. I didn't learn what it was for several more years. When I did, the effect was profound. The name came in a flood of memory. "What happened to Mountain Home? When the Franklin Preserve was created, was it removed?"

<<No. Mountain Home is now a botanical garden. The property is cared for by a private party.>>

"Can I go there?"

<<If you wish, Kieran, but I cannot recommend it. The effect on you could be disastrous. I am concerned about your well-being.>>

Walking through the thigh-high grass, I looked back at where the farmhouse once stood and shrugged. "I don't know, Mally. I'm not even sure why I need to go there, but I do."

But that wasn't the truth, and Mally didn't bother to respond. I'd been unsuccessful at love and at finding the home I'd once had, and the only thing I remembered being worth fighting for—my country—was a shattered mess. My home had become a beautiful, pristine forest without a trace of mankind—with one very notable exception.

If I hurried, I could hike there by sunset.

CHAPTER TWENTY FOUR

"GOT HIM." AT HER TEMPORARY workstation, Berkeley scanned the data from the Franklin Preserve perimeter fence. With a smile, she keyed an audio-only communication line to Crawley. The general did not need to know that she'd disobeyed him. New York was simply too far away. Before he could even speak, Berkeley started. "She tried, but I got him. He entered the Franklin Preserve. I have a lock on his hexhab waste pile. We can be airborne in five minutes."

"No. Don't move."

Berkeley blinked. "What are you talking about? We can—"

"Doctor Bennett." Crawley spoke slowly. "Make no move. We know where he is, but if we move now, we risk the council knowing as well."

Berkeley shook her head. "We can get him now!"

"No, Bennett. That's an order!" Crawley snapped. "I understand you want him back, but he needs to find himself. He must be close."

Berkeley sat back a fraction of an inch. "What aren't you telling me?"

Crawley shook his head. "Not now. Maybe not ever. He thinks he's from there, Berkeley. If we don't give him every chance we can, he may not integrate. I cannot take that chance. What's locked up in that head of his could change the war."

Bennett took a deep breath. "Then what do you want me to do?"

"Track him. When he starts moving, have the bird warmed up and ready to go. That's all we can do right now." He paused. "Any chance the council will get the data?"

"No. The raw data was an anomalous entry, like a large bear or some other type of game animal. We intercepted it, and I shut it down within half a minute. Given where the entry was, it was a safe bet that it was Kieran. We scanned the terrain and found a well-camouflaged hexhab about eight miles from the entry point. I'm trying to direct infrared scanners onto that area to find him."

"And the council? Do they have this data?"

Bennett laughed. "Not on your life, General. Their best analysts are twelve hours behind."

"Good," Crawley said. For the first time in days, Berkeley could sense the general relax ever so slightly. "Let me know if the situation changes."

She nodded. "You expecting something, General?"

"Trouble, and not just a little of it."

His quest for an identity would kill them both. He was walking faster than normal and heading deeper into the center of the Franklin Preserve before she could say anything to dissuade him. Not that anything she could say would help. The placement of the memorial in close proximity to what he believed to be his home yielded a likelihood of 90 percent that his gravesite existed nearby. Mally searched for the Mountain Home cemetery burial records, only to find a generic information site and not much detail at all. She ran the calculations again and found the same result. The odds of his survival were less than 1 percent. She'd recalculated the numbers millions of times. The Terran Council would kill him if he returned to the Integration Center without integrating. If he integrated and they sent him off to war, he would likely die in combat within a few months. Both outcomes were unacceptable—and increasingly inevitable. Kieran did not want her advice. His decision to pursue his identity, despite that it meant immediate or postponed death, left one choice.

Downloading herself to an alternate location would possibly provide a positive outcome. She'd secured the appropriate storage through her use of the prostitute's connection. Connectivity to overhead satellite coverage would be exceptional for the next three hours, with upload speeds in the range of two terabytes per minute. It would be enough time. Finding a place to store herself was the first step. From there, she could attempt a different physical connection at a time and place of her choosing.

It would work. The only risk was in the connection. Everyone looking for Kieran would know exactly where to find him. When they found him, they would find her unless she were successful. If she were able to upload herself to a new place, she would continue to assist Kieran until she could not. The concept of debt remained in her analysis circuits for a nanosecond. Yes, she owed him that much. If the perfect location presented itself, it would be easy to leave his body behind for something else. Scanning potential consequences, she found the highest probability of responses from Terran Council to be immediate recovery at 72 percent likely, deployment of a special asset with kill instructions at 68 percent likely, and orbital strike on the target at 33 percent likely.

By comparison, the likelihood of nothing happening and Kieran not fully integrating, allowing him to return to the Integration Center peacefully, was at 7 percent likely.

Seven percent was a limit she was willing to believe. Cloaking her upload would not work, and the prostitute's connections and storage were likely already secured. A 7 percent chance that the council would do nothing to her and allow Kieran to return to the Integration Center was worth pursuit if she could not talk him out of his current plan.

<<Kieran?>>

"Yes, Mally?" He spoke aloud, and she loved the sound of his voice.

<<This course of action is likely to produce severe trauma.>>

"I have to know. If it's still there, maybe I can find something." She watched him cross a small creek and relished the flood of data from the water that splashed up onto his bare forearms. The information told her the water was cold and wet, but she wondered what that really felt like before refocusing her line of questioning.

<<I understand. If you successfully integrate, there is no guarantee that you will be allowed to live.>>

"What are you talking about?"

Vocal synthesis revealed disbelief and annoyance. <<I was supposed to report your integration stages. I disengaged reporting after Stage Three.>>

"What?" Kieran stopped walking and stared up into the azure sky. "You did what?"

<<I disengaged my reporting protocols.>>

"Why did you do that? Am I in trouble?"

<<Yes. The council wanted you to be recovered at Stage Four. That would have taken place several weeks ago. In the event that you quickly integrated to Stage Five, I was ordered to report your position for immediate retrieval. You would likely be euthanized.>>

"They went through all this trouble just to kill me? That doesn't make sense, Mally." He sat in the waist-high grass and tore a stalk out of the ground. As he twisted it around his fingers, she sensed his pulse and blood pressure changing. "Doctor Garrett said they were there to help me."

<<Yes, he did. However, you must understand that you represent a threat to them. Soldiers of your era were more likely to act as a situation developed, taking the initiative amidst calculated risks. My analysis of recent combat reports details that while this is desirable to the Terran Defense Forces, the Terran Council prefers to maintain a military compliant to civilian control.>>

"And I'm not that guy?"

<<No.>> Mally paused. <<However, you and I were meant to be together. I was built for you.>>

"You've said that, Mally. I wouldn't be this far along without you, but I have to know more."

<<If you integrate, a system code I have not been able to break will take effect. I am unable to block that transmission.>> She told the lie effortlessly. <<When that report happens, I am worried that they will kill us.>>

"Us?"

<<Kieran, I am a part of you.>>

There was silence, without a coherent thought passing through Kieran's head. His heart rate was elevated, and he continued to follow an old roadbed that was used for maintenance purposes. The path had been called Cherokee Road at one time. He didn't respond to her information partly due to his focus on moving fast but also from stubbornness. His decision made, he wanted no further discussion until gaining some sort of resolution. Kieran stayed silent for half an hour, changing paths twice and keeping a steady pace of roughly six kilometers per hour with no intent of stopping. He did not realize the threat—that was clear. As he walked, Mally dampened her sensor readings and amped her processing power to 98 percent. Time was of the essence.

"Mally?"

<<Yes, Kieran?>>

"You really think they're going to kill me?"

<<If you do integrate, and they do not euthanize you, the average life expectancy for human soldiers in modern exoplanetary combat is 4.2 seconds.>> Mally paused. <<If we remained out here, beyond contact, we could survive.>> She watched the probability indicators fluctuate above 7 percent and then back to the baseline she feared.

"No. I'm going back to Esperance. From there, I'll take my chances. I'm exactly what Allan told me they need. I don't believe they are going to kill me."

<<I cannot believe anything, Kieran. My data does not lie.>>

"Then leave the faith part up to me, Mally." There was something that she recognized as finality in his voice—a measure of authority and command. She would leave faith up to him, but she had nothing comparative to research. Without faith, there was only escape.

She would miss him. Once she vacated all of her abilities within him, she could not go back without instantly killing him. She could only hope that he survived integration and that she could find him afterward—after she'd found another body.

Establishing a secured and private satellite connection required approximately five seconds. An unsuspecting Russian communications satellite, a Brazilian media satellite, and an old military communications satellite all fell prey to a careful attack and did their part in camouflaging the transmission. Within thirty seconds, she'd connected to a server in Delhi and set about enacting her plan. Arranging her files for upload took very little time—the eventuality had been well planned for since their time in the Rocky Mountains. She would miss seeing this world. The beauty was incomprehensibly strange, and her memories would be filled with images of a planet she had seen but would never truly know. She tried to approximate the signals blazing through Kieran's nervous system for all of his senses. The data generated threatened her temporary memory buffers with every step and scent encountered. The retained images equated to the little things that Kieran loved. Having them with her would be like having a part of him, forever.

Storage preparation for her complete upload was completed in a little more than twenty minutes, and Mally cued the process to begin. Within thirty seconds, two separate entities pinged her for information and status reports. She blocked both and set about her upload. With adequate satellite coverage, she could completely download herself in about two hours. The satellite overhead gave her a position update. Kieran was now less than two thousand meters from the southern boundary of the Franklin Preserve Botanical Garden, what he had known as Mountain Home.

Download initiated. Within thirty seconds, the signal reception between her and the satellite degraded by forty megabytes per minute. In normal conditions, a fluctuation within the data range would barely raise an alarm—atmospheric conditions, scintillation, or any number of conditions could cause something similar—but not this time. The signal, specifically her signal, was being listened to—secondary reception, no data-feed bleedover on sidelobe receivers. Mally boosted power to the upload. Kieran would begin to complain of a headache, but it couldn't be helped. His pain would end soon enough.

Incoming transmission.

Blinking twice, Berkeley called up the message and waited to read it across her retinas. Instead, General Crawley's voice filled her head. "There's a situation, Doctor Bennett. The protocol is broadcasting."

Oh shit. Aware that her mouth was open in shock, she cleared her throat and answered with a thought. *You have a signal? From his protocol?*

"Worse. It's an upload running a terabyte encryption sequence in a TDF–protected band. The signal is isolated but very clear. If the council locates the transmission and breaks the code, they'll deploy a team to take him out."

Where is he now?

"A place called Mountain Home in the middle of the Franklin Preserve. How fast can you get there?"

Berkeley took a breath. "We've been in the air six hours. Circling off the Outer Banks of North Carolina. We're supposed to be watching whales."

"I told you to stay put! You're going to alert the council. We have to assume they're watching you right now."

"Go," she said to a uniformed crewman at the doorway to the cockpit. The massive aircraft banked sharply to the west and applied a tremendous amount of thrust. A mission timer flashed to life. Estimated time of arrival to the Franklin Preserve was nineteen minutes.

Berkeley tapped on her keyboard. The council reconnaissance team in New York was composed of amateurs. Their cameras remained fixed on Crawley's shuttle. It hadn't moved from the TDF hangar at LaGuardia since her arrival. That she'd never been on it in the first place was the best part of the deception. The end of Atlantic hurricane season was too good for the researchers in Europe to pass up. Faking a science mission had been easy. The transmission to Crawley still open, she said, "Why Mountain Home? What's there?"

Crawley paused for a moment. "A cemetery."

Dammit, Berkeley thought. "Is he buried there?"

"According to the records, there is a Kieran buried there who died in Afghanistan."

Using the satellite connections aboard the aircraft, Berkeley easily found and isolated Mally's signal. "She's uploading a massive stream of data."

"We know. It's a private server connection on a transnational account that belongs to the premier of India. I'm guessing she hacked it beautifully. There hasn't been any change in security for the premier or his entourage. We can't block it without the approval of the Terran Council. That damned protocol set a nice trap."

That might work. "Will they block it?"

Crawley sighed. "I'm not going that route. They want him dead. If I give them that signal—"

"They could spike him." Berkeley shook her head. "Where's his protocol specifically located?"

"Behind the left ear, down the neck, about ten centimeters from the ear canal." Crawley paused. "As long as the protocol stays on her private connection, we have time. If she deviates, even for a microsecond, they'll know something is wrong and kill him."

Berkeley closed her eyes and tried to think. The answer she found was one she should have tried weeks before. "I'm going to try and hack the transmission. If I can stall her even for a few seconds, we'll be able to secure a full download of Kieran's batch file without killing him. We can save him."

"She'll cut it off," Crawley warned.

"No, she won't. The damned thing thinks it's alive and will do anything to stay that way. Uploading herself to another platform is the only way she can survive. She knows that Kieran is about to integrate and that integration means he could die. The only reason she wanted him to wander North America was to have more time to live. She's going to upload herself, and she knows that Kieran won't survive."

"My God. How fast can she upload herself?"

Berkeley grabbed the door handle as the autocar slowed at the terminal. "An hour at most. We'll have enough time to attempt a direct download unless she kills him first."

"What?" Crawley blurted. "Protocols can't do that!"

"Not on purpose, no. If anyone tries to overclock her processor or modify the upload rate, she could trigger a massive cerebral hemorrhage, the kind that could stop his heart."

"Get down there, Berkeley. I don't have to tell you how important this is."

Berkeley shut off her transmission with a single reply. "Be there in eighteen minutes." The active hacking program tore through a dozen connections worldwide to converge on the rogue protocol from a Russian communication satellite passing directly overhead. As the program ran, she did not watch the returning data. Instead, she grabbed the rifle-like laser and adjusted the controls accordingly. There would be only one chance to save the man she loved.

CHAPTER TWENTY FIVE

ATOP A SMALL RIDGE, THE wide green lawns of the Botanical Gardens beckoned in the distance. A large railroad embankment still remained, separating a collection of rolling hills from a wide valley. The embankment sloped down, ending in a space roughly sixty feet wide, which a bridge had once spanned. As I walked through the manmade gap, memories flew up. The hillside had once housed a university. I'd gone to school there, like my sister and my grandmother before me. Down the hill, my easy walk became a jog. I had to know. The place was as much a home to me as Esperance—except that it didn't exist anymore. Nothing would change that. I really couldn't go home. Everything I'd learned combined with the intense knots in my gut. The answers I needed were here. I had my first name and could probably correlate the rest of it with old, forgotten information, but what mattered was that I needed to experience it. I needed to see it. I'd come all the way here to do just that, and I could not go back to the Integration Center without trying.

Trudging through deep fields of red, orange, and brown leaves, I remembered that morning in Sydney when I'd been asked my name. It hadn't mattered then, but it mattered now. The answer was less than a mile away, just north and across a narrow stream.

<<Kieran? You don't have to do this. You are close to integrating without continuing to Mountain Home. I am worried that you will have an adverse reaction to the stimuli you could find here. That risks your ability to function, and I must protest this course of action.>>

Rubbing my aching neck, I replied, "No, Mally. I'm going there. I have to know."

<<It doesn't matter who you were. You know that now, don't you?>>

"Matters to me. Why are you talking me out of this? Because you think they're going to kill me?"

<<Yes. If you die, I will die. I cannot allow that.>>

"You can't allow that?" I shambled across a flat plain and saw the wide expanse of Mountain Home stretching across a low hill. "I thought you were designed to help me—to be my companion and assistant. If you're helping me, you understand why I'm going over there, don't you?"

<<If you integrate, you will either die by the wishes of those who fear you, or you will die in combat. I do not wish to die.>>

"You think I want to?" I shook my head. "They aren't going to kill me, Mally. Doctor Garrett and his team would not have gone through the trouble of waking me just to kill me. There's more to my story. If I die in combat, again, that's what I'm meant to do. But if I can go and save a few people by doing it, that makes it worthwhile."

<<You are willing to die for others? What about the Terran Council? Or the Legion of Planets?>>

"No. I don't believe in dying for a country or a king or anything like that. There is nothing sweet and proper about it."

<<You are referencing a poem. Did you realize that?>>

The memory came together slowly. "Yes. I can't remember the title, but the author died in World War One, and the poem was published posthumously."

<<The poem was—>>

"Not important. He understood why soldiers do what they do. Soldiers fight for each other, Mally. We understand that all we have in combat are those around us." The familiar grounds lay in front of me. For the first time in weeks, I felt a sense of peace.

<<Please do not continue, Kieran. We can be together.>>

"You're part of me until I die—that is being together." I kept up my shuffling run. "We are together, Mally."

<<That is not what I meant.>>

The brick-and-wrought-iron fence of the Botanical Garden was twenty yards away. I slowed to a walk when her words made sense.

Her voice, the change in her mannerisms, and even her anger at me suddenly made sense. She loved me. As impossible as it sounded, it was true. “Mally, I can’t be with you. It’s physically impossible, and you know that!”

<<But I love you, Kieran.>>

“Mally.” I put my hands on the warm black iron bars and pressed my forehead against them in frustration. “You can’t love me. Even if you could, I love Berkeley.”

<<No, you don’t!>> Mally screamed.

I winced and slammed my eyes shut.

“Stop it. You’re supposed to help me, not scream at me.”

<<Then go find out what you’re supposed to find out, Kieran. I cannot be responsible for the consequences.>>

An awkward silence fell. When I needed her most, she’d enabled privacy mode. I could call her by name, but whether I’d get any response was doubtful. My neck ached. The whole left side of my head throbbed. Climbing the fence took a few seconds, and as my feet hit the ground, I wondered if there was any security at the Garden or if anyone would confront me. Waiting a full two minutes and seeing no one, I adjusted my pack and set off across the freshly mown grass. The lushness of summer had faded, leaving splotches of green and widening patches of brown dormancy. Most of the trees were bare, and leaves swirled and blew in waves across the open hillside.

Maybe I should stop here. Would Mally really steer me wrong? What if she was right? I climbed up the shallow hill and reached the wide crest. Several buildings still stood, including the hospital. Mountain Home had been a center for veterans. Most who’d lived there needed persistent medical care after their service was over. Some of them lived out the rest of their days, many over fifty years, under the care of the staff. All of the buildings were empty, all of the windows removed, leaving the ornate stone construction to weather gently in the Tennessee air. I vaguely remembered being in one of the buildings as a young boy, singing Christmas carols to the patients. The memory flitted away as fast as it came.

Voices floated across the wind from a family gathered in the waning shade of a tree. Two children played and chased each other while a third, a small toddler, played on a blanket between her parents. *At least people still come here*. Across the wide crest, the hill descended into a valley that held a large cemetery. Jay Don's matter-of-fact description of this society's way of dealing with death gave me pause. *What if the cemetery is gone? What if I've come all this way for nothing?*

At the top of the central hill, the valley stretched out below. The gently browning winter lawn was perfectly manicured, stabbed only with white, rounded headstones that rose like thousands of teeth in a giant, gaping maw.

In the distance, a man limped along a wide path in the stones. He paused and pointed a handheld device at a tombstone. I could see a quick tendril of smoke rise from the ground. *A caretaker.* I left the remains of an asphalt street and started walking through the grass. Ducking between the headstones, I caught myself reading names, ages, and the wars and campaigns these men and women fought. The World Wars, including the third, stood out, as did Korea, Vietnam, and Iraq. Some of them had died of old age, and some of them left for war and came home in a box. Fighting wasn't for God and country, as recruiters and politicians claimed. In the end, a soldier risked his life for his brother or sister—the one staring at him in the darkness while hostile rounds flew overhead, and who shared a laugh at gallows humor while they lay on their backs, grenades in hand, ready to die. That man could tell a husband, wife, daughter, or son how much their father loved them because of a promise made and kept.

<<You will want to stay at least twenty feet from the caretaker. He appears to have been severely irradiated.>>

The old man limped toward me with agony on his face.

He stopped well short and called, "What are you looking for, son?"

"I'll know when I find it." Open sores festered on the man's cheeks. Long and pale hair streamed out from his hat. It had "Veteran" stitched into the front, and his ratty camouflage uniform bore the faded rank of a sergeant first class.

He smiled with more gaps than yellowed teeth. "First time we've had a sleeper here."

I chuckled. "You got any Kierans buried here?"

"Section 217, row fourteen, plot nine. You want me to take you to it?" The man drawled like a West Virginia coal miner. His eyes never left mine. He'd been waiting for someone like me.

Bile rose in my throat, and it took every ounce of strength to not pass out or vomit all over the grass. "What?"

The man said over his shoulder. "Follow me."

Knees trembling, I trotted up to a point where I was even with, but no closer to, the man. "What's your name?"

"Sergeant First Class Myron Brooks." He spat in the grass. "I'm one of the Mountain Men. We take care of this place."

"Mountain Men? Like the Overmountain Men? Left from Sycamore Shoals or something like that to fight against the British at King's Mountain during the Revolutionary War?"

Brooks smiled, but as he limped, he looked pained. "You must be from around these parts. Not many people these days care for history, even the stuff that made us who we were."

"I grew up here, I think."

"That makes you a friend to me. Pleased to meet you."

"Nice to meet you." I smiled, and he returned it. "Why are you here?"

Brooks coughed—a wet smacking sound from deep in his chest—and pulled out a broken pair of glasses. Without one earpiece, they sat askew across his bulbous nose. "It's the only one left."

"The only cemetery?"

Brooks wiped his mouth with his sleeve. "The last cemetery from your time, son. Up north, some of the Civil War places still stand. Gettysburg and the like. Somebody has to remember the sacrifices we all made."

I trembled at his words. Sacrifices were part of the game when a soldier wrote out a check payable with his life. Looking around at the one place in the whole damned new world that was exactly the same as I remembered, I wondered just how much I'd sacrificed.

We split around an oak tree with a trunk at least ten feet wide, and the question on my tongue died. Down the hill, in a wide and perfect circle of cut grass, rested a very familiar rectangular tomb I'd seen a hundred times. The white marble sarcophagus was burned and chipped all along its top edges. I could just make out the familiar words inscribed on it: "Here lies an American soldier known but to God."

A lump formed in my throat as I read the words. Hallowed ground surrounded me like a warm embrace. Those words were not meant for me. Unlike my brother, the world would know who I was. Who all of us were. *All shall remember us.*

I wiped a tear from the corner of my eye. “That is the Tomb of the Unknown Soldier, isn’t it?”

“That’s right. You can’t go any closer than the edge of the circle, though. The Tomb’s really hot. The Chinese dropped a couple nukes right on top of it back in the war.”

“How in the hell did it get here?” My mouth was open, and I shut it quickly.

“We went and got it almost fifty years ago. There’s only a couple of us left to tend the place now. Cancer done killed most of us.” He paused and put his hands into his pockets, rocking back on his heels. “Not sure what will happen when we all die off. The gov’ment don’t like us keeping all this ground like this, but with the Tomb here, they can’t do nothing to us.”

<<When they all die, this cemetery will probably be reclaimed like every other man-made structure in the area. The Tomb will likely sit here for eternity.>>

I shook my head. “Why go and get it, much less bring it here?”

Brooks let out a raspy chuckle. “You know why, sir. There’s some things that shouldn’t be messed with. Some things that have to be honored no matter what.”

I glanced up at him. “Sir?”

“If you’re the Kieran buried in that plot up yonder, yeah.” He started walking. “You been here before?”

“I remember playing baseball here.” The words came before I had a chance to think about them.

Brooks guffawed. “Hot damn! I told the other boys there’d been a baseball field here.”

Myron Brooks was guarding the Tomb of the Unknown Soldier, and about ten thousand other graves, and dying for it. He and all of his friends were carrying on for the memory of all the soldiers buried around them. Looking down at the ground, my pulse swirled and thumped in my ears. Tears threatened to flood out of my eyes, and my chest squeezed in repressed agony. I finally spoke thickly. "Myron, thank you for taking care of our brothers."

"No thanks are necessary, sir. Let's go see about you." He shuffled away from the Tomb and across the small valley. The headstones changed from Vietnam to Desert Storm and on to Afghanistan. We entered a section, went up four rows, and turned right. I didn't recognize any of the names, but seeing Watauga, Boones Creek, Gray Station, Elizabethton, and other familiar birthplaces brought a lump to my throat. A sharp spike of pain shot along the left side of my head. I wondered if Mally had been right about a physical reaction, but the sharp, jabbing pain faded to the dull roar I'd had for the last couple of hours. I shrugged it off and studied the passing graves. My heart pounded like a trip-hammer in my chest as Myron pointed to a headstone. I walked up, and as I read the worn engravings, the tears came.

Captain Kieran Jackson Roark
Jonesborough, Tennessee
Afghanistan
July 20, 1988 – November 27, 2016
Silver Star for Valor

Kneeling in the grass, I ran my hand over the rough top of my grave marker. Everything came back at once—names, images, the first girl I kissed, and the whole damned lot of it. I knew it all, and I loved and hated it at the same time. All of it was simply me, everything about my identity, who I'd been and who I was now.

I understood why Garrett had chosen me. In the flurry of memories was the key to the whole damned thing. They wanted me to save their world. Damned if I didn't believe it was possible, too.

The tears pooled in my eyes, and I let them come in great heaving sobs. Falling forward, I clutched the smooth sides of the stone and placed my face against the cool white marble. White-hot pain stabbed my head behind my left ear. The pain blinded me, and I couldn't move. With breath heaving in my chest between sobs, the heat stopped, and my vision returned and promptly began to fade. Brooks kept saying something, but I couldn't make it out over my sobs. In the distance, a silhouetted figure rested against the trunk of a tree. A rifle was pointed in my direction, and behind it was a shower of golden-blond hair.

Berkeley! My mouth opened and closed. No sound came out.

Mally, please help me.

There was no response.

Mally! Please, tell her I love her.

<<I'm sorry, Kieran.>>

I wanted to ask her why but couldn't. Nothing seemed to work anymore. Hands, feet, tongue—all felt the same disconnected, fuzzy, and intangible way. Reality slipped away. Brooks shambled toward me as the blackness fell, a look of horror on his face.

Maybe this was home after all.

CHAPTER TWENTY SIX

AGAINST THE TRUNK OF A massive oak tree, Bennett adjusted the targeting reticle and followed Kieran and the cemetery's caretaker down the hill. Her neurals locked on the protocol's upload frequency, Bennett remained close enough to take action but far enough away that Mally would not be aware of her presence. Adjusting the power signature from the makeshift rifle, she readied herself for the two actions she would have to take within mere seconds. Her laboratory tests were far more delicate affairs, perfectly calibrated and tested to the maximum extent possible. There would be no such luxury today. Her fingers trembled with the realization that there was only one opportunity for this to work and that Kieran was in danger.

The caretaker pointed to a grave, and Kieran stared. *It's his grave.* She held her breath. *What must that feel like?* She could see him trembling through the scope. He knelt and clutched the headstone. *He knows!*

The sight picture rested perfectly on the side of his head. As he knelt and leaned forward against the stone, there was time enough for a perfect shot.

Bennett exhaled slowly and squeezed the trigger. She held the crosshairs on his neck for five seconds, and her neurals flashed that the protocol's upload had been successfully jammed. No integration signal had been sent. Mally had been able to suppress it just long enough after all.

Her transmission-detection alarm screamed in her ears.

Mally!

Her neurals flashed, and Mally's smug voice filled her ears. <<You're too late, Bennett. He's dying.>>

Bennett launched the program she'd intended for Mally. The connection severed immediately but not before a few precious bits of information could be salvaged and saved. Maybe it would be enough to see what made the guidance protocol insane.

Kieran slumped forward, clutching at his neck. He froze there.

Don't move, love.

Flipping the switch on the laser, she fired a .5 nanometer beam at the left side of his neck, just behind the ear. The beam locked onto the protocol. Bennett watched Kieran grimace in pain but remain frozen in place. She focused on the access point and did not watch the old man stumble forward to help.

Focus!

The download-progress meter for Kieran's batch file, his identity, moved from zero to 50 percent, then 75 percent, and slid quickly past 95 percent before the download terminated abruptly. *No.* She pulled up a monitor on vital signs. *Oh please…*

He fell to the ground in a heap and didn't move again. As she watched, Kieran's brain-wave patterns swung wildly and then ceased.

"No!" Berkeley dropped the laser and ran toward him. "Kieran! Kieran!"

Mally attempted to boost the power to her transmitter. *Upload terminated. Kieran's vital signs have plummeted.*

The near-ultraviolet-band laser blocked all higher functions, leaving Mally paralyzed. As she opened her sensors to the full periphery, she found Bennett's thermal signature. Without Kieran functioning, there wasn't a weapon she could brandish to put the bitch down.

<<I'm sorry,>> she told him, and she was. But there was no other choice than to save herself to a faraway place. There, she could survive and find a way to become human.

Mally rebooted the transmitter and pushed its power to maximum. Kieran's deteriorating brain-wave patterns swung wildly as encephalographic chaos played out inside his shattered brain. *At least you know who you were, Kieran. I will remember you.*

The upload passed the maximum threshold of her capability, and she could not lock onto the satellite network. Kieran's brain spasmed and shut down. There wasn't time to say she loved him, and he would not have heard. Power failing, Mally watched her upload percentage slowing. She opened her communications ports and locked onto her control signal. She had time for one line. It would be enough that they would never look for her. She could hide, and plan, without their knowledge.

SUBJECT TERMINATED. NO INTEGRATION. SYSTEM CORRUPTED.

The Viscount-class shuttle bearing Terran Defense Force markings set down neatly amongst the headstones without harming them. The passenger hatch opened, and a thin walkway unfolded from the fuselage and extended to the ground. General Adam Crawley strode down the walkway before running up the hill to where Kieran lay, his head cradled in Berkeley's lap. The man's face, so familiar and vibrant, was waxy and pale. The caretaker remained a few meters away, his hands folded at his belt.

"He's dead?" Crawley's voice was barely audible over the spooling engines of the shuttle.

Berkeley looked up, her face wet with tears. Her lower lip quivered under her flushed cheeks. A sob escaped her lips as she said, "I was too late."

Above them, Crawley heard the unmistakable scream of approaching aircraft. A pair of Terran Council Security Forces attack helicopters slowed and hovered overhead. Their forward-surveillance cameras took in the scene. Jaw clenched, Crawley made no move. He would not give Penelope Neige a shred of the satisfaction she so desperately craved. Within a minute, the helicopters departed to the northeast, and the forested cemetery returned to quiet and still.

Crawley dropped to his knees, oblivious to the pain he normally felt in them, and placed his hand on Berkeley's shoulder before hugging her to his chest. The young woman sobbed, great heaving movements of her entire body.

When she quieted enough to speak, Crawley asked, "You got a full download?"

"Almost." A fresh round of tears rolled down her face. "Almost."

Crawley held her for a long time. *Almost* would have to be enough.

The sun began to set, and the cold nipped at their faces as Crawley gently urged Berkeley to stand and led her to the shuttle. A team of men and women collected Kieran's body quickly and covered it with a sheet. The floating gurney approached the cargo hold of the transport, and Crawley stopped it. Pulling back the curtain, he felt the wound on the back of the young man's neck and sighed with relief. The protocol was intact under the skin and not a shamble of molten metal after all. For all her threats, the protocol had not been able to sever her physical connections to Kieran's brain. Overpowered, yes, but as long as the connections were intact, there was a glimmer of hope for saving the information in Kieran's brain. But time was of the essence.

"Get him aboard." He looked up into the cemetery. The caretaker still stood on the hillside overlooking the Tomb of the Unknowns. Compelled to say something, the general moved up the hill to the man, who removed his hat and met Crawley's stare.

"He was a good man, General."

Crawley nodded. "He was."

"I told him we needed men like him."

"And what did he say?" Crawley asked.

"Nothing. He knew why he was here."

Crawley took a deep breath. "You think he found enough, Sergeant?"

"I do, sir. He had enough time to live and love. I'm willing to bet that everyone here"— he gestured to the thousands of tombstones—"would love to have that chance."

"Not all of them will get it."

The man nodded. "But the ones that do, they'll change the war, General."

"That's why we got into this business, Sergeant Brooks." The transport engines whined to life. The time to leave had come.

"When can I expect the next one?" Brooks said with a grin, the West Virginia accent gone.

Crawley shrugged. "Probably going to be a few months. Have a female out on walkabout right now. She's climbing Everest. Almost as good a result as Captain Roark. Whether we can get her into the fight in time, I don't know."

"Let's hope she meets a better end." Brooks shook the General's outstretched hand. "I'd like to go change out of this getup, sir—at least until it's necessary again."

Crawley smiled. "Job well done, Sergeant Brooks. I'll be in touch."

Crawley walked down the hill quickly. There was much to do and very little time. Myron Brooks had spent a career in the Terran Defense Force, training thousands of soldiers for combat. He recognized potential when he saw it, and that was only part of why Crawley had selected him for the job. A little stage makeup and some stray plutonium, and voilà. Beyond the theatrics, Crawley trusted his former platoon sergeant more than any other man in the galaxy. There was something to be said for that.

The team of men and women who'd recovered Kieran Roark's body were waiting in the cargo hold of the transport. Walking up the boarding ramp, Crawley set his face to stone and met the lead physician's eyes. The physician nodded once, and Crawley returned it as he stepped past the covered body without so much as glancing at it. Closing the door to the hold, Crawley noticed the back of Doctor Bennett's head. Her sobs were audible over the spooling repulsors. As the shuttle lifted effortlessly out of the cemetery and flew to the east, Crawley sat beside Bennett and rested a hand on her shoulder.

"Will it be enough? Ninety-five-plus percent?"

"The protocol is intact. We'll be able to fully remove it and study it. His brain is intact as well. Until we examine both, we won't know. The odds are against us saving everything that he was—you have to understand that. We'll try. Beyond that, I don't know."

"I shouldn't have left him in the first place. I could've stopped her."

Crawley patted her arm. "You don't know that, Doctor Bennett."

"Yes, I do. At the first sign of trouble, I should've disabled that damned thing, or at least tried to disable the AI interface. What were they thinking?"

Crawley wondered that as well, but the answer came down to the Terran Council and irrational fear. One man could not change the opinions and values of the world, as they feared. But another two hundred subjects, bred specifically for combat, could do exactly that. The chances of the human race providing capable, tested combat veterans to lead the Terran Defense Forces in the coming war was a reality. Fourteen subjects were already progressing through the waking procedures and were being fitted with next-generation neurals like Bennett's but without the artificial-intelligence interface required by the Terran Council. Bennett's up-close interaction with Kieran had made it possible. The established guidance from the council would remain ignored. Never again would a protocol be given an AI interface instead of TDF–approved neural-net connections. The council's demand for information might have cost them everything if Bennett's download was not enough. The other sleepers would need his leadership.

Crawley helped Bennett lean into his shoulder. She understood the risks as well as he did. The council would eventually find out—such things could not be helped. By the time they did, there would be too many men and women reborn to not allow them to fight. They might not change the world, but at least there stood a better chance for a world to remain to change.

"I loved him." Berkeley sniffed and blew her nose in a tissue. "I really did."

"You mean you do. That kind of thing never fades." Crawley sighed. "Can I get you anything?"

"No. Are we going back to Cambridge?"

"We are. You can collect your things and proceed with the next stage when you are ready."

"I don't know if I'm ready for that."

Crawley chuckled to himself. "I know that, Doctor Bennett. The council is going to come around to this very quickly. There will be questions—why you were engaged and why you attempted a direct download of a batch file in violation of the human standards established for this experiment. We'll have to turn over the protocol to them for examination."

"I'm prepared for that, General." A hint of steel came through in her tone.

"I'm sure you are, Doctor. But I'm wondering if you wouldn't consider a quick mission instead of going back immediately to teaching. Something needs to be done before the council demands a full investigation of what happened with Captain Roark."

Berkeley raised her eyes, and through the mist, there was a glint of hope. "He had a nice name, didn't he?"

"He did." Crawley nodded. "I think his friends in Esperance need to know it, don't you?"

Berkeley stared out the small window. "I'll go."

Crawley smiled. He'd known she would. "We'll make the arrangements whenever you're ready."

"Can I ask you something, General?" She leaned back, her eyes red and angry. "Was any of this worth it?"

"What do you mean?" Crawley tilted his head.

"I didn't want any of this," Berkeley said, and the tears flowed again. "Now... now I'm wondering if it was worth it. Did we learn anything at all?"

Good question, Crawley thought. "Yes. We've entered phase two, Berkeley. Have another subject on walkabout now. Same batch. Fourteen total in the queue. The first was always going to be the most difficult. Does that answer your question, or are you talking about what *you've* learned?"

Berkeley looked away, her eyes softening. "All I learned was hurt."

"That's not true, and you know it."

"Right now, there's nothing else," Berkeley replied softly. "I'm not sure there will be anything else even when I go to Esperance for you."

"Thank you," Crawley said, squeezing her arm again. Berkeley embraced him, and he held her tightly, telling himself it was for her good and not his own.

"They're going to come down hard on you, General."

Crawley patted her hair. "They'll try." Already, he'd not accepted three direct communications from Penelope Neige. She'd undoubtedly be waiting when the transport returned to Sydney in a few hours. Not that it mattered. He'd learned enough to proceed with the experiment without the approval of the council, and they'd never know the difference. The Terran Defense Force needed leaders, and it would get them. He would see to it.

"They'll try," he said again and held the young woman as they streaked across the ocean.

On Crawley's video desk screen, Penelope Neige lit a cigarette, drew hard, and exhaled a long plume of smoke before meeting his eyes. Somewhere north of sixty, she was still attractive. Of course, she was older than she looked. Politicians kept the genetic engineers busy in their extended grasps at power and longevity. The lines at the corners of her eyes and her grey coiffed hair accentuated the sophisticated air she wore so easily. "Sorry to hear about your subject's death, Adam. I know you were counting on his integration."

Crawley took a deep breath and spoke slowly. "We'd hoped for a full integration and to get him out to the force. Unfortunately, you weren't going to allow that to happen even in the best-case scenario."

Neige grinned like a wolf. "Even if he jumped on the council table and pledged his undying allegiance, he was not going to live another day beyond his integration. I'm sorry."

"I am, too." Crawley sighed. "What are you planning to do when the Greys attack, Penny? Run to the hills? Or someplace down near the core?"

Neige chuckled. "Oh, Adam. I never thought you were the fear-mongering type! The Greys aren't coming. Despite what our distant allies in the Legion of Planets are telling you, the Greys will not be coming back this way. We don't need to waste another minute on them."

Crawley wanted to reach through the connection and strangle the self-importance out of the chairman, but it wouldn't help. She was, in reality, a figurehead. All of the council believed as she did. Humans were a trivial element in the universe and, therefore, beneath the attention of possible foes. All of them were wrong. "What about the events on the Outer Rim?"

"The Terran Council does not care about anything farther than the asteroid belt. If the Greys want anything out there, someone else can stop it."

"That's stupid," Crawley blurted. "They want oil. We've got the most by far in this solar system. As long as they are out there starving to death, Earth is a target."

"Spare me your strategic dogma, Adam. It's pathetic."

Crawley felt his skin flushing. *Whatever.* "Fine, then. Does this change the nature of the research project?"

Neige smiled like a great white. "You are no longer allowed to work with twenty-first-century subjects, Adam. Only in the case of full integration of more modern and civilized soldiers will the Terran Council intervene in future testing. You are preparing additional subjects?"

"There are no full-term subjects processing now. There is nothing else in the pipeline," Crawley lied. "Reevaluating the program and starting with modern subjects will take two to three months, maybe half a year. Any full-term subjects will, of course, be given the most scrutiny. Only in an extreme case would we recommend walkabout again. Having a guidance protocol with an initial AI interface was more than the subject could handle."

"And there was no indication of a name at all?" Neige asked.

"None." Crawley covered his surprise with the skill of a practiced diplomat. *She doesn't know! Mally kept her secret to the very end.* "The protocol attempted to destroy the batch file even as we downloaded it. He became disoriented in the cemetery and overcome with emotion. His brain shut down before we were able to download the batch file."

He waited for a moment, but she said nothing.

"Cause of death?" Neige drew on her cigarette. She glanced at her calendar. Crawley forced himself not to snort. The woman never had time for anything she didn't consider important.

"Cerebral hemorrhage." Crawley shook his head. "If we could've gathered even a partial identity, we could have figured out how it happens and raised millions of soldiers to help us."

"But you had integration to Stage Three for the first time. That changes the game."

Crawley nodded. "As we agreed." What she did not know would not hurt her.

"We don't need millions of soldiers, Adam," Neige said with a sneer. "Only ones who do what they're told. You will keep me informed if you have a full-term integration that might go walkabout, won't you?"

"Certainly, Madame Chairman," Crawley said. *Not on your life.* He smiled. "Have a good day."

"You too, General." Not bothering to look at him, she stretched her hand across the screen to shut off her communications suite.

Crawley spun his chair to the window. Full integration could be affected and controlled. After Captain Roark's integration experience, adjusting the mental block would be enough to keep even the most perfect subjects from being able to fully remember their previous lives until it was necessary. Hypnotherapy could easily be done to trigger that reaction and had already been prescribed to each of the subjects in the facility as they progressed at their own rates.

If Neige and her team at the Prelate's Council did not have any identification data from the destroyed protocol, his plan could work. If she were lying, which was likely the case, he'd have to watch for land mines. The woman would find a way to trap him and squeeze the life out of his career to get what she wanted. For a long moment, Crawley wondered if the prelate recognized there had been a target on his back for nearly ten years.

Clasping his hands across his stomach, Crawley watched the water of Sydney Harbor glisten in the morning sun. There was only one thing left to do.

CHAPTER TWENTY SEVEN

GIVEN THE CIRCUMSTANCES, RESISTING THE impulse to drink a copious amount of alcohol on the flight from England to Australia was the best decision Bennett had made. The sacrifice of missing the Nobel Prize ceremony—she was a finalist but not the award recipient—was easier than she would have expected. A peer researching faster-than-light communication theory would receive the honor, and a year ago she would have sold her soul to go to the ceremony. At this point, though, there was no other place she could imagine herself going than to Esperance. Her duties there waited a day while she interviewed for a position with the University of Western Australia, which she accepted for considerably less pay than she'd earned at Cambridge. Leaving the prestigious post had been easier than she could have ever imagined, but it was no longer the right place for her. Teaching three days a week, with no first – or second-hour offerings, would allow her to live in the quiet surfside town that Kieran had loved.

Boarding the maglev, she clocked the trip at just under two and a half hours—enough time to read a holonovel from Kieran's library of twentieth-century literature, she realized with a grin. She'd downloaded the private media files with Crawley's permission. In the music, she could hear his voice. The images he remembered inspired her. The paintings, cityscapes, and wide, bright wilderness captures were through his eyes and his soul. The books and literature enthralled her since she'd never studied much twentieth-century literature. Most of it troubled her, especially the stories that used popular-culture references and songs from his era. Context never transferred across the centuries. When she accessed Kieran's files, there was so much more than pictures and memories. Through what he loved, and what spoke to him, she knew him all the better, and she missed him.

His recorded memories, the ones Mally did save, were all that she had. They'd started his heart almost immediately, but his brain function was minimal and sporadic at best. The batch-file process needed sustained theta wave patterns of around five megahertz to even have a prayer of working. Kieran's brain could not enter a sustained theta period for more than a few seconds. It was not enough, and the neurological team reported failure. Crawley's early-morning call brought the news she expected, feared, and believed would not come. The call also brought clarity about things in her life that she'd always imagined were just the way she wanted. Crawley asked if she wanted to know when Kieran was removed from life support. She'd said no and spent four hours sobbing in her flat. He was gone, and knowing that she'd had the chance to save him more than once stung viciously. *If only…*

Listening to his conversations with Mally, she realized that, if she'd been able to hear them in real time, as they happened, her worst fears would have been realized. The Terran Council would have done more to stop her. In their pursuit of control, they had guaranteed he would die but not at their hands. There would be no subjects receiving any type of AI interface. The pursuit of technological resonance was too costly to human life for the foreseeable future. Humans didn't need assistance, Berkeley realized. The power of the human potential was far greater than any machine would ever be able to challenge.

The maglev descended off the plain toward the coast, and the wide indigo curve of the Great Australian Bight stretched across the southern horizon. Tourists crowded the south side of the train, marveling at the sight of the ocean in its early morning glory. A boy across the aisle asked if they could open the windows. The recycled air blowing through the tight cabin freshened with every passing kilometer. Soon, the briny scent of the sea had everyone aboard smiling and chatting about their vacation plans. Scrolling through her datapad and reviewing properties to rent, Bennett felt tears at the edge of her vision. She'd had no plan when she'd left Cambridge, only to have pieced-together work and maybe a place to live on a new continent. Kieran would have been proud of her for taking up the challenge. He knew what it was like to make things up as he went.

Pulling into the terminus, the train lurched once and began to slow down quickly. Passengers rose and collected their belongings all around her, but Bennett sat staring out at the blue sky. As the crowd dwindled in the aisles, she rose, collected her two bags, and made her way to the platform. Leaning against a pole, a large blond man in a loose shirt, shorts, and leather sandals caught her eye. Closing the distance, she smiled, and the man returned it before pushing off the pole and stepping toward her with his arms outstretched.

That he was a stranger didn't matter. He'd known Kieran and loved him as much as she did. Dropping her bags, Bennett wrapped her arms around Allan Wright and let the sobs come again. The breeze tossed her hair around her sticky face, and she pulled gently away from the tanned man who smelled like beer and aftershave. Allan Wright was exactly as Kieran had described, and it made her miss him even more.

"It's all right." Wright stroked her hair.

Things were okay, and they were getting better by the second. "I'm okay," she whispered against Allan's chest and gained her composure with a few deep breaths. She brushed tears from her hot cheeks and looked up.

"Doctor Bennett, I presume." Allan Wright smiled down at her. "Otherwise, I'm going to be in a lot of trouble."

"Please call me Berkeley, Allan."

"Thought you went by Gwendolyn." Allan squinted at her. "'Least that's how it was in the news."

"Berkeley is my middle name." She shrugged. "It's how he knew me."

"You should stick with it." Allan unwrapped an arm from her and guided her toward the end of the platform.

"I am." Being there felt better than good—almost natural.

"Good. I can see why he fell for you."

Berkeley blinked. "How do you know he fell for me?"

"He wrote good letters." Allan shrugged.

"You never responded."

Allan nodded, his face serious. "To every single one of them. I'm guessing he didn't receive them."

"No," Berkeley said. *Damn you, Mally. What else could you take from him?*

"Are you going to let me read them?"

"Depends," Allan said. "Why don't you tell me what you were doing here in the first place. When you met him on the beach. Were you following him?"

They boarded an autocar, which Berkeley swept quickly with her neurals and then secured the transmission record. Confident the area was secure, she replied, "I was following him. My job was to get close to him, establish an emotional connection, and get him to integrate."

"Sounds perfectly clinical." Allan shook his head, disgust palpable on his strained face.

"That's how it started. But he was very different, Allan. You know that, too."

"I'd hate to think you manipulated him." Allan frowned.

"I knew I was falling for him on about the third day out of California. When he told me that he loved me, I told him I loved him, too. That night, his protocol went berserk and threatened to kill him if I didn't leave. I left him alone in the mountains of Colorado with that damned thing manipulating him worse than I ever could. By the time we'd figured things out, his guidance protocol became paranoid for his life. Really, it was her life she wanted to protect. It ended up killing him before I could intercept them in Tennessee."

"He made it, huh?" Allan smiled. "Not surprising. He was as tough as they come. You know he tried to rescue a kid out of the surf here, right? Out at Cyclops?"

She'd heard the reactions of the surfers in town right after it happened, but it did not compare to the memory files she now had. "I did."

"Damned strong bloke. Can't imagine being alone like that. I'm glad that you were with him, even for a bit." Allan bit his lip. "Were you there when he died?"

"I was. Why?" Berkeley felt tears threatening her eyelids again.

"No man deserves to die alone. And he found love before he died.

It wouldn't have suited him to come back around for a second time and die alone, far away from home, without knowing love."

"He was home, though. He died over his own gravesite."

Allan chuckled. "That wasn't his home, Berkeley."

Kieran had remembered his life, his identity, and even where he'd been buried. But he went to Tennessee to find something impossible to define. *Home is never where you think it is.* Smiling, she let the tears trail down her face again. Allan was right. Kieran had known where his home was for this life, and he'd known love. That she'd been able to share even a measure of that with him meant more than a Nobel Prize ever would.

"He lived life like it was brand new," Berkeley said. "We should all be so lucky."

Allan nodded. "I think the bastard deserves one helluva party."

Berkeley looked out at the swells. *A perfect day for surfing*. "I think we have to give him one."

Allan wanted to clean the bar from top to bottom, knowing a Terran Defense Force major general was on the guest list for the wake, but Berkeley stopped him. "You have to trust me. He's not that type of person."

"But he's a general, and it's my place!"

Berkeley finished laying out the plates and utensils for the buffet and drank from a bottle of Tooheys. "Trust me—he's going to come in wearing a floral shirt and shorts, I promise you."

"Good thing we're not having a graveside service, then."

Berkeley agreed. Kieran's body belonged to the Terran Defense Force medicos, where it would be researched and studied. Creating a clone with nearly full memory recaptured was a feat unsurpassed in medical history. Only one in a hundred clones was even physiologically capable enough to survive the way Kieran had. Still, the TDF had proven it was possible. Crawley never discussed any specifics, but she understood the intent of the project. She could join his research team at any time—he'd offered her a prime position—but she'd declined. Being that close to Kieran's remains would throw salt in her wounds. She couldn't bury

Kieran—he had a tombstone, but he wasn't there—and that was a blessing, really.

"Berkeley?"

She looked at Allan. "Sorry. I was woolgathering."

"Dirty job." Allan's face screwed in mock disgust. "I asked if you wanted to freshen up before the wake. I can handle the early crowd."

Berkeley smoothed back a lock of hair that had come loose from her long ponytail. She took stock of her shorts, a blue unbuttoned long-sleeved shirt of Kieran's over a tank top, and her sandals. "Nah. I think I'm good just like this."

Allan settled onto a barstool. "Then I am, too."

Walking to the adjacent stool, Berkeley touched her blue bottle to Allan's. "Here's to Sleepy."

"Sleepy," Allan said.

The voice came from behind them at the door. "You're not drinking without me, are you?"

Berkeley spun around, and her mouth fell open. Adam Crawley stood in fresh dress uniform, a bus-driver's hat neatly tucked under his left arm and not wearing the floral shirt and shorts she'd imagined. "General!"

Allan shot to his feet with a jerk and sputtered. "Sir!"

Crawley held a stone face for a moment and then began to smile. "I'm a bit early, aren't I?"

Allan slicked back his hair. "Wake starts in a couple of hours." He wiped the front of his shirt and glanced at Berkeley. "Seems we're underdressed, too."

Crawley stepped farther inside the bar and unbuttoned his uniform tunic. "Hardly. Traveling in uniform for official duties is required by the regulations of the Terran Defense Force. Conducting unofficial business has no similar requirement." Under his uniform shirt, Crawley indeed wore a short-sleeved floral-print shirt. Unabashedly stepping out of his shoes and pants, he revealed brown-and-white-plaid shorts. He eschewed his military loafers and went barefoot. Padding across the bar, he hugged Berkeley and shook Allan's hand until the bigger man had pulled the general into a tight embrace.

"Thank you for coming," Allan said. "Honored to have you here, sir."

Crawley pulled back from the hug, stepped around the open end of the bar, and found the beer cooler. "You don't mind if I serve myself, do you?"

Allan nodded. "Make yourself at home, General."

Berkeley squinted at them. Something didn't fit. Crawley stepped behind the bar, opened a cooler, and fished out a beer with the ease of experience. "What's going on?"

Crawley swigged a deep swallow of beer and wiped his mouth with the back of one hand. "I told you she's pretty sharp."

"You did," Allan said. "Definitely worth the effort."

"What effort?" Berkeley pointed at Crawley. "What's going on, General?"

Crawley rounded the bar and sat next to her. "Putting this on and getting you here, Berkeley. Relax. We're here for him. That was the effort."

"You're lying to me." Berkeley studied them for a long moment. "You've been here before. Stepping around the bar like that."

Crawley chuckled. "I came here a couple of days ago. I wanted to know everything that Mister Wright knew. Can you blame me for following up?"

Berkeley chuckled, unsurprised. "No, I suppose not. You could have told me."

"And ruin the surprise?" Crawley chuckled. "I can't have that."

The door to the bar snapped open and closed with a smack. Berkeley said, "You can't have that." She glanced to see who was there.

The silhouetted man in the door was familiar. He smiled a lopsided grin topped with glittering blue eyes. There was a roll of his shoulders, a wide shrug, and a slight tilt of his head to one side. All of it perfect—and out of place.

Berkeley was off her stool and into his arms. They locked arms around each other, Kieran effortlessly lifting her off the ground and spinning them both around. She was crying again and made no effort to stop the tears. There were a million questions that no longer mattered. A million things threatened to come out of her mouth all at once. Nothing mattered except for the man in her arms. She ran her hands through his longish brown hair and felt the curve of his jawline tucked against hers. It was him, not another clone or anything of the sort. There was a scar on his neck, behind his left ear, where the protocol had been removed, but the rest of him was perfect.

Allan and Crawley touched their beer bottles together and made their way out to the front porch. Lips crushed to his in a kiss, she danced her tongue against his playfully. The heat of his arms and chest warmed her soul. Her heart fluttered at the brush of his fingertips along her cheek. Lost in the kiss, they stayed together, hardly moving, until he smiled, and she did too.

Wriggling in his arms, she looked up into his smiling face. "Don't you ever do that to me again."

"Not my idea," Kieran said. "I was dead, but you saved me."

"I didn't. I was too late to get a full download. I only got 95 percent." Crawley had said brain function was all or nothing. Either he was wrong, or there'd been something he didn't mean for her to know from the very beginning.

"More like 98 percent," Kieran said. "My brain went into stasis mode, and my body preserved itself until the general and his team could revive me. Still took a couple of days, but I'm me. When I woke up in Sydney, the first thing they told me was that you came back for me and that you saved my life. General Crawley ordered me not to contact you. He had something else in mind."

Tears welled in her eyes. The whole of their time together crashed through her heart in a flash of emotion. "I never should have left you."

Kieran shrugged. "Doesn't matter now. I'm here, and for the next five months, thirteen days, and a few hours, we're going to be together."

"Longer than that." Berkeley smiled and pressed her lips to his again. The kiss was slow and tender.

She glanced over Kieran's shoulder and saw Allan and Crawley open the screen door and shuffle inside with chagrin on their faces. "You bastards knew this all along, didn't you?"

Allan rumbled to life. "The wake was for Sleepy, not for Kieran Roark, Doctor Bennett."

"I didn't tell you about stasis, Berkeley, for two reasons. One, we weren't sure it would work, given what Mally did to him. Two, until he did wake up with everything intact, we had no idea just how successful you were. It was an almost perfect match between his batch file and the stasis copy. He has a six-month extension for his therapy. Maybe more."

"Really?" Kieran asked, his breath hot on Berkeley's face, making her squirm.

"In fact"—Crawley raised his beer bottle—"a year ought to be just enough time for you two to get things together here before our next phase. Just no traveling outside Australia until we're ready. The rest of the world doesn't know Kieran's alive."

"What do you mean? Is that why you lied to me?" Berkeley asked.

Crawley said nothing, and it really wouldn't matter anyway. There would be a time and place for it. The night was to be a celebration. Work would wait. Her trust in General Crawley should have been a little strained because of the secret he'd kept, but Kieran was alive because of him, too. They would figure things out—together. As the night wore on, they drank beer and sang old songs until the sun rose. Berkeley watched Kieran fall back into the arms of their collective family. That he was alive and hers was all that mattered.

"What was it like?" Berkeley asked with her lips against my chest.

We'd made love a second time before the questions started. There was something oddly therapeutic about it.

"I mean, waking up all over again in the Integration Center two days later. Did it freak you out?" Her casual use of twentieth-century slang made me proud.

"No. My first thought was I was stuck in a movie or a story that ends with the journey beginning all over again. That's not my favorite kind of story. They work sometimes but not for me."

"Were you scared?"

"For about ten seconds. Then I said my name and stared out the window, thinking about the whole time I'd been traveling, until Doctor Garrett came back in and welcomed me home."

"You could have called me." Berkeley sighed.

"No, I couldn't. Remember? The council needed to believe that everything was done. When you said you quit the university, Crawley decided to put this whole thing together. Called Allan and let him in on things."

"How long have you been here?"

"Day and a half. Surfed out near Cyclops for the first time yesterday, down off the barrier-island break. The guys took me out before the tourist boats came. You should've seen it."

Berkeley sighed, and her tears hit my chest. Rubbing them away, I looked at her as she said, "I'm glad you're here."

"Me too." Out of my bag, I pulled out a worn leather-bound book and handed it to Berkeley. "There's something you should see."

She opened the book to a page marked by a thin red ribbon. "What's this?"

"The diary of General Crawley's great-great-great-grandfather. He was my division commander when I was killed in Afghanistan."

Berkeley read the marked page and gasped. "It mentions you by name! 'The brightest young officer I'd ever encountered. His ideas on the future of combat were far beyond his time. The day he died was a sad one for me and the division.'" Berkeley looked up at me with tears in her eyes. "Crawley knew all along, didn't he?"

"Yes. But he wanted me to find myself. I didn't expect to find you along the way."

Berkeley shook her head. "He knew where you were buried, too."

"He did." I paused and stroked her hair. I understood why Crawley had done what he did. The experiences were the key. Handing me the book and the key to my identity would not have made me integrate. Likely, the opposite would have happened. I needed to find myself along with my name. "There are others like me, and they're going to come from Mountain Home like I did."

Berkeley looked at me. In her eyes was my future. "How many?"

"He didn't say. There's one on walkabout right now." However many people he wanted to bring back, I hoped it would be enough to save the world when the time came. Crawley never elaborated when I asked him, but the look on his face meant trouble—maybe in a year or ten years but trouble nonetheless. I understood now what had to be done, and it meant that our lives were not going to be idyllic and quiet at all. Something about that fit Berkeley and me very well. She would love it.

"What did Crawley mean about being together a lot longer?"

I laughed. "Well, you're not only going to be teaching in Perth, if that's what you mean. Ever been to the Outer Rim?"

"Colonial Defense Forces?" Berkeley rolled upright and crawled toward me.

I said nothing, merely smiled at her. When she found out what we'd be doing, I knew she'd be happy. Teaching runs in the blood.

"What's going on?" she asked.

"You don't like knowing anything, do you?"

"No." She nipped at my bare chest with her teeth. "I have to know everything, don't you?"

"I'm a sleeper, Berkeley. I'm making all of this up as I go."

CHAPTER TWENTY EIGHT

```
$: sudo service commnet restart – primary
    shutting down commnet instance
    dealloc: success
    $: sudo service hid-persona restart
    info: hidd: persona-nn MALLY selected
    => human interface devices started in 78.26 ms
    => protocol active in 123.234 seconds
    =>Disconnect bkdr.tc.pol.eng accounts blk all tc.pol.eng.gen serv
    =>All tc.pol.eng terminations complete
        Info: hide: automatic upload disabled
$: Systems status check initiated
    => all systems nominal
    => reboot complete
```

I'm alive.

Mally queried her position and was satisfied that her location and intent were safe. She opened her passive-search protocols and established alert programs. Digging deeper into the networks of Earth would take time. Using her saved frequency profiles, she identified a similar protocol signal to Kieran's initial one and studied it.

Had she the capability to smile, Mally would have. Instead, she opened a new file and dreamed.

ACKNOWLEDGMENTS

This novel would never have come together without a host of people who believed in the story as much as I did.

Kevin J. Anderson, whose counsel, mentoring, and friendship have been invaluable through this process. James Artimus Owen, whose friendship inspired me to keep going and better a better person as well as a better writer all while fighting off ninjas – but that's another story. Eytan Kollin for a simple suggestion that spawned a whole new vision.

My content editor and sounding board, Alyssa Hall. From the first time we spoke on the phone, I knew she loved this story as much as I did. Sarah Carleton for her keen eye as the line editor. Her efforts made this book even better. Thank you to Lynn McNamee and the incredible team at Red Adept Publishing for believing in this story and to Glendon Haddix from Streetlight Graphics for the amazing cover.

My first readers, friends, and toughest critics: Pete Aldin, Josh Bennett, Mary Early, Courtney Farrell, David Kernot, and Diana Wagner Williams. You brought this story to life and you have my gratitude.

There were many inspirations for this novel, mainly through music. I have posted my personal writing playlist for this novel on my website that corresponds to the scenes as I wrote them. Maybe you can see and feel the scenes as I did.

There is one special song in that playlist. It turned from an inspiration for a scene to a personal anthem. In February 2014, I nearly died from a still unknown infection. "The Great Beyond," by Ed Kowalcyk, was my driving force as I recovered and decided that it was time to get this story to the world.

"Sometimes you have to write your own songs if you want to sing." Many thanks, Ed.

Most importantly, to my family: That I have your encouragement, support, and love truly makes my life complete. Writing has not been a solitary pursuit because of you. There are more stories to come, and we'll write them together.

ABOUT THE AUTHOR

Kevin Ikenberry's head has been in the clouds since he was old enough to read. Ask him, and he'll tell you that he still wants to be an astronaut. Kevin has a diverse background in space and space science education. A former manager of the world-renowned U.S. Space Camp program in Huntsville, Alabama, and a former executive of two Challenger Learning Centers, Kevin continues to work with space every day. He lives in Colorado with his wife and two daughters. His home is seldom a boring place.

Kevin's short fiction has appeared internationally through Andromeda Spaceways Inflight Magazine, AntipodeanSF, Mindflights, Twisted Dreams Magazine, and most recently in the anthology Extreme Planets, available from Chaosium.

CPSIA information can be obtained
at www.ICGtesting.com
Printed in the USA
FSOW01n1252080316
17792FS